The Second Midnight

ALSO BY ANDREW TAYLOR

An Old School Tie
Our Fathers' Lies
Waiting for the End of the World
Caroline Minuscule

The Second Midnight

A Novel

Andrew Taylor

Dodd, Mead & Company
NEW YORK

No part of this book may be reproduced in any form
without permission in writing from the publisher.
Published by Dodd, Mead & Company, Inc.
71 Fifth Avenue, New York, New York 10003
Manufactured in the United States of America
Designed by Suzanne Babeuf
First Edition

1 2 3 4 5 6 7 8 9 10

Library of Congress Cataloging-in-Publication Data

Taylor, Andrew, 1951–
The second midnight : a novel / Andrew Taylor.
p.   cm.
I. Title.
PR6070.A79S4   1987

ISBN 0-396-09193-8

For C. and L.T.

Contents

Prologue

George Farrar got his first inkling that something was wrong when he collected his room key from reception.

The manager himself was behind the desk. He was a plump Viennese, almost as small as Farrar himself, and he always wore a flower in the lapel of his black coat. He was also a compulsive talker.

Tonight, however, he produced the key as soon as Farrar reached the desk and slapped it down on the counter between them. Immediately afterward he bent his head over the register, as if the pressure of work prevented him from exchanging pleasantries with his guests.

"Any messages?" Farrar said. He was hoping that William McQueen might have telephoned.

The manager didn't raise his head. "No, Herr Farrar."

Farrar noticed that the white carnation was beginning to wilt. He also noticed that the manager's face was shiny with sweat. Still, it was uncomfortably warm in the foyer.

He said good night and took the lift up to his floor. A tall man wearing a camel hair overcoat came up with him. He was smoking a cigar and had small, sad eyes. ·

They both wanted the same floor. The tall man gave a polite little bow when they reached it, indicating that Farrar should leave the lift first. Farrar smiled his thanks.

The long corridor was empty. Farrar walked quickly to his door; behind him he could hear the soft, slow pad of the other man's footsteps. He unlocked the door and opened it; his hand brushed against the light switch.

Everything happened very suddenly. A hand slammed into the small of his back, propelling him into the room. Simultaneously, he saw that the carpet was strewn with his belongings. Another man was lying on the bed, with his hands behind his head. He was smiling. When Farrar tripped over his own upturned suitcase, the smile became a chuckle.

Behind him, Farrar heard a click as the tall man locked the door.

The man on the bed stopped chuckling. Farrar's stomach lurched as he recognized the Bavarian he had met last night.

The Bavarian raised his heavy black eyebrows. "And how is our lovely Gretl this evening?"

Farrar groped for his glasses, which had slid to the foot of the bed. Camel hair brushed his cheek. A large brown shoe stamped on the glasses and twisted them into the carpet.

The tall man sucked in his breath. "Ach," he said. "I am so clumsy."

"What a pity," said the man on the bed. "Still, accidents happen."

Farrar got slowly to his feet; his muscles tightened, ready to receive a blow from the tall man. He moved more slowly than he needed, pretending the fall had winded him. His own stupidity angered him: last night he had assumed that the man on the bed was nothing more than a tourist who had had too much to drink; he should have known better. He remembered the manager's behavior, and realized that his visitors must be police of some sort: German, not Austrian. He was a fool to have run any unnecessary risks before he had seen William McQueen.

"Gretl," the man on the bed said conversationally, "won't be lovely for much longer." Without any change of tone he added, "This room is a pigsty. Tidy it up, Farrar."

Did they know? Had they found it?

Farrar had the answer to the second question as soon as he picked up the suitcase: it was appreciably lighter than it should have been. He scooped up a pile of shirts and threw them into the case.

Sweet Jesus, he thought. *Please not the Gestapo.*

"Neatly, Farrar. You get so much more in if you pack neatly, don't you?"

"Look, I'm sorry about last night," Farrar said quickly. His German was fast and fluent, and he had a salesman's confidence in the power of his own voice. "I'd had a bit to drink, and the girl—"

The tall man slapped him. "Silence, please," he said politely.

Farrar picked himself up again. Some clothes went in the suit-case, others in the wardrobe and the chest of drawers. Meanwhile, the man on the bed leafed through Farrar's order book. Farrar noticed that the thieving bastards had even been at his brandy: the bottle, nearly empty, was on the bedside table; beside it was a tumbler with a couple of inches of brandy still in it.

The man on the bed looked up. "Business has not been good lately?"

Farrar nodded. There wasn't much demand for boxed sets of British Grenadiers in the Third Reich. That was one reason why he had taken the other job when they offered it to him.

"I expect you find it hard to make ends meet."

Again, Farrar nodded. It seemed safer to agree. Besides, the man on the bed was quite right. He wondered whether they were going to beat him up before they arrested him, or wait until they had him in custody.

Escape was out of the question. His captors' combined weight was three or four times his own; and both men would be armed. The door was locked. Even if he could open the window and dive through, he doubted if he would survive the dive of fifty or sixty feet to the street below. Shouting for help would be useless, for it was obvious that they had the cooperation of the manager.

But they wouldn't kill him—he was sure of that. A murdered British citizen would lead to awkward questions, even in Vienna. They would interrogate him, of course, and if he was dead he couldn't tell them anything. But the worst he had to fear was a jail sentence, and perhaps a little preliminary suffering. They might not realize the significance of what they had found.

The man on the bed tore a blank page from the order book and wrote something on it with a silver pencil.

Farrar bundled a pair of shoes into the bottom of the wardrobe. At last the room was clear.

The man in the camel hair coat patted his shoulder. *"Gut,"* he said encouragingly. *"Sehr gut."*

"Have a drink," said the man on the bed. He beckoned Farrar closer and jerked his head toward the tumbler. "Go on, drink," he said irritably. "It may be your last chance for some time."

Farrar picked up the glass. The probable consequences of throwing its contents into the Bavarian's face chased through his mind.

The Bavarian shook his head. "Don't be silly, Farrar. There are two of us."

"Hurry, please," the man in the camel hair coat said. He looked ostentatiously at his watch.

Farrar shrugged. He picked up the glass and had his last drink.

George Farrar died on Wednesday, February 15, 1939.

The fact that he had died was more important than how and why, at least to Michael. But, much later, Michael became curious about all aspects of the little man's death. This was because he came to see the murder of Farrar as the starting point for what came afterward. He realized that this was an arbitrary choice—equally logically, he might have chosen Farrar's birth, or the Anschluss, or even (to stretch a point) the Great War.

But, being an artist of sorts, he considered that human beings had a fundamental need to create patterns from the chaos of history and from their own messy lives. A pattern had to start somewhere: even the author of Genesis had had to face up to this problem: *In the beginning God created the heaven and the earth.*

So Michael's pattern began with Farrar's death. If Farrar had reached London the following weekend, a world war might have taken a slightly different course; his death sent ripples even further into the future; it touched, perhaps marginally, on the rise and fall of empires.

In the final analysis, however, Michael was more concerned with the effects of Farrar's death on himself and on people he was later to know. That was where it mattered. Michael took things personally, which was why he was never particularly successful at his job. Uncle Claude never made that mistake.

Despite the fact that Michael had never met Farrar, he came to feel an almost proprietorial interest in him. In the years to come, he collected information about him.

At the time of his death, Farrar was thirty-five. He was five feet two and reputed to be hot-tempered. He had a widowed mother who lived in Worthing. Some time afterward, Michael checked to see if His Majesty's Government had seen fit to grant Mrs. Farrar a pension. He was not surprised to find that it hadn't. HMG, probably in the person of Uncle Claude, had used a Gestapo lie to avoid spending a few hundred pounds on an old lady who could give nothing in return. That was typical.

Farrar had worked as a traveling salesman on the Continent since 1936. He was employed by a struggling British toy firm which had built its reputation on the manufacture of toy soldiers. Z Organization had recruited him as a courier in Zurich on December 8, 1938.

Those were the salient facts about Farrar's life. The facts about the manner of his death were more difficult to establish. Michael had access to Z Organization's files, but these were sketchy at the best of times, and they were particularly bad for Vienna after the Nazis took over. Later he was able to use the SIS Registry, but here the facts were even thinner on the ground. It was true that the Vienna Station had more or less recovered from the disruption of the Anschluss by this time. The problem was that no one there had any interest in Farrar; they had no reason to disbelieve the official story, and hence no reason to investigate it. In 1939, few people in the service were aware that SIS was operating in tandem with a changeling half brother called Z.

Eventually Michael was able to consult the Vienna police file, though that was useful more for what it omitted than for what it included. According to the civil police, George Farrar died around midnight in room 47 of the Hotel Franz Josef on the Plosslgasse. The body was found the following morning by the chambermaid. Farrar was fully dressed, and lying supine on his bed; there were cherry-pink patches on his skin. The gas was on but unlit, and the cracks around the door and the window had been clumsily sealed with newspapers and towels. The chambermaid turned off the gas and fetched the manager; the manager called the police.

The police found the remains of a bottle of brandy, an empty glass, the room key, and a scrap of paper on the bedside table. Four English words had been scrawled in pencil on the paper: *I can't go on*. There was no reason to doubt that they had been written by the dead man, though the only standards of comparison were a few notes in Farrar's order book and his entry in the hotel register.

Further investigation showed that Farrar's financial affairs were in a bad way. The manager and the chambermaid testified that Herr Farrar had seemed distraught and depressed. Another witness came forward—a public-spirited Bavarian tourist, who claimed to have met Farrar in a café on the Ringstrasse a few hours before he died. According to the obliging Bavarian, Farrar had been drunk and talking of suicide; he blamed his problems on the international Jewish conspiracy.

Michael didn't dispute the evidence in the police file, except perhaps the testimonies about Farrar's state of mind. Of course it was curious that no one had thought to test the body for traces of cyanide—for cyanide, like carbon monoxide, left patches of lividity on a corpse. It was curious but not necessarily significant. The Viennese police sent Farrar's belongings to the British Embassy, which transmitted them to Worthing. They were itemized with Teutonic thoroughness on the file—right down to *Handkerchiefs, 6, Pair of Glasses (Broken),* and *Book Entitled* The Black Gang *by Sapper.*

But someone had been careless: there was no mention of a pencil.

Z Organization had a man in Vienna—indeed, William McQueen had intended to contact Farrar on the Thursday to pick up the gold. McQueen's cover was at risk, but he made cautious inquiries after Farrar's death. He found a waiter from the Franz Josef who admitted, when suitably primed with alcohol, that something odd had gone on that night. The manager had taken over the receptionist's evening shift. There was a rumor among the staff that two men from the Hotel Metropole had been seen in the Franz Josef on Wednesday night.

The Hotel Metropole was the Vienna headquarters of the Gestapo.

The gold was no longer among Farrar's belongings, but that was only to be expected. Uncle Claude and everyone else drew the obvious inference: the Gestapo had somehow identified Farrar as a courier; they had killed him and taken the gold. The fact that they had killed him—rather than used him as bait—suggested that they already knew for whom the gold was intended. Perhaps Farrar had talked before he died. As a result, Uncle Claude decided his resources were better used elsewhere: McQueen was transferred to Basle, and the Z network in Vienna never amounted to much.

The real irony only became apparent years later, when Michael was interrogating a Gestapo officer who had made something of a name for himself in wartime Holland. Knowing that his prisoner had previously served in Vienna, Michael threw in a question about the Farrar affair.

The officer, who was in the talkative, confiding phase of his interrogation, remembered it well, because of the gold. Farrar, it seemed, had been a womanizer whose bravado was in inverse proportion to his height. On the Tuesday night he had quarreled with a man he believed to be a German tourist. The cause of the dispute was the favors of a prostitute; and the scene of it was that bar on the Ringstrasse. Farrar had won.

The following evening, the plainclothes man and a colleague had paid a visit to the Franz Josef, intending merely to teach Farrar a lesson. Farrar was out, but the manager gave them a passkey to his room. While they were waiting, they discovered the gold concealed in his suitcase. The presence of undeclared gold marks worth nearly a thousand pounds sterling didn't suggest to the two policemen that Farrar was engaged in espionage. Why should it have done? In those days, plenty of people were trying to move hard currency out of Austria for the most personal of reasons, and foreigners, with their relative freedom to cross the frontiers of the Reich, were often used for the purpose.

On balance, it was safer to kill Farrar if they wanted to take the gold. The manager of the Franz Josef was persuaded to cooperate; he didn't want to lose his job and possibly his liberty. The officers had to give Michael's captive a percentage of the proceeds, because his authority was needed to ensure that the civil police drew the right conclusions.

The police did as they were told. It was, they were informed, a political matter which concerned the security of the Reich. And there was the irony: the lie was perfectly true.

George Farrar was murdered in Vienna on February 15, 1939: that was the beginning of Michael's pattern.

It was an arbitrary choice, yes: but at least it made the whole affair seem personal—and therefore easier to bear. It showed that affairs of state were ultimately dependent on the motives and actions of apparently insignificant individuals. What happened after Farrar's death was made somehow more intelligible by the idea that it could be traced back to the greed of two secret policemen, the whim of a Viennese whore, and the libido of a commercial traveler in toys.

I

Prewar
1939

One

The ivory ruler snapped in two as it hit the top of the desk. Three inches of it ricocheted off the polished oak and landed on Hugh's shoe. He jumped backward. The remaining nine inches stayed in Alfred Kendall's hand.

His father's knuckles, Hugh noticed, were the same color as the ruler.

Alfred Kendall turned slowly in his chair. He was still dressed in his City clothes, which lent an odd formality to the proceedings.

"Do you mean to tell me that the headmaster is *lying?*"

"No, Father." Hugh's hands clenched behind his back. His body was treacherously determined to tremble. "Mr. Jervis was mistaken. I—"

"Don't lie to me, boy. I've known Mr. Jervis for a good ten years. He isn't a fool." Kendall tapped the letter in front of him. "Nor is he the sort of man to fling around wild accusations."

Hugh's vision blurred. "I didn't do it."

The words came out more loudly than he had intended. For a moment his father stared contemptuously at him. Hugh tried to look away. It was almost with relief that he saw his father begin to gnaw his lower lip with a long, yellow tooth. This was almost invariably a preliminary to speech.

"Never did I think I should read such a letter about a son of mine." Kendall's voice hardened. "You don't seem to realize that you've brought shame on the entire family."

Hugh shrugged. It was a gesture of discomfort, not insolence, but his father interpreted it otherwise. Kendall's slap caught Hugh unawares: he reeled back against the table.

"That," his father said slowly, "is just a foretaste of what you should expect. Don't snivel. Listen to what Mr. Jervis has to say about you. 'Dear Captain Kendall, It is with deep regret that I have been forced to expel your son Hugh from the school, with immediate effect. One of his classmates had foolishly brought a ten-shilling note to school. Just before luncheon, the boy reported it had been stolen. It was subsequently found in the pocket of Hugh's overcoat. Hugh, I am afraid, made matters worse by trying to dissemble his guilt. For the sake of the other boys in my charge, I cannot permit a pupil who has proved to be both a thief and a liar to remain for a moment longer than necessary. I will forward the termly account at a later date.'

"The *termly* account, you note. In the circumstances, Mr. Jervis is quite within his rights to charge for the entire Lent term. Have you any idea what the fees are like for a first-rate prep school like Thameside College? Your brother used his time there to win a scholarship. But you have wantonly wasted your opportunities from the first. I scrimp and save to give you the finest education available in England—and this is how you repay me. Do you think that's fair? Do you think that's reasonable? Answer me, boy."

Hugh's eyes were heavy with tears. Humiliation bred anger, which in turn created a brief and desperate courage.

"I . . . I thought—"

"Don't mumble at me. And don't you know that tears are unmanly?"

"I thought Aunt Vida was paying my fees."

Purple blotches appeared on Kendall's face. He jerked himself out of his chair and towered over Hugh.

"You impudent little wretch," he said softly. "You will regret that, I promise you."

Hugh's courage evaporated. He had been stupid to mention Aunt Vida. None of the children was supposed to know that she paid their school fees. But Stephen had found out years ago from their aunt's housekeeper.

This time the blow was a back-hander. The edge of Kendall's wedding ring cut into the skin over Hugh's cheekbone. He cannoned into the table and fell to the ground.

"Get up. And don't you dare bleed on the carpet."

Hugh got slowly to his feet. He touched his cheek and looked at the smear of blood on his fingers.

"Handkerchief."

Hugh pulled out the grubby ball of linen from his trouser pocket.

4

He dabbed his face, conscious that his father was still looming over him. Adults were so unfairly large.

"You despicable little animal," Kendall whispered. "You're no son of mine, you know. You must get it from your mother's side."

Hugh held back a sob with difficulty. He knew he would cry sooner or later, but he was determined to put it off for as long as possible. What was happening to him was unjust; yet for some reason that didn't seem important beside the fact that he disgusted his father. He was bitterly ashamed of himself. He wished he was dead.

"Bring me the cane. The thinner one."

The two canes were kept in the corner between the wall and the end of the bookcase. Hugh sometimes daydreamed of burning them. The thicker one, curiously enough, was less painful. The thin one was longer and suppler; it hissed in the air, gathering venom as it swung.

He handed it to this father. It was part of the ritual that the victim should present the means of punishment to the executioner.

Alfred Kendall tapped the cane against one pin-striped trouser leg. "You know what to do, Hugh. Waiting won't make it easier for you. I can promise you that."

Hugh turned away and unhooked the S-shaped metal snake that held up his trousers. His fingers groped at the buttons. When the last one was undone, the trousers fell to his ankles. He shuffled across the room to the low armchair where his mother sat in the evenings. He could feel a draft from somewhere on the back of his knees.

The chair had a low back, Hugh stretched over it, extending his arms along the chair's arms for support. His mother's knitting bag was on the seat of the chair. He could see the purple wool of the jersey she was knitting for Stephen.

His father's heavy footsteps advanced toward him and then retreated. This, too, was part of the ritual: Alfred Kendall was a man who liked to take measurements. Hugh knew there were four paces between the desk and the chair. To be precise, there were three paces and a little jump. After the jump, his father would grunt like someone straining on a lavatory. Then would come the pain.

The footsteps returned, and Hugh held his breath. The first blow caught him by surprise, as it always did. In the interim between beatings, you forgot that it hurt so much.

The cane wrapped around his buttocks. It felt like a branding iron. Despite himself, Hugh yelped. He pressed himself forward against the back of the chair. His hands dug into the arms.

The footsteps slowly retreated. Once again, they advanced.

The cane seemed to land on precisely the same spot. This time, Hugh cried out. His father said nothing, though his breathing was more labored than usual; he never spoke when administering punishment.

Hugh tried to concentrate on counting. You never knew in advance how many strokes you were going to get. Four was probably the average, at least for himself and Stephen, though it was at least a year since Stephen had been beaten; Meg usually had three, but then she was a girl. Five was by no means unknown. Stephen boasted that he had been given six on two occasions.

Five—Six. Hugh stirred, but even the slightest movement made the pain worse. His arms and legs were trembling. To his horror, he realized that the footsteps were again coming toward him.

Seven.

Eight.

Hugh's legs buckled. He was crying now—the pain was so great that he no longer cared. His tears glistened on the purple wool.

"Stand up," snapped his father. "Can't you even take your punishment like a man?"

There was a clatter as his father returned the cane to its corner. Metal and flint rasped together, and the smell of tobacco filled the air.

Hugh levered himself into an upright position. For a few seconds he stared stupidly at the trousers which shackled his ankles. He bent down with difficulty and tugged them up to his waist. The pain was no longer blindingly acute; it had softened, if that was the right word, to a dull, angry throb. Every movement made it worse.

Alfred Kendall was leaning on the desk; he held the Gold Flake in his left hand. His thumb and forefinger were stained yellow, like the ragged fringe of his military mustache.

He exhaled a lungful of smoke in the direction of his son. "Well?"

Hugh had missed his cue. The ritual demanded that the victim should thank the executioner. It was an exquisite refinement: you thanked someone for inflicting pain on you, thereby implying you deserved or even desired it. It suddenly became very important to Hugh that he should not make the required response.

"I am waiting, Hugh."

6

His father walked slowly toward him. With him he brought his characteristic smell—a compound of stale tobacco, hair oil, and a musty, sooty odor which Hugh associated with suburban trains. Without warning, Kendall nipped the lobe of Hugh's ear between finger and thumb and twisted it through ninety degrees.

Hugh gasped and tried to pull his head away.

"You always were a weakling," his father observed. His grip tightened on the lobe. "A real boy of your background would have learned to stand punishment years ago. I'm still waiting."

It was at this moment that Hugh decided never to forgive his father in any circumstance. Aloud, he said, "Thank you, sir."

Alfred Kendall released the ear and nodded toward the door. Hugh, who was expert at interpreting his father's nods, opened the door and stood aside to allow his father to pass through first. Kendall set great store by the courtesy that men owed to women, and the young to their elders and betters. It was a sign, he often remarked, of good breeding.

His father flung open the kitchen door and motioned to Hugh to stand beside him in the doorway.

They were all in there. The opening of the door had cut off both their conversation and their movements, leaving a strained, still silence. Hugh's mother was standing by the gas cooker, stirring the contents of a saucepan; the rich smell of mutton stew made his mouth water. Meg, still in her school uniform, was at the kitchen table doing her homework. Stephen sat opposite her; he had changed since he got back from the bank, and the *Star* was spread open in front of him. Hugh was sure that they had been talking about him. He knew from experience that the sound of a caning was clearly audible from the hall.

Kendall sucked on his cigarette. "Hugh will go straight to bed. He will have nothing to eat tonight, and no one will visit him. Do I make myself clear?"

Mrs. Kendall covered the saucepan with its lid. "Alfred, perhaps I should—"

"I've made up my mind, Muriel. The boy's enough of a namby-pamby as it is, without you trying to make it worse. We'll have dinner at the usual time."

He laid a heavy hand on Hugh's shoulder, turned him around, and pushed him toward the stairs.

The stairs were a form of torture. Hugh climbed slowly, clinging to the banister; his body protested at every step. He heard his

7

father go back into the dining room and close the door.

From the landing another flight of stairs wound upward to the attic where Meg slept. Hugh could just remember the time when the room had belonged to a maid. On the right was the big bedroom at the front, where his parents slept; Stephen had the room opposite. Hugh's was farther down the landing toward the back of the house, next to the bathroom over the scullery.

His room was small and cold, but at least it was his alone. He shut the door behind him and closed the curtains. He was crying again now no one could see him—softly and wearily. His body ached. As he shrugged himself out of his jacket, his teeth began to chatter.

Usually his mother gave him a hot-water bottle when he came to bed; such luxuries were out of the question tonight. His pajamas felt clammy. He pulled them on and rolled gingerly into bed.

It was obviously impossible to lie on his back. He discovered that lying on his side was almost as bad. The problem with lying on his front was that it brought the weight of the bedclothes on to his back. On the other hand, without the blankets he stood no chance whatsoever of warming up.

Hugh had forgotten to switch out the light, but for the moment he lacked the energy to get out of bed again. There was a line of lead soldiers deployed on the mantelpiece. Soldiers were a little babyish, but he still enjoyed playing with them in private. Major Hugh Kendall (VC and bar) was leading a daring patrol through no-man's-land, attended by his faithful batman Hiawatha the Red Indian. Hiawatha was Hugh's oldest soldier; most of his paint was gone, and his costume looked a little incongruous beside the Great War uniforms of the rest of the patrol. But Hiawatha always had to be included. Perhaps he was working as a secret agent, and was therefore in disguise; Major Kendall's job was to infiltrate him through the enemy lines.

Hugh tried to make the story continue in his mind, but it was no use. Instead he found himself thinking about the war his father had said was coming. With luck his father might get killed. He hugged the thought guiltily to himself.

The hours slipped slowly by. Every quarter of an hour, chimes from the clock in the drawing room filled the house. His mother spent hours cleaning that clock. It was in the form of a black marble triumphal arch, upon which two modestly attired cupids were frolicking; it had been a wedding present to his parents.

There were other sounds that signified the passage of time.

Hugh's room was directly over the kitchen. He could hear the clatter of pans and plates as the meal was prepared; and occasionally the scrape of a chair and the murmur of conversation. From half past seven onward, there was nearly half an hour of silence: everyone was in the dining room. Suddenly he felt very hungry.

Food would have warmed him, as well as satisfied his hunger. The cold seemed to be seeping into his bones. His muscles were stiffening up. With immense effort he wriggled out of bed, knowing that to leave his light on was to risk another beating. Before getting back into bed, he picked up Hiawatha. As he lay there shivering, the little lead figure grew warm in his hand.

At a quarter past nine, he heard footsteps shuffling down the landing. It was Meg's bedtime, and she was coming to use the bathroom. There were familiar sounds—the running of water, the flushing of the cistern, and the small explosion as she drew back the bolt.

Her steps paused outside his door. Hugh heard the faint creak of the doorknob rotating. Meg came into the room and closed the door behind her with great care. She tiptoed slowly across the floor to the bed. Hugh tensed and then relaxed. He began to cry again, this time with relief: at least someone cared enough about him to come and see him.

The springs groaned as Meg sat on the edge of the bed. She bent down, and her long dark hair brushed his cheek. Hugh stretched out his hand and felt the thick flannel of her dressing gown. Her breath was fresh with toothpaste.

"Are you all right?" she whispered. "How many did you get?"

"Eight." Hugh felt a certain pride in this. "It hurts all over. And I'm starving."

"I managed to save you a bit of bread."

He crammed the bread into his mouth. It tasted delicious. He also ate some fluff which the bread must have picked up from Meg's pocket. He swallowed the last mouthful with regret.

"Where are they?" he asked.

"Father and Mother are in the dining room. Stephen's gone out, the lucky devil. We haven't been allowed to mention your name all evening."

"What's going to happen to me?"

"How should I know?" Meg's weight shifted on the mattress. "Can I come into bed with you? I'm freezing."

Hugh made room for her. She slid into bed beside him. He felt embarrassed, which was odd because they had often cuddled up together to keep each other warm; but for some reason they hadn't done it as much in the last couple of years. Meg used to want to play Mothers and Fathers, which he thought was a girlish game.

His sister gurgled with laughter. "Your feet are like ice. Here, put them against my legs." As she spoke, she put an arm around him. He could feel her warmth from his shoulders to her feet.

"It's all right for Stephen," Meg said. "He can get away from it. He said he was going to the pictures, but I bet he's going drinking. Father would kill him if he knew what Stephen gets up to. I wish I were a boy."

Hugh sniffed. "It's not much fun."

"Not like you, silly. Like Stephen. Did you know he started smoking? He buys those Turkish cigarettes, the oval ones. And since he started work at the bank he's hardly ever at home. In the evening he usually goes out."

"Where does he go?" Hugh didn't really want to know, but it was comfortable to have Meg whispering in his ear. He didn't want to give her an excuse for going.

"I'm sure he goes to parties and shows and restaurants." Meg's voice was bitter. "I know he sees a lot of people he knew at school. Especially Paul Bennet: you know the one—his father's filthy rich and they've got a Rolls-Royce. The friends Stephen chooses always have pots of money—have you noticed that?"

Hugh snuggled closer to his sister. His shoulder was against her breasts. He was beginning to feel drowsy. When she spoke again, her whisper was so low he could hardly catch what she was saying.

"You know Mary? She's awfully nice—she's in my form at school and we do *everything* together. She saw Stephen and Paul on Sunday, in Richmond Park. They were with *girls*. Mary said they had their arms around their waists. She said the girls looked terribly common and—you know—flashy."

Hugh wasn't quite sure what she meant, but he grunted encouragingly. Meg sounded strangely breathless, as if she found the subject absolutely fascinating. He forced himself to find a question to keep the conversation going.

"Are you going to go out with chaps when you grow up?"

Meg wriggled beside him. "Of course I am. They'll be rich, too—perhaps they'll have titles. They'll take me to nightclubs, you know, and we'll drink champagne and dance very close to each other." She made a sound which was halfway between a sob and a sigh. "The trouble is, I never get a chance to meet anyone. Father keeps us cooped up like prisoners. He never lets us invite anyone home. Mary's people are always having parties. And her brothers bring their friends. They had a tennis tournament last summer and Mark (that's her elder brother) brought a friend from Oxford. He was called Gerald and looked like Robert Donat. He kissed Mary, in the summerhouse. And it was a proper kiss, too, not just a peck on the cheek."

Hugh wondered what a proper kiss was: presumably it was a peck on the mouth.

"Sometimes," Meg hissed in his ear, "I feel so jealous of Mary I could burst. She knows such a lot about men already." Her arm tightened around Hugh. "I say," she said casually. "Eight must have hurt an awful lot. Can I see it?"

"It's dark," Hugh protested sleepily. "We can't put the light on again. Besides—"

He stopped, aware he couldn't put his other objection into words, even to himself. In any case, he didn't want to offend Meg.

She seemed to understand what was in his mind. "Don't be an idiot. You're my little brother—I used to help bathe you. Anyway if it's dark, I wouldn't see anything. I could just touch."

"If you like." Hugh tried to make himself sound indifferent. "But be careful: it's jolly painful."

Meg's free hand moved slowly down his spine. She hesitated when she came to the top of his pajama trousers. He had left the cord untied in the hope that it would be less painful. Her hand slipped underneath.

Hugh winced as her fingers gently touched the line of welts. His father's aim had been good: most of the strokes had fallen on the same spot. She touched one of the scabs and sucked in her breath sharply.

"It bled quite a lot," Hugh said proudly.

"You poor darling."

Meg's hand moved on. It cupped one of his buttocks for an instant, and then stroked the top of his thighs. Where she touched the welts, it was painful; but elsewhere it made Hugh tingle. He felt a warmth growing inside him. Her hand slipped down between his legs.

Suddenly they both heard footsteps coming along the land-ing.

Hugh and Meg held their breath. They knew it must be their mother—she walked slowly and lightly, while their father's step was brisk and heavy. As his mother reached the door of his room, Hugh clutched Hiawatha so tightly that one of the Indian's arms bent beneath the strain.

But the footsteps passed on to the bathroom. As soon as the bolt shot across, Meg began to wriggle out of bed. In her haste she scraped a fingernail across one of the scabs; Hugh nearly cried out. A long, bare leg rubbed against Hugh's arm. Meg put on her slippers and bent down to Hugh.

"Don't make a sound. I'll wait behind the door until she's gone back downstairs."

Next door, the lavatory flushed. His mother's footsteps paused outside Hugh's door, but moved on after a few seconds. Hugh didn't know whether to be relieved or hurt: his mother's fear of his father was greater than her desire to comfort him.

Meg waited a moment and then left without even saying good night. Hugh half wished she would come back to bed, despite the risks. Her visit had made him both warmer and happier. He stirred in the bed; he was suddenly conscious of his body as something outside himself. He realized that other people could give it pleasure as well as pain.

"We'll survive old fellow," he whispered to Hiawatha. "The enemy may have won the battle, but he hasn't won the war."

There would be a respectful grin on the usually impassive face of his batman. "Yes, sir. The men are all in good spirits. Permission to kip down?"

"Granted," Hugh said. He laid Hiawatha beneath the pillow, but kept his hand on top of him.

Hiawatha may have gone to sleep at once, but it took Hugh much longer. His drowsiness seemed to have gone. He heard his parents come to bed just after eleven. Neither of them came in to see him.

The last thing he was aware of was the clock downstairs striking midnight.

Alfred Kendall always went into the office on Saturday mornings. The journey by train and bus from Twickenham to the City marked the transition from the problems of home to the problems of work.

Sometimes he could distract himself from them with a newspaper or a thriller, but not today.

Kendall and Son occupied two rooms of a building in Sweetmeat Court; in palmier days they had rented the entire first floor. Miss Leaming, the angular secretary whom Kendall had inherited from his father, was in the outer office. She was the firm's last employee: Kendall kept her on solely because a younger and more efficient secretary would have required a higher salary.

Miss Leaming fussed ineffectually over his wet overcoat.

"I hope you've done the post," Kendall said.

She avoided his eyes. "Yes, sir. It's on your desk."

Kendall turned down the gas fire. "We're not made of money, you know," he said over his shoulder as he went into the inner office.

The letters he found on his blotter soured his mood still further. The new director of the Nuranyo glass works at Pilsen announced that he was unable to fulfill some foreign orders, including Kendall's, owing to a change in company policy. Kendall snorted: a lot of Czech companies had altered their policy since Hitler annexed the Sudetenland, the strip of Bohemia adjoining Germany, last September.

Kendall's bank manager had written to remind him that the firm's overdraft now stood at £343 6s. 9d.; he drew Mr. Kendall's attention to the fact that the original overdraft facility had been for £250, to be repaid at the end of January, nearly three weeks ago. A letter from Kendall's solicitor discussed the bankruptcy of Kendall's one important creditor; it looked as though Kendall and Son would be lucky to get three shillings in the pound.

Kendall and Son. Even the name of the firm was a reminder of failure. Kendall had always imagined that Stephen would follow him into the business one day. But one didn't take passengers on board a sinking ship. Stephen was better off at the bank: at least his job was secure and he had prospects.

There was one more letter. As its envelope was marked *Private and Confidential,* Miss Leaming had not opened it. Kendall frowned when he saw the address at the head of the paper: his correspondent was a member of White's.

Kendall would have given a great deal to be able to use that stationery himself. Every time he passed through St James's Street he looked up at the club's great bow window and yearned to be on the other side of the glass.

He glanced at the signature and tugged his mustache uneasily.

He knew Sir Basil Cohen by repute, of course, and had met him briefly at one of the annual dinners of the British Glass Association. Sir Basil was Jewish, but Kendall was forced to admit that an unfortunate—well, ungentlemanly—racial background counted for little in comparison with the man's immense wealth and influence. Cohen was not only chairman of Amalgamated British Glass: his business interests ranged from films to diamonds, and extended over four continents.

The letter was short, but it took Kendall several minutes to decipher Cohen's ornate but nearly illegible hand.

Dear Kendall,

You may recall that we met at the BGA dinner in '37. I wonder if you could spare the time to see an acquaintance of mine, Michael Stanhope-Smith. He is looking for a man with your qualifications to undertake a small commission for him. His work is of national importance; and I fancy that he is in a position to offer some sort of honorarium, should you accept his proposition.

I understand that he intends to telephone you at your office on Saturday or Monday.

Yours sincerely,

Basil Cohen

Kendall's hand trembled slightly as he lit a cigarette. He was in the grip of an unfamiliar emotion: it took him a moment to realize that it was hope. There was more to this than the prospect of earning some money. An international financier was asking a favor of him; he, Alfred Kendall, was needed for work of national importance.

The nature of the commission continued to puzzle him, since his only qualification was a thorough knowledge of the glass-importing business. Perhaps Stanhope-Smith was a senior civil servant at the Board of Trade (and possibly a member of White's himself). A government inquiry might be in the air—and not before time. Stanhope-Smith might have asked Sir Basil to recommend an experienced man to help frame the inquiry's terms of reference.

Who knew where it might end? One thing could so easily lead to another, once one's face was known in the right places. He was in the prime of life: he could still go far. He drifted into a reverie that involved Sir Basil and Stanhope-Smith congratulating him on his appearance on the New Year's honors list.

Just as Kendall was considering the respective merits of the various orders of knighthood, the telephone began to ring.

"Kendall and Son." Miss Leaming's cracked voice was clearly audible through the partition wall. "I'm sorry, sir: I didn't catch your name."

Two

After church on Sundays, the Kendalls called on Aunt Vida. Stephen said it was just like their father to pay his respects to God and Mammon on the same morning.

Aunt Vida lived in Richmond. The Kendalls went there by train from Twickenham. Mr. and Mrs. Kendall walked together from the station, together but never arm in arm. The children trailed behind. Hugh always walked the short distance to Richmond Green with his head held unnaturally high. This was because his mother considered that a clean Eton collar was pleasing in the sight of the Lord and Aunt Vida; it chafed his neck mercilessly until it wilted.

Wilmot House was in a small street near Maid of Honor Row. Prim black railings and a narrow strip of flowerbed separated the pavement from the red-brick Georgian façade. A brass knocker shaped like a mermaid twinkled incongruously on the chaste, olive-green front door.

Hugh always enjoyed the change of atmosphere when he stepped into the house. Outside, everything was bright and regular; but the interior was dark and full of secrets. The hall was nearly a foot below ground level outside. It was stone-flagged and paneled in dark oak. The glass in the fanlight was green with age, which gave the hall the appearance of being under water.

Mrs. Bunnings, the housekeeper, answered Alfred Kendall's knock. She gave a nod and held the door open as the family trooped into the hall.

Mrs. Kendall said, with an apologetic twitter, "And how is Mrs. Lane today?"

"As well as can be expected, ma'am," Mrs. Bunnings said grimly.

"The mistress is in the drawing room."

She disposed of the Kendalls' hats and coats and announced them ceremoniously. In the unimaginably far-off days of her youth, Mrs. Bunnings had been a parlor maid in the household of a baronet; an Edwardian stateliness still distinguished her public manner.

Aunt Vida awoke with a start as they filed into the drawing room. As usual, she was wearing a shapeless gray dress beneath a thick gray cardigan. Around her neck were three gold lockets, each with its own chain. Each contained a photograph and a lock of hair: one was a shrine to the late Mr. Lane, the others to their sons, George and Harry, both of whom had been killed at Passchendaele.

Alfred Kendall shook her hand and mumbled a vague inquiry about her health into his mustache. She didn't bother to reply. The rest of the family kissed her cheek; it smelled of lavender water and felt like tissue paper.

"Run along to the kitchen," Aunt Vida said to Hugh and Meg. "Give them a glass of milk, Bunnings, and then you can bring in the sherry."

Meg and Hugh followed Mrs. Bunnings out of the room. Until last year, Stephen would have gone with them. But when he left school, Mrs. Bunnings started to call him Mr. Stephen rather than Master Stephen; she made it quite plain that he was now too grown-up to have the freedom of her kitchen.

In her own domain, Mrs. Bunnings became a different person. She told jokes; she gossiped; she pried indefatigably into their lives. She also gave the children scones, which was contrary to Mr. Kendall's strict instructions that their appetites should not be spoiled.

She left them for a moment to take the sherry and biscuits into the parlor. When she got back, she tapped Hugh on the shoulder.

"What's all this, young man? I heard your dad saying you'd been expelled from that school of yours."

Hugh flushed. "I have. Someone stole some money and they thought it was me. But it wasn't—I promise."

Meg dabbed at the rim of milk around her lips with a handkerchief. "Father gave him eight of the best," she said ghoulishly. "He had nothing to eat on Friday night, and he was only allowed bread and water yesterday."

Mrs. Bunnings snorted. "I know who I'd beat if I had half a chance. Have another scone, you poor lamb."

When alone with the children, the housekeeper never made any secret of her dislike of their father. Miss Muriel, Mrs. Lane's niece, had been as happy as the day was long before she married him: and look at her now. Their father only bothered with these weekly visits because he wanted to get his hands on Mrs. Lane's money. Mrs. Bunnings didn't know why he troubled to come since, when he got here, he just sat there and grunted.

"What will he do with you now? Has he found you another school?"

"I don't know." Hugh avoided Mrs. Bunnings's eyes. His fingers traced the reassuring shape of Hiawatha in his trouser pocket.

"Father says that if Hugh was a few years older he'd pack him off to Australia and have done with him." Under the table, Meg put her hand on Hugh's knee; it made him shiver. "He really means it."

Hugh shifted uneasily. Sitting down was still uncomfortable, and he wished Meg would remove her hand. Mrs. Bunnings might see. The long, low kitchen was like a hothouse; Mrs. Bunnings had insisted on keeping the old-fashioned range. The heat, the food, and even the sympathy combined to make him feel drowsy.

A bell jangled over the door. It was precisely twenty minutes after they had entered the house. Mr. Kendall always timed their visits with meticulous care. At the end of the twenty minutes, he would stand up and announce they had to be going, usually when his wife was in mid-sentence.

Mrs. Bunnings escorted the children back to the drawing room to say good-bye. Mr. Kendall was waiting impatiently by the door. Hugh had often wondered why his father seemed always to be in a hurry to be somewhere else; when he reached the somewhere else, he was always in a hurry to leave there as well.

For once, Aunt Vida seemed reluctant to let them go. She made Mr. Kendall make up the fire for her. She suddenly remembered that she wanted her niece to get her some wool; the commission involved a great deal of explanation, during which Mr. Kendall jabbed angrily at the fire with the poker. He consulted his watch.

"We shall miss the train if we don't hurry."

"Off you go then." Aunt Vida paused. "Hugh, come over here. I want a word with you."

Alfred Kendall turned in the doorway.

"Hugh can run after you," Aunt Vida said firmly, before he could protest. "Please close the door behind you."

Kendall gnawed his lower lip but said nothing. He shut the door behind him; with a little more force, it would have been a slam.

Aunt Vida beckoned Hugh toward her. "I hear you've been in hot water again."

Hugh nodded. There was nothing he could say.

"Bring me my handbag. It's on the bureau."

Like his father, Aunt Vida was always giving orders; Hugh found it odd that he wasn't afraid of her. His parents and Meg were afraid of her—even Stephen was wary of what he said and did in her company. He fetched her the battered black bag and stood patiently while she rummaged in it. He watched her face with fascination: her skin was a maze of wrinkles; there were more cracks than surface.

Suddenly she glanced up at him. "Don't you know it's rude to stare at a lady? Hey?"

Hugh grinned. He heard the front door closing with a bang; Mrs. Bunnings was glad to see the back of her visitors.

Aunt Vida nodded in the direction of the sound. "Don't let it get on top of you," she said gruffly. "These things pass. Worse things happen at sea, not that that's much consolation. When your father asks why I kept you, say I was telling you to be a better boy in the future. Here, hold out your hand."

Hugh looked down. On his palm was a half-crown.

"Kendall?" Colonel Dansey stared with distaste at his plate; it was difficult to tell whether it was the omelet or the name of Kendall that was responsible for the irritation in his voice. "Who the devil's he?"

"He's a glass importer, sir." Michael Stanhope-Smith sipped his burgundy appreciatively. Early in their acquaintance, he had learned that it was a mistake to deluge Uncle Claude with information; Dansey himself never made that mistake, and he expected those who worked for him to be equally sparing.

Michael glanced over his shoulder to make sure that no one was in earshot of their table. The dining room at the Savoy was still moderately crowded, but it had definitely passed the Sunday lunch-time peak.

Dansey arranged his knife and fork neatly on his empty plate. He adjusted the dark-rimmed pebble glasses on his large, curved nose. "You know that I don't encourage people to indulge in recruiting off their own bat. Recruit in haste and repent at leisure."

Michael flushed. He was twenty-five; he was two stone heavier and six inches taller; but Uncle Claude could still make him feel like a schoolboy who hadn't washed behind the ears.

"I haven't actually interviewed him yet. I telephoned him yesterday; we've arranged to meet tomorrow."

"I see. And why this unseemly haste, may I ask?"

"You haven't heard? Farrar's dead. Apparently he killed himself—sealed the drafts and turned on the gas in his hotel room. The signal came in from Vienna on Friday night."

Dansey said nothing. He appeared to be concentrating on adjusting the red carnation in the buttonhole of his dark blue suit.

Michael swallowed. "William McQueen talked to a waiter at the hotel. He said that Farrar might have had a couple of visitors in his room the evening before he died. Probably Gestapo, though we've had no confirmation of that. You know how difficult it is to get hard information out of Austria these days."

Dansey gave a scarcely perceptible shrug. "It's immaterial. Farrar couldn't have told them anything. He hadn't been briefed."

In the pause which followed, Michael sipped his wine to cover his confusion. It was brutally obvious to him that Dansey didn't care that Farrar had in all likelihood been killed. It was at most an inconvenience. A newly recruited courier was of little weight in Uncle Claude's professional scale of values. If this was professionalism, Michael thought bitterly, he wished he was an amateur.

"Do go on," Dansey suggested. "You were about to explain why you found it necessary to circumvent the standard recruitment procedure."

"Farrar was due to return to London, and then go on to Prague at the end of the week. You said the Prague trip was vital, sir. I would have contacted you, but you were on a train somewhere between Zurich and London. I thought I'd better act on my own initiative."

"And how did your initiative lead you to this man Kendall?"

"We need someone with a bona fide reason to go to Prague—preferably a commerical one. I thought Prague—Bohemia—glass; and then I remembered Sir Basil Cohen."

"You know Basil?" Dansey said sharply. "How did that come about?"

"I was at Cambridge with his younger son. I stayed with his people down in Gloucestershire once or twice."

"I see." For once Dansey sounded almost amiable.

Michael's mind immediately made a connection. Cohen had been very helpful, right from the start. Dansey had been cultivating the friendship of the wealthy and the powerful for nealy half a century. Many of them were now unobtrusively helping Dansey's Z Organization in a variety of ways. It was not inconceivable that Cohen was among them. In that case, Sir Basil must have derived a great deal of private amusement from Michael's claim that he was working for the Foreign Office trade section.

A muscle twitched in Dansey's cheek. In a lesser man, it might have been a grin.

"I telephoned him—luckily he was in town. He was dining at White's, but he said he could spare me a few minutes there after dinner." Michael glanced quickly at Dansey and hurriedly continued. "I—well—implied I had some sort of FO connection. I said we needed an unofficial trade representative in Prague—someone who made regular trips there and could combine his own work with a little confidential work for us. Sir Basil asked a few questions, of course, but I was as discreet as possible."

A waiter moved tentatively toward the table. Dansey waved him away. "What do you know about Kendall?"

"He works from an office in the City. He buys mainly from Czechoslovakia. His main customers in this country are provincial department stores. It's an old-fashioned firm, run on prewar lines. Apparently Kendall's in a bad way financially—Sir Basil reckons he must be on his last legs."

"Does Basil know him personally?"

"They've met, sir, but that's about all. I rather gathered that Kendall isn't quite . . ." Michael's voice trailed away. He believed that all men were equal but had long since discovered that most of his friends and colleagues paid only lip service to the notion. He despised snobbery; but he was intelligent enough to realize that it couldn't be ignored.

Dansey nodded understandingly. "Any war record?"

"Yes, sir; I checked with the War Office. Enlisted in the Pay Corps in 1915 as a private. Commissioned in 1918. He ended the war as an acting captain, after four years behind a desk in Whitehall." Michael made his voice as neutral as possible. "It seems that he likes to be called Captain Kendall."

Dansey's eyebrows rose. "Despite the fact he never held a regular commission?"

"Yes, sir."

The eyebrows fell back into place. Dansey poured out the last of the burgundy and signaled to the waiter to bring their coffee. He was not in the mood for pudding or cheese and he assumed, correctly, that Michael would be content to follow his lead. By now they were almost alone in the big dining room, except for tail-coated waiters who swooped like swallows among the empty tables, clearing them with deft, darting movements. Michael could feel the hard edges of his sketchbook in the pocket of his jacket. He had a sudden urge to draw what he could see, to record an instant in the life of the Savoy in black and white. He would use lots of heavy shading, and soften the outlines as much as possible.

He grinned into his burgundy at the thought of what Dansey would say if he started to draw. It was well known that Dansey considered that the chief purpose of art was to be a tool of espionage: it was a convenient means of creating a visual record of enemy installations. The old man knew that Michael had once wanted to be an artist. What he didn't know was that Michael still did.

The waiter brought their coffee and withdrew. Dansey produced a cigarette case and offered it to Michael. As Michael lit their cigarettes, he noticed that Dansey's hand was speckled with brown liver spots and trembled slightly. The hand reminded him that Dansey had already reached the age when most men were thinking of retirement.

"I'm dining with your godfather tonight," Dansey said abruptly.

It was not a social observation. Michael's godfather, Admiral Sinclair, was head of SIS, the sponsor of Z Organization. If it hadn't been for Sinclair, it was unlikely that Michael would now be at the Savoy with a decent suit on his back. In all probability he would have been teaching history, art, and games at some godforsaken little prep school. Sometimes Michael wished he was.

"Do give him my regards," Michael said.

As always, Dansey's words had at least two layers of meanings. He was hinting that he would take the opportunity to protect himself in the event of something going wrong with Kendall: Michael was the precooked scapegoat, ready for eating if the need should arise. But there was another implication: Dansey was tacitly accepting what Michael had done; it was the first time that Michael had been allowed to make an independent decision; and that, he supposed, might be construed as progress.

"You're meeting Kendall tomorrow?"

"Yes, sir—for lunch."

"If you do decide to take him on, you are to act as his sole control. I want him to have no contact with anyone else in London.

He's not to be given the emergency addresses in Vienna or Budapest or Zurich—is that clear? You can offer him his expenses plus fifty pounds; he can have fifteen pounds now and the rest when he returns. And get receipts."

"How much should I tell him?"

"As little as possible, of course." Dansey's eyebrows rose once more. "My dear Stanhope-Smith, surely your artistic temperament hasn't prevented you from grasping that simple principle? All the man has to do is take something to Prague and bring something back. Unless you're even more foolish than you look, you won't mention Hase to him. Just teach Kendall one of the standard recognition drills and tell him to go to his usual hotel. You can then inform Hase of the arrangements independently by telegram. I'm sure you will be able to resist the temptation to wire direct; it really would be much wiser to route it through Zurich and Budapest."

Michael almost flinched at the quiet savagery which had suddenly invaded Dansey's voice. At first he was inclined to attribute it to the bitterness which Dansey felt because Michael had been forced on him by Sinclair; then he noticed the lines of pain in Dansey's forehead, and the tiny beads of sweat on his temples. He felt an unexpected stab of pity for the man opposite him: combining a job like his with an ulcer must be an impossible task.

Dansey stubbed out his cigarette, precisely in the center of the ashtray. Only when the last shred of tobacco was extinguished did he speak again. "This is important, you know. There's very little time. The Czech *Deuxième Bureau* is really very good. They estimate that Hitler will move within a month—six weeks at the outside. Then there will be no Czechoslovakia—just another province of the Reich. We have to be in place by then."

"May I ask a question, sir? If Czech military intelligence is so good, they must be making their own contingency plans. Why aren't we coordinating with them?"

Dansey shrugged wearily. "We are. Colonel Moravec and Gibson—he's the SIS Head-of-Station in Prague, you know—are practically blood brothers. But Moravec's an intelligence-gatherer, not a guerrilla chieftain. His idea of a resistance movement is based on the Boy Scouts—and his political masters think the same. The other problem is geographical: a resistance movement needs a foreign base. Moravec naturally thinks of us and France, though God knows why after what we did to them at Munich. But it's over two hundred miles between the French and Czechoslovak borders at their nearest points. And that's as the crow flies across the Reich."

Michael suddenly understood what Dansey was driving at. "But there's another potential anti-Nazi ally whose border is far closer? And that's why Hase is so important?"

"Not just Hase. God help us, even Kendall could be important." Dansey's thin lips twisted. "In the circumstances it's probably just as well you used your initiative." He gave Michael no time to savor the unexpected compliment. "Where are you intending to have lunch with him?"

"I thought perhaps the Berkeley Grill. Get him in a good humor."

"I think not, Stanhope-Smith. Catering to the sybaritic whims of its junior employees is not one of the purposes of this organization. I'm told that one can find a very decent lunch at a Lyons corner house."

Dansey pushed back his chair and stood up. The movement triggered a flurry of activity among the waiters near the door. Michael stepped to one side to allow Uncle Claude to precede him.

He glanced at Michael as he passed. "I wish you wouldn't carry a sketchbook in your jacket pocket," he observed waspishly. "It ruins the cut."

After dinner on Sunday evening, Mr. and Mrs. Kendall listened to the news. When it had finished, Kendall prowled at high volume through the air waves of Europe.

"It's all damned rubbish," he said. He turned off the wireless and began to ream a pipe with unnecessary violence.

"Yes, dear," said Mrs. Kendall automatically. She decided that now was not the moment to mention the possibility of a rise in her housekeeping allowance.

Kendall rapped the pipe against the side of the ashtray; a small shower of carbon fluttered on to the arm of his chair.

"I suppose I'll have to come to some decision about Hugh soon. I've always said you spoiled him, Muriel: I hope you're satisfied. What that boy needs—"

The front door slammed. Mrs. Kendall looked up; there was a smile on her face.

"It'll be Stephen," she said. "He's earlier than usual."

"It's about time he got to bed at a respectable hour." Kendall

25

chewed his pipe stem. "And it's a bit much, him going out on a Sunday, don't you think?"

Stephen pushed open the door with a little more force than was necessary. He swayed slightly as he stood in the doorway; Mrs. Kendall hoped his father wouldn't realize he had been drinking.

"Hello. Any tea left?" Stephen pulled up a chair to the fire. Mrs. Kendall refilled her husband's cup and poured another for her son.

"Have you had a nice evening, dear?"

"I met Paul Bennet up in town." Stephen draped an arm along the back of his chair; there was a scowl on his thin, dark face. "He's finally decided to go up to Cambridge this autumn. His father's promised to give him a car—one of those little MGs."

Muriel Kendall prayed silently that Stephen would say no more; it would only infuriate his father. Downing College had offered Stephen an exhibition to read modern languages, but he had been unable to take it up because his father refused to find the rest of the fees. The decision had provoked one of the rare open quarrels between Stephen and his father. Her elder son had always been adept at concealing his feelings. Only ambition and, more recently, alcohol allowed one a glimpse of what was going on in his mind.

"Ridiculous to give a car to a boy that age. When I was nineteen, we thought ourselves lucky to have a bicycle."

To his mother's surprise, Stephen said nothing to this. He finished his tea and stared into the fire. His next words were spoken in such a casual tone that Mrs. Kendall was immediately suspicious.

"A lot of chaps at the bank are saying there's sure to be a war by the end of the year."

Kendall grunted. "They're probably right."

"One or two of them have already joined the Territorials. I was wondering if I should, too. With my background they'd probably give me a commission, wouldn't they? And if there's a war, we'll all be called up in any case."

Alfred Kendall nodded slowly. There was a flicker of interest in his eyes at the thought of his son becoming an officer and a gentleman.

"I asked Mr. Horner and he thought it was quite a good idea. He said it's always best to get to the head of the queue."

Muriel Kendall suppressed a smile. Stephen knew exactly what he was doing. First he had played on Alfred's gentlemanly aspirations; then he invoked the powerful name of Horner, the submanager at his branch—and also, incidentally, the man who had approved the overdraft for Kendall and Son. She would be surprised if Stephen's briefcase didn't contain an application form, all filled in except for the space where his father's signature was needed.

"I'll think about it." Kendall often deferred family judgments, chiefly on the principle that his decisions seemed weightier when they were finally delivered.

Stephen nodded gravely; his expression implied that he would be happy to accept whatever his father decided; he knew as well as his mother that he had already won his point.

Shortly afterward, Kendall announced that it was time for bed. Stephen went up first, while his father made up the fire and his mother washed up and laid the table for breakfast. Kendall unlocked the sideboard and poured himself a nightcap. He sat beside the dying fire, sipping his whiskey and smoking a last cigarette.

There was a pile of ironing on the kitchen table. Mrs. Kendall took it upstairs with her, balancing her hot-water bottle on top. She wrapped her husband's pajamas around the bottle and began to put away the ironing. Her movements were slow, as they generally were when she was alone; in the last twelve months, it was as if her limbs were turning gradually from flesh to lead. She put the children's clothes to one side. There was no point in disturbing them.

Halfway down the pile she came to one of Hugh's shirts. It prodded her memory: she had forgotten to lay out Hugh's weekday suit and give him clean clothes for the morning. It would be just like him to come down to breakfast in a dirty collar and his Sunday suit; and it would be just like his father to seize the opportunity to go berserk.

She padded down the landing to Hugh's door. The room was in darkness, as she had expected, but there was enough light from the landing for her to see the chair on the far side of the fireplace. She tiptoed across the floor and laid the clothes on it.

The sense that something was amiss took her by the throat. Although she scarcely admitted it to herself and never to anyone else, Hugh was the dearest of her children. She glanced around the room, her eyes straining to make out the darker shadow which was the bed. Then the realization hit her.

There was no sound of breathing.

She knew at once that he was gone, though she flipped on the light by the door to confirm it. His bed was empty, but the covers were rumpled. His Sunday suit was hanging behind the door; the rest of his clothes were on the chair. His dressing gown was gone.

27

Panic invaded her mind. She had a vivid picture of Hugh running away from the house in a blind attempt to escape from his father's persecution. The cistern flushed in the bathroom, breaking into her nightmare. Hugh must have gone to the lavatory. Just as she reached the landing, the bolt shot back and Stephen emerged.

"Is Hugh in there?" she demanded.

"Not that I noticed." Stephen was wearing a purple dressing gown which he had acquired at a Christmas sale in Richmond; when he wore it, he tended to model himself on the characters of Noel Coward.

Muriel pushed past him to make sure. Stephen shrugged elaborately and walked slowly along the landing toward his bedroom. He was curious about what was happening, but the dressing gown prevented him from showing it too obviously.

His mother rushed downstairs and into the dining room. Alfred was slumped in his chair, a cigarette smouldering between his fingers. The nightcap had turned into two, as it so often did these days.

"Alfred! You must help me—Hugh's vanished."

Hugh was asleep.

This evening, Meg had suggested that he come to her room rather than the other way around, as on the two previous nights. It was difficult to refuse. With the possible exception of Aunt Vida, Meg seemed to be the only person who cared that the bottom had fallen out of his world. She was certainly the only person who dared to talk to him; his father had decreed that, as part of Hugh's punishment, he should be sent to Coventry until further notice. Another reason was that being with Meg made him warm. A third reason was that it was hard to refuse Meg if she asked you to do something when she was in a certain mood: her dark eyes had a sparkle to them which communicated her excitement to you; her charm was something you could almost touch.

When she had finished in the bathroom, she tapped lightly on his door before going on to her bedroom in the attic. Hugh counted to sixty before he moved, as she had suggested. They had both enjoyed these conspiratorial details; Hugh pretended as he counted that he was a secret service agent preparing for a rendezvous with one of his spies.

He scrambled out of bed and put on his dressing gown. "If I'm not back within two hours," he whispered to Hiawatha on the bed-side table, "you'll find a file marked *Top Secret* in my dugout. Take it to the general at once. Make sure you hand it to him directly—not to one of the ADCs."

"Right, sir." Hiawatha would add gruffly, "You will take a revolver, sir, won't you?"

"Not tonight. Shooting would give the whole show away." Major Hugh Kendall glanced down at his muscular hands. "There are other ways of keeping the enemy quiet."

Hugh walked quietly along the landing. He paused by the stairs. The wireless was booming away in the dining room. He climbed up to the attic. The third stair creaked loudly, so he avoided it; the other treads were all right, as long as you kept to the sides of them.

Meg's room was in darkness. As he opened the door, its characteristic smell swept out to meet him: it reminded him of Aunt Vida's garden in autumn.

"Come into bed," she whispered.

She moved over to make room for him. He could feel her warmth through her nightdress.

"Does it still hurt down there?" Her hand burrowed under his dressing gown and stroked his buttocks.

"A bit."

"Come on top of me, then. If you're face downward it won't be as bad."

They wriggled into the new position. Hugh found it surprisingly comfortable, and Meg didn't complain about the weight. She ran both hands down his back, from the shoulder blades to the top of the thighs, and stirred gently beneath him. Hugh's face was buried in the crook of her shoulder. It seemed to be hard to breathe. He raised his head, and Meg gave a little giggle.

"You know Gerald? The one who looks like Robert Donat? Mary said he didn't just kiss her—he put his hand on her breasts."

Hugh yawned. Why Gerald should have wanted to do a thing like that was beyond him. He knew, of course, that ladies' breasts were somehow taboo: you weren't supposed to look at them or touch them.

"You try," Meg whispered. A trace of irritation came into her voice when he hesitated. "Go on, silly—you're too young for it to matter."

Stung by the reference to his age, Hugh laid his hand on Meg's left breast. To his surprise, it felt quite firm—he had expected it to be fragile. Meg squirmed beneath him, forcing the pressure to increase.

"Put your hand inside my nightie," she said. "That's the proper way to do it." She fumbled with the buttons, seized Hugh's hand, and thrust it inside.

"I'll make you cold," Hugh objected.

"It doesn't matter. Rub it."

He obeyed. Beneath his hand, the nipple grew hard. When he pointed this out to Meg—he was worried that he was damaging it in some way—she said it didn't matter: nipples often went like that when it was cold. His hand warmed up, but the nipple remained hard.

Two late nights had left them both with a backlog of tiredness. Their breathing became slower and heavier; Hugh's mind slid sideways into a waking dream. Suddenly he jerked awake.

"I'd better go."

Meg's arms tightened around him. "Stay for a bit longer, Hugh. You're lovely and warm."

"Just another minute."

This time sleep enveloped them both completely. Hugh dreamed that he and Hiawatha were at Buckingham Palace, receiving medals from the king. Neither of them heard the slam of the front door when Stephen came in, or the movements downstairs as he and their parents prepared for bed.

Neither of them heard anything at all until Meg's door was flung open and her room was flooded with light.

A quite extraordinary thing happened just before breakfast: the telephone rang.

Alfred Kendall was upstairs in Hugh's room at the time. He broke off in mid-sentence and hurried downstairs. But Muriel got to the dining room first and he was forced to listen to one incomprehensible side of the conversation which ensued. Meanwhile, the smell of burning bacon grew stronger.

"I'll come at once," Muriel said; her voice was unusually decisive. "Meg can pack for me and come over later with the suitcase."

"Who was that?" Kendall demanded before his wife had time to replace the receiver. "Where are you going?"

She pushed past him into the smoke-filled kitchen and turned off the gas ring.

"It was Bunnings, dear. Aunt Vida had another one of her turns in the night. A minor stroke, probably."

The same thing had happened last year. Aunt Vida refused to go into hospital and Muriel had spent two weeks in Richmond looking after her.

Kendall grunted. "You'll have to go, of course."

It was damned inconvenient but he had no alternative. He knew what women were like: Vida was quite capable of leaving her money to a home for sick parrots, just to spite him; and she would as well, if she felt the Kendalls weren't giving her the attention she deserved. He also suspected—though he barely admitted the suspicion to himself—that Muriel would go to Richmond whatever he said.

"I don't know how long I'll have to stay. But Meg will look after you—she's quite a good little cook now. Besides, you'll get your main meal at lunchtime."

"What about Hugh?"

"He'll have to look after himself during the day." She avoided his eyes and wiped her hands on the apron. "After all, you'll be there in the evenings."

"Mr. Stanhope-Smith?" The voice sounded doubtful.

Michael looked up. Kendall hovered over him with an anxious smile on his face. Obviously he had been expecting a man of his own age.

"Captain Kendall?" Michael stood up, his hand outstretched. "How d'you do?" He hadn't described himself over the phone; he had merely said that he would be sitting alone at a table near the band in the Coventry Street Lyons, with a copy of *The Times,* open at the crossword but upside down, in front of him.

They sat down and Michael passed him the menu.

"I haven't ordered yet. I don't know what you'd like to drink. I don't think much of their wine list, but they certainly know how to keep their Bass."

He steered the conversation into neutral channels until their food arrived. Kendall said little at first, but Michael persevered; he listened in deferential silence as his guest gave his opinions about the state of the weather and the deficiencies of modern youth. By the time the soup arrived, Kendall's nervousness had evaporated and he was giving Michael the benefit of his views on the servant problem.

He sucked noisily his soup. "I blame the war, you know," he confided. "It gave the working classes a grossly inflated view of their own value."

Michael seized the opportunity to introduce another topic. "Sir Basil tells me you were in the Pay Corps, sir."

Kendall nodded. "They also serve, eh? Of course I applied to be sent to France, time and time again. They always turned me down on the grounds I was more useful where I was."

"Of course." Michael tried to look sympathetic. Then he abandoned finesse. "You're probably wondering why I asked Sir Basil to arrange for me to meet you."

Kendall laid down his soup spoon. "He said it was something of national importance."

"Perhaps I should explain, sir. But I must stress that what I'm going to say is completely confidential, and must remain so. I'm connected with the Foreign Office and I have a proposition for you. If you decline it, which of course you may, I must ask for your word that you will immediately forget this meeting has taken place."

"You can rely on my discretion entirely, Mr. Stanhope-Smith."

"Then may I begin by asking you a few questions?"

Kendall nodded gravely. He sat up straight in his chair and wiped his mustache with his napkin.

Michael cleared his throat to conceal his desire to smile. "Do you make regular visits to Czechoslovakia on business?"

"Until very recently, I've been going two or three times a year. Bohemian glass is my bread and butter, you understand—and my father's before me." Kendall chewed his lower lip. "But I don't mind telling you that fellow Hitler's made my life damned awkward in the last few months. I'm thinking very seriously of taking my business elsewhere."

"But even now, if you were to visit Czechoslovakia for a week or two, it would hardly seem strange to the authorities there?"

"Not at all." Kendall looked away. "In fact, I wish I could afford to do so. One or two of my contracts have been canceled recently. I've a feeling that, if I could see the people concerned on the spot, I might be able to get them to reconsider their decisions. At least I'd have a sporting chance."

"Do you speak Czech?"

"I can get by—both in Czech and German."

Michael nodded. "Excellent. Now—you don't mind me asking what your views are on Hitler, do you?"

Kendall shrugged. "Why should I? At first I thought these fascists had a lot of good ideas. Look at Mussolini, for example—at least he's made Italian trains run on time. Their methods seem to get results. But after the *Anschluss,* I began to change my mind. Only a fool would think that Hilter means to stop with Austria and the Sudetenland. Churchill's right: the only argument the Boche respect is cold steel."

"Quite so." Michael paused while the waiter brought his lamb cutlets and Kendall's steak. The interruption gave him time to consider his tactics. It would be better not to mention the money, he thought, not at this stage. He was able to fit Kendall into a category now: the warlike attitude was often found in men of his generation who had done no actual fighting in the Great War; the bitterness of combat was an abstraction to them, as it was to Michael himself.

Kendall waggled his fork in Michael's direction. "Mark my words, we shall be at war before the end of the year, whatever that fool Chamberlain thinks. My eldest boy is joining the Territorials already. I've always said—"

"The more preparations we can make beforehand, the better our chances will be," Michael cut in. "You agree?"

"Of course. If only—"

"And preparations have to take place right across the board. We at the FO, for example, are not concerned with the purely military aspect, naturally. Our fundamental purpose is to gather information from abroad. In wartime, the purpose remains the same but the—ah—methods of collection have to be adapted to meet the circumstances. Particularly in those countries where we can have no formal diplomatic representation."

Michael chewed a mouthful of lamb, covertly watching Kendall's face. The man looked as if he nourished his inner self on a diet of John Buchan and Sapper: surely he wouldn't be able to miss such an obvious appeal to pick up a cloak and dagger for his country?

Kendall stiffened in his seat; his nostrils flared. "Does this mean you work for the—"

"It's better not to mention names," Michael said quickly. "Even in private." This was one of Dansey's recruiting principles: that one should leave as much as possible to the recruit's imagination.

"What do you want me to do?"

Michael leaned forward. "Our concern is to establish channels of communication which will remain open when the usual ones are closed. At present we need someone to act as a courier—to take a small package to someone at the other end, and to bring back something else. It may be just the one time—or there may be others. You'll appreciate that it's difficult to be definite in these matters. There's no risk involved, but it's vital that the courier should be a man whom we can trust absolutely—and who has a cast-iron reason for going there in the first place."

Kendall gave a little grunt of satisfaction. Michael decided that, if one was going to lay on flattery, there was no point in being niggardly about it.

"When I consulted Sir Basil, yours was the first name he mentioned." As he spoke, Michael wished he could afford the luxury of a job where lying was not part of the stock in trade. *Try Kendall*, Cohen had said. *He's a wretched little man, but he'll fit your bill.*

"Could I have a day or two to think things over?"

Michael shook his head. "I'm sorry, Captain Kendall. Time is the one thing we haven't got. I need a decision now. If you turn it down, I'll try someone else. I must get a man in Prague by the weekend."

Michael's bluff partly succeeded: Kendall looked faintly aggrieved at the thought that there might be other candidates for the job.

"Would you be able to leave at such short notice?"

"My passport and visas are all in order, if that's what you mean. And it wouldn't take long to tie up any loose ends at the office. But there is one problem . . ."

"If you accept our offer, we would naturally take care of your expenses." Michael smiled apologetically. "And we usually make some sort of token payment for such services."

Kendall sawed violently at his steak. "I don't deny the money would be useful. But it's not that. You see my wife had to go away this morning to nurse an aunt of hers. Going to Prague this weekend would mean leaving my younger son alone. I can't do that: he's—ah—he's not at school at present."

There was a curious inflection in Kendall's voice, and it puzzled Michael. It was almost as if the man was afraid of what his son might do if left alone, rather than of what might happen to him.

"I deeply regret," Kendall said through a mouthful of pink meat, "that I may have to decline your offer."

34

The solution to the problem suddenly occurred to Michael. It would remove Kendall's little difficulty at a stroke—and it might even increase his professional cover in Czechoslovakia. Dansey could hardly object.

He took a long swallow of his beer and wiped his mouth with his napkin. He waited until Kendall's jaws had stopped moving.

"There's no reason why you shouldn't take the boy with you."

Three

"For God's sake!" Kendall snapped. The Czech matron at the next table looked curiously at them. He lowered his voice to a hiss. "Has no one ever told you that it's rude to stare?"

Hugh looked away from the crowd in the hotel foyer. The sight of his son's bowed head brought Kendall's exasperation to the boil: at that moment he could have willingly strangled the boy. He lit another cigarette from the stub of the old, and glanced once again toward the revolving door which led to Vaclavske Namesti. Everyone in Prague seemed to be here except the man he wanted.

The presence of Hugh was only part of the reason for his irritation, but he was a convenient focus for Kendall's discontent. Hugh was simply not to be trusted: he was a thief and a liar; and after Sunday night Kendall had begun to suspect that he was something worse as well.

His mind shied away from the memory of finding his son in his daughter's bed. It seemed to Kendall that whenever he closed his eyes he was doomed to relive that instant when he turned on Meg's light.

Two heads, one fair, one dark, on the same pillow: two bodies entangled—

According to Hugh, he had crawled into bed with her to get warm; and she had been so soundly asleep that she hadn't woken up. According to Meg, on the other hand, she was the one who had been cold; and she'd persuaded *him* to come to bed with her.

Kendall had beaten them both: they were lying; they were conspiring against him; they were breaking his rule forbidding one child to go into another's bedroom. He felt instinctively that Hugh must have taken the initiative—after all, he was the boy.

The top of Meg's nightdress was unbuttoned. It looked almost as if Hugh's hand was inside, resting on her—

The thought was monstrous, and Kendall tried to push it away. But one thing was clear; Hugh needed strict and constant discipline. Kendall could not risk leaving him in Twickenham while he was away. Meg would have been completely at his mercy.

After they returned from Prague, he would have to find a long-term solution to the problem of Hugh. It was as if the boy had a highly contagious disease: it was imperative to isolate him from the rest of the family. Kendall wondered whether the merchant navy might be a possibility.

He pulled out his watch: it was nearly three o'clock. He suspected that Stanhope-Smith's man was going to let him down again. It would be the third time. Stanhope-Smith had told him to wait in the foyer of the Hotel Palacky for an hour after lunch and an hour after dinner, until the contact made his approach.

The big glass door revolved. Cold air swept into the lobby. Kendall swore under his breath as three women filed in.

"Can't you sit up straight?" he said to Hugh. "Don't slouch."

"Smim si pripalit?" said a husky voice behind him.

Kendall swung around. His eyes widened when he saw that it was a woman. She was short, and her plumpness was accentuated by a heavy fur coat with an upturned collar; she had a snoutlike snub nose and a faint but distinct mustache. At first Kendall thought her words must be a coincidence. But then he saw that she was tapping the butt of her cigarette against a silver case. The case was angled toward him so he could see the design of four interlocking lozenges engraved on the side.

"Prosim," he muttered politely, fumbling in his waistcoat pocket. His fingers shook slightly as he opened the silver matchcase. He nearly forgot to let her see the lozenges on its lid.

"What is your room number?" she murmured in English just before the match touched the tip of the cigarette.

"Twenty-three."

She blew out words and smoke simultaneously: "Meet me there in twenty minutes." Her voice returned to its normal speaking level: *"Dekuii."*

Kendall bowed. She turned and walked to the bar. From the

back she looked like a hedgehog in patent-leather high-heeled shoes.

The fat woman with the overpowering scent stood in the center of the hot and ill-proportioned room which Hugh shared with his father. She jabbed her thumb toward Hugh and broke into a rapid stream of Czech.

His father replied haltingly in the same language, but she interrupted him before he could say more than a few words. As she spoke she gestured toward Hugh; he wished he could understand what she was saying.

At last his father shrugged. "Hugh, I want you to go for a walk for an hour. You can take the guidebook. And make sure you behave yourself."

Hugh grabbed his coat, scarf, and cap and almost ran out of the room. He was so relieved to get out of his father's presence that he hardly bothered to wonder why he had been sent away. He ran down the stairs, through the lobby, and into the street.

For a moment he stood at the head of the steps which led down from the revolving door, savoring the sights and sounds of freedom. It was the first time he had got away from his father since they had left London. At the far end of the broad road he could see a statue of a man on horseback. The strangeness of everything gave him a jolt of pleasure. He darted down the steps and began to run toward the statue.

The pavements were crowded and slippery. As he dodged between a linden tree and a stall selling spicy sausages, he skidded on a pile of dirty snow. At the last moment he clutched at the tree and saved himself from sprawling on the surface of the road. A car swerved to avoid him. A bicycle bell jangled angrily.

Hugh laughed aloud and ran on.

"We could have talked in Czech," Kendall said peevishly. "The boy wouldn't have understood."

Madame Hase settled herself in the only armchair that the room possessed. "My English is much better than your Czech. Besides, if we talk in English, there is less chance that an ear at the keyhole would be able to understand." Her voice hardened. "Why did you bring the boy? It is very foolish. I was not warned."

"It was decided in London," Kendall said curtly. He was

39

annoyed that his contact had proved to be a woman, largely because the fact surprised him. Her haughty attitude made things worse; he was damned if he was going to let a female talk to him like that.

"You have brought the package? There was no trouble with customs?"

Kendall nodded. He crossed the room to the basin in the corner and picked up the shaving brush which stood on the glass shelf above it. The handle was made of metal. He unscrewed the base and extracted the small chamois leather bundle.

"It's stitched together. Do you want me to open it?"

"Of course."

He slit the neck of the bag with the blade of his penknife. Madame Hase snatched the bag from him and upended it over the palm of her hand. Seven cut diamonds, small but flawless, trickled out. She sucked in her breath sharply. For the first time she smiled.

"Satisfied?" Kendall asked with heavy sarcasm.

"Perfectly." Her pudgy fingers clenched around the stones, as if she was trying to squeeze the virtue out of them. "But we may have a problem at the other end of the transaction."

"What do you mean?" Kendall had assumed that she would hand over the papers now she had the diamonds; he knew nothing about possible problems. Now he came to think about it, he knew very little about this whole business. Stanhope-Smith hadn't been very informative.

"I have not yet obtained the information." Madame Hase's English might be fluent, but she pronounced it as if it was a dead language, with equal stress on each syllable and without inflections. "The principals with whom I am dealing lack confidence, both in me and in London. They do not trust me because I am a woman, and because my origins are bourgeois. And of course they have only my word that London is the source of these." She unclasped her hand and prodded the little pile of diamonds.

Kendall shrugged. "I'd've thought diamonds were diamonds wherever they come from."

"Not if they come from Berlin. That is their worst fear, I think. But these men see enemies everywhere. Can you blame them? England and France were our allies; they guaranteed to maintain our borders; and then they betrayed us at Munich because of a ranting bully with a big stick. Or perhaps they think these diamonds come from closer home. The *Deuxième Bureau* has never loved us, and Moravec is a man who likes to hold all the strings in his hand. No one trusts our government anymore: those fascist toadies dissolved the Communist Party just before Christmas."

Kendall took his time over filling and lighting a pipe. A familiar sense of helplessness swept over him; and that as usual made him angry. As far as he could see, the only course open to him was to return to London, empty-handed. He had a shrewd suspicion that Madame Hase meant to keep the diamonds whatever happened. He could hardly force her to return them; she would probably shriek the place down and accuse him of trying to rape her.

If he returned to London without those papers (whatever they were), he would be back to square one: he would have failed Stanhope-Smith; there would be no more lucrative little jobs. Worst of all, England would suffer because of his failure.

"Is there nothing we can do to convince them that we're all aboveboard?" He spoke more loudly than he had intended; Madame Hase looked at him sharply.

"Perhaps," she said after a pause. "We have one strong card in our hand: they need help from somewhere. Any resistance network needs money, and it needs access to the outside world. We thought Moscow would provide both, but they are being dilatory and time is running out. You are here and you can offer what they want."

"Would it help if I met them?"

"It might. But that would take time to arrange—and there might have to be several meetings." A fit of coughing interrupted her. "It would help if you were more important. They may consider that a mere messenger boy can have nothing useful to say to them."

Kendall's face became mottled. Madame Hase appeared not to notice.

"But of course they do not know what your rank is," she continued. "Nor do I. I simply draw inferences."

"I fail to see—"

There was a tap on the door.

Madame Hase snapped open her handbag, dropped in the diamonds, and pulled out something else. A sense of unreality caught Kendall by the throat, making him literally gasp for breath. She was holding an automatic pistol.

This time it wasn't a tap: it was an impatient double knock. Madame Hase concealed the pistol in the folds of her fur

41

coat and signaled to him to open the door.

It was almost with a sense of anticlimax that he found one of the pageboys waiting in the corridor.

"*Pan* Kendall?" The youth held out a dented silverplated salver. On it was a flimsy gray envelope addressed to Kendall at the Hotel Palacky.

Kendall took the letter, dropped a tip on the tray, and closed the door. He ripped open the envelope and extracted the single sheet of paper it contained. Madame Hase returned the automatic to her handbag.

"Oh, my God." Kendall suddenly sat down on the edge of the bed. "What the hell are we going to do?"

When Hugh had looked at the statue, he went on to the end of Vaclavske Namesti. The broad avenue ended in a T-junction. He turned right, hoping eventually to reach the river.

Before he came to the Vltava, he emerged into a rectangular open space. He consulted the guidebook and decided he might be in Charles Square. The center was laid out as a public park. The snow was still thick on the grass, contrasting bleakly with the bare branches of the trees.

A covered fiacre clopped passed him; the nearside wheels of the carriage sprayed his legs with slush. Hugh wiped it off as best he could with his handkerchief. He was beginning to feel cold. He sidled nearer to a brazier on the corner of the park, hoping to steal a little heat. Chestnuts cracked and sizzled above the glowing charcoal. Hugh's mouth watered. It was a long time since lunch. He wished his father had given him a little pocket money. Aunt Vida's half-crown wouldn't be much use here.

A small van pulled over to the curb and parked. Two men got out, both wearing faded blue overalls. One of them opened the back of the van and appeared to be rummaging around inside. The other came over to the brazier and held his hands over the fire. He was tall and thin, with very large blue eyes. Hugh backed away: this looked like a real customer.

"*Dobry den,*" the newcomer said to the owner of the brazier.

That meant "Good day" in Czech, according to the list of useful phrases in the back of the guidebook. Hugh felt pleased: already he was learning to swim in strange waters.

The man said something else, and was given a cone of newspaper filled with chestnuts, which steamed in the cold air.

He paid for them and sauntered over to Hugh.

"English?" He held out the cone. "For you. Take."

Hugh made a halfhearted attempt to explain in sign language that his parents had told him never to accept presents from strangers. But the man was insistent, and it seemed easier to take the cone, just to keep him happy. Besides, Hugh told himself, this was Prague, not London: the old rules were no longer so important.

The first chestnut burned his fingers and scorched his mouth; but it tasted wonderful. Hugh politely offered the bag to his benefactor.

The man shook his head. He laid a hand on Hugh's arm. "Come. My friend speak English good." With his other arm he gestured to his friend at the back of the van.

Hugh hesitated: his parents had also told him never to go anywhere with strangers, either. But a few paces across a crowded pavement was surely a different matter. It seemed churlish to refuse.

The other man turned as they came up. He was built like a bull, with thick shoulders and a massive head. The van doors were open, but the interior was still sheltered by a pair of canvas curtains.

"Hello, my friend." He smiled and pantomimed with finger and thumb that he would like a chestnut.

Hugh moved a step closer, holding out the cone. The first man was close behind him; on either side were the doors; in front was the van itself.

The smile vanished. Two hands grabbed him around the waist and threw him bodily through the curtains. Before he had time to think, he was sprawling on the ridged metal floor of the van. Chestnuts rattled around him like hailstones.

The doors slammed behind him. A few seconds later, the engine coughed into life and the van began to move. The floor vibrated uncomfortably beneath Hugh: they were traveling over cobbles and the rudimentary suspension of the van couldn't cope.

Hugh bit his lip in an effort to keep back the tears. For once his parents had been proved right. He pulled himself up, using the side of the van as a support. The van, now traveling at some speed, took a sharp turn to the left. Hugh lost his balance and careered over to the right. His fall was partially broken by a large, unyielding object that hung along the far side of the van. It was cold, firm, and sticky.

Both his hands and one cheek felt clammy from its touch. Hugh lifted one hand to his nose and sniffed cautiously.

It smelled of blood.

Madame Hase hailed one of the taxicabs which lurked in wait outside the Palackys' door. She pushed Kendall before her into the back, and scrambled in after him. Her skirt—far too short for Kendall's taste—rode up, exposing sturdy legs; wiry black hairs poked through the flesh-colored silk stockings.

She told the driver to take them to Nadrasi Dejvice, a suburban station on the other side of the river, just north of the great hill of Hradcany. "We can walk from there," she whispered to Kendall. "It would be foolish to drive straight to the shop."

"Whose shop?" Kendall was too angry to keep his voice down.

Madame Hase patted his knee reprovingly. "Jan's, of course," she said in an undertone. "Your letter was in Bela's handwriting, so it's the obvious place. Jan and Bela are on the Provisional Committee for Prague." She giggled incongruously. "They do everything together, you see."

"It's damnable," Kendall burst out. "Do you Bolsheviks make a habit of kidnapping the sons of British subjects?"

"No, no, my friend." She patted his knee again, and Kendall edged away. "You don't understand: the fact they took your son is good. It means they think you are worth taking seriously. We have a proverb: in English it would be something like 'You don't mark the pack if you don't want to play cards'."

Kendall looked blankly at her. "I don't see why you're so cheerful. If they're just going to give Hugh back, why bother to take him in the first place? It's perfectly obvious they're going to use him as a lever to blackmail me."

She shook her head and leaned closer to him. "First they did it to show you they are strong men, men you must respect. Next they did it to make sure your son is really English. But, most of all, they did it so that you would hand over the diamonds to them at a place which they choose, not you. Once you have exchanged the diamonds and the boy, we can all get down to business."

"How did they know where I was staying? How did they know the one time that Hugh was going out by himself? It was your suggestion that he should go for a walk."

Madame Hase ignored the suspicion in his voice. "I had to tell them your name and where you were staying. They wouldn't just take my word, you know. They've been watching you since you arrived. There will be plenty of Party members at the Palacky to act as their eyes and ears. Communism makes a simple emotional appeal to waiters and bellboys and that class of person."

Kendall realized that he had no option but to trust this latter-day Mata Hari. But where did her loyalties ultimately lie—with the British secret service or with her communist comrades? Stanhope-Smith might at least have told him whom he was working for. It was so damned unfair. His mind digressed for a moment: it was typical of Hugh to have got them both into this mess; the boy had a genius for causing trouble.

Madame Hase squeezed his knee. "Leave the talking to me, as much as possible. We will offer them two of the diamonds in exchange for the boy; they do not know how many you have brought."

"What if they search you?" Kendall objected.

This time she nudged him in the ribs. "Two diamonds are in my bag. The others are in a hiding place only ladies have." She tittered and snuggled closer to Kendall. "Jan and Bela are not the sort of men who enjoy searching the intimate parts of ladies."

Kendall blushed and cleared his throat. It was difficult to imagine anyone less like a lady than his present companion. To his great relief she pulled away from him.

"You must say very little—be cold and angry and very British gentlemanly. I want to make them feel that they have gone too far, that they have been rash in offending you so casually." She broke off and studied Kendall thoughtfully for a few seconds. "Yes, I think I shall say you are the head of the Middle European network of SIS. That should impress them."

Kendall had never heard the acronym before. He guessed it might refer to the British secret service. He felt a sudden spasm of hatred for this domineering woman beside him. He drew out a cigarette and tapped it deliberately against his case.

"That, madame, is precisely who I am."

When the van stopped, Hugh wiped his eyes with the back of his hand and stood up. He had been crouching for so long that his knees screamed with agony.

The doors opened and the curtains were pulled back. The bull-like man beckoned him to come out.

Hugh jumped down and glanced around. He was in a cobbled yard. On three sides were sheds; on the fourth was a brick wall, ten feet high and topped with a row of spikes. The other man had his back to them: he was barring the heavy double gates in the middle of the wall. During the journey, the afternoon had turned into evening.

His captor seized Hugh's ear between a huge thumb and forefinger and led him over to one of the sheds. He shot back the two bolts, undid the padlock, and pushed Hugh inside.

A match rasped and flared. The tall, thin man followed them in and closed the door behind them; his colleague lit a paraffin lamp. The wick was untrimmed, and the lamp sputtered fitfully, throwing out a flickering yellow light.

The shed was about five yards square. It had a concrete floor and was lined with crudely built shelves of unvarnished pine. There were piles of tins on the shelves. All the tins which Hugh could see bore the same picture—a garishly pink joint of ham.

The picture connected in his mind with the blood on his face and hands. He might have fallen against a pig's carcass. The thought made him feel slightly better.

The taller man pointed at Hugh's face and said something in Czech. Both men chuckled.

Their laughter made Hugh feel a little bolder. "Why have you brought me here?" he demanded. "Who are you?"

Neither of them replied. The bull-like man, who seemed to be the leader, said something else in Czech. He walked behind Hugh and grabbed him by the shoulders; the grip was firm but not painful. The younger man knelt in front of Hugh and methodically emptied his pockets.

One by one, Hugh's possessions formed a little pile on the concrete. Some items aroused little interest, but others, including the guidebook and Hiawatha, were obviously considered important.

Hugh tried to work out the motive for their search. When the thin man passed his purse, containing Aunt Vida's half-crown, to his colleague, the answer suddenly occurred to him: they were interested in anything that suggested he was English. The guidebook had the stamp of a London bookshop on the flyleaf; underneath Hiawatha's base were the words *Made in England*. The hypothesis seemed to be confirmed when the two men exclaimed excitedly over the school outfitter's label inside his jacket.

The conclusion intensified his fear: perhaps they were going to strip away all evidence of his name and nationality as a preliminary to murdering him.

When the search was over, the big man released his shoulders.

46

Hugh backed away until he came to the shelves. He knew he had to do something before it was too late. One of those tins might make a weapon. He could knock over the lamp and make a break for the door. Plans chased feverishly through his mind, all nullified by the sheer impossibility of carrying them out.

But nothing happened to him. After a rapid, incomprehensible conversation, the men left without a word to him. They took the lamp with them. The bolts shot home and, a few seconds later, he heard the van's engine. The roar of the motor grew louder, and then gradually diminished into silence.

Once he was alone, Hugh began to tremble uncontrollably. It was cold in the shed, but he knew that was not the only reason why his teeth were chattering. It was also completely dark. The only sound he could hear was the distant grumbling of traffic.

He edged across the floor, using his feet to probe for his belongings. When he found them, he stuffed them back in his pockets. Hiawatha remained in the palm of his hand.

"Well, sir, they say it's always darkest just before dawn," his batman would say in the gruff voice he reserved for tight spots. Somehow Hiawatha seemed less reassuring than usual.

Hugh tried to act as Major Kendall, VC, would do. He made a reconnaissance, which in this case meant looking in vain for a window and banging helplessly on the door. He laid an ambush: having chosen half a dozen tins of ham, he stood behind the door and waited for the enemy to return. As he made his preparations, he knew it was hopeless: Major Kendall lived in a different world from the two Czechs.

Of course it was possible that they didn't intend to murder him: perhaps they were going to hold him to ransom, in the mistaken belief that his father was a wealthy British businessman. But his father wasn't wealthy; and, even if he were, Hugh rather doubted that he would spend money to ensure the safe return of his son.

After five minutes of waiting in ambush on his feet, Hugh decided that he could wait just as well if he sat on the floor. He was tired; and he might feel warmer if he clasped his hands around his knees. He would have plenty of time to stand up when he heard the van's engine in the yard outside.

His head fell forward, and he dozed.

The door cannoned into him, waking him abruptly.

Men were laughing; an unbearably bright light shone into his eyes. He turned his head away from the glare. His hand closed around one of the tins.

A woman's voice said, "But there's blood on his face."

"Get up, boy," his father said.

A hand grasped one of his lapels and hauled him to his feet. The torch swung away from his face. Hugh recognized the fat woman with the fur coat and the two Czechs behind his father. Everyone seemed to be grinning, and there was a heavy smell of spirits in the air.

His father cuffed him lightly. "What's that mess on your face? Have you been crying again?"

Hugh shook his head automatically. He had learned long ago that admitting weakness to his father was always rash.

Alfred Kendall turned to the woman. "He's a regular mother's boy." The tone was jocular; in private he often used the same words in an entirely different way.

"He needs a bath," she said judiciously. "And perhaps food."

His father laughed. "What he needs is a bit of self-discipline. Perhaps this tutor will make him pull himself together."

It occurred to him that they were talking about him as if he wasn't there. The four white faces above him seemed to be revolving, receding from him as they spiraled. The motion made him feel giddy; the acrid taste of nausea flooded his throat. One of the Czechs said something to his father, but the words were too faint for Hugh to catch.

His body crumpled into darkness.

"It is all arranged," Madame Hase said.

Alfred Kendall pushed aside the remains of his breakfast. After last night, he had a splitting headache and Madame Hase's voice made it worse.

"When can he start?"

"This morning. I told him Hugh would come every day except Sunday, between nine in the morning and five in the afternoon. He can have his lunch there—that will be included in Dr. Spiegel's salary. Hugh can go to and from the apartment by tram. It is an easy journey—the number seven will take him almost from door to door."

"I hate to think what this is going to cost."

Madame Hase sat down and reached for Kendall's coffee pot. "Spiegel's in no position to bargain. Besides, if money is short we can

48

use one of the diamonds to cover these extra expenses. I know a jeweler who will give us a good price.

"But that money is for—"

"The diamonds are there for a purpose. They may legitimately be used for anything that helps to achieve that purpose. We can't afford to have Hugh under our feet for the next week or so. You made a good start with Jan and Bela last night, but we still have a long way to go."

"I'd better tell Hugh." Kendall pushed back his chair. "There's no need for me to come, is there?"

Madame Hase put down her coffee cup and reached for her cigarette case.

"The less Spiegel knows the better. This time I'll take Hugh. Afterward he can travel to Zizkov and back by himself. How is he this morning?"

Kendall shrugged. "None the worse for wear as far as I can see."

"He is upstairs?"

"In our room, mooning around as usual. I'll bring him down." He glanced around the dining room and lowered his voice still further. "Look here, are you sure we can trust this Spiegel chap? He's not one of your lot, is he?"

Madame Hase squinted at him through a cloud of smoke. "Ludvik Spiegel was a friend of my father's. He's a man of no account—a learned fool. I can twist him around my little finger."

When they reached the terminus, Hugh followed Madame Hase out of the tram. She led him in silence down a narrow street, lined with small factories. Without warning she turned left through an archway. Hugh found himself in a large, rectangular courtyard, around which was an eight-story block of flats.

Dr. Spiegel lived in a top-floor apartment whose door gave on to the communal balcony. The balcony was an obstacle course of clotheslines, dustbins, and bicycles.

"This is not a nice neighborhood," she said over her shoulder to Hugh. She rapped on Spiegel's door. "You must not talk to people on your way here."

The door opened with a screech of unoiled hinges.

"Good morning!" boomed Dr. Spiegel.

He was a tall, thin man whose beard straggled over his bow tie. He ushered them into what was evidently his living room. It was

49

crowded with dark-stained furniture, and there were piles of books on most horizontal surfaces.

Madame Hase declined to sit down. She spoke rapidly in Czech to Spiegel; it sounded as if she was reeling off a string of orders. She left abruptly, without even glancing at Hugh.

"*Pan* Kendall, we must introduce ourselves," Spiegel said in English. He held out a bony hand with ragged nails. "How do you do?"

"How do you do, sir?" Hugh and his tutor shook hands ceremoniously.

Dr. Spiegel tilted a chair, sending a pile of newspapers to the floor. "Please sit down. I would advise you to keep your coat on for the time being. I do not light the stove in the mornings. You must pardon me for forcing you to share the brunt of my domestic economies."

For the next five minutes, Spiegel strode up and down, his frock coat flapping behind him, describing with nostalgia his experiences in the British Museum reading room at the turn of the century. Hugh felt himself relaxing.

"And now, Mr. Kendall, we must consider our curriculum. We need not trouble with English, since I'm sure you know more about your delightful language than I could ever do. I think we may safely ignore mathematics and the natural sciences for much the same reason. Latin and Greek, on the other hand . . . . But I forget my manners: I should begin by asking your opinion. Is there something that you would like to learn which is within my competence to teach?"

For a moment Hugh said nothing. His mind was full of what had happened yesterday. It wouldn't have been so bad if he could have understood what the two men were saying.

"I'd like to learn Czech."

"Indeed? An interesting choice. You think you may be here for some time?"

"I don't know, sir. But I'd like to know more of what's going on."

"That, my dear Kendall, is a desire which does you credit. Most people prefer to know less rather than more. I wonder if we should add German to our syllabus? It is a language which is often heard in Prague. And of course you will need to have an idea of the historical background. Languages are not static things; they exist in time; they grow, flourish, and decay like organic matter. In a word, languages are alive. Like plants, their development is intimately connected with the soil and climate in which they grow." He smiled at Hugh, revealing an ill-fitting set of discolored false teeth. "Yes, I think we have our modern trivium: Czech, German, and history."

Hugh looked blankly at him. Dr. Spiegel appeared not to notice.

"You will remember, of course, that the trivium provided the foundations of learning in the Middle Ages. Every scholar began with its three subjects, the essential tools of grammar, rhetoric, and logic. But—*mutatis mutandis,* as it were—other subjects are essential if one is to live in contemporary Prague. It is most unfortunate, but these days one must be practical. At least I am well qualified in this respect: my mother was Czech, my father a Sudeten German, and my lifelong study has been history."

Dr. Spiegel stirred in his chair. His mouth moved as if he was talking silently to himself. He pulled out his watch and consulted it. His hand shook so much that he had to steady it against his leg.

"Before we begin, I think we should drink a toast to our joint enterprise." He peered anxiously at Hugh. "Would this meet with your approval?"

Hugh nodded. It seemed a little early for elevenses, but perhaps the routine was different in Czechoslovakia.

Dr. Spiegel went into the next room; before the door closed, Hugh caught a glimpse of a sink piled high with crockery. The door's catch failed to engage, and the door swung six inches back into the kitchen. Hugh saw his tutor take a brown, unlabeled bottle from a wall cupboard; he took a long swallow from it and put it away. When he returned to the living room, he was carrying another bottle and two large teacups, neither of which had saucers.

"Glass breaks so easily," Dr. Spiegel said apologetically. Taking great care to avoid spillages, he poured precisely the same quantity of a translucent golden fluid into each of the cups. He raised his cup in salute and drank with solemn concentration. Hugh took a sip and blenched: the taste was bitter.

Dr. Spiegel refilled his own cup. "Czech, of course," he remarked suddenly, "is a Slavonic language in origin, though much influenced by German. It emerged as an independent language in the Middle Ages, at much the same time as the Czechs achieved political independence. Indeed, our progenitors used a single word, *jazyk,* to denote both "language" and "nation." As you know, it is written in Latin characters; this was an early development, despite the problems associated with the transliteration of specifically Slav sounds—"

"Please, sir," Hugh said desperately. "I don't understand."

The excitement drained away from Spiegel's face. "Forgive me, *Pan* Kendall. I was giving you a condensed version of the introductory lecture I used to deliver to my first-year students. Perhaps it is not altogether appropriate to our present circumstances." He drank again and stared into the cup as if enlightenment was hidden there.

"Sir, I really want to be able to understand what people are saying on the streets—what the signs mean—to know how to ask for something in a shop."

"Ah. I see you favor the practical approach." Dr. Spiegel looked relieved. He poured himself another cupful, which emptied the bottle. He flicked a fingernail against the glass. "I have an idea. We shall further your education and, if you have no objection, my convenience at one and the same time. If you return to the road and walk to the left, you will come to a shop on the corner. There you may purchase our lunch. A humble collation—bread, a few slices of sausage, and some more of this excellent Pilsener. The modern Czech, my dear Kendall, makes two things superlatively well—guns and lager."

The first day established a pattern that they followed with little variation for the next few weeks. In the mornings they studied languages—Czech or German, according to Spiegel's whim. The afternoons were devoted, at least in theory, to general knowledge and history.

The old man proved to be a surprisingly efficient teacher, particularly in the first few hours of the day. He gave Hugh a grounding in the grammar of the two languages, but for most of the time they concentrated on speaking them.

Dr. Spiegel revealed a talent for mimicry. He would invent little scenes, and he and Hugh would act them out. He gave Hugh a dictionary and a grammar, and made him puzzle out the main stories in the newspaper. Hugh often did his tutor's shopping.

Dr. Spiegel drank his way steadily through every day. His main source of nourishment seemed to be the strong export Pilsener, which he had produced on that first morning. On later occasions, Hugh drank sweet black tea which he made himself in the cramped and evil-smelling kitchen. His tutor rarely drank tea; but he would sometimes bring out the little brown bottle between cups of lager.

As the day wore on, Dr. Spiegel's step would become unsteady, and his eyes had difficulty in focusing. But his courtesy to Hugh remained unchanged; nor did the alcohol affect his speech.

In the afternoons he talked. Most of his monologues concerned two inextricably entwined subjects—himself and the recent history of central Europe. He spoke with nostalgia of the heady days of the Great War when he had fought with the Czech Legion on the Allied side. He described the early years of the newly created republic of Czechoslovakia and the democratic constitution he had helped to frame. He was particularly proud of the course on Czech nationalism which he and his wife had founded at the Charles University.

But there were bad days as well, when the nostalgia was supplanted by bitterness and the brown bottle came out of the kitchen and stood beside Dr. Spiegel's chair. He was obsessed by the weakness of his country—an infant democracy surrounded by increasingly hostile neighbors; its allies, Britain and France, were hundreds of miles away, and lacked both the will and the means to intervene. Across the border was Germany, gleefully exploiting her neighbor's political problems and racial divisions.

"Hitler wants to carve us up like a big sausage," Spiegel said on one afternoon, early in March. "Our minorities rush to join the feast. They do not realize that they will be eaten, too."

The rape of the Sudetenland, Spiegel claimed, was but a symptom of what he regarded as a wider evil—Hitler's perversion of the sacred traditions of nationalism.

"With all the means at his disposal, that foul little man has encouraged the separatist nationalist movements in our Slovakian and Ruthenian provinces. Quite simply, he plans to undermine Bohemia and Moravia, which form the core of Czechoslovakia." Spiegel raised a trembling hand and hammered it down on the arm of his chair. "Once he invades us, Hitler will be exposed as the fraud he is: all his previous conquests could be justified, if only speciously, on the grounds that they brought Germans into the Reich. But Bohemia and Moravia are chiefly inhabited by Czechs, not Germans. You grasp my point, my dear Kendall?"

Hugh nodded; what puzzled him was his tutor's uncharacteristic vehemence.

A few hours later he discovered the answer. Madame Hase had dined with the Kendalls at the Palacky. She was in a confidential mood after the better part of a bottle of wine and several brandies. Hugh was puzzling his way through an illustrated magazine when he heard his tutor's name.

"You would not believe that Spiegel was once a friend of

53

President Masaryk, would you?" Madame Hase was saying. "Today he is nothing more than a political fossil. At one time my father believed he would succeed him as professor of history, but he destroyed his career when he wrote that pamplet about Nazi tactics in the Sudetenland. So foolish—what did he hope to achieve? He lost all sense of proportion after his wife disappeared. Jewish, you know. She went to visit relatives in Berlin in the spring of 'thirty-eight, and never came back. He spent thousands of crowns trying to find her. We thought he was going insane."

As March progressed, Dr. Spiegel's behavior became more erratic. He developed a craving for the news. Hugh gathered that the government had proclaimed martial law in some parts of the country; but in Prague life went on much as before.

On March 14, they heard that Slovakia had declared itself to be an independent state.

"The fools have changed masters," Spiegel said. "They prefer Berlin to Prague."

Later the same day, the Czechoslovak president took the train to Berlin. The following morning, the German Army flooded smooth-ly across the border into Bohemia and Moravia.

As usual, Hugh reached his tutor's apartment at nine o'clock. For the first time in their acquaintance the old man was unshaven and he forgot to shake hands. He stumbled back to his chair. The brown bottle was already within reach.

"It is the Ides of March," he murmured as if to himself. "Today a country has been murdered."

Four

Colonel Dansey continued writing when Michael came into his office; with his free hand he pointed to the chair in front of his desk.

Michael rubbed his bloodshot eyes and sat down, grateful that there was no immediate need for him to make intelligent conversation. He had spent most of last night in the company of Betty Chandos, proving yet again that lack of sleep and an almost exclusive diet of champagne cocktails created a five-star hangover. Up here, on the eighth floor of Bush House, the rush-hour traffic in the Aldwych was mercifully muted.

Dansey capped his pen and used his blotter on the letter before him.

"No news from your man Kendall yet?"

"No, sir. I can't understand—"

"It doesn't matter now. You can forget him."

"I don't follow you, sir." Michael's tongue seemed too large for his mouth. "If Hitler—I mean, since yesterday—we need . . ."

"If I were you, I'd start again," Dansey said.

Michael flushed. "Bohemia and Moravia are now part of the Reich. More than ever we need all the Czech allies we can find. I admit that Kendall and Hase have probably failed, but there's still an outside chance."

Dansey picked up a newspaper and tossed it to Michael. It was yesterday's *Times*. A small news item, ringed with pencil, announced the arrival of several unnamed Czechs at Croydon Airport.

"Someone blundered," Dansey said sourly. "There was even a photograph in some of the papers. Not that it really matters."

"Who are they?"

"Colonel Moravec and fourteen of his intelligence officers. We chartered a Dutch plane for them. They left Prague just before the Germans arrived, with the cream of their files and all the money they could lay their hands on." Dansey permitted himself a prim smile. "Which happened to be quite a substantial sum. SIS handled the operation through Gibson and the embassy."

Michael felt himself beginning to sweat. What Dansey had told him seemed to have no bearing on Kendall and Hase.

Dansey took off his glasses and polished them with his handkerchief. "Neither Z nor SIS has much interest in Czech Communists at present. They're a disorganized rabble with little access to useful information; they're too far away for us to control with any degree of certainty; and in any case they'll always give Moscow right of way over London. But Moravec naturally sees them from another angle. He's spent half his career fighting the Bolsheviks, and of course he wants to know what they're doing in his own country."

"Do you mean we were just going through the motions to oblige Moravec?"

"Precisely. That was the sole purpose of the exercise. Your godfather and I knew the *Deuxième Bureau* would have to transfer its headquarters abroad sooner or later. Moravec had two choices—London or Paris. The Hase business was designed to woo him over here. Now he's here, he'll find it very difficult to move on." Dansey restored his glasses and looked directly at Michael. "Which means, of course, that we have achieved our real goal—direct access to A-54."

A-54?

Michael knew he was now expected to ask who or what was A-54. But Dansey's reply was unlikely to be very informative: either he would yet again have the pleasure of reminding Michael of the need-to-know principle; or his answer would lead to a bewildering vista of further questions that would leave Michael no better informed than he had been in the first place.

Michael mulishly decided to say nothing. He pulled out his case and lit a cigarette with a great show of concentration. As he looked up, exhaling a cloud of smoke, he caught an unfamiliar expression on Dansey's face, just before it vanished.

On another man's face it might have been a smile of approval.

Dansey stood up; and Michael obediently followed suit.

56

"So, Stanhope-Smith, from now on you may leave Czechoslovakia to SIS and the *Deuxième Bureau.* In the meantime—"

"But, sir, what about Kendall? I recruited him, and I do feel to some extent responsible. And it was my idea that he took his son."

Dansey clicked his tongue against the roof of his mouth. "You and I no longer have any responsibility for the Kendalls. You didn't compel *Captain* Kendall to take the job. He knew there were risks: he must take the consequences."

"We could at least alert Gibson and the embassy. And what about—"

"Stanhope-Smith," Dansey snarled with a ferocious hiss of sibilants, "will you be quiet? I want you to spend the rest of your valuable time this morning compiling a brief political and economic analysis of Poland, using the material in the B files. By brief, I mean about five hundred words. And make it not only succinct but simple enough for even a politician to understand. If it helps you, imagine you're writing for the eyes of our revered prime minister. I want it on my desk by lunchtime."

"Poland?" said Michael dully. His mind was still full of the Kendalls.

"Yes, *Poland.* It may interest you to know that, according to A-54, Poland will be Hitler's next target."

On the evening of March 15, twelve SS officers moved into the Hotel Palacky and the Kendalls moved out.

Most of the officers were young. Their fresh, healthy faces made a mockery of the black uniforms and the sinister insignia they wore. They tipped well, smiled a lot, and went out of their way to be pleasant to the other guests. Hugh secretly thought they looked rather heroic.

Later that evening Madame Hase came to their room unexpectedly; most people, both staff and guests, were watching Hitler's imperial entry into Prague. She was flushed with excitement and looked happier than Hugh had ever seen her.

"You must leave the hotel at once. The staff will have registered your arrival with the police. Checking on foreign visitors is one of the first things the Gestapo will do."

Alfred Kendall shrugged. "Does it matter? Britain's not at war with Germany. My papers are all in order. I've a perfectly legitimate reason for being here."

"Fool!" Madame Hase drew herself up to her full height of five foot two. "Half the staff in this hotel are Nazis. If they weren't before, they will be now. Servants talk, my friend, and my name is bound to come up. Have you never heard of guilt by association?"

Her urgency infected Kendall and Hugh. While Kendall paid their bill, she helped Hugh pack; they were out of the hotel within ten minutes of her arrival.

She directed the taxi across the river to Mala Strana, a part of Prague that lay just south of the castle; Hugh had never been there. On the way, she explained that she could not take them to her home—that would be too dangerous. They would go to the house of one of her cousins; the cousin was away but the servants knew her and would do whatever she asked.

The house came as a surprise to Hugh. It was built around a cobbled courtyard and covered an area of roughly the same size as the entire apartment block where Dr. Spiegel lived.

There were only two servants, an old man and his wife, who grudgingly agreed to open up a few rooms for Madame Hase and her guests. The palace had been shut up since the previous autumn. The furniture was shrouded in dustsheets and cobwebs. Candles were the only form of light available, which made the huge rooms seem still larger.

They ate an impromptu supper in a dining room whose ceiling was so far away that it might just as well not have been there. Scratches and rattles came from the walls.

"Rats," said Madame Hase. "One gets used to them in an old barn like this."

Shortly after the meal, Hugh was sent to bed. He lay there, trying not to listen to the sounds behind the skirting boards, and wondering whether there were many Communists like Madame Hase.

They spent the whole of the next day at the palace. In the afternoon, Jan and Bela arrived in the butcher's van at the tradesmen's entrance. They joined Kendall and Madame Hase in a large room that had been a library before the ceiling collapsed. It was not a comfortable place to sit, but its windows covered the whole of the courtyard, including the great entrance gates, and it had the additional advantage of a small staircase which led down to a side entrance. As Madame Hase said, they could not afford to be careless.

Without consulting Kendall, she sent Hugh to sit in the anteroom before the library. Kendall stood in the doorway and watched as she settled him down on a tiny chair upholstered with dusty velvet. Opposite them was a grimy, twelve-foot-high mirror. Their reflections swam in the murky world behind the glass. For an instant Hugh's eyes met his, and then looked away. Kendall felt an inexplicable sense of loss; since it was inexplicable, he ignored it.

As if by prearrangement, the four adults veered away from the easy chairs around the smoldering fire and sat around the table in the center of the room. Above their heads a chandelier creaked and tinkled faintly in the draft.

Kendall tried to seize control of the meeting. "We must review the situation," he began. "Events have moved so quickly that—"

"Perhaps I should do it, Alfred," Madame Hase interrupted. "I am the only person here who is fluent in both English and Czech."

Kendall winced. It was the first time she had called him by his Christian name. He was both offended and thrilled by the careless intimacy it implied. He was the natural person to chair this meeting; but, on the other hand, Madame Hase was the cousin of the Slovakian countess whose husband owned this immense place.

Madame Hase briskly reviewed the military and political situation. Bohemia and Moravia were solid with German troops, particularly in the major cities and along the frontiers. Slovakia, now nominally independent, had asked for Hitler's "protection"; the Wehrmacht, ever obliging, was already crossing the border. A new government had been announced, which consisted solely of Nazis from Berlin or the Sudetenland.

"And you, my friend," she said to Kendall, "are going to find it very difficult to leave the country. It will be just like Austria after the Anschluss. Foreigners will be one of the first targets the Gestapo choose. And you have already compromised yourself by your activities in the last few weeks."

As she translated what she had said to Jan and Bela, Kendall gnawed his lower lip. He felt a pleasant sense of superiority: the others were so afraid of the Germans—and of the Gestapo in particular. No doubt they posed a problem, but there was no need to be theatrical about it. When Madame Hase had finished, he leaned forward, tapping the table to draw their attention.

"Look here, it's about time you decided whether or not you're going to trust me. You can't dither any longer. You need funds, and England can supply them. But we must have cooperation in return.

And that means information, not to mention a way of getting me out of your blasted country."

Madame Hase blinked. She talked rapidly in Czech for a moment.

Jan shrugged his heavy shoulders and said slowly in the same language, "We need money now, not promises, *Pan* Kendall. I trust you as far as I can see you. Maybe we can get you out of the country—but how do we know you will come back?"

"Very well." Kendall had only one thing left to offer. "I can give you three more diamonds. And I give you my word as an English gentleman that I will be back within a few weeks."

Jan's head was lowered. He shook it slowly from side to side, which gave him the appearance of a bull about to charge. Bela glanced quickly around the table and then out of the window.

"Good faith—that's what it comes down to." Madame Hase's beringed hand wrapped itself around Kendall's wrist. "Alfred! I have an idea. There's only one way you can prove to our friends that you really mean to return. Leave the boy behind in Prague."

High above him, from the ridge of Hradcany, the great bell of St. Vitus' Cathedral tolled midnight. In the still air, he could hear other bells broadcasting the same message. Tomorrow had already become today.

Kendall shivered and stepped from the balcony into his bedroom. He closed the window with difficulty—the wood was warped—and drew the heavy curtains. The room seemed as cold as the outside world. He knew he should try to sleep, but the bed, despite its imposing appearance, was as hard as concrete; he had already discovered that the sheets were damp.

It was hardly worth going to bed in any case—Bela would be collecting him at four-thirty. Kendall preferred not to think about the journey ahead of them. For the first time in his brief secret service career, he would be adopting a disguise and actually breaking the law.

For the first time, he was afraid.

The plan was very simple. Bela, though he had lived and worked in Prague and Brno for many years, was a Slovakian. The authorities were used to him paying regular visits to his family in Presov. Kendall, suitably equipped with false papers, was to play the part of Bela's half-witted cousin. Once they reached Presov, Bela would be in his home territory; he had access to the smuggling routes through the mountains into Hungary.

It was obvious that the faster they moved, the better their chances would be. Germany's control over its new protectorate and its Slovakian satellite was not yet complete. In a way, Kendall was glad that they had to hurry—it left less time for reflection.

Time and again, he told himself that he had no option but to leave the boy behind. Stanhope-Smith had strictly forbidden him to contact the Prague Embassy. If the Kendalls tried to leave the country under their own names, the Gestapo would pick them both up at the border. Kendall was left with a choice between two evils: either he stayed with Hugh, in which case his mission would be a failure and the two of them would be fugitives in Prague; or he returned to England, in which case the mission would succeed. Hugh would be in good hands, and he would only be alone for a few weeks. Kendall was sure that Stanhope-Smith would send him back to Czechoslovakia in the circumstances. In the meantime, Hugh would be safer than if he and his father tried to escape on their own initiative.

He imagined how he would put it to Stanhope-Smith and possibly even to Muriel: *It wasn't an easy decision, of course. But when one took a common sense view, patriotic duty and one's paternal responsibility really left one with no alternative.* Perhaps he would add as a casual afterthought: *I left Hugh at the Michalov Palace—the countess is Madame Hase's cousin, you know.*

Kendall felt a little more cheerful. He removed his jacket, tie, and waistcoat, and put on his dressing gown. His clothes and the rest of his luggage would have to be left behind—Bela would be bringing him the clothes and possessions appropriate to a laborer at a Brno munitions factory. Madame Hase had assured him that his own belongings would be safe in the cellars of the palace.

A wing armchair in front of the empty fireplace looked more comfortable than the bed. He settled into it with a pillow and a couple of blankets, intending to smoke a last pipe before blowing out the candle. Just as he had succeeded in insulating himself from the main drafts, there was a tap on the door.

His instinctive reaction was to panic. But, even as he was struggling to free himself from the blankets, it occurred to him that the Gestapo would be unlikely to knock.

"Alfred!" Madame Hase rattled the handle. "Let me in."

Kendall unbolted the door. She burst into the room, despite his half-hearted attempt to keep her on the threshold. His sense of propriety was outraged: what would the servants think?

Madame Hase had discarded her fur coat, for the first time in their acquaintance; she wore a pink quilted dressing gown and a pair of pale blue mules with two-inch heels. The smell of musk was stronger than usual.

She put down her candle next to his on the wine table and settled herself into the armchair.

"Sit down." She pointed to a footstool. "We must talk—there will be no time in the morning."

"It *is* the morning," Kendall pointed out. "Where have you been all evening?"

"Making arrangements about Hugh. He can't stay here—the servants would talk, and it might be difficult if my cousins return. But Ludvik Spiegel is willing to take him for a month."

"What about his neighbors? They must know Hugh is an English boy."

Madame Hase shook her head. "Spiegel sees very little of his neighbors. Most of them are young, working-class couples, and they're out to work when Hugh is there. Besides, if we give Hugh a haircut and another set of clothes, he won't look English anymore."

"But he'll need identity papers and so forth, won't he? The Boche run a tight ship."

"True. Jan may be able to help with that. I think he knows a clerk in the Ministry of the Interior. But there might be an easier method. Hugh could become my nephew."

Kendall sucked angrily on his pipe. He said, with exaggerated patience, "But everyone would know—"

"It's not so foolish as it sounds. My sister married a Hungarian, a banker. They had a son—he was born in 'twenty-seven. The whole family died in a car crash last year—near Budapest, where they lived. The shock of it killed my father."

"So the boy's dead?"

Madame Hase patted his knee. "The point is, Rudi had dual nationality. His death was never registered in this country. It was done in Hungary, of course, but not here. With my father dying, I had too many things on my mind. Hugh could use Rudi's identity. I have all the papers. Perhaps Jan's friend at the ministry could help bring them up to date."

"Anyone who talked to the boy would immediately see he was English."

"Foreign, yes; but not English necessarily. If everyone thinks he spent most of his life in Hungary, that would be quite understandable. It may not arise—Ludvik says that Hugh is making very rapid progress in Czech."

"Hugh? Nonsense—the boy's as thick as two short planks."

"As you say. But you must not worry: we will equip him well enough to pass a street check, if need be. It will only be for a few weeks."

There was a moment's silence, during which Kendall fervently wished his hostess would leave. But she settled herself deeper in the armchair and fumbled in the pocket of her dressing gown.

"Here." She passed a silver flask to him. "It is cognac. We must drink a toast to your safe return."

Kendall's face brightened. "I'll get you a glass. I'll use the cap."

They drank to a safe return; they drank to England and Czechoslovakia; Kendall poured another drink and they drank damnation to the Nazis.

Then Madame Hase proposed another toast: "To us."

Kendall blushed and drank.

The conversation took a personal direction. Madame Hase talked about her husband, a young German of good family whose political career had been cut short with tragic finality by tuberculosis in 1931. Had he lived, she implied, neither Germany nor Czechoslovakia would be in its present appalling condition. She dropped tantalizing hints about her own family's connections with the old nobility of Bohemia and Saxony.

"The trouble with people like Jan and Bela," she said confidentially, "is that they cannot appreciate what was good in the old values; and that means they don't understand the *poetry* of communism."

Kendall didn't understand it, either, but he nodded nevertheless; it seemed to be expected of him. In any case he was watching her rather than listening to what she was saying. The candles were kind to her: her skin lost its pallor; the lips were no longer flabby, but sensuous; her plumpness might almost be described as voluptuous.

Desire stirred within him, engendered by the sheer romance of his surroundings. What would *it* be like, he wondered, with a beautiful aristocrat in a Bohemian palace?

Madame Hase leaned forward, holding out her glass. "Is there more in the flask?"

"Of course, madame." As he took her glass, her hand brushed his. He nearly dropped the glass.

"I call you Alfred," she said with a touch of petulance. "Why do you not call me Josefina?"

"I—very well." Kendall cleared his throat and took the plunge. "Your glass, Josefina."

When she took the glass, her hand again touched his. She put it untasted on the table. Kendall refilled the cap. He was very conscious of her presence; out of the corner of his eye, he could see that a tendril of black hair was swaying only inches away from the sleeve of his dressing gown.

"Tell me, Alfred," she whispered huskily. "Are you really a senior officer of SIS? The head of the Central European Section?"

"Of course." Kendall sipped his cognac. At this moment, he almost believed he was. In any case, it was essential to maintain the pretense, both to Madame Hase and to Jan and Bela. His safety—and Hugh's—depended on him being able to play the part convincingly. "Do you really think a job like this would be handled at a lower level?"

"Ah."

Madame Hase suddenly slumped forward on to her knees. Her dressing grown fell open, revealing a nightdress of black silk, trimmed with lace. She clasped Kendall's legs and rubbed her body against him.

"Love me, Alfred."

"Good God!" Kendall leaped to his feet and broke away from her. She tried to seize him again, but he palmed her away.

"Alfred, *milacek*—"

"Madame, I must ask you to leave." Kendall backed away and took refuge on the far side of the bed. These foreigners were sex-mad. "I insist that you go," he pleaded. "Josefina, *please.*"

Madame Hase stood up; she was lopsided, because one of her slippers had fallen off in the struggle. She refastened her dressing gown, found the missing slipper, and picked up her candle. Kendall hastened to open the door for her.

"You must understand, Josefina," he said as she passed him with her face averted. "I am married; I am here on duty—"

"You English." She looked up at him. The candle turned the tears in her eyes to glints of fire. "You have no romance in you."

Dansey lowered himself with great care into the armchair nearest the fire. "Just imagine I'm not here."

"That won't be easy," said Michael dryly. "Would you like a drink?"

"No, thank you. If you have to introduce me, call me Mr. Hayward. Has the report from Moravec come in yet?"

Michael nodded. "The DB can confirm at least half of the information from their own sources. They seem to think the rest is at least plausible."

"But none of it is particularly significant?"

"Well, no. It identifies a few names which were new to the DB on the provisional regional committees. There's a sort of shopping list which starts with gold and ends with tanks. But there's no firm information about what the Bolshies plan to do."

"That is probably because they don't know themselves."

Dansey fell silent and glanced around the small sitting room. Michael cringed inwardly: this was the first time Dansey had visited his rooms in Dover Street, and Michael felt that his possessions—and hence his private self—were unfairly at the mercy of Uncle Claude. He wished he had removed his own paintings to the bedroom. But that would have been worse: Dansey would have noticed the lighter patches on the wallpaper and drawn his own conclusions.

He was suddenly ashamed of the shabby, comfortable room with its oversized furniture. The furniture was part of his past—he had kept back a few pieces from the sale after his mother's death—but most of it looked ridiculous here.

"Extraordinary," Dansey said. He was looking at a painting over the sideboard. First he looked through his glasses and then over the top of them. "Not one of yours, I hope?"

"No, sir. Chap called Chagall."

"Glad to hear it. I've known children with a better sense of perspective. And I wonder why he found it necessary to give the man green hair." Dansey changed the subject without warning, or even altering his tone. "How's Kendall taking it?"

"Better than I'd expected. Of course he thinks the information he brought out was vital—perhaps that's some consolation. I think I was more upset about the boy than he was. He's one of these people who keep their emotions very tightly battened down."

"I hope he doesn't think we're going to send him back by the next train to collect the boy? You've made that clear?"

Michael got up to fetch the cigarette box from the sideboard. When he replied, he was safely out of Dansey's sight. "Not in so many words, sir. I thought I'd leave it until today."

Dansey refused a cigarette. "That was foolish of you."

"I hadn't the heart to do it."

Kendall had come off the boat train at Victoria yesterday afternoon. The little man had been wearing a baggy Hungarian suit; he had no luggage, apart from the contents of his pockets; he had so little money left that Michael had had to give him the cab fare home. His return journey from Prague had taken him the better part of a fortnight. Despite all he had gone through, he had been pathetically happy—full of himself like a dog who believed he had earned his master's approval.

"I hope your heart's in better shape this afternoon." Dansey glanced at his watch. "He's late."

At that moment, they heard the doorbell. A moment later, Mrs. Granger, Michael's landlady, showed Kendall into the room. He bustled in, shook hands with Michael, and looked inquiringly at Dansey.

"Mr. Hayward," Michael said with a wave of his arm. "A colleague of mine." A spurt of mischief made him add, "Just imagine he isn't here."

Kendall was about to hold out his hand, but Dansey confounded the move by giving him the slightest of nods and becoming lost in contemplation of the fire.

When he had settled his guest in a chair and given him a cigarette, Michael produced an envelope from his inside pocket. He handed it to Kendall.

"It's rather more than the sum we agreed on," he said awkwardly. "You've done a very good job. Had I known it was going to be so difficult we wouldn't have asked you to go."

And I certainly wouldn't have suggested you took the boy with you.

Kendall stuffed the envelope in his pocket without looking at its contents. "Only too glad to be of use," he mumbled. "Hope you don't mind that I had to pretend I was a —ah—senior officer. It was the only way to get those chaps to cooperate."

"Not at all."

It made it all the worse, Michael thought, that Kendall had done so well. He had been recruited as nothing more than a courier on the lowest of levels, but he had had to deal with problems which would have taxed an experienced agent. It was hardly his fault that his job had lost what little importance it originally had when Moravec arrived in London.

"When do you want me to go back?"

"Captain Kendall." Michael paused, wishing Dansey was at the other end of London. "As a matter of fact, it would be better if you didn't go back. Your face is known, you see. You couldn't go back under your own name, because there's no exit stamp on your passport. The Gestapo has almost certainly circularized your description. Quite frankly, your return could jeopardize the whole operation— destroy the value of the work you've done for us."

Kendall sat there with his mouth open as he grappled with the meaning of Michael's words. He sagged in the chair: the jauntiness had been sponged out of him.

"But what about Hugh—my son?"

Michael glanced at Dansey, but Uncle Claude was still staring at the fire. "We'll tell the embassy about him. You can let us have his address? I'm sure they'll get him home almost as soon as you could. It'll have to be carefully handled, of course."

Kendall nodded, apparently satisfied. Michael felt a sudden revulsion for the man's stoicism. Did his warped sense of patriotism obliterate his affection for his son? It was uncanny: Kendall was less concerned about his son than about the fact that His Majesty's Government didn't propose to send him back to Prague.

Kendall scribbled Spiegel's address in his pocket book, tore out the page, and passed it to Michael.

"Then there's my luggage," he said. "Can the embassy send someone around to the Michalov Palace? It's only just around the corner."

"Of course." Michael stood up, hoping that Kendall would take the hint. "One of our people will telephone you in the next few days and arrange a meeting. We'd like to get your firsthand impressions in detail of the invasion."

But Kendall remained in his chair. "I notice a lot of changes here since I got back. Even Chamberlain seems to realize that war's inevitable. Does this mean you'll be expanding your permanent establishment?"

"It's a possibility." Michael moved slowly toward the door. It was more than a possibility: he knew for a fact that both SIS and Z Organization were actively trawling for recruits—and had been since Munich.

Kendall got to his feet. "Then I wonder if you'd consider myself and Stephen—my eldest boy. He's a bright lad—and good at languages, too. St. Paul's, you know."

"I'll mention your name, of course. Naturally I can't promise anything—it's not my department."

Michael showed Kendall out. When he got back to the sitting room, he found Dansey jabbing the coals with a poker.

"I think I'll take that drink now, Stanhope-Smith."

Michael crossed to the sideboard. "What do you think of Kendall's offer?"

"I think we can get along quite well without the services of *Captain* Kendall or his wretched son. Even if he has been to St. Paul's. We may be moving on to a war footing, but there are limits."

Michael handed Dansey a small whisky and soda. "About the other son: shall I approach the embassy through the FO or get on to SIS?"

"Neither." Dansey finished his drink in a single swallow and wiped his mustache with his handkerchief. "Now I must be off. If necessary you can get hold of me through the PM's office."

"But we can't just abandon the boy."

"Why not? He's of no importance. Kendall's not going to make a fuss, especially if he thinks you might give him a job. Even if he did make a fuss, we could muzzle him with the Offical Secrets Act."

"But we do have a moral obligation—"

"Our moral obligations, as you choose to put it, lie elsewhere, Stanhope-Smith. Getting that boy out would be a purely sentimental gesture. I'm sorry, but the risk is unacceptable. The FO wouldn't cooperate for a start: they've had to tread very carefully in Prague for the last fortnight. And I've no intention of compromising either SIS or Z. I wouldn't be at all surprised if the Germans have already got the boy and his Communist hosts under observation."

"We could send in a nursemaid to bring the boy out—an amateur like Kendall."

Dansey picked up his hat and coat. "When I need your advice I shall ask for it. Don't bother to come down: I'll see myself out."

When Dansey had gone, Michael kicked the sofa until the pain forced him to stop. He had known before that he was involved in a dirty business, but this was the first time that Dansey had rubbed his nose in it quite so hard.

For a moment he toyed with the idea of resignation. But that would rebound on his godfather's head, especially at a time like this when the country was readying itself for war. Michael tried to ignore the thought that it would also be financial suicide: his rent was due tomorrow, on the first of the month; both his tailor and his wine merchant had presented him with extraordinarily large bills; and Betty Chandos was proving an expensive hobby.

But he had to do something—anything to prove to himself that he had not sold his soul entirely to Uncle Claude. He picked up the telephone and dialed the number of a house in Queen Anne's Gate. He used the private line to the flat, rather than the switchboard number for the rest of the building. Dansey would be furious, but with luck he wouldn't hear about it until it was too late.

"May I speak to Admiral Sinclair? It's Michael Stanhope-Smith."

He breathed a sigh of relief when the secretary said his godfather was in. If he didn't do it now, he suspected that he would never find the courage to try again.

"Uncle Hugh? It's Michael. I've found two possible new boys for you. I wonder if you could let them know downstairs."

II

War
1939–45

Five

The bullet, which was fired from above, punched into the crown of Dr. Spiegel's head at an oblique angle. The impact blew away the back of his skull.

Unable to move, Hugh gaped down at his tutor. Spiegel sprawled on the cobbles like a discarded toy. What was left of his head pointed toward the Vltava which flowed, gray and swollen with the autumn rain, toward the Manes Bridge. Around his head was a red halo that grew larger every second. There were white splinters and gray islands in the blood.

It made it worse that there had been no intermediate state. One moment Spiegel had been hurrying Hugh away from the crowd outside the Clementinum; the next moment he simply wasn't there. Nothing else had changed: the students were still shouting, "Germans go home!" while the men in gray were on the outside of the crowd, methodically controlling the civilians' movements, like dogs among sheep.

"Halte! Komm doch her!"

A soldier in helmet and greatcoat clattered down the steps from the road to the embankment. He carried his rifle across his chest. Behind him there were three more shots, and someone began to scream.

The scream unlocked Hugh's muscles. He began to run in the direction of the Charles Bridge. The soldier shouted again but made no move to follow. After fifty yards, Hugh glanced back: the German was standing over Dr. Spiegel, his arms flung wide and his body arched in a parody of a bow to his victim's corpse.

Twenty yards later, Hugh realized what he had seen: the murderer was being sick.

He ran on to Narodni Street. The trams were still running, and he was lucky enough to reach the stop just as a number seven came over the bridge. He sat by the exit, trying to control his breathing. It had become desperately important to look normal. He was Rudi Messner, a Czech-Hungarian boy who was blessed with a German surname and ancestry. He lived with his old Uncle Ludvik—who was fortunate enough to be half German—in Zizkov. Uncle Ludvik's flat had been his home since his parents died in Budapest. He was going home.

It was only when the tram turned into Vaclavske Namesti that he realized that he no longer had a home. Within an hour or two the Gestapo would have identified Dr. Spiegel and arrived at the flat. The Rudi Messner story and Hugh's command of Czech were adequate for routine security checks but they would never stand up to the Gestapo.

Hugh got off at the next stop. The tram deposited him within a stone's throw of the Petschek Palace, a bleak modern building that had once housed a bank. Now it was the headquarters of the Prague Gestapo.

The only place he could go to was Old Town Square; and the quickest route would lead him past the Petschek Palace, if he chose to go on foot. He rummaged through his pockets, finding a handful of small change. It would be wiser to save what little money he had for emergencies. He thrust his hands in his pockets and walked fast with his head down, like someone with somewhere to go.

In Old Town Square Madame Hase rented a narrow but immensely high house on the north side, near the monument to John Huss. Dr. Spiegel had taken him there one afternoon in June, when his father's money ran out. Madame Hase had told him that there was no more money, and that it didn't look as if his father would be coming back. He didn't expect she would welcome him, but perhaps she might be prepared to help. If he didn't find shelter for the night, the police would pick him up.

It was nearly five o'clock by the time he reached the square. There were soldiers and police on every corner. Two boxlike armored cars were parked with their engines still running outside the Old Town Hall.

Madame Hase's front door was at the top of a small flight of steps. Hugh rang the bell and waited. He fixed his eyes on the doorknob, willing it to turn. At any moment someone might ask him for his papers.

Bolts rattled and the door swung back a few inches. Madame Hase herself peered through the gap; in June an elderly housekeeper had answered the door. She wore no makeup and looked much smaller; Hugh realized that for the first time he was seeing her without high heels.

"What is it?" Her eyes slid past him to the soldiers in the square. Then she saw who it was and the door began to close. "Go away," she muttered. "There is nothing for you here."

In his desperation, Hugh acted without thinking. He jammed his foot over the threshold and pounded on the door.

Once again the door opened to the limit of its chain.

"Don't do that, for God's sake." In her panic she spoke in Czech. "You'll draw attention to us."

Hugh had a flash of inspiration. "Then let me in. Or I'll shout until someone comes to see what's happening."

Madame Hase's face tightened with fear. "All right. Wait."

She unlatched the chain and opened the door just widely enough for Hugh to slip inside. "Down the stairs. Quickly."

He found himself in an untidy basement kitchen that for an instant reminded him of Mrs. Bunnings's domain in Wilmot House. There were books and newspapers on the big scarred table. A tap dripped into the sink in the corner. A single armchair had been drawn up to the stove.

Madame Hase came in after him and closed the kitchen door behind her. He noticed that there were streaks of silver in the black hair.

"Why aren't you in England?" she snapped.

"After we saw you in the summer, Dr. Spiegel took me to the embassy. But the guards wouldn't let me in because I didn't have a passport. I came here on my father's, you see."

She sank into the armchair. "Where have you been all this time?"

"At Dr. Spiegel's. There was nowhere else."

"The man always was a fool. Where is he now?"

"He's dead." Hugh clenched his hands behind his back. "A soldier shot him this afternoon. It was near the Clementinum—the students were protesting and we were trying to get away."

Madame Hase nodded toward the radio. "It was on the news just now. The SS are pleased: it's given them an excuse to shut down the universities and polytechnics."

She spoke calmly, as if the events they were discussing were remote from them both. Hugh wondered if she had heard him. He tried again.

"Dr. Spiegel was *killed* today."

"So? We shall all die soon. I think the Gestapo will come tonight."

Hugh frowned. "How do you know?"

"The riots. The Germans will use them to justify a purge. They always do. Many people will disappear in the next few days. Communist intellectuals will be among the first."

"Can't you escape?"

Madame Hase shrugged. "Where? How? The Provisional Committee might have helped—you remember Jan and Bela? But they turned against me when your father did not keep his promises. They think I'm a traitor. No one wants me."

To Hugh's embarrassment she began to cry. She wept with abandon, making no attempt to control or conceal her tears. Hugh sidled nearer the stove.

Eventually the sobbing died away. She looked up at Hugh, her lips still trembling.

"I could have been a heroine, you know. But no one would let me. I made my housekeeper go—she was Jewish. My mother was half Jewish. Oh, my God, my God—"

"Madame Hase," Hugh said abruptly. "May I stay here?"

She emerged from the private world of her fear. "If you want. It does not matter to me. But the Gestapo will find you when they come tonight."

Madame Hase was wrong: the Gestapo did not come.

In a sense there was no need for them to come, for Madame Hase had already made herself a prisoner; she had not left the house for weeks. Later that evening Hugh asked her for money and bought some bread and cheese for them.

She no longer bothered to wash herself. Her fur coat was stained and matted, and its lining trailed along the ground when she walked, but it never left her back, day or night. She lived and slept in the kitchen.

Hugh explored the upper floors of the house and found little beyond flaking plaster, bare boards, and rat droppings. Madame

Hase had sold or given away most of her belongings over the summer; she planned to escape via Hungary to England. But war broke out in September: travel became more difficult for everyone and many passports, including hers, were confiscated.

Now—two months later, in November 1939—the Wehrmacht had shot Dr. Spiegel and Madame Hase was no longer capable of caring. Hugh soon discovered that when she wasn't weeping or sleeping, she was talking; he could hear her even when he was out of the room. Sometimes she spoke in German or English, but mostly she used Czech.

She didn't comment on his knowledge of Czech and German—perhaps, Hugh thought, because she never really listened to what he said to her. But the fact that he could understand most of what she said was a secret source of satisfaction to him.

For the first time in his life he realized that he was alone. No one would make the decisions for him. The future nagged him like a decaying tooth.

The worry kept him from sleeping for most of the first night at Madame Hase's. Huddled in a dirty blanket, he lay on the floor near the stove. Madame Hase, wheezing heavily, slept in her chair a few yards away. Hugh stuffed his hands in his pocket in an effort to warm them. His fingers touched the familiar metal outlines of Hiawatha.

The Red Indian was the only reminder that Hugh possessed of his old life in England. Everything else, from the clothes on his back to the contents of his pockets, had been made in Czechoslovakia. Hugh had grown out of toys, but the little lead figure had become a talisman—tangible evidence that he had not always been a fugitive in Prague.

During the night there were times when he wondered whether he should simply give himself up to the police. Then he would have to make no more decisions. Surely the German's wouldn't harm someone of his age, whatever his nationality?

That would have been the sensible choice. But, every time he closed his eyes, he saw Dr. Spiegel lying by the Vltava, while his killer vomited beside him. That was why he could not risk being sensible.

He slipped into a doze, which lasted until dawn. With the daylight, his head cleared. For the time being he was safer in this house than on the streets. It was possible that Madame Hase had exaggerated her importance in the eyes of the Germans. Perhaps in a few weeks he would be able to escape from Prague and make his way toward Hungary. He thought there would still be a British Embassy in Budapest.

In the meantime, however, he needed to know more about his immediate surroundings in case Madame Hase had been right about the Gestapo. Before breakfast, he slipped out of the back door and explored the yard at the rear of the house.

It was a cobbled area, bisected by a sagging clothesline and bounded on two sides by the high, windowless walls of a neighboring church. There was a door in the third wall. Hugh eased back the bolts and found himself in a weed-infested graveyard. He investigated cautiously: an archway on the far side of the graveyard gave on to an alley which ran on an east-west axis to the north of Old Town Square. He had found a possible escape route if trouble arrived at the front door.

Considerably relieved, he returned to the yard. From this angle he could see the whole of the rear elevation of the house. A large grating set in the wall caught his eye. Its top was perhaps two feet above ground level, and it was partially obscured by a pile of empty tins. He examined it more closely, and realized that the grating continued beneath the level of the yard. The iron stanchions had rusted: most were still solid, but one had broken off. The gap was just large enough for Hugh to squeeze through.

He was in a large, dimly lit cellar. A flight of steps climbed up to what must be the kitchen floor. The steps ended with a massive flagstone. Judging by the position of the end wall, he guessed that the flagstone was near Madame Hase's armchair. There was no other exit. The cellar was potentially a trap.

As he turned to go, Hugh stumbled; one of the flagstones was set slightly higher than the rest. His foot slammed down on it in his effort to keep his balance.

Instead of the slap of shoe leather on stone, he heard a dull, metallic boom.

He dropped to his knees and scraped away the dirt. Underneath was a square of blackened iron, divided diagonally into four triangular sections. He prised one of them open, breaking a nail in the process. A current of cool air swept up into the cellar. He peered into the opening.

There was nothing but darkness beneath—darkness and the ripple of running water.

On the second night, in the early hours of November 19, Hugh woke from a nightmare to find that Madame Hase had the muzzle of a pistol in her mouth. She held the gun upside down, with her thumb on the trigger. Her eyes squinted down the barrel toward the hand-grip.

"Don't shoot, madame—*please!*"

The words burst out of him as he scrambled to his feet. Madame Hase lowered the pistol with a frown; she wiped the end of the barrel on her coat.

"Why should you care?" She cradled the gun in both hands. "Besides, I was only trying it for size. This is a Mauser—a good German pistol."

"I do care." Rather to his surprise, Hugh realized that this was true. "There's still time to escape. Anyway, perhaps the Gestapo won't come, perhaps they've decided—"

"Death will come," she said harshly. "Don't you understand? I've run out of time. Everyone has betrayed me in every way they can. Even Stalin made a pact with that Austrian monster—the man who should have led the fight against fascism. And your father spurned me as a woman—you know that?" She drew herself erect in her chair and flung out her arm toward Hugh; the pistol pointed at him like a finger. "One day you will find out: life is a series of betrayals which end in death, the greatest betrayal of them all."

Her arm waved in a gesture that dismissed life as an insignificant tragedy and narrowly missed knocking over the candle. Hugh bit back a desire to laugh. He sensed that Madame Hase was to some extent acting—and even enjoying—her despair. She reminded him of his father being haughty with shop assistants—both of them were somehow in their own audiences, observing their performances.

A dull thud shook the house.

Hugh looked up. "What was that?"

There was a second thud, followed by a third. Wood splintered somewhere above their heads.

"The Gestapo, of course. I told you they would come." Madame Hase stood up. Her face was suddenly gray, and her theatrical manner had vanished. "They often use a sledgehammer. Would you like me to kill you?"

Hugh backed away, his hands outstretched as if they could ward off a bullet.

"No? Then I shall shoot some of them and then myself."

For the first time that evening, Hugh had no doubt that she was telling the truth. He bumped into the back door and automatically fumbled at the bolts. Madame Hase ignored him. She stood by the range, staring at the door which led to the stairs and the hall.

The two doors opened simultaneously. Hugh glimpsed two tall men in leather trench coats; there were more men, in uniform, behind them. Madame Hase raised her gun. There was a deafening *crack* and one of the leather-clad men was flicked backward on to the stairs behind him.

A large black-and-tan Doberman hurtled down the stairs, its claws rattling on the bare boards. Someone shouted. There was another shot.

In one fluid movement, the dog bounded from the doorway, across the kitchen and into the air. Its jaws closed around Madame Hase's throat. Its flailing body knocked over the candle.

A woman's scream rapidly became a sexless gurgle. Then there was a blessed instant of silence.

Hugh threw himself into the yard, slamming the door behind him. He was about to run for the gate into the graveyard, when he heard voices and saw lights on the far side of the wall. There was a burst of automatic-weapon fire and the gate bucked on its hinges. Hugh changed direction and scuttled toward the grating in the wall of the house. He dived headfirst through the narrow gap and fell heavily on to the flagstones beneath. The jagged edge of the broken stanchion gouged into his leg, just above the knee.

The cellar was completely dark. The blood trickled down his leg leaving a smear of temporary warmth.

For a second he thought he was safe. No adult could get through that grating. Then he remembered the dog, and what it had done to Madame Hase. Outside he could hear confused shouting. At any moment they would discover the grating.

The first triangle of the manhole came up easily. But the second, welded into place by generations of dirt, refused to budge. He abandoned it and moved on to the third iron segment. He tugged at it desperately with both hands. It lifted so easily that he fell backward.

The shouting outside increased in volume. Someone shone a torch full on the grating; light flooded into the cellar, glinting on the splashes of blood. Hugh stumbled toward the manhole.

Beneath his feet, the invisible water rustled. The dog barked.

Hugh closed his eyes and jumped.

★   ★   ★

"Betty, this is Stephen Kendall. Stephen, this is Lady Elizabeth Chandos." Michael bent down and pecked her cheek. "You'd better call her Betty. Everyone else does."

Lady Elizabeth held out her hand. "In that case I'll call you Stephen, and we can start on an equal footing. Come and help me with the toast."

Stephen took the toasting fork she offered him and, having hitched up his trousers, knelt awkwardly beside her.

Michael sat on the sofa behind them, with his legs draped over one of the arms. He was glad that Betty was here: it gave him an excuse to postpone what he had to say to Stephen. He pulled out a sketchbook and began to draw the Adam fireplace and the two figures crouching in front of it like votaries before the sacred flame. He started to draw merely to distract himself; but as he continued his interest grew.

Betty kept up a stream of chatter, most of it addressed to Stephen. She was tall and slim, with short dark hair and a tendency to gurgle with laughter at the slightest provocation. As Michael watched, she set Stephen at his ease with the casual social efficiency that came from generations of practice.

There was a knock on the door and Burton came in with the tea tray. The old man had forgotten to shave again, and there was a puddle of tea around the tarnished Georgian teapot. Nevertheless, few butlers could have rivaled the sonorous perfection of his diction.

"Tea is served, my lady."

"Thank you, Burton. Oh, damn! How did I get all this butter on the hearthrug?"

By now the pale November daylight was rapidly fading. Michael got up to draw the curtains across the tall windows overlooking Hill Street. First he pulled down the blackout blinds: the air-raid wardens were ridiculously officious about their duties and even a chink of light was asking for trouble. Betty turned on a heavily shaded standard lamp. The big drawing room suddenly shrank and became cavelike.

"This *bloody* war." Betty always added a quaint emphasis to a swear word, as if it was a foreign word daringly introduced into an English sentence. "We get all the inconveniences but none of the excitement. Not even a real air raid. I just wish someone would do something."

Stephen handed around the cups and plates. "It's a war of

81

nerves. Perhaps Hitler's waiting for us to drop the first bomb so he can say we started it."

"Then I wish the RAF would stop dithering. At least a few bombs would be some consolation for this wretched blackout. The streets are a positive deathtrap after dark. Look." Betty extended a shapely leg and pointed to a discolored patch on the shin. "I came out of the Ritz last night, and it was so dark I walked straight into the sandbags they've got outside the entrance. It's too tiresome—if the bombs don't get us then the sandbags will."

"I rather like the blackout," Michael mumbled through a mouthful of toast. "On clear nights you can see the stars from Piccadilly. I doubt if anyone's been able to do that for a couple of hundred years."

"Darling, not all of us share your artistic sensibilities. Personally, I'd much rather see the pavement beneath my feet. What do you think, Stephen?"

Stephen was in favor of the stars and for a few minutes he and his hostess wrangled amiably about it. Michael finished off the toast and poured himself his third cup of tea. He listened to the others, occasionally throwing in a word to keep the conversation going.

He was relieved that Betty and Stephen had taken to each other. Michael was always hesitant about allowing his private and professional lives to overlap. But Stephen Kendall was more than just a colleague: he was in some sense a protégé. It was largely due to Michael's recommendation that SIS had taken the boy in the first place. Stephen had started in April, on the same day that Michael had joined SIS himself; Uncle Claude had not forgiven his championship of the Kendalls and had arranged for him to be transferred from Z Organization. Michael knew he had been lucky—if Admiral Sinclair had not been his godfather, he might have lost his job altogether.

Both Michael and Stephen had been assigned to Section V, which dealt with counterespionage; Michael was Stephen's immediate superior. After the excitements of Z Organization, the work itself seemed tedious. They spent most of their time analyzing material relating to Germany's intelligence and security services. As Michael saw it, their job was to provide the bricks and mortar; their senior officers had the fun of doing the building. Stephen was showing an unexpected aptitude for the job: he had a gift for seizing on the one relevant item in a mass of irrelevancies, and a positive genius for linking facts with suppositions. He was a hard worker, too—in his spare time he was studying Russian and Arabic; he was already fluent in French and German, and had a good working knowledge of Spanish and Italian.

Betty laid a hand on his arm. "Stop brooding, darling, and give me a cigarette. What are you doing at Christmas?"

Michael offered her his case. "I have to stay in town. Work, you know."

"Too tiresome," said Betty sympathetically; she knew little of his work beyond the fact that he was vaguely attached to the Foreign Office. "I'll be in Ireland, of course. No rationing and no blackout. If it weren't so dreadfully boring, I think I'd stay there for the duration. But if I'm under the same roof as my father and my brother for more than twenty-four hours, I start turning to drink. Talking of which, is it too early to have a cocktail?"

It was, but they decided to have one anyway. Michael rang for Burton, but the old man failed to appear. Betty said he was probably asleep—either that or pretending to be deafer than he was. She decided that it would be quicker to go in search of the materials herself.

When she had closed the door behind her, Stephen said, "Is there any news about the succession?"

Michael repressed a sigh. Stephen was also showing a natural talent for office politics. "It's almost certain that Menzies will get it," he said shortly. The subject was still painful to him. "They were offering ten to one in the office yesterday."

On November 4, Admiral Sinclair had died in the London Clinic; his death was variously attributed to a malignant tumor or fifteen years of overwork. Menzies, previously a section head, had taken over as acting chief, but it was by no means a certainty that he would be appointed the new CSS; the Admiralty was pushing hard for its own candidate. It was rumored that Dansey's support had tipped the scales in Menzies's favor. Uncle Claude had a lot of influential friends. Once Menzies was on the throne, Dansey would become the power behind it. It was an arrangement that would suit both of them.

Stephen got up to fetch the lighter from the mantelpiece; he glanced at himself for a shade too long in the big mirror above it. Michael's lips twitched. He derived a good deal of amusement from the secret pride that Stephen took in his appearance. He had also noticed that Stephen's taste in clothes had changed in the last six months. At first the boy had alternated between two suits at work: one made him look like an aspiring city gent, the other like a trainee

83

bookie. Recently, however, he dressed in the flannels and tweeds that Michael himself favored; after a few botched attempts he had succeeded in knotting his tie with the same Double Windsor; even his handkerchief protruded precisely the same distance from his breast pocket as his mentor's. It was endearing, Michael thought; imitation was the sincerest flattery.

"Have Betty's people got a big place in Ireland?" Stephen asked casually.

"It's a great big white elephant. Her grandfather had a fit of the Balmorals. That's why they're all as poor as church mice." Michael saw the look of surprise, instantly repressed, on Stephen's face. "Don't be taken in by the house in Mayfair and the butler. The house is on a ninety-nine-year lease which ends in June. And Burton's only kept on because it's less trouble than getting rid of him. You know what these old servants can be like."

Stephen nodded eagerly. He was about to ask another question when the door opened and Betty came in, carrying a tray of martinies.

"No olives, I'm afraid. There's a war on."

Half an hour later, Michael and Stephen left the house. As they strolled toward Berkeley Square, Michael realized that he really couldn't put it off any longer. If he didn't tell Stephen now, he might never get around to doing it. Stephen would hear the news at secondhand, probably at the office tomorrow.

"Stephen," he said abruptly. "There was some other news yesterday."

The blackout made it hard to see the expression on Stephen's face; Michael was grateful for the small mercy.

"There was the usual Saturday meeting of section heads. Apparently that business at Venlo was even worse than we thought. In fact it's so big a disaster that the bosses can't hide it from the rank and file like us."

"Venlo? I thought that was over and done with." Stephen's voice was as light and precise as ever.

They turned into the square. The great plane trees in the central garden were black against the lighter darkness of the sky. Michael stopped so abruptly that Stephen cannoned into him.

"I'm afraid it's far more serious than that. The Nazis were lucky: they captured one senior officer from SIS and one from Z Organization. The odds are that they didn't even know that Z existed. But they will now. The SD's interrogation methods are damned efficient."

Stephen immediately grasped what Michael was trying to say. "You mean that the damage won't be confined to the Dutch networks?"

"Security was bad. Both men knew too much about other stations, and about London. Captain Best—he was the Z man—has been in this business for years. He knows literally hundreds of names."

Stephen stirred beside him. "Why are you telling me all this now? Why not wait till tomorrow?"

"Best recruited several people for Z. One of them was that Hase woman your father met."

"So? She's not exactly vital for the war effort, is she?"

"She was the only person in Prague your brother could have turned to. If she's been arrested, we can only assume that the Nazis have got Hugh as well."

There was a moment's silence. Michael tried to find words of consolation, but found none.

"Stephen," he said in a voice that was little more than a whisper, "I am sorry."

"It's the war, isn't it? These things happen in war."

Six

Hugh swam through the nightmare. It was too terrible to be real, yet too immediate to be truly frightening; it left him no time to think.

He swam with the current. Sometimes his hands scraped against a rough stone vault above his head. He glanced back twice at the cone of light which descended from the manhole in the cellar. At first he heard shouting, and there was a single burst of machine-gun fire which boomed along the culvert, temporarily drowning the roar of water.

The culvert must have made a shallow turn. The next time he looked around, he could see nothing. His arms and legs ached, so he turned on his back and floated. Unidentifiable objects jostled him in the stream. At one point he could have sworn that something ran over his chest. At first the stench was overwhelming; but later his nostrils became clogged, so he could smell nothing. When he began to swim again, one of his flailing legs touched the bottom of the sewer. The water was becoming shallower—it was less than four feet deep.

He drove himself onward, ignoring the fear, the cold, and the pain in his leg. The culvert sloped gently downward. At intervals, other streams cascaded into the main channel.

The height of the roof varied; often it was easier to walk than to swim. The worst moment was when Hugh walked into an arch that spanned the culvert. Feeling with his hands, he discovered that the water flowed beneath, through a gap which was barely two feet high. He sucked the foul air into his lungs and dived.

For seconds that felt like hours he moved forward, half scrabbling and half swimming. When his head burst out of the water on the far side of the arch, the air smelled sweet.

Above his head were the dim outlines of a manhole.

Hugh made other discoveries. Iron rungs led down from the manhole to a deep, brick-lined recess, a foot above the water level. Within the recess he found a metal trunk which contained, among other things, a pair of dry leather overalls and an electric torch.

There was a bottle of colorless liquid. He knew it was vodka, the drink to which Ludvik Spiegel had always referred as "my medicine." Hugh drank and, despite the disgusting taste, the vodka spread fire through him. His teeth chattered and he had to fight back a tendency to retch, but he drank again.

He tore off his soaking clothes as quickly as his numb fingers would allow. The leather overalls fitted him better than he had expected and they were lined with heavy cotton.

Nevertheless, the cold seemed to grow worse: his whole body began to shake. He glanced up at the manhole. He must wait until daylight showed. By then the curfew would have ended and it would be safe to move.

In the meantime, he was cold. He swallowed another mouthful of fire.

His mind was a jumble of impressions and memories. Sometimes he wondered if he was imagining them; at other times he was convinced that they must belong to someone else.

There were often voices on the edge of his range of hearing. They spoke in many languages. He tried to identify the owners of the voices, but this was usually too difficult for him to do with any certainty. Once he was sure he heard Aunt Vida arguing about the price of vodka with Meg; the strange thing was that they were talking in Czech. It was even odder when Meg suddenly turned into Madame Hase.

Another voice was often telling him to drink something. This was good, because he was always thirsty. He thought he might be lying in a flat desert beneath a broiling sun; the sands stretched away on all sides to what would have been the horizon if his eyes were open. He was alone, except for the voices.

The voices were good, too, for they spoke in many languages. And languages made you free.

Suddenly the voices became quiet.

Hugh opened his eyes. He shut them immediately because the light was so bright. After a while he tried again. This time it was easier.

He was lying on a small bed in a narrow room that he had never seen before. There was a window in the far wall, through which he could see a dull gray sky.

Beside the bed was a table on which stood a carafe of water and a glass. Everything was very clean. He thought he could hear dance music somewhere, perhaps from a wireless.

A movement caught his eye. A sparrow landed on the window-sill. It looked toward the room and then away. It skipped eighteen inches along the sill, glanced again at Hugh and vanished.

It was very strange. Hugh closed his eyes and fell asleep.

It was evening when he awoke. The curtains were drawn and a tall, thin man was bending over him. Hugh stirred.

"Good, you are awake. Now you must drink."

The man supported Hugh with one arm and used his free hand to lift a cup from the table. He held it to Hugh's lips. The liquid was warm and tasted of meat. Hugh swallowed it greedily, wishing the cup held twice as much. Afterward, the man settled him gently against the pillows and turned out the light.

"Now you must sleep."

"Where am I? Who are you?" Hugh croaked. He spoke in Czech without thinking; the man had used the same language.

"Sleep now. We'll talk later."

The door closed behind him. Hugh puzzled over his host's identity. The voice, with its Slovakian vowels, was faintly familiar; but the light had been dim and behind the man, so his face had been a shadow.

He abandoned the mystery after a few minutes. His mind was clear now, but very tired. It was as if it had returned from a long journey: it was glad to be home but very weary.

Sleep caught him unawares.

In the morning Hugh was already awake when Bela came in with a glass of sweet black tea. While Hugh sipped it, Bela sat on the bed and smoked a cigarette. His large blue eyes stared thoughtfully at Hugh, but he made no attempt to start a conversation.

At last Hugh could bear the silence no longer. "How long have I been here?"

Bela's long, fair lashes fluttered. "Six days. Today is November the twenty-fifth."

"But what happened?"

"Jan found you outside the yard. You had a fever and you thought he was a Gestapo officer. You were wearing a sewage worker's overalls and carrying your own clothes." Bela wrinkled his nose. "Everything stank of shit."

"I was running away from the Gestapo. They killed—"

Bela stopped him with a wave of his hand. "I know. For the first few days you did nothing but talk, in English and Czech. You were a little mad, I think. We expected you to die."

Die? Hugh felt instinctively that death was something that happened to other people. *Dr. Spiegel. Madame Hase.*

"Maybe," Bela continued, "it would have been simpler if you had. Jan couldn't just leave you on the streets: you were talking too much. So he put you in the van and brought you here."

"Where's here?" Hugh demanded. There was desperation in his voice.

"In the apartment above Jan's shop in Bubenec. You remember? Near Dejvice Station? It's near the yard where we took you that first time."

Hugh nodded. It was a relief to find that some of his memory was clear. He could remember everything up to the point where he jumped into the sewer. After that it was all blurred. He must have left the sewer and set off blindly in search of the only other people he knew in Prague. He knew the street where the yard was, because he had overheard Madame Hase mentioning it to his father. He shivered at the thought of the risks he must have run—crossing the city in the early morning in stolen clothes, and talking about the Gestapo.

Bela produced a saucer from beneath the bed and flicked ash into it. His movements were delicate and precise, like a cat's. "Jan thinks we should kill you," he said conversationally.

"No! You can't do that! What have I done?"

"It's not what you've done." Bela smiled. "You can die for what you are. He says we have to think of our safety."

"I promise I won't talk to anyone." Hugh bit his lip; the futility of what he was trying to do overwhelmed him.

"But Jan is impetuous." Bela's smile broadened. "If we kill you, that is that: you can do no harm to us; but neither can you do us any good."

"My father is a very important man."

The words sounded a lie even to Hugh. But to his surprise, Bela nodded.

"That is true. It might be useful to us. In a war like this, sometimes your friends become your enemies, and your enemies become your friends. That's what I said to Jan: look what Stalin did to us in August. One day perhaps we will need friends in London. Stranger things have happened in war."

Hugh tried to keep his bewilderment from his face. *Languages can set you free.* "You don't speak English well. If you keep me here, I can translate for you."

"Maybe. And in the meantime you can help us. Children can sometimes do what adults cannot. If we are careful, there will be no danger—your papers are in order."

Bela laid a large clean hand on the blankets above Hugh's thigh; he pressed down until he was gripping the leg itself. He brought his face close to Hugh's; his features were finely drawn with the exception of the nose, which looked as if someone had squashed it out of shape with a blow; the skin was as smooth as a woman's; the eyes seemed to have no need to blink.

The hand tightened its hold. Hugh grunted with pain and tried to squirm away.

"And you would be very, very good," Bela cooed, "wouldn't you? Because if you weren't, my friend Jan would pick up his big knife, the one he uses on pigs, and do *that!*"

Bela sliced his free hand across Hugh's throat, grazing the Adam's apple.

In Bubenec, the days drifted into weeks; winter grudgingly gave way to spring.

Once again Hugh's life found a routine; and the routine mercifully deadened sensation. They allowed him a couple of days of convalescence. After that he was told that he would sleep in a tiny room under the eaves, because his bedroom was needed for other things. There was no bed in the attic: Hugh made do with a pile of evil-smelling blankets. In a while he no longer noticed the smell: perhaps it merely became his own; there was little opportunity to wash.

Much of his life and many of his dreams revolved around dead pigs. The war seemed to have made little difference to Jan's business. He was a specialist pork butcher who selected his own pigs from farms to the north of Prague. He killed them and cut up the carcasses in one of the sheds in his yard. Most of the cuts were then sold to other butchers for a comfortable profit. Jan retained the legs and the neck ends and cured them in another one of his sheds. The bulk of his hams were tinned; there was a steady demand for them all over the Reich. But some of the hams were sold in their natural state to customers in Prague.

Hugh soon realized that Jan took a fierce pride in his hams. They were the best (and most expensive) on the market. The business might be small, but quality was more important than quantity. He was particularly pleased that they had a regular account with Hradcany Castle, the seat of the government. Baron Konstantin von Neurath, the *Reichsprotektor* himself, was said to have commended Jan Masin's hams.

But—as Hugh soon discovered—there was more than one reason for the weekly trips to the castle. The van delivered hams; on some occasions it also took away small packages wrapped in oilskin. Hugh always knew when one of these was due: Jan took care to have a bucket of fresh offal in the back of the van. Sometimes the sentries would make a routine inspection on arrival and departure; but none of them cared to rummage through the bloody mixture of hearts, livers, and lungs. The Nazis, as Jan once said with a chuckle, did not like to get their hands dirty.

Hugh had never been so busy in his life. For the first few weeks his body was reduced to a mass of aching muscles. He worked for twelve or thirteen hours a day—lifting, carrying, sweeping, cleaning, and running errands. Jan was a hard taskmaster. Once, when the slaughterhouse floor had not been swabbed to his satisfaction, he seized Hugh by the scruff of the neck and plunged his head into a bucket of pig's blood. At the time Hugh thought he was going to drown.

In time he grew used to the labor. Physical work made it easier to bear the lack of heating. At night he was so tired that neither cold nor fear kept him from sleeping. The food was plentiful and unexpectedly good—Jan demanded a lot of it and Bela had a talent for cooking; Hugh benefited indirectly from both these facts.

As his body hardened, so did his mind. For one thing he began to realize that Jan and Bela were not quite the same as other men he had known: it was almost as if they were man and wife. They shared the vast double bed in the room beneath Hugh's attic. At night Hugh often heard the bedsprings creaking; sometimes there were other sounds—moans and raised voices. When they were not in public, they touched each other much more than men usually did; and both of them—usually when they thought Hugh was out of hearing—occasionally called each other *milacek,* which was the Czech for *darling.*

It was very strange. At first Hugh wondered if he was misinterpreting what he heard and saw: after all, this wasn't London; they did things differently in Prague. Perhaps *milacek* when used between men was like *mate* in English. Perhaps it was quite normal for Czechs to live with a male friend instead of getting married. Then he remembered how Jan sometimes looked at him when Bela wasn't around. For some reason that look made *him* feel ashamed. It was very strange.

One night shortly after Christmas, Hugh was awoken by Jan bellowing his name from the apartment below. Jan was alone in the living room, with a bottle of slivovitz on the table in front of him. He beckoned Hugh to come nearer and poured out a second glass.

"Rudi!" He belched, and plum brandy fumes rolled toward Hugh. "We must drink to the death of the old year, eh?" He gripped Hugh's wrist and pulled him on to his lap. The slivovitz made Hugh cough. He could feel Jan's lips nuzzling his hair.

Without further warning, Jan grabbed Hugh's crotch and squeezed. Hugh screamed—from pain, fear, embarrassment, and panic. It was at that moment Bela returned.

Hugh was sent upstairs. He heard them fighting. Then the bedsprings creaked, and there were moans. In the morning, Bela had a black eye; Jan had a bandage on his arm and scratches on his face. They seemed the best of friends, and Jan ignored Hugh except when he had to give him orders or tell him off.

He frequently fell foul of both Jan and Bela for the way he spoke their language. He pronounced it in the wrong way; he used too many long words; he knew nothing of the argot which his hosts used.

Jan would cuff him around the head. "Speak like a worker, for Christ's sake. Who do you think you are?"

And Bela would twist his ear in a way that was oddly reminiscent of his father. *"So* gratifying," he would murmur. "Such an education for us."

All around them, there was news of the war—on the wireless, in newspapers, on the streets, and in cafés. Customers mentioned it when they came into the shop; Jan and Bela would talk about the same news items in an entirely different way after work—when they were alone and when they met their innumerable and usually anonymous friends. As far as Hugh could tell, there was a great deal of talk about very little. After the Germans and the Russians had sliced up Poland in the autumn, not much seemed to have happened. A few ships had been sunk. On the western front, the British, French, and German armies appeared to be having cold feet about the whole affair. In Prague—for all the speeches, parades, and feverish preparations—life had changed very little since September.

If this was war, Hugh wondered what all the fuss was about.

Winter that year was savagely cold.

In the first few months of 1940, Hugh began to suspect that there was another war in which he was somehow in the front line. This war was waged in Prague and in secret; people talked about it very little, though the *Reichsprotektor* sometimes issued proclamations about the arrests and executions of agitators and enemies of the state.

In January, Bela and Jan started to use him for errands. Often he was uncertain whether they concerned the business or the private war. At first he seemed innocuous—a letter to be left at someone's apartment, or an enigmatic verbal message to be collected from a *parky*-seller in Vaclavske Namesti.

But one day Bela took him in the van to a farm which did not keep pigs. They parked in a barn. The farmer stood like a sentry outside the door while they loaded heavy wooden crates into the back. The crates had markings, but the alphabet they used was unfamiliar to Hugh; it reminded him slightly of ancient Greek.

They drove back to Prague, crossed the Vltava, and headed east into the working-class suburb of Karlin. As the van rattled down Sokolovska trida, Bela nodded toward a shuttered house which they were passing.

"That was the CP headquarters," he said as quietly as the engine would allow him, "until the bastards closed us down in 'thirty-eight.'"

Bela drove to a warehouse near the river. A man in oil-stained overalls came out to meet them; he staggered as he walked; he stuck his head into the cab, bringing with him the stench of stale brandy.

"You got them?" he said hoarsely. "All of them?"

"Shut your mouth," Bela snapped; he jabbed a thumb at Hugh. "He's—"

"How many of them?" In his enthusiasm, the man sprayed spittle into the van. He was so drunk that Bela's interruption hadn't registered. "Come on, man, you can tell old Ota. How many machine guns have we got?"

Ten days later the Ides of March came around again—the anniversary of Hitler's entry into Prague.

Hugh spent the morning rehearsing what he was to do with Bela. Time and again, Bela took him every step of the way. Hugh was made to repeat the few words he had to say so often that he lost all sense of their meaning. Bela spent over an hour discussing the various contingencies that might threaten the success of the plan. If the manager, for example, asked him what he was doing, he would use one response; if it was a waitress, he would use another; if the one-armed man was not at his usual table, Hugh was to ask the nearest waitress. It was all perfectly simple.

"But *why?*" Hugh asked. "Why all the fuss?"

"My friend wants to talk with him, that's all. He can't go in himself because the last time he was there he didn't pay his bill." Bela smiled and touched Hugh's throat with his forefinger: it was an unmistakable reminder of Jan's pig-killing knife. "Tell me again what you do afterward."

Jan pulled out of the traffic and parked the van outside a bank. On the other side of the road a church clock chimed three. Both Jan and Bela stared diagonally across the road toward Panska, a street that ran parallel to Vaclavske Namesti.

There was a man in a tweed overcoat on the corner. Hugh saw him smack his leg, as if swatting an invisible fly. Some of the tension left Jan and Bela.

Jan leaned across Bela and pushed Hugh's shoulder with the palm of his hand. "Go!"

Hugh crossed the road. By the time he reached the corner of Panska, the man in the overcoat had vanished and the van was lost among the traffic. As usual the street was crowded with shoppers and businessmen; among them were a number of officers, both German and Czech. It was an oasis of affluence. It seemed hardly possible that places like Karlin and Bulbenec could be in the same city.

No one noticed him, though he felt he could hardly be more conspicuous if he was seven feet tall and wearing no clothes. A woman in furs, who reminded him fleetingly of Madame Hase, walked straight at him as if he wasn't there. He hastily got out of her way. He looked exactly what he was, Hugh realized—a tradesman's errand boy. For an instant, he understood why these people made Jan and Bela so angry.

He found the Dutch Mill's doorway without trouble. The café-restaurant was on the first floor. No one stopped him as he padded up the stairs; the thick carpet seemed luxurious to him. On the walls were huge paintings in heavy gilt frames. He presumed they were Dutch; they were windows into another world which seemed infinitely preferable to Prague.

A gabble of words and music poured out as he pushed through the swing doors at the head of the stairs. A waiter hurried toward him.

"Yes?" The man's brows were drawn down in a V-shaped frown.

"Urgent message for *Pan* Spinka." Hugh stumbled over the words, but at least they were intelligible. "His mother—"

"Give me the message." The waiter held out his hand. "I will see that *Pan* Spinka gets it."

"No, you don't understand. I have a taxi outside for him. His mother is very ill."

In his panic, Hugh had raised his voice. People at nearby tables looked up. It was this, rather than anything he had said, that seemed to influence the waiter.

"Over there," he muttered. "End table on the far wall. And don't take all day about it."

So Spinka was at his usual table. Hugh hurried toward it. The tables were separated from one another by low partitions; and each table had its own wireless. The room seemed to be full of Wehrmacht officers. According to Bela, the Dutch Mill was a popular place with the Germans; that was why Spinka was there.

There were three men at the end table. Two of them were young and blond; Hugh knew they were German immediately, despite the fact they were in civilian clothes—it was something to do with the set of their mouths and the way their heads sat on their shoulders. Hugh touched the arm of the third man.

His fingers felt nothing but fabric. Hugh jumped back; he could feel himself blushing; his embarrassment temporarily blotted out his fear. He had tried to touch an arm that wasn't there.

"*Pan* Spinka, you must come quickly. Your mother has had another attack. Your brother has sent a taxi for you."

The words flowed out perfectly, thanks to Bela's training. But Hugh's mind was elsewhere—on the absence of Spinka's arm, on the Hitler mustache he wore, and on the toupee which failed to match the rest of the hair.

Spinka was rising to his feet before Hugh had finished. While he was still half sitting and half standing, he abruptly froze. His brown eyes stared imploringly at the two Germans.

"You permit?"

The older one flicked his eyes toward the ceiling: it was as if he had spoken the words aloud: *How absurdly hysterical these funny little Czechs are.*

But he gave a curt nod. "As long as you're at the Petschek Palace by nine, I don't care where you go."

Spinka thanked him—in German—and followed Hugh toward the door. He tried to question Hugh on the way; but Bela had warned him about that. Hugh shook his head and said, "Quick." He took the stairs three at a time.

He could hear Spinka panting after him.

By the time Hugh reached the street, he was a good five yards ahead of Spinka. He waved once, as if pointing to the taxi, and darted away. As he ran, he saw the man in the tweed overcoat emerging from a tobacconist with his hand in his pocket. Jan, Bela and the van were nowhere to be seen.

Hugh sprinted toward the tram stop, where a number 21 was waiting. In those few seconds, his mind was possessed with a harsh clarity. Bela's friend didn't want to talk. Moreover, Jan and Bela had taken the opportunity to make sure of Hugh's loyalty. The waiter, the two Germans, and dozens of other people in the café had seen his face. It was almost as if Bela was whispering the words in his ear: *If you betray us, you will betray yourself as well.*

Then the grenade went off and the screaming began.

"He collaborated with the Gestapo, you see." Bela ladled an extra large helping of goulash on to Hugh's plate. "Because of him, three of our comrades have been arrested; two have been shot already."

"Little rat." Jan broke off a piece of bread and stuffed it into his mouth. "I wish I'd had him alone for five minutes first."

Bela tapped Jan's wrist. *"Naughty* boy. We mustn't be selfish. A nice public execution does wonders for morale. Spinka could have set a very bad example to some of our weaker comrades. And we wouldn't want that, would we, Rudi?"

Hugh pushed aside his plate and stumbled from the room.

Muriel Kendall took the weight off her feet. She sighed with relief and allowed herself the luxury of closing her eyes for a few seconds.

She had done everything. There was really no need to wait. Indeed, the only reason to stay was the allure of the temptation to go. But she had spent half her life avoiding awkward scenes, and it was time to change.

In a way, the decision had been made easier by the changes all around her. The familiar pattern of the prewar world was breaking up with astonishing speed. The war itself was refusing to conform to the pattern laid down by the earlier war to end all wars. The Germans had flicked the British Army back into the English Channel at Dunkirk. France had been reduced from a world power to the western province of Hitler's empire. England itself had become another country—with a new government, new rules, and new priorities. So why should she not become a new person?

As she heard the key in the front door, Muriel stiffened automatically. Trained reflexes died hard: it cost her an effort of will to relax into her armchair; it would have been so much easier to leap up and rush into the hall.

The door of the dining room opened.

"Muriel, my dear." Alfred Kendall crossed the room to the sideboard; he fumbled for his key chain.

She didn't need the unexpected endearment to know he was pleased with himself. You couldn't live with someone for twenty years without developing a sixth sense about their moods.

"Some bloody fool's keeping a cab waiting outside. The Joneses, I suppose. The way they waste their money!"

He took out the decanter and poured himself a careful measure of whiskey. This was confirmation of his mood: usually, by now, he would have noticed that tea wasn't ready; and he saved the whiskey until later in the evening.

"Alfred—"

"Not a bad day." He flung himself into his chair and lit a cigarette. "We were inspected by Dalton—the minister, you know—this afternoon. In fact, he was rather complimentary about our section's work. He's only had the job since May, but by God he's made himself felt. Talk about a new broom. The ministry's done more in the last two months than in the rest of the war put together. Of course, some of that's Churchill's influence."

"Alfred, that's my taxi."

"There's a rumor that our lot's going to be expanded. Which means that there's a very good chance that people like myself—the experienced chaps—will move a few rungs up the ladder."

Yes, he's probably had a drink on the way back from the station, as well as the ones at lunchtime—

"Alfred, I'm leaving you. That's my taxi." Now that she had spoken the words, she became two people—an actor mouthing words that had no meaning, and a fascinated spectator.

"Your taxi? Have you any idea how much it costs to keep a cab hanging around— *Leaving?"*

"I'm going to live with Aunt Vida. Meg's already there." She caught sight of her hands: the red, chapped skin generated a welcome spurt of anger. "As for the taxi, I'm paying for it. Or at least I will when I've earned enough to pay back Aunt Vida. I'm going back to nursing."

She knew that this would be another body-blow—almost as bad as the announcement that she was leaving him. She had trained and worked as a nurse during the last war; but of course her marriage to Kendall had put an end to that. The idea of his wife going out to work *for money* was naturally anathema to him, for it implied that he was incapable of keeping her. That the implication was true was neither here nor there. Voluntary work would have been quite acceptable, providing it was suitable to her station in life. It had always amazed Muriel that he saw nothing demeaning in forcing his wife to become a household drudge, unpaid in either monetary or emotional currency.

"Oh, for Christ's sake, don't be so stupid."

"Stephen's got a room in town now. Meg's coming with me. As for Hugh—"

She broke off; her lips were trembling, despite her efforts to keep calm. She would never forgive Alfred for leaving Hugh behind like so much excess baggage in Prague. *Never.* By now the loss of Hugh should have been easier to bear; but both the sorrow and the anger she felt for Alfred remained unchanged. She had nothing left of her younger son except what was in her handbag: half a dozen toy soldiers which she had found on his mantelpiece. The rest of his toys and all of his clothes had gone to the church bazaar, the profits of which were going to the war effort.

Kendall's face was mottled. "I wish you'd stop crying over spilt milk. I told you, I had no choice. Damn it, I was doing work of national importance. Anyway, if you had any sense you'd realize—"

It was his turn to stop. Muriel knew what was in his mind. Alfred had been thinking it for months, but even he hadn't dared to say it to her: *Hugh was an impossible problem: and now that problem's been solved forever*.

Muriel swore: she had never used that particular word before, though she had heard it often enough in her hospital days. She could have laughed at the surprise on her husband's face.

"National importance?" An immense scorn buoyed her up. "Is that what you call it? You came back preening yourself like a peacock. And you met a countess there, didn't you? I heard you dropping hints about it to someone on the telephone. Terribly aristocratic, wasn't she? Well, I hope you did better with her than you used to do with me."

He slapped her hard on the cheek. He was trembling from head to foot as he stood over her. Muriel wondered how she could ever have lived in fear of this pathetic little tyrant. Her thrust about the woman must have gone home, because his next words sounded almost like a plea.

"Look, there's a war on, Muriel. We've all got to pull our weight. Look at me—I've had to sell the business and go to the Ministry of Economic Warfare. Your place is in the home: you've got to stick to your guns."

Does he mean all that? Is he really so stupid?

"You had to sell the business anyway. You had no choice. Even so, Aunt Vida had to pay off your overdraft." She stood up, gloves in one hand and handbag in the other. "My place is where I want it to be."

"Muriel—look here, I know we've had our ups and downs. Everyone has. I can't manage this house without you—"

"We just had downs." She pulled on her gloves and walked toward the door. "You'll easily find something in town, nearer your job. Everyone's moving out of central London these days."

She reached the hall. In the drawing room, the ornate marble clock struck seven. She would never have to clean that beastly wedding present again.

"You haven't heard the end of this," Kendall shouted after her. "It's desertion, that's what it is. I'll be seeing my solicitor."

"I wouldn't do that. When Aunt Vida paid off your overdraft, it was a loan, not a gift. She made you sign something this time, didn't she? You're paying it off at five pounds a month; and she's got the right to demand the balance at any time."

"You bitch."

She opened the front door. The evening sunshine burst into the house, along with the smells of a suburban July. People said this summer of 1940 was one of the best they could remember. The cabbie saw her and started his engine.

As she opened the gate and stepped out onto the pavement, she heard behind her a sound which was unbearably reminiscent of Hugh.

Alfred was crying.

It was a good summer in Prague as well. The bathing stations along the Vltava were crowded almost every day. Hugh was allowed to go a few times, usually with Bela. This was a relief not only because he loved swimming but also because the hot weather made the smells worse.

Bela visited the *plovarnas* only partly for recreation. The bathing stations were also useful for meetings. All sorts and conditions of people went to them; and when people took off their clothes, as Bela was fond of pointing out, they also shed the outer layers of their identity.

It was as a result of one of these meetings in early August that Bela decided to visit Slovakia for a few days. The Provisional Committee for Prague was trying to establish links with all the underground Communist organizations in what had once been Czechoslovakia; only then would concerted action on a national scale be a real possibility.

Since March 1939, when Germany had declared Bohemia and Moravia a protectorate of the Reich, Slovakia—the eastern end of the prewar republic—had been technically an independent state; in reality it was run by a fascist government which took its orders from Berlin. But the government was less efficient than the protectorate's, and life was less regimented. The Provisional Committee of Prague pinned a lot of hopes on their Slovakian comrades.

Bela was an obvious choice as one of the emissaries. He had a cast-iron reason to visit the country since his family were in Presov. Jan's contact at the Ministry of the Interior was able to help with the exit visa. Bela already knew personally a number of the leading comrades on the other side of the border.

He left by train on August 11. Hugh and Jan saw him off at the station. Jan waved as the train hissed and clanked out of the station. Then he dropped his arm and draped it like a yoke along Hugh's shoulders.

"So, little one," he said softly as they walked out of the station. "We shall have to look after each other, won't we?"

A year ago, Hugh would have talked it over with Hiawatha; but that was impossible. He had swaddled Major Kendall's erstwhile friend and batman in a scrap of rag, and hidden him in a crack between the wall and the window frame in his attic.

He had to make his own decisions now. He had a fair idea of what Jan wanted: his information had been gathered piecemeal— from his observations in the flat, from gossip among other errand boys, from watching the animals on the farms. It was like a jigsaw puzzle: and now the pieces made a picture.

The possibility of succumbing could be discarded right away. That left him with two options: flight or fight. The former had little in its favor —he was with Jan during the day and locked in the flat with him at night; besides, where could he go? He prepared as best he could for the second alternative by stealing a small, little-used knife from the shop downstairs. He sharpened it and kept it beneath the winter coat which served him as a pillow.

Bela was to be away for ten days. After the first five had crawled away without incident, Hugh began to relax. Perhaps he had over-estimated Jan's lust and underestimated his loyalty to Bela. Bela's absence meant that both of them were kept very busy: maybe Jan had no time to spare for that sort of thing.

They spent the morning of the sixth day in the shop: Jan was doing the accounts in the small back room which he used as an office, while Hugh served all but the more demanding or important custom-ers in the front. Jan Masin's fame as a pork butcher was increasing, largely because of the castle patronage. Nearly half of their customers that morning were German.

Around midday, Ota the warehouseman paid a social call. He and Jan retired to the backroom to sample some French cognac which had flooded the black market in Prague since the fall of France.

Ota and Jan spent an hour together and managed to drink the whole bottle between them. Ota boasted proudly of his achievement to Hugh as he passed him on the way to the door.

Jan, having waved good-bye to his friend, staggered back

through the shop. Without warning he seized Hugh with an armlock around his neck and dragged him into the office.

It was a hard lesson, but Hugh learned it fast: *when you make a plan, first examine the assumptions on which it rests.* He had assumed that, if this happened, it would happen at night, like last time. His knife was two stories away.

He rammed his elbow into Jan's stomach. The butcher grunted; but his grip on Hugh's neck tightened rather than slackened. He yanked at Hugh's hair, tugging back his head, Hugh screamed; he swiveled in the armlock and jabbed lower.

Jan cried out and recoiled, losing his grip on Hugh. For a few seconds, he was bent double with his hands cradling his crotch. Hugh would have darted for the door, but Jan's bulk, formidable even when temporarily immobilized, was between him and the exit.

Instead he looked desperately for a weapon. The knives were all in the shop or the meat store next door. His eyes swept around the office. The pen was too small; the empty cognac bottle was too near to Jan; the account book wouldn't hurt anything larger than a mouse; the chair was too heavy.

Then he saw the cleaver. It was one of several; Jan had taken it out of the shop because the blade needed regrinding. Only a few inches of the haft were visible—the rest was obscured by the account book and a pile of invoices.

There was no time for subtlety. Hugh seized the cleaver and, holding it in both hands above his head, charged at Jan.

In that instant, Jan straightened up. One huge hand clamped over both of Hugh's on the cleaver's handle; the other took him by the throat. There was a brief, unequal struggle. Hugh was forced backward until his thighs collided with the desk. Jan twitched the cleaver out of his hands with insulting ease and tossed it onto the filing cabinet. At the same time he continued to push, bending Hugh's body backward like a bow.

He rubbed himself against Hugh. His hand dropped to the waistband of his trousers. His heavy belt clattered on the uncarpeted floor and his trousers slid down to his ankles. Hugh gagged at what he saw, and struggled to pull himself away.

Jan merely shifted his grip and worried Hugh's belt. He tugged the strap through the buckle. Hugh was shouting—in Czech and German, even in English; but he knew that the walls were thick and that the neighbors had long ago learned to keep their distance from

Jan and Bela. The butcher was panting like a thirsty dog.

From the shop came a *click* and a *scrape*.

A customer had opened the street door into the shop. Jan must have been too drunk to lock it when he said good-bye to Ota.

Hugh screamed.

Jan rammed himself against Hugh, as if the scream had intensified his excitement. The little office darkened slightly: someone must be standing in the doorway.

"What is this?" a man snapped in German.

Jan released his hold so unexpectedly that Hugh slithered to the floor. The butcher spun around with surprising speed to face the intruder; his right hand brushed the top of the filing cabinet as he turned; he scooped up the cleaver.

Hugh glanced up at his savior; and what he saw killed the hope that had been rising within him. In the doorway stood an elderly Wehrmacht officer; he was immaculately turned out, small and rather stout; his hands were empty. As Hugh watched, a monocle fell from his left eye.

"Drop it," the officer said calmly.

Jan snorted and charged.

Events now became so fluid that Hugh could no longer separate one from the other. The officer's hand dived toward the holster at his waist. *Too late.* The office was too small for Jan to be much hampered by the trousers around his ankles. Hugh lunged at the butcher's legs: in his mind was a confused memory of a rugger game at Thameside College: *Go for the legs, Kendall! Don't funk it!*

Jan's bare legs felt as rough and as strong as tree trunks. Even as Hugh wrapped his arms around them, he knew it was no use: the room was too small and Jan too strong. The German seemed to be moving in slow motion.

But Hugh's abortive tackle diverted Jan's aim by several inches. The cleaver missed the officer's head and shoulders. But it sliced into his leg just below the knee. Jan, having missed his expected target, lost his balance and stumbled against the wall.

To Hugh's amazement, the German did not collapse, shrieking and bleeding, on to the floor. Instead he steadied himself against the doorpost, unstrapped his holster and drew out a Luger. The butcher, dazed by the fall, scrambled on to his hands and knees; he was still holding the cleaver.

The German bent down and put the muzzle in Jan's ear. His

mouth tightened, as if he had felt a twinge of pain. Then he pulled the trigger.

The echoes died away. Outside in the street someone was shouting. A soldier with grizzled hair ran into the shop.

The officer reholstered his pistol and replaced his monocle.

"It's all right, Hans," he said testily to the soldier. He turned back to Hugh. "Thank you, my boy," he said in careful, textbook Czech. "You saved my life."

Seven

It was excellent cognac, there was no doubt about that.

Von Neurath had given him a case for his birthday last month. The baron might be unsuited to his present job—as a moderate, he was criticized from both sides, but no one had ever criticized his palate. At least there were a few advantages to be gained from the wanton destruction of a civilization; for example, the officers' social club at the Michalov Palace was offering cases of champagne at a very reasonable discount. Colonel Scholl rolled another drop of cognac lovingly around his tongue. And then of course—when communications were back to normal and France had settled down again—there would be the possibility of some really good claret.

He turned his head as the door opened. Eva came in, followed by one of the maids with the coffee. The maid put down the tray on the table in the big bay window, bobbed her head awkwardly, and withdrew.

Eva sighed. "These local girls. They take so long to train."

"At least they seem willing," Scholl said mildly. "Have the children settled down?"

"Just about. Heinz was rather sulky—he wanted to go on with his Führer scrapbook. Magda's curious about the gardener's new boy. If you come to that, so am I? Why were you so mysterious about him at dinner?"

Scholl sipped his coffee. "The full story wasn't suitable for children's ears. As a matter of fact, it was all rather shocking."

He stared out over the lawn, which by now was vanishing into the twilight. Five or six miles away to the north was Prague, its lights smothered by the blackout. It was extraordinarily peaceful.

"Helmuth! Don't be so infuriating."

"It was all because of your ham," he said with a grin. "You remember that ham we had at the castle last week? I thought I'd get you some. In the event I got you the butcher's boy instead."

In the end, she wormed the whole story out of him, as he knew she would. He tried to keep the precise nature of Masin's brutality from her, but it was no use. It was equally impossible to hide the fact that he might have been killed.

"I would have been, if it hadn't been for the boy. The cleaver did a bit of damage to the prosthesis—I'm wearing the spare now— but that's all."

Eva frowned. "It must have jarred the stump. Have you had it looked at?"

Scholl shook his head. "Hardly worth it."

"Nonsense. I'll have a look at it tonight when we go to bed; and I think you should see Dr. Wirth tomorrow."

"But—"

"No buts." The smile she gave him stripped the years away from her: once again he saw the girl who had met him at Dresden Station in 1918, when the hospital train brought him back from the Front. Once she saw her point had been gained, she abruptly changed tack. "Why did you bring the boy here?"

"Nowhere else for him to go. He's an orphan—parents died in Budapest before the war. There was an uncle, I gather, but he died last year. Masin had some connection with the family. I think he simply seized the chance to get some slave labor. I checked the ministry's files: technically Masin was the boy's guardian."

"I still don't see why we should have him."

Scholl began to clean his monocle; it was a favorite trick when he wanted to avoid his wife's eye. "The poor kid's in a state of shock. If I hadn't taken him, he would probably have spent a night or two in the local police station; then they'd've shunted him off to some institution."

"Another of your lame dogs." Eva's voice was resigned. Her husband was usually the most biddable of men, but she knew it was futile to argue with him when his conscience was involved.

"Miroslav does need help in the garden." Scholl replaced his monocle. "He's quite a strong lad for his age—about fourteen, I should say, the same as Magda; and he certainly seems willing enough. I've told the office to sort out the paperwork. One advantage of being on the *Reichsprotektor*'s staff is that you get instant cooperation from bureaucrats."

"Are you sure he's not—I mean, that he won't be a bad influence on Heinz?"

Scholl shook his head. "I trust the boy. He told me that nothing like this had happened before, though he suspected that Masin was—well, inclined that way."

The expression on Eva's face told him that she wasn't satisfied.

"Oddly enough he's got German blood in him—his name's Rudi Messner, though his mother was Czech and his father Hungarian."

"Austrian, I expect, rather than German." Frau Scholl's voice was a trifle disdainful: after all, the Austrians were not exactly Germans in the true sense.

"He speaks some German, too." Scholl pressed on, gallantly determined to display the bright side of his new acquisition. "And what there is of it is quite cultivated; I wonder if his family have come down in the world. It occurred to me that Heinz and Magda might be able to pick up a bit of Czech from him. We're going to be in Prague for the foreseeable future, and it might be useful for them."

Frau Scholl said nothing as she refilled her husband's cup. She couldn't help thinking that it would be much simpler if the Czechs learned German.

In the distance a clock chimed midnight.

Hugh was on the borders of sleep when he heard it. Probably, he thought the clock belonged to a church in Zbraslav, just up the road; *Oberst* Scholl's villa—it seemed more like a palace to Hugh—was on the outskirts of the little town.

He stretched luxuriously. For the first time in months he was lying on a bed between real (though rather coarse) sheets. And he was clean as well. Old Miroslav, who lived in the cottage at the end of the old stable block, had insisted on him having a thorough wash in the tin bath that he kept in his kitchen. He had also insisted on burning Hugh's old clothes.

A heavy perfume flooded through the open window: there was a bank of honeysuckle below. The privacy was as much a luxury as the physical comfort. Below him was an old coach house which was now used as a garage for the *Oberst*'s Mercedes. Miroslav's quarters were twenty yards away. The villa itself was even farther; the stables were shielded from its windows by a clump of chestnuts and ash trees.

It was almost as if he had been reborn into another life. He had saved only two things from the old—Hiawatha and the knife which he had stolen from Jan. He planned to make a primitive sheath for the knife; it was small enough to carry on him. *Be prepared.* He grinned in the darkness: he was learning to place an entirely individual interpretation on the Boy Scouts' motto.

There was a whirring above his head.

Hugh jerked awake. A sweet, cracked bell began to chime. He relaxed: it was only the stableyard clock. It was at least a couple of minutes behind the church clock.

A second midnight. He toyed with the idea that the space between the two midnights was a sort of no-man's-land in time: anything could happen then; it was outside the usual rules.

The stairs creaked.

Hugh's hand snaked beneath the pillow and grasped the knife. They creaked again: someone was coming up. It couldn't be Miroslav or Colonel Scholl—they would have switched on the light, or called up to him.

Bela.

That was irrational—Bela was in Slovakia. *He might have come back.* He couldn't have known where Hugh was. *He might have found out; he has friends everywhere.* One thing was certain: whoever it was had no desire to advertise his presence.

As these thoughts were chasing through his mind, Hugh was slithering inch by inch over the edge of the bed. Fortunately he had not tucked in the blanket. He lowered himself down to the floor, praying that the bare boards would not creak like the stairs. There was just room for him in the narrow space between the window and the bed. The bed was between him and the door.

As the last note of the second midnight sounded, the door swung open. Hugh could hear someone drawing breath sharply; there was a whisper, followed by a *shhh!* So there were two of them.

A torch came on. Hugh judged its beam must be full on the pillow.

"He's not there!" The voice was a high childish treble; it spoke in German.

"What's that on the pillow?" The second voice was older: it sounded like a girl's.

Hugh realized with the shock of anticlimax that it must be the two Scholl children. The *Oberst* had mentioned their names on the drive from Prague, but they hadn't registered in his memory.

"It's a toy soldier." The owner of the first voice was very near now. "A Red Indian."

"How babyish," said the girl calmly.

It was the hauteur in the girl's voice that made up Hugh's mind for him. He didn't mind if these kids wanted a midnight prank. But if they were going to involve him, he would give them a little more than they had bargained for.

"Wer sich in Gefahr begibt," he announced in a low sepulchral voice, *"kommt darin um."*

It was one of the few German proverbs he knew: "He who puts himself in danger perishes therein." Dr. Spiegel had been fond of using it.

The boy gasped and the beam of the torch wavered.

But the girl was made of sterner stuff. "Who's that? Where are you?"

The torch found him almost at once. Hugh sat up, blinking. He took care to tuck the knife under the bed.

"What do you mean by trying to scare us?" the girl demanded angrily—so angrily that Hugh thought he had probably succeeded. "You've got no right, do you hear? We'll see what my father has to say about this."

Her German was rapid, but Hugh could follow it. Speaking it was more difficult, but she had given him such a perfect opening that he had to try.

"So your father knows you are here? The light on my face is too bright."

He knew that he had found her weak spot when the torch beam slipped from his face to the floor. This was an illicit outing. But the girl was a fighter: she merely switched her attack.

"What's your name?"

"Rudi Messner. What's yours?"

"He's impertinent," the boy piped up. "He's a servant. He should call you Fräulein."

The girl ignored her brother. "Magda Scholl. And this is my brother Heinz."

"Are you a Czech?" the boy asked suddenly.

Hugh shrugged. He wished he could see more of them than two shifting shadows. "I'm a mixture: Czech, Hungarian, and German."

"So," Heinz sounded as if his worst fears had been confirmed. "A mongrel."

"May I see you?" Hugh was suddenly irritated with these two arrogant children. Who did they think they were? "You've seen me."

"All right." Magda turned the torch on her brother. Hugh saw a skinny, fair-haired boy, dressed in shorts and a shirt. He looked about eleven. In his belt he wore the dagger of the *Hitleriugend*. His teeth were too big for his face. He was making a brave attempt to sneer.

The torch cut away from him and flashed upward. Hugh caught a glimpse of blond hair and regular features, lit from below; for an instant he could have sworn that Magda was smiling. Then she switched off the torch.

"It is safer. We're not meant to be here." The admission was a peace offering of a sort. "How old are you?"

"Fourteen. Last June."

"So am I."

Heinz shuffled his feet. "What does your father do?"

"He's dead." Hugh noticed that Magda made an almost imperceptible movement with her arm, just like Meg used to do when he had said something tactless. "He was a banker."

"My father's a hero. He's got the Iron Cross First Class *and* the *Pour le Mérite*. He was decorated by the emperor himself. My uncle's a hero, too."

Bully for you. Eighteen months ago Hugh would have been impressed; now he thought that two medals in exchange for a leg weren't much of a bargain.

"Come on, Heinz." Magda tugged her brother toward the door. "Rudi needs his sleep." Something in her tone told Hugh that the thaw in her hauteur had been only temporary. "Good night, Rudi."

Hugh waited until they were on the stairs. "Good night." He added, in a softer voice, "Fräulein."

"Please, Mrs. B. *Darling,* Mrs. B."

"Oh get along with you." Mrs. Bunnings picked up the rolling pin and waved it like a sword. "I can't abide having people underfoot in my kitchen, and that's a fact. I just don't know what your mother's thinking of, allowing a girl of your age to titivate herself like that."

Meg held her ground. "I'd do it myself, of course. But no one sews a seam like you do. And then there's the hem: I can never get them straight. You wouldn't like all Stephen's grand friends to think I looked like a scarecrow."

"All that glitters isn't gold—you mark my words, young lady." Mrs. Bunnings—apparently satisfied that she had won a moral victory—put down the rolling pin and waddled across to the dresser where she kept her sewing box. "Have you pinned it?"

"Sort of. It's a bit hard when there's only one of you. I was going to wait until Mother got back from St. Thomas's, but it'll be too late then."

Mrs. Bunning put out a hand for the dress. She tried first one cotton then another against it, clicking her tongue when they failed to match. "Don't you go bothering your mother. She's tired out these days. Working herself to a frazzle. How long have we got?"

"Stephen's meeting me under the clock at Waterloo, at six."

"Ridiculous." Mrs. Bunnings lowered herself into the chair by the range and threaded a needle. "If you were my daughter, I wouldn't allow you to go gallivanting off to London in the evening, especially with all these bombs about."

Meg filled the kettle at the sink. "Stephen says it probably safer in London than anywhere else," she said over her shoulder. "They're only nuisance raids, you see. I think the sirens are worse than the bombs: I hate those Wailing Willies."

"I just sleep through them." Mrs. Bunnings' disdain for a world war was as massive as her person. "But they keep the mistress awake. If you ask me, they should drop a few of them Wailing Willies on Berlin. That'd teach old Adolf a lesson."

Meg's mind was temporarily diverted from the absorbing prospect of her first grown-up outing. "Mrs. Bunnings—is Aunt Vida all right? She looks so gray at present. Like a ghost. It is just the sirens?"

"It's everything, love. She's getting on a bit. She deserves a bit of peace at her age." Mrs. Bunnings glanced across the kitchen at Meg. "If you must know, I think she misses your brother more than she lets on."

"Hugh might not be . . ."

"Don't you start, love." The housekeeper's broad red face lost its laughter lines. "I seen it all before. The mistress was just the same when Mr. Harry was posted missing in the first war. They never did find his body. Half of her still hopes that one day he's going to walk in the door. And now it's all starting up again with Master Hugh."

Meg looked away; she could feel tears pricking her eyelids. It seemed quite impossible that she would never see Hugh again. How dare Mrs. Bunnings say such a thing? It wasn't right.

"You mark my words, young lady: living in hope brings nothing but grief."

On the evening of Saturday, September 7, Michael found it hard to pinpoint the precise moment when he knew he had made a mistake.

It was a gradual realization. The sounds were the same as usual: the bombers droned overhead; the antiaircraft batteries chattered away; the sirens were even worse than the explosions. The lights flickered in the bar of the Café Royal; and sometimes there were tremors that set the glass chinking.

On the surface Michael and his three guests carried on as if the air raid wasn't happening. Most other people in the bar did the same. No one enjoyed going down to those squalid shelters. Besides, running for cover unless it was absolutely essential had somehow become bad form. A fatalism had developed—a feeling that, if a bomb had your number on it, there was nothing you could do to avoid it; as a corollary there was no need to avoid bombs that didn't have your number on it.

But the conversations—both theirs and those at the nearby tables—were all about the war. Michael derived a certain pleasure from the way that his countrymen treated a world war as if it was a cricket match. The newspaper placards announced the figures—of deaths, of enemy planes shot down, of our own planes lost—in much the same way as they used to announce the test match scores.

People also took a personal pride in the war, as if their individual experiences of destruction and suffering were somehow worth boasting about. At the table next to Michael's, two businessmen from the suburbs were bragging competitively about the size of the bomb craters in their neighborhoods; a year ago they would have been bragging of their roses.

It struck Michael that the British, himself among them, had achieved something of a miracle: they had domesticated a world war.

But tonight was slightly different from other nights. The knowledge crept like a chill through the crowded bar. In consequence, people drank a little more, and talked a little more loudly.

There was a stir by the door as a young pilot officer shouldered his way into the bar. His face was flushed and chubby; his limbs had that hint of uncoordination that went with adolescence or alcohol or both. He looked about sixteen.

Dear God, Michael thought. *We're letting children fight this war for us.*

To Michael's surprise, the airman waved toward their table and barged over to their corner.

"Paul!" Stephen got up and grabbed a free chair from the next table. "Come and join us. We must celebrate: I see you got your wings."

The young man blushed and touched the bright new badge on his RAF tunic as if reassuring himself it was still there. "On Friday, actually." He sat down heavily. "I've been celebrating already."

"This is Paul Bennet," Stephen told the others. "We were at school together. "Paul, this is Lady Elizabeth Chandos; you must have met my sister Meg; and this is Michael Stanhope-Smith—we work together."

Michael signaled for a waiter.

"You're another pen-pusher, eh?" Paul said to Michael. "Each to his own, that's what I say. How d'you do, Lady Elizabeth?" He appraised her figure with frank pleasure. Then his eyes widened as he focused them on Meg. "I say! Last time I saw you, you were in pigtails. Where's Stephen been hiding you?"

Meg smiled but said nothing. She gave a tiny shrug. The movement seemed to ripple through her body to her face. For the first time Michael saw her as a person, rather than as Stephen's kid sister who had come along simply because Stephen didn't have a girlfriend to make up the numbers. In this light her skin looked so creamy you could almost eat it. Michael noticed how the neck met the shoulders; he wished he could paint that shadow along the collarbone.

Betty was looking at him curiously. He turned away with relief as the waiter came up for their order.

"Whisky!" said Paul Bennet. "Bring the bottle. It's on me."

"I think I'll stick to champagne," Michael said. Betty, with a glance at Meg, backed him up. After some discussion and much diplomacy, Paul Bennet was persuaded to make do with a treble Scotch.

A wave of explosions, much nearer than the previous ones, hit the bar. Conversations stopped; several people hurried from the room.

Bennet abruptly lost his euphoria. "This isn't just a nuisance raid, you know: this is the big one. The sky's as red as a furnace out there. By the look of it, the East End is taking the worst of it."

"That's not surprising, is it?" Betty said fiercely. "The Germans learned that in Spain. A bomb in the working-class area kills more people, destroys more homes, and puts more strain on the relief services. The Nazis aren't fools—just *utter bastards*."

Both Stephen and Paul looked shocked—less by the sentiments than by the swear word. Michael was more surprised by Betty's vehemence.

Meg glanced first at Betty, then at Michael. "I must go and powder my nose." Suddenly she seemed much older than she was. She touched Betty's hand. "Can you tell me where the ladies is?"

"I'll come, too." Betty scraped back her chair; the men politely began to rise. "Don't bother to get up."

Michael watched them cross the room. They made an attractive pair. Especially—it occurred to him with a momentary flash of embarrassment that he was admiring the wrong pair of legs.

"If you ask me, old Goering's trying for a knock-out blow." Bennet hit the tabletop twice with the palm of his hand; drinks slopped and ash scattered. "Pow, pow, like that. Send in the Luftwaffe to smash London and then it'll all be over. That's what he's thinking. This is the heart of the empire, gentlemen, and he wants to cut it out."

"I think Goering could be making a mistake." Stephen was drunk, too, though not as much as his friend. "The Luftwaffe's only got finite resources, just like the RAF. He should keep throwing everything he's got against our air bases. Once he's got command of the air he can do what he likes with our cities. Why, only this afternoon—"

Michael kicked Stephen on the ankle. The boy talked too much when he got drunk. This afternoon, Colonel Vivian—the head of the Counter-Espionage Section where they worked—had been holding forth at an indiscreet volume about a top-secret Air Ministry assessment of the damage sustained by bases in the southeast.

"Only this afternoon," he said smoothly, "we were saying that London's got off relatively lightly so far."

He kept the conversation in safer channels while they waited for Betty and Meg. He was beginning to wonder if this party had been a mistake. The evening had been designed to celebrate his recent promotion with the section; Vivian liked Michael because Dansey, Vivian's bête noire, was known to dislike him. He had included Stephen—and later Meg—in the invitation because of the old guilt: the surviving Kendalls deserved whatever he could give them.

More bombs fell while they waited; by now the bar was emptying rapidly. When the women came back, Michael suggested that they move on to a shelter.

"Where's the nearest?" Meg asked. "Piccadilly Circus?"

"I'm not going there!" Bennet brayed with laughter. "It's a thrupenny dosshouse. Having a party on the southbound platform of the Bakerloo line isn't my idea of a night out."

Stephen sniggered. "I'd rather have a thousand bombs than all those germs."

The younger men roared with laughter. Meg looked away, biting her lip.

"We don't have to go there," Michael said. "We can use the cellar of the house where we've got digs. It's not far—Dover Street."

"And I've got some Scotch," Stephen said. "Let's go home."

After some persuasion from Michael, his landlady Mrs. Granger had found a room for Stephen at the top of the house.

The presence of Scotch in Dover Street was the clinching argument as far as Bennet was concerned. In a few minutes all five of them were walking up the broad sweep of Regent Street. Glass crunched under their feet. There was little traffic apart from the vehicles of the emergency services. Searchlights slashed across the sky, particularly to the south and east. It should have been a clear night, but a red haze hung over the city.

The sound of the antiaircraft guns was receding. The bombers came in waves, which, as far as Michael could judge, were ten to fifteen minutes apart from one another. You could track their approximate whereabouts by estimating which batteries were attempting to deal with them.

A sense of unreality swept over him: the familiar city of London had been transformed into an infernal nightmare. He and his friends—tin hats on their heads and gas masks on their arms—were skulking in the shadows of an urban no-man's-land. It couldn't be happening.

Betty slipped her arm through his. "Looks like the West End's been spared the worst of it."

"It's hard to tell. I'm sure our turn will come."

They walked as quickly as possible; even Bennet stopped chattering and concentrated on not falling over. As they turned the last corner, Betty's grip tightened on Michael's arm. There was a barrier across the road.

A very young police constable and a very old ARP warden blocked their way. Dover Street itself was full of ambulances and hurrying people. Toward the Piccadilly end someone was crying as if he or she would never stop.

"I'm afraid you can't go through, sir—"

"Don't be ridiculous," Michael said. "I live here, and so does Mr. Kendall."

"Which number?"

At that moment an incautiously shielded torch swept over what had once been Mrs. Granger's house. It was still there, propped up between its neighbors; but it no longer had a façade. In front of it on the pavement and on the road was a mound of rubble. It was as if a giant had stooped down and removed the front of the house as casually as a child removed the front of a dollhouse.

Paul Bennet slumped against a wall and was violently sick.

The officials allowed Michael and Stephen to go through; the authorities needed to know who might have been in the house. Meg and Betty slipped in after them.

The inhabitants of the nearby houses were being evacuated. Some of them were still in their pajamas; most carried suitcases. A dozen stretchers were lined up on the opposite pavement. All of them were occupied.

Stephen nudged Michael and pointed to the top story. "Lucky I wasn't at home."

But Michael could not tear his eyes away from his own sitting room. A cross section of his private life was on public exhibition. Apart from the fact there was no longer any barrier between it and the street, the room seemed untouched. He could see a side view of his bureau and the back of the sofa. The Chagall was still hanging on the wall. It was fortunate that he had hung only his own pictures on the window wall.

"I say! Wait for me." Bennet managed to evade the policeman at the barrier and stumbled up the street toward them; he was apparently under the illusion that they were trying to get away from him.

"Meg, darling—you wouldn't leave me?"

He lunged toward Meg. Michael stepped between them. Bennet ran into him with his arms outstretched. His legs crumpled; he sat down in the road and began to cry.

Meg was still edging away, retreating from the onslaught. One of her high heels caught on the curb. She tripped and fell backward onto the rubble.

Then she screamed.

Michael was the first to reach her. He lifted her gently to her feet. A part of his mind sardonically noted that he took pleasure in touching her body, even at a time like this.

"It's alive." Meg huddled against him. "Something down there's alive, I tell you. I felt it."

A nearby fireman heard what she said. He raked his shaded torch over the pile of rubble. The beam paused and returned to the spot where Meg had landed.

Stephen whistled. "Jesus Christ!"

It was a solitary arm, severed just above the elbow. The hand was splayed open, resting palm downward on a fallen slate. A worn gold wedding band and an engagement ring were on the third finger. The fireman knelt beside it, bringing the torch closer. The stone in the ring was an opal.

"It's an opal, sir," Mrs. Granger had told him. He had offered her a drink on Christmas Eve and, trying to make polite conversation, had commented on her ring. "I'm a Libran, so it's my birthstone. It's unlucky for anyone else to wear opals."

The fireman looked up. "Any idea who it belongs to?"

"The landlady—Mrs. Granger," Michael said.

Meg's body shook with silent sobs. Her hands burrowed beneath his jacket. Michael thought she was trying to hide herself in him. Anyone would have done: he just happened to be the nearest.

"Hush now, it's all right." He stroked her hair—she had lost her helmet when she fell. "Hush now, it's all right."

Hugh knew he was in for trouble as soon as they got on the steamer at Zbraslav.

It started when Magda bought three second-class tickets. Heinz

119

complained bitterly: he felt that he and Magda should travel first class, which would entitle them to the use of the saloon, while Hugh could go third class, which would have left him on the open deck behind the funnel. Magda said she wasn't going to travel inside on a day like this. When Heinz continued to grumble about the indignity of it all, she pointed out that, since Hugh was carrying their bags and the picnic basket, there would be a considerable risk of getting smuts on their bathing costumes and on their lunch if he traveled third class. First-class tickets, moreover, were absurdly expensive; if they bought two of them, they wouldn't be able to afford a trip to a café in the afternoon. She clinched her case by reminding Heinz that their mother had given her the money for the outing: if he wanted to go first class he could pay for it himself.

While this was going on, Hugh stood at the rail and gazed at the wooded hills on the other side of the river. He was embarrassed because he was the cause of their quarrel; and he was angered by the way they treated him purely as a beast of burden.

The steamer chugged slowly down the river through the green suburbs of Prague. Hugh had never come into the city by water before and the strangeness took him by surprise. Gulls formed an aerial escort for the steamer; they swooped around the boat, crying for food. The buildings and hills of Prague took on a menacing quality when seen from the water. The skyline in front of them was dominated by St. Vitus' Cathedral, squatting like a slumbering monster above the castle.

They landed at the Palacky Bridge. There was a bathing station just south of the steamer port, on the other bank of the river. But Heinz objected to it on the grounds that it was too crowded. He wanted to go on to the *plovarna* at Letna.

Magda shrugged her agreement. She glanced at Hugh; there was a glint of amusement—even of complicity—in her gray eyes: *Heinz lost the last battle. Shall we let him win this one?*

Hugh turned away, ignoring the look. He wished she would make up her mind. Over the last month she had alternated between treating him as a slave and treating him as an equal. The uncertainty was not only bewildering: it was humiliating.

A tram took them northward along the right bank of the river. The bathing station was on the opposite bank, a few hundred meters downstream from the Manes Bridge. Magda paid for them to go in and gave Hugh enough money to hire a bathing costume.

Hugh was grateful for that, though he wished she had not done it in the manner of a lady bountiful dispensing alms to an undeserving beggar.

He took his time getting changed. He put his clothes in the wire basket and took them to the attendant. She was an old lady with three warts on the left side of her face. She was knitting something long, green, and shapeless. Her needles continued to clack as Hugh deposited his basket on the counter.

"Hardly worth me being here today." The warts jumped as she spoke. "I doubt if we'll get more than thirty people in the whole day. No one's hired a boat since Sunday. It's enough to make you cry."

Hugh nodded sympathetically. He could see the line of flat-bottomed boats chained to the pier; none of them was out on the water. There were fewer than a dozen swimmers, and most of them looked as if they were in the water for the sake of their health rather than for pleasure.

The attendant gave Hugh a numbered rubber bracelet in exchange for his basket and took up her knitting again. "I said to my son: why do we bother to open midweek in September? Everyone's at work and there's already a nip in the air."

"I must be going." Hugh tried to look away from the warts. "My—my friends will be waiting for me."

The needles stopped. The woman looked directly at Hugh. "Bloody Germans," she said. "They're bad for business."

Hugh turned and ran along the pier. He took a running dive into the water. After the initial shock it still felt warm from the summer. He did ten strokes underwater and then surfaced, gasping for air. He could hear the buzz of a motorboat approaching from upstream.

"Rudi!"

He looked back at the pier. Magda was there, gesturing for him to come ashore. Hugh swore under his breath and swam slowly toward her. He used a clumsy breaststroke, just to irritate her. She wasn't to know that he had won the crawl race at the Thameside College swimming sports for two years running. The maneuver had the additional advantage of allowing him to look at her at his leisure. It was the first time he had seen her in a bathing suit. He hadn't realized that anyone's legs could be so long and smooth. It was a pity that the cap covered up her hair.

She was waiting by the head of the steps as he hauled himself out of the water. "Have you seen Heinz?" She jumped back as he dripped on her bare feet.

Hugh suppressed a grin. "No. I thought he was with you."

"I was sunbathing. I thought he was out here with you."

"I haven't seen him since we went to change."

"He promised not to go in the water until you came out."

The motorboat was much nearer. They both had to raise their voices to be heard above the whine of its engine. It was towing a woman on an aquaplane; she was almost concealed by the spray.

"Well, he must be somewhere." Hugh turned and scanned the river. He had good long-distance sight. Magda, he suspected, was a bit shortsighted; no doubt her vanity kept her from wearing glasses. The sun glinted on something golden in midstream.

"Isn't that him? Over there?"

In her anxiety, Magda was standing very close to Hugh. He felt her bare arm brush his. His mouth suddenly went dry. His heartbeat seemed faster and louder than ever before.

"Where?" She gripped his arm: Hugh felt as if the end of the world had come. "He's trying to swim across the river. Oh, God, I told him not to try. He's never done more than about fifty strokes, and that was in a proper swimming pool."

The motorboat changed course, swinging away from the *plovarna* toward the opposite bank. Its wake and that of the aquaplane became double curves. The woman on the board shrieked with laughter. The wash, Hugh realized, must be looping around Heinz, buffeting him into the water. Even for a good swimmer it wouldn't be much fun. The blond head bobbed out of sight. When it reappeared it was facing the *plovarna*. Heinz waved once, and vanished.

"Get a boat out. *Now,*" Hugh said.

He caught a fleeting but immensely satisfying glimpse of the shock and surprise on Magda's face. Then the water surged around him.

It was a racing dive—as good a one as he had ever done. He paced himself to a strong, regular crawl. The kid must have underestimated the distance to the other bank. It was easy enough to do, especially on water. The river here was about two hundred yards wide. *(It's almost half as wide again by the Palacky Bridge: perhaps that's why Heinz wanted to come here.)* That meant he had a hundred yards to go. *Less now.* He tried to remember all he had ever heard about lifesaving. All he could think of was that giving the kiss of life to Heinz was not something to look forward to. *The stupid brat.*

In the event, Hugh nearly missed him. If the motorboat hadn't chosen to cut its engine, he definitely would have done. In the silence that ensued he heard a faint, high-pitched voice calling his name. He turned upstream; the current had carried him farther down than he had anticipated.

Heinz was still afloat, treading water—and spitting it out, too. His face was gray with fear or tiredness. The pale hair was plastered over his skull. The teeth looked more prominent than ever.

"Float on your back," Hugh gasped. He tried to say it in German, but failed; he said it in Czech; somehow Heinz understood. "Lie still. I'll tow you ashore."

Before they had gone thirty yards, help arrived simultaneously from two directions. The motorboat roared over from the far bank with insulting ease. Magda and the *plovarna* attendant arrived in a heavy, flat-bottomed rowing boat; rowing side by side, they made an unlikely but surprisingly efficient team.

They hauled Heinz over the gunwale. The old lady, clucking gently, wrapped him in towels. The boy's face was pinched with cold and exhaustion, but he was otherwise unharmed. Magda knelt down beside him.

He gave her a faint smile. "I nearly did it, didn't I?"

The first midnight began to strike.

Too excited to sleep, Hugh sat on the end of his bed with his elbows resting on the sill of the open window. He was smoking a hand-rolled cigarette which Miroslav had given him.

The cigarette was making him feel slightly queasy; but there was compensation in the fact that Miroslav's stinginess with tobacco was notorious among the servants. Hugh knew he had been honored.

As the strokes of the clock continued, Hugh found the events of the day were flashing through his mind in a series of split-second mental images. Magda in her bathing costume on the pier gave way to Heinz's half-drowned face. Once again he could sense the fear with emanated from the old lady with the warts and the couple from the motorboat when Magda told them that her father was the deputy military attaché on the *Reichsprotektor*'s staff. Scholl himself, summoned by telephone from the castle, had collected them from the *plovarna* in his Mercedes; the car smelled of leather and cigar smoke.

At the villa, Hugh was treated as a hero, much to his embarrassment. Frau Scholl kissed him on both cheeks and instructed her cook to give him the best meal the kitchen could offer. The colonel doubled his admittedly minuscule wages. Early in the evening, Scholl took Hugh upstairs to see Heinz. Heinz was in bed, propped up on three pillows. His room was a shrine to National Socialism: pictures of the Führer, cut out from the illustrated papers, decorated much of one wall; *Mein Kampf* was on the bedside table beside the Hitler Youth dagger. Heinz limply shook hands with Hugh and thanked him for saving his life.

Much to Hugh's surprise, Scholl had shown no inclination to blame anyone for the incident. Magda had made a clean breast of what had happened: she had been irresponsible; Heinz had been stupid; and if Hugh hadn't been there her brother might well have drowned. Frau Scholl spoke a few sharp words to Heinz; but the colonel was simply grateful that the accident had been no worse. Hugh couldn't help imagining how his own father would have reacted in a similar situation.

It was undeniably pleasant to be a hero, though he realized that this exalted state was unlikely to last. There was also a satisfaction in having repaid Scholl for saving his own life; Hugh didn't enjoy being under an obligation. On a more practical level—and he fully understood the need to be practical if he was going to survive—saving Heinz's life must have consolidated Hugh's position on the staff. Frau Scholl, for example, was completely won over; and he was no longer just another lame dog as far as Colonel Scholl was concerned.

But what about Magda? In front of her parents she had thanked him like someone reciting a lesson. Didn't it mean anything to her? The memory of her touching his arm on the pier made him feel both sick and excited, rather like he used to feel on Christmas Eve when he was very young. It was most puzzling—and curiously upsetting.

"Don't you know that smoking stunts your growth?"

The voice rose from immediately beneath his window. From the first word he knew it was Magda's. He was so surprised that he dropped the cigarette; the glowing tip turned and twisted through the honeysuckle until it vanished into darkness.

"I don't usually smoke." His own voice started high and ended low. "Miroslav gave it to me."

He could just make out the paler darkness of her hair. She must be wearing rubber-soled shoes.

"I wanted to say thank you," she whispered abruptly. "I couldn't do it properly with all those people around. Do you understand?"

"I think so." Hugh leaned out farther. Above him, the stable clock began the familiar preliminary whir. He seized on it, grateful for an excuse to move to a neutral subject. "It's going to strike in a few seconds."

"I know. It's like a second midnight."

The uncanny echo of his own thoughts jolted Hugh still further.

He said before he could stop himself, "Anything can happen in the space between the midnights."

The first chime rang out.

As the clock struck, she turned and ran almost soundlessly back across the lawn to the villa.

Eight

The next twelve months were the happiest that Hugh could remember.

Miroslav made more than sure that he earned his keep. The old man was a perfectionist; he was always grumbling that the younger generation—which in this case meant anyone beneath the age of sixty—didn't know the meaning of work.

But Hugh gradually won the old man's grudging approval. After the sheer drudgery of his life with Jan and Bela, working in a garden was almost a pleasure. There was another reason to work hard: the fear of dismissal never entirely left him. He had found a secure haven in an otherwise hostile land, and he was determined to cling to it.

Moreover, he found the Scholl household an endless source of fascination. It was unlike any other family he had known. Magda and Heinz weren't afraid of their father. Frau Scholl treated her husband in private in much the same way as she treated the children.

It was even more extraordinary because they were Germans. Dr. Spiegel, Madame Hase, Jan, and Bela had all in their different ways led him to believe that the Germans were a race of monsters. But the Scholls were just an ordinary family—if anything, rather nicer than most. Apart from Hans Bruckman, the soldier who doubled as the *Oberst*'s batman and chauffeur and considered himself a cut above the rest of the staff, the servants were Czech. Hugh had hitherto understood that the vast majority of Czechs loathed the Germans, but his fellow servants seemed to like their work and respect their employers.

In one of his rare communicative moments, Miroslav gave

Hugh a hint of the reason for this apparent contradiction. They had spent a crisp November afternoon raking up leaves and burning them in the kitchen garden. The old man suddenly spat into the flames of the bonfire.

"At least this lot notices when the lawns are clear," he said. "It's enough to break your heart when no one cares what you do." He shook his head with gloomy satisfaction. "You should have seen some of the folk we've had here."

"Have you worked here long?" Hugh asked the question idly, largely to prolong the break from work.

"Man and boy since eighteen ninety-two. I've seen them come and go. We had a count once, before the war—the big war, that is, not this one. Big Austrian bloke—he served with the imperial garrison. He only took this house because it was near the race course. He kept a full staff here all the year round, but I doubt if he spent more than a week or two here in any one year. *Yoh!* We've had some rum ones."

Hugh threw a dead branch on the fire. A shower of sparks went up. "Some better than others?"

"The worst one was a furrier—we had him from 'thirty-six until the Germans came. Treated us like shit, and his wife was worse. Jumped-up guttersnipes." Miroslav spat once more. "At least our Kraut's a gentleman."

Perhaps, Hugh thought, only people were important in the end. There were different nationalities, religions, races, and political creeds—huge abstractions that were too slippery for his mind to grasp. When the abstractions took flesh—and he thought of the deaths of Dr. Spiegel and Madame Hase—they became like deadly diseases that swept through whole populations. But somehow they didn't amount to much beside an elderly alcoholic who had risked his life to shelter you, or an employer who thanked you when you did him a service.

Hugh's work was not confined to the garden. Colonel Scholl's job included liaison with units of the former Czechoslovak Army which had been absorbed into the armed forces of the Reich. He was also partly responsible for contingency plans for the defense of the protectorate. These two aspects of his job involved him in a lot of traveling and in dealings with many Czechs who did not speak German. Official interpreters were of course available, but occasionally Scholl would take Hugh instead, if the meetings were at short notice and reasonably close at hand. The Bureau of

Translators, he explained, was very overworked.

Hugh occasionally wondered whether there was more to it than this. He had once overheard the colonel complaining to Frau Scholl that the bureau was practically a subdivision of the Gestapo. Scholl's conversations were never remotely treasonable, but perhaps—Hugh thought—he disliked being spied upon; or perhaps he wanted to be sure that he was hearing what the Czechs were really saying to him, rather than what the official translators wanted him to hear.

Everyone, including Hugh, was surprised by the rate at which his command of German improved. Hugh privately attributed it to the solid foundations that Dr. Spiegel had laid. He also suspected that the more languages you knew, the easier it became to learn others. His accent, according to Magda, was that of an educated Saxon; the Scholls came from Saxony.

His employers would have been less surprised by Hugh's fluency if they had known how much their daughter was talking to him. It began in a small way—a few words about the weather when their paths crossed in the garden. Hugh had Sunday afternoons free, and he often used to spend them in the pine woods around Zbraslav. When he was walking there near the end of October, he ran into Magda. Nothing was said about meeting again, but the following Sunday he returned to the same place and found her there.

There were other regular opportunities. Magda had weekly lessons in Prague with a retired violinist who used to play in the orchestra of the *Narodni Divadlo*. The violinist's apartment was in Smichov, and Frau Scholl refused to allow Magda to travel there alone. If the car was not available, Hugh would be sent to keep her company.

It was a strange and often strained relationship. She was by nature impetuous, while Hugh's experiences had left him stolid and cautious, at least on the surface. Everything they said and did was colored by the inescapable fact that she was the master's daughter, and he was the master's gardener's boy. From the start she addressed him as *du,* the familiar form of the second person singular which one used for servants, pets, family, and God, but he used the respectful *Sie* to her, even when no one else was around.

Hugh had never known anyone like her before. Everything about her was fascinating, down to the minutest details of her appearance. Even Heinz seemed larger than life, simply because he was privileged to be her brother.

Sometimes in his dreams, both waking and sleeping, Hugh would tell Magda who he really was, and he would announce—with the assurance of a social equal—that he was going to call her du. After that the dream became blurred.

He knew of course that he could never do it. Magda would have to tell her father. The colonel had a soldier's sense of duty: if he learned that Hugh was an enemy alien he would not let personal considerations stand in the way of reporting him to the authorities. The authorities would presumably intern him for the rest of the war. He doubted if anything very terrible would happen to him—unless there was some truth in the servants' gossip about the Nazis' secret camps.

But he would never see Magda again.

That was unthinkable. In consequence he buried his nationality as deeply as he could: he willed himself to forget that he was English. Magda asked him once if he knew any other languages besides Czech and German. He said that he had a little schoolboy French and Latin, which was true, but that he had forgotten most of the Hungarian he had once known. When Magda said she thought everyone in Europe learned a little English these days, he lost his head and denied that he knew a word.

In the winter of 1940–41, Hugh began to read again. Reading had not been an activity which Jan and Bela favored, but for the Scholls it was as automatic as breathing. According to Magda, her father had been a journalist between the wars; he had been recalled to the army in 1935 when the sudden decision to expand the armed forces put experienced officers at a premium. Her grandfather, she told Hugh with some pride, had been professor of history at Leipzig.

On one of their Sunday meetings Hugh asked her if he could borrow a book or two to improve his German. She found him a couple of children's stories that had belonged to Heinz; they were part of a series from Eher Verlag, the Nazi publishing house. Both of them featured a tall, blond Aryan hero who foiled the vicious conspiracies of Jews and Bolsheviks with a combination of superhuman strength and stern moral rectitude. Hugh found them rather boring, but he was pleasantly surprised by the ease with which he read them.

They were the first of many. Magda was surprised by the appetite he developed for the printed word. He had been starved of it since Dr. Spiegel died, and now he became a glutton. He read everything—newspapers, novels, plays, and poetry. The fact that much of it was incomprehensible to him made no difference. Much later, he realized why books were so important to him then: books, like languages, could make you free. They offered another technique to transcend the limitations of the present.

Hugh struggled through the first quarter of *Mein Kampf*—nearly two hundred pages—but had to admit defeat. Magda was not surprised.

"We've got four copies in the house, but no one actually reads it except Heinz. My mother always makes sure there's a copy in the drawing room when we're having visitors."

Magda told Hugh that she was going to be an historian like her grandfather. But, she confided, it was a very difficult subject because there were two sorts of history—the sort she learned in school and the sort she found in some of her father's older books—and they often didn't agree.

"I asked Papa about it once. He said it was important to use the textbooks for school and examinations . . . that the government doesn't approve of the other history."

"Did he say why?" Hugh asked.

Magda shrugged. "Only that the end sometimes justified the means. But he made me promise not to talk about it at school."

Magda's school was in Mala Strana, not far from the Michalov Palace. It was of course a German institution, created for the children of high-ranking party officials, senior civil servants, and army officers. Hugh was astonished by the regimentation that surrounded the lives of the children, even outside school hours. Heinz of course was a member of the Hitler Youth; at present he was in the *Jungvolk;* he was eagerly looking forward to graduating into the seniors when he was fourteen. Even Magda was a member of the *Bund Deutscher Maedel,* the League of German Maidens.

"It's horrible," she said. "They're always going on about how we should train ourselves to be healthy mothers of healthy children. I don't want to be a mother: I'll be too busy as an historian, I expect."

Hugh blushed. They were climbing through the woods to a hill from which you could get a spectacular view of the Vltava in its gorge. He was grateful that the path was narrow at this point, so they were walking in single file.

"Still, it was worse last year." Magda glanced back over her shoulder. "I was in the *Jungmaedel* then: we had to wear the ugliest uniform you ever saw and great big marching boots."

She ran on up the path, offering Hugh a tantalizing glimpse

of brown calves beneath a swinging skirt.

On June 22, 1941, the Germans invaded the territory of their ally the USSR without the courtesy of a declaration of war.

Helmuth Scholl had been expecting it. It had been obvious to him from the start that the German-Soviet Non-Aggression Pact nearly two years ago was merely a temporary expedient. It made military sense, of course: Germany had learned the dangers of fighting on two fronts in the last war. He agreed with the logic of Hitler's strategy—knock out France, the one significant land power to the west of the Reich, and then concentrate on the Wehrmacht on the east. He was amazed that some of his fellow officers had ever taken the Pact seriously. Hitler had made it clear from the beginning—in *Mein Kampf*—that the bulk of Germany's *Lebensraum* would have to come from the Slav lands. And Hitler was consistent in this if in nothing else—that his policies since coming to power were based on the crackpot ideas he outlined in *Mein Kampf.*

Colonel Scholl had had firm knowledge of the impending invasion for nearly six months before it happened. Hitler's Directive 21 for Operation Barbarossa inevitably involved the military staff at the castle in a great deal of work. The movement of men and munitions was only part of the problem; the worst headache was the need to coordinate the preparations of the Reich's allies, Slovakia, Roumania, and Hungary.

The sheer size of the attack worried Scholl. Hitler was concentrating the forces at his disposal into three huge army groups: one hundred and twenty divisions would attack on a broad front that stretched from the Baltic to the Black Sea. Everything depended on speed and the quality of the Russian defense. The strategy might be impeccable, but the tactics, in Scholl's view, had an unnecessary element of risk about them.

Hitler wanted too much and too soon. Scholl remembered a line from the American philosopher Santayana: *Those who do not remember the past are condemned to relive it.* At times he was terribly afraid that the Führer had forgotten Napoleon. Russia was not like other countries.

And the Russians were not like other soldiers.

The telephone call came four days later. Scholl was in his office in the castle, sipping the strong black coffee which he always had at ten-thirty. It was not a direct line, of course. The news had filtered back from the headquarters of Army Group North, somewhere in

Lithuania, to the Army High Command in Berlin. The news was unofficial at this stage—the colonel had a friend on Brauchitsch's staff—but it was nonetheless accurate for that.

He left his coffee unfinished and didn't even touch the pastry that came with it. He ordered his car and told the secretary in the outer office that he wouldn't be in for the rest of the day. His manner was as courteous as ever, but the secretary claimed that she knew something was wrong from the instant that she saw that untouched pastry; the colonel's sweet tooth was notorious.

Bruckman drove him home. The chauffeur had known the *Oberst* since 1917, and he recognized the expression on his face. For once there was no conversation during the drive.

At the villa, Scholl went straight to his study, leaving orders that he was not to be disturbed. But Eva, who had been upstairs supervising the maids, had seen the car arrive. He wasn't surprised that she ignored his order. He was even grateful.

"What is it, Helmuth? Why are you back so early?"

He looked up at her. His face was streaked with tears. He was sitting at his desk with the monocle lying on the blotter. In his hand was a photograph.

She was beside him in an instant, cradling his head against her breast and crooning nonsensical words of comfort. There was no need to ask what had happened. The photograph showed a small, lightly built man striding down the Rue de Rivoli, past the garden of the Tuileries; he was arm in arm with a very pretty girl, and he was grinning at the camera; he wore the uniform of a major in a panzer regiment.

Scholl turned over the photograph. On the back was a penciled scrawl: *Hope the girls in London are as pretty as this.* The message had been typical of Franz Scholl. He was fifteen years younger than his brother Helmuth and relished flaunting his hedonism at his staider relatives. It was a joke they had both understood very well.

But Franz's regiment hadn't gone to London: it had been transferred to the east.

"*Liebling*—"

"It's not just the fact he's been killed, you know. It's how they did it." Scholl sat up and wiped his face. "Franz's tank got too far ahead of the others. There was something wrong with the radio, they said. They must have stopped to find out where they were. Then they were ambushed and—killed. They were found the next day when the rest of the advance caught up."

Eva squeezed his shoulder as if she was trying to squeeze the full story out of him. "How did he die?"

"We mustn't tell the children. The barbarians slaughtered the whole tank crew. Franz was crucified against a barn door; then they disemboweled him and left him to die."

"It's too tiresome," Betty Chandos said. "But Michael wants me to be nice to some American this evening. He's something at the embassy—Wilbur Cunningham. *Wilbur!* I ask you."

"It doesn't matter." Meg closed the *J–Mc* drawer of the card index and wandered back to her desk. "Everyone says the play is going to have a long run. We can go another night."

Betty snapped open her handbag, took out the mirror, and stared critically at her own lips. "I wish I could get out of it, but I suppose being nice to Americans is all part of the war effort. Did you see that piece in the *Daily Express?* They want every house to fly the Stars and Stripes next week to celebrate the Fourth of July."

She ran the lipstick expertly along the line of her lips.

"What are you going to wear?"

Betty shrugged. "God knows. It's that *bloody* clothes rationing. Anyway, there's nothing left to buy these days."

"Wear your black," Meg suggested.

"I daren't. The neckline's too risky. For all I know Wilbur will turn out to be a geriatric puritan. Michael's never met him."

"At least he'll speak English. Look on the bright side: it might have been a Russian."

"Michael's probably saving the Russian for next week." Betty grinned. "It's comic how the Russians have suddenly become respectable since last weekend. The next thing we'll know, the BBC will be playing the "Internationale" along with the other Allied anthems on Sunday."

Meg laughed and went back to her typing. Despite the open windows, the office was stiflingly hot. They were on the top floor of a converted house on Kensington High Street. It served as the headquarters of one of the semivoluntary organizations that addressed itself to the endless task of trying to house the homeless. Betty had worked there for nearly eighteen months. There had been a vacancy for a clerk-cum-typist just as Meg had finished the typing and shorthand course she had taken after leaving school. At present, neither of them was eligible for call-up—only women aged twenty and twenty-one were being conscripted; Betty was too old, and Meg too young. It was more than likely that the authorities would in any case decide that they were more useful where they were—unless, of course, the present lull in the bombing turned out to be permanent.

It was too hot to work. Betty buffed her nails instead, refusing to be shamed by the clatter of Meg's typewriter. She glanced across at the girl's dark head and felt a sudden pang of envy. Did Meg have any idea just how attractive she was? It wasn't that she was beautiful, or even pretty. It was something to do with the way she moved and the way she reacted to people. She radiated a sort of animal warmth. And then of course there were the eyes. *Bedroom eyes.*

Betty knew that Michael was attracted to the girl. You couldn't have an affair with a man on and off for nearly three years without knowing when his attention was otherwise engaged, however much he tried to hide it.

She doubted if Michael admitted the attraction, even to himself. He would feel it came under the heading of cradle-snatching; and there would be a tangle of guilt in his mind as well—disloyalty to Betty and that curious sense of responsibility he seemed to have for the entire Kendall family. Michael's problem was that he had a conscience.

Her problem was that she wanted Michael. He had asked her to marry him once—long ago, before the war, and she had rejected him with a laugh and a kiss. Just because you liked—even loved—someone and went to bed with him, it didn't mean you necessarily wanted to marry him. But the war had gradually changed her mind for her. She wanted a home and children; and above all she wanted Michael. The war, she thought, had made her realize that these three things would not come to her as if by right, as soon as she asked for them. All around her people were losing their homes, their children, and their husbands.

But Michael had never asked her again, and she was too proud to take the first step toward what she felt would be an inevitable rejection. It was better to hang on to what she already had. At present she was safe with Michael. He hadn't noticed the sly little glances that Meg gave him when she thought no one was looking; he couldn't know how Meg's attention would suddenly tighten if someone mentioned his name in conversation.

The telephone on her desk began to ring. She put down the nail file and answered it.

"Betty? It's Stephen here."

Oh, God. She hadn't seen him since that dreadful evening last month when he had tried to make a pass at her. She had seen it coming for months. He had taken her out to dinner and then to a nightclub, neither of which he could really afford. He had taken her home—she had rented a small flat in Bayswater since the lease on the Hill Street house ran out—and maneuvered her into asking him up for coffee. The only surprise was that he had started to paw her as soon as they were inside the door. Usually they waited until she had put the kettle on. She had quenched Stephen's ardor by her customary tactic: having slapped his face she told him the address of a brothel in Great Windmill Street. As far as she knew, the brothel didn't exist, but the gambit never failed to silence the most persistent of her unwanted suitors.

"Betty—could I meet you after work? It's rather important."

"No. I'm afraid you can't."

"Look, it's not what you think. I've just had some bad news."

Despite the warmth of the room, Betty shivered. Stephen's voice was light and pleasant; it matched his dark good looks. But there was an undercurrent of menace: *bad news*—

"It affects Meg, you see," Stephen said. "I think it would be better if you told her. Why don't we have a drink this evening? I can't talk on the phone."

"Yes you can," Betty said firmly. "You've managed very well so far: keep at it."

Meg? Her mother? Her aunt? The typewriter hammered away in the background. Had it been anyone but Stephen, she would have agreed to meet him, if only for Meg's sake. But his brotherly concern didn't ring true. He treated Meg as an encumbrance, not as a responsibility.

Stephen didn't give up. Betty sat there, repeating the word "no" into the receiver at regular intervals. After a while Meg stopped typing. Betty was tempted to put the phone down, but something stopped her. She wondered idly whether it was due to vestigial good manners or whether some of Michael's responsibility for the Kendalls had rubbed off on her.

"Oh, very well," Stephen said at last. "Would you tell her that Paul Bennet's bought it? I know it'll be a terrible shock to her. Unofficially, the word is that he was shot down over Normandy. He didn't bail out."

Betty snorted with laughter before she could stop herself. She was sorry for Paul: she supposed he had died a hero's death even if he was an objectionable young puppy. But he had been pestering Meg ever since that night at the Café Royal, and Meg had never concealed her dislike for him. Stephen had chosen an absurdly transparent excuse for trying to see her.

"Right," she said briskly. "I'll tell her. Good-bye."

Meg looked up as Betty put down the phone.

"Who was that?" she asked. "And what's the joke?"

Toward the end of September 1941 there was a small but significant addition to the skyline of Prague. The SS flag flew over the castle.

Helmuth Scholl was not entirely surprised. It had been evident for some time that von Neurath was not fully in control of the situation. He had failed to damp down the sporadic eruptions of Czech nationalist feeling. Scholl's contacts in the *Abwehr* assured him that the underground resistance movement was in a flourishing condition. The industrial strength of the protectorate made it crucial to the war effort. Hitler needed a stronger man at the castle; and Scholl—as a patriot and a soldier—agreed with the Führer.

It was tactfully done. On September 21, the Czech press agency carried the story that von Neurath had requested the Führer for an indefinite period of leave, owing to ill health. Hitler had graciously granted the petition; he had also named as acting *Reichsprotektor* SS *Obergruppenführer* Reinhard Heydrich.

Scholl was privately dismayed by the appointment. Heydrich was Himmler's deputy in the SS; he was the head of the RSHA, the central security bureau of the Reich; he was a fanatical Nazi whose ruthlessness was legendary; his nickname was "Hangman Heydrich." The protectorate needed a strong man, but Scholl would have preferred a soldier to a secret policeman.

His fears were confirmed at this first meeting with Heydrich. The new *Reichsprotektor* summoned all his senior officials, both civil and military, to a meeting in the Cernin Palace, on October 2. Scholl was familiar with the man's appearance from photographs. He was a tall, fair-haired man who could have modeled for one of Eher Verlag's illustrations. The one surprise was the voice which belonged to this imposingly Aryan exterior: it could only be described as a high-pitched bleat.

But the mind belonged to a wolf, not a sheep. Heydrich began by declaring a State of Emergency in the protectorate. Then he outlined what he called the final solution to the problem of Czech nationalists and Jews. "This entire area," he said, "will one day be definitively German . . . we will try to Germanize these Czech vermin."

And what of those Czechs who remained Slav? Scholl wondered; and what of the Jews?

The executions began at once. Heydrich enjoyed variety: people were hanged, beheaded, or shot. Scholl knew few of the details—he was not directly involved with the Gestapo, the SD, and the SS, the three organizations that Heydrich used for his work. If the truth were told, he was glad of his ignorance. He did not conceal his doubts, but he did not publicize them, either. He sometimes felt that he was acting as a moral coward. On the other hand, courage could be a thinly disguised form of selfishness: it was easy for a bachelor to be brave.

In the circumstances, however, it was strange that Heydrich went out of his way to be pleasant to his deputy military attaché. Heinz and Magda were occasionally invited to children's parties at Panenske Brezany, the château outside Prague where Heydrich lived in some state with his family. Eva was on calling terms with Frau Lina Heydrich. Heydrich's quasi regal rule was marked by many official and semiofficial gatherings; and at these Scholl was generally allotted a rather better seat than he used to have in von Neurath's day.

At Christmas 1941, Scholl's doubts came to a head. He and Eva attended midnight mass at the cathedral on Christmas Eve. It was a grand affair: most of the congregation seemed to be wearing dress uniforms or fur coats. Scholl—a nominal Catholic at best—wondered whom they were really worshiping: the Führer in the sky or the Führer in Berlin. Afterward, Lina Heydrich kept Eva chatting for several minutes.

Scholl was silent during the drive home through the snow. At the villa there was a log fire in the study. He poured glasses of brandy for himself and his wife.

She peered at him over the rim of her glass. "What's wrong with you? Cheer up."

Scholl threw another log on the fire. Sparks fled up the chimney.

"I don't like Heydrich," he said abruptly. "Or his family. Why are they so sociable to us? It just doesn't make sense."

Eva, still in her fur coat, curled up in an armchair. "Why shouldn't they be? Lina says that Reinhard admires you tremendously."

"Oh, don't be absurd!"

"But she does. For a start, there's your war record. I don't think Reinhard was ever on active service, so naturally he looks up to people like you."

"Heydrich doesn't look up to anyone."

"*And* he says your military analyses are first class. You're politically reliable—"

"I joined the Nazi Party in 'thirty-eight for your sake, and for the sake of the children." Scholl stamped across the room to the brandy bottle; when he was angry, he used his prosthesis like a hammer. "All right, it was for my sake as well. But carrying a Party card doesn't make you politically reliable. Heydrich of all people knows that."

Eva held out her empty glass. Somehow she managed to make the gesture seem as if she was brushing aside both his anger and his words.

"Another thing in your favor is your fencing," she said chattily.

"I haven't fenced since—"

"I know, darling, but you won the Army Championship in 'thirteen, and you know what the Nazis are like about fencing. They think it's such a *knightly* thing to do."

It was the way she was sitting that gave her away. Her head was sideways and lowered, with the chin tucked into the collar of her fur coat. She had sat like that on the evening she had maneuvered him, a cripple just invalided out of the army, into proposing to her.

Scholl took her glass and put it down on a sidetable. He cupped her chin with his hand, forcing her to look at him.

"Now, my dear," he said gently, "tell me the truth."

"But I have." She took his hand and cradled it against her cheek. "Most of it. There's only one other little thing. Do you remember when I first met the *Reichsprotektor*—at that concert in October? I just happened to mention that it was nice to meet him again."

Scholl lost his monocle. "You knew him before?"

"Ages ago—it was just before the first war, or just after it started. He can't have been more than nine or ten. I was staying with my grandparents in Halle. The Heydrichs lived there. His father ran a music school."

"I thought Heydrich's father was a composer."

Eva nodded. "Wagner and water. But I don't think he ever made any money from it. He made his living from teaching—taught

139

my mother her scales. Grandpa and I went to a concert, and we sat next to Herr Heydrich and young Reinhard. Herr Heydrich spent most of the interval trying to butter up Grandpa. I remember it because I was wearing—

"Come to the point, my love."

"Herr Heydrich was rabidly anti-Semitic and right wing. But the story was that his father was a Jewish carpenter." She grinned. "Just like Joseph. People in the streets used to shout *Jewboy!* at Reinhard."

The mystery of Heydrich's benevolence evaporated in an instant. In a sense, it was irrelevant whether or not Heydrich had Jewish blood. Just the rumor of it was enough. The fear of it becoming public knowledge must have haunted the *Reichsprotektor* all his adult life. Powerful though he was, he could hardly muzzle everyone who lived in Halle and its environs. It would be neither easy nor worthwhile for him to exterminate a relatively well-connected couple like the Scholls.

There was an irony here which would have appealed to Scholl's father, the professor. History was not inert: it cast long shadows into the present, affecting even those who were trying to remold it in their own image. *Jewboy Heydrich.*

"Why are you smiling?"

Scholl bent down and kissed her on the mouth with a passion that surprised them both. "It doesn't matter. Let's go to bed."

The study was forbidden ground to the children, unless they had been specifically invited to come in. The prohibition included the windowless bookroom, the only access to which was by a door to the right of the study fireplace. Hugh had only once been inside the study; and he had never seen the bookroom.

"There's a big safe in it," Magda said, "and Father's guns. And there are hundreds of books, of course—all the interesting ones he doesn't like visitors to see."

It was a rainy Sunday afternoon toward the end of March 1942. It was too wet to go out—the ground was a mixture of mud and slush, for the snows were melting fast. They were in the coach house, sitting on the running board of the Mercedes. Both were bored.

Hugh grunted, but said nothing. He was trying to conceal the immensely embarrassing fact that he had an erection. If being two feet away from Magda had this effect on him, what the hell would it be like to touch her? At least he no longer had to worry about the fact of the erection itself. For a time he had thought that this sudden—and frequent—expansion and hardening of a part of his body was both shameful and unnatural. It was connected in his mind with the butcher Jan and—more remotely, like a half-remembered nightmare—with his sister Meg. But scraps of conversation in the servants' hall and his own observations had gradually persuaded him that this was not the case. He was normal: he was having a natural reaction to Magda: and that was the trouble.

"Wake up!" she said sharply. "I'm talking to you."

Hugh stared at her, biting back his anger. "I'm sorry. What were you saying?"

"I said why don't we have a look at it? The bookroom, I mean. I know where Papa keeps the key."

"It's too risky. Someone will see us."

"No they won't. Heinz is out at his meeting. Papa and Mama always spend Sunday afternoons in the drawing room listening to the gramophone. All the servants except Hans have the afternoon off, so they won't be wandering around the main house. Besides," she added grandly, "if we're caught, I shall take full responsibility."

Hugh shook his head. Magda might offer to take full responsibility, but, if they were caught, he doubted if her offer would be accepted. And you could sack a servant but not a daughter. Moreover, prying in the bookroom seemed a rather shabby thing to do.

"You're scared," Magda said coldly. She stood up, brushing the seat of her skirt; Hugh looked away. "I'll just have to go by myself."

The key was in the Chinese vase which stood on the colonel's bureau. While Magda got it out, Hugh stood on the hearthrug, cursing the stupid pride that had brought him here.

The ormolu clock ticked away on the mantelpiece. Through the partly open door of the study came a trickle of distant music; Magda said it was a Mozart Divertimento. On their way to the house, Hugh had peeped through the window of the butler's pantry: Hans Bruckman was cleaning the silver.

Magda turned the key in the lock and opened the door. Hugh followed her in; he was anxious to get this over with as soon as possible. The room beyond was scarcely more than a cupboard. It was about six feet square. Once there had been a window, but it had been bricked up by a previous tenant. The air was fresh, for there was a ventilator in the wall above the safe.

The book titles leapt out at them when Magda flicked on the light. Most of the volumes on the shelves nearest to Hugh seemed to be in English or French. He noticed two by H.G. Wells—*The Shape of Things to Come* and *War of the Worlds;* a one-volume edition of Shaw's plays sat next to Bertrand Russell's *In Praise of Idleness* on the one hand, and Sassoon's *Memoirs of an Infantry Officer* on the other. His eyes fell to the shelf below: it was almost filled by a set of books called *A la recherche du temps perdu* by someone called Marcel Proust. He stretched out his hand toward the first volume.

"Proust's Jewish," Magda whispered. She was very close to him; he could feel her breath on his cheek. "He wrote about—"

At that moment, the air was filled with the roar of engines. The sound rapidly grew louder, drowning the faint notes of the music.

"Quick!" Hugh seized Magda's arm and pushed her out of the bookroom.

But they were too late. The colonel was already in the hall. A door banged as Bruckman rushed through from the servants' quarters, pulling on his jacket.

"It's the *Reichsprotektor,* Hans." The colonel's voice was clearly audible from the study. "If he's here for any length of time, you'd better look after his driver and escort."

Hugh acted instinctively. Their escape was blocked. They had to hide. He pulled Magda back into the bookroom, switched off the light, and closed the door. Perhaps it was a social call: that meant they would use the drawing room. Magda was trembling by his side; his own fear was dwarfed by the need to protect her.

A moment later, he realized he had made a mistake. There were footsteps in the study. A door closed with a snap.

"I regret having to disturb you at home, Scholl." The voice didn't sound regretful: it was cold and as high as a woman's. "I have something to discuss which is both urgent and private."

Magda nudged against Hugh. "It's Heydrich," she whispered; her lips moved like electricity against his ear. Without thinking, he slipped his arm around her.

"There are too many ears at the castle," Heydrich continued. "Even the switchboard—that's why I didn't have them telephone ahead. By the way, have you met Inspector Abendschon?"

Scholl and the inspector exchanged the usual courtesies. Abendschon's voice was gruff and abrupt. Every word spoken in the study could be heard in the bookroom; the thin panels of the intervening door acted as sounding boards. Springs creaked as the men sat down.

"Carry on, Abendschon," Heydrich said.

"Well, sir, I expect you know Paul Thümmel?"

"Of course," Scholl said. "The *Abwehr* chap. He's been here almost as long as I have."

"Former baker," the inspector intoned, as if reading aloud from a file, "born 1902; has worked for the Party since 1928; transferred to the *Abwehr* in 1933; posted to the Dresden office, 1934; sent to Prague in March 1939 by personal order of Canaris; responsible for networks in the protectorate, Slovakia, the Balkans, and the Middle East; Party number 61574, and holds the Party's gold badge—"

"I think I know the man you mean." There was more than hint of sarcasm in Scholl's voice. "Thickset and pop-eyed."

"Just so, sir. Thümmel has a Czech mistress—a Madame Figarova—who lives at twenty-seven Dlouha. I expect you know the street, sir—just off Old Town Square?"

"And we must not forget," said Heydrich softly, "that Thümmel is on terms of friendship with Admiral Canaris and indeed with my own superior in the SS—Herr Himmler." After a pause—as if that last name was so important that it needed to be digested in silence—Heydrich continued. "And this man, my dear Scholl—this well-connected *Abwehr* officer—is a traitor."

"Good God," Scholl snapped. "But he must have had access to—"

"Precisely." A chair creaked: Heydrich must have stood up; Hugh could hear footsteps pacing up and down, close to the door of the bookroom." We have suspected a highly placed traitor in Prague for at least six months. There are no rotten apples in the SD, thank God; nor in the Gestapo. Abendschon here has had his suspicions of Thümmel for some time. He's had the wretched man in for questioning. There were unexplained links with Czech terrorists, you see—Thümmel claimed he was trying to infiltrate them. But now there are no more doubts: he has confessed, and we have interrogated him in depth."

"How long has this been going on?" Scholl demanded.

"Since February nineteen thirty-seven. Fill him in, Abendschon."

"Sir!" Papers rustled: perhaps the inspector really had a file on his lap. "Thümmel volunteered his services to Colonel Moravec of the Czech *Deuxième Bureau;* his motives seem to have been financial rather than ideological. Moravec skipped to London in March 'thirty-nine, but Thümmel continued to feed him with high-grade information. And not just the Czechs, of course—Moravec's hand in glove with the British secret service. Thümmel's identity was closely guarded—he was codenamed A-54. We've evidence that Thümmel started to deal directly with the British after the war broke out. Gibson—he was the British man in Prague—was made Head of Station in Istanbul. Thümmel made a number of legitimate trips to Turkey on *Abwehr* business. He had to stop his trips outside the Reich last year: he was promoted, you see, and Canaris and Himmler considered him too important to be allowed to travel abroad."

"Ironic," said Scholl.

"No doubt, sir. More to the point, it forced Thümmel to rely on local terrorists to get his information to London. That's how we got him in the end. We've got the home turf pretty well mapped out by now."

"But not well enough," Heydrich said. "Men, money, and arms are still getting through from London; and information's getting out. Thümmel's just the tip of the iceberg: you'd do well to remember that."

"I'm going to sneeze," Magda whispered.

"Rub your upper lip," Hugh mouthed back. He brought his other arm around Magda and tried to bury her face under his jacket.

Scholl said calmly, "I take it you want me to assess the military damage which Thümmel might have done?"

"Yes—and immediately." By the sound of it, Heydrich had regained control of his temper. "I'll give you a lift back to the castle now. Your priority must be the current stuff. We know the damage that Thümmel has already done—everything from the Wehrmacht's order of battle in France to the exact composition and timetable of Army Group South. If it's any consolation, the SD and the *Abwehr* are even more compromised than the army. And I must order you to work as secretly and as rapidly as possible. More than the army is at stake here—think of the potential propaganda damage."

"Yes, sir." Scholl's voice was purged of emotion. "Will you be at the castle this evening? I could bring you my interim report."

"Good. Seven o'clock." Heydrich sounded fainter: he must be moving toward the door. The others must be on their feet as well. "And not a word to anyone, my dear Scholl. Remember, there may be political ramifications."

The study door slammed behind them. Engines came to life outside in the drive. Magda sneezed.

"Are you all right?" Hugh muttered.

He felt rather than saw her nod. They stood there without moving in each other's arms. Both of them were clammy with sweat. The Hangman had been just a few feet away. It occurred to Hugh that fear was an antidote to his erection: in the circumstances it was just as well.

Magda stirred in his arms. "Rudi? Did you know you called me *du* just then?"

May 27, 1942 began for Hugh like any other day at the villa. He was up by 6:30; he did an hour's work in the garden with Miroslav; they had breakfast with the other servants and then returned to their work. An hour after breakfast Miroslav went back to the house to receive the day's orders and to do battle with the cook over what he would allow her to have out of the kitchen garden.

Miroslav came back grumbling from the villa; this was nothing new.

"You're wanted up at the house," he told Hugh curtly. "Some bloody errand. *Yoh!* It's always the same—they think this garden tends itself."

Hugh was secretly pleased rather than otherwise, though he knew he wouldn't see Magda at this time—she had already left for school. But there was a good chance that he would have a morning's jaunt in Prague; it was certainly better than working.

Frau Scholl herself was in the kitchen, waiting to give him his orders. She wanted him to go into Liben, the suburb to the northeast of Prague, and collect a leather coat she was having made for her.

"I'd send Hans, of course—it'd be far quicker; but the *Oberst* will need him all day. I'll give you the money. Mind you get a receipt."

Hugh took a series of trams across the city. It was a fresh, clear morning: despite the heavy overnight dew it promised to be a fine day. The streets were already crowded. Many women were in summer dresses. The bright colors matched Hugh's holiday mood. He enjoyed the journey and was almost sorry when the last tram rumbled over the river and began to climb the broad, gently winding hill which led to Liben.

The tailor's shop was near the top of the hill, not far from the crossroads. Long ago, Hugh had come here with Dr. Spiegel: if you turned sharp left at the junction, you came to the Bulkova Hospital.

The hill was lined with gardens. In most of them the lilac was in full bloom; even the smell of the traffic couldn't drown the scent. A woman was sunbathing in one of the gardens. Beside the tailor's was a hardware shop. Two men were unloading cases of furniture polish from a van.

The tailor had already parceled up the coat. Hugh paid him and asked for a receipt. While the man was writing it, there was an explosion outside.

The tailor looked up. A muscle was twitching beneath his eye. "What in God's name was that?"

Hugh shrugged. "Perhaps a truck burst a tire." He stuffed the receipt in his pocket and picked up the parcel. *"Na shledanou."*

"Good-bye," the tailor said absently. He followed Hugh to the door and peered up the hill. Everything seemed normal.

Hugh turned up the hill. He was in no hurry to get home, and there was another tram stop near the corner. He could dimly remember a café in one of the side streets; he would have a glass of tea there in memory of Dr. Spiegel.

The road twisted, and suddenly the crossroads were in sight. People were shouting; there were two gunshots. Pointing down the hill toward him was a black Mercedes—a big, open sports model. It was listing badly on its near side. The air was thick with dust, but Hugh's long sight could pick out the swastika pennant on the bonnet.

Two men were running away—one up the hill toward the hospital, the other in the opposite direction. The former was being chased by a man in an SS uniform with a pistol in his hand.

There was another man in an SS uniform. He, too, had a gun in his hand, but his other hand was pressed into his side. Drops of blood gathered on his black tunic, seeping around the splayed fingers. He was trying to stagger in pursuit, brushing aside a policeman who wanted to support him.

The face was curious: it had turned yellow with shock, but the features were entirely impassive. The blue eyes might have belonged to a fish.

Ever afterward, the scent of lilac turned Hugh's stomach: it reminded him of Reinhard Heydrich.

He turned and ran. There was no time for calculation. The reflexes he had learned during his time in Prague dictated flight. Someone had tried to kill the *Reichsprotektor,* and it would be folly to linger at the scene of the crime.

A tram came rattling down the hill. He leapt aboard just as it was pulling away from the stop. Still clutching the parcel, he fell into a seat. Most of the passengers were staring up the hill toward the crossroads. Several people looked as if they wanted to smile, but no one liked to smile in a public place these days.

A large, clean fingernail tapped the parcel on his lap, just below the place where the tailor had written Frau Scholl's name and address.

"So *that's* where you've been hiding yourself," a voice beside him cooed. "How *naughty* of you not to keep in touch with your old friends."

Hugh looked up.

Bela smiled at him.

Nine

"I am an optimist." Inspector Abendschon chuckled; cigar smoke oozed like ectoplasm from his parted lips. "Who can doubt that the ways of providence are fundamentally benevolent?"

Colonel Scholl reminded himself yet again that he could not afford to antagonize this man. He said dryly, "I wonder if Heydrich would agree with you."

"But he is a case in point, my dear Colonel. In death he has achieved what he was trying to achieve in life. Our justifiable reprisals have given us a chance to spring-clean the protectorate."

Abendschon chuckled again. He was a man of many noises, Scholl thought sourly: when the policeman wasn't talking, he was laughing; when he wasn't laughing, he was sucking his teeth or smacking his lips.

Their car was in the center of a Gestapo motorcade which was elbowing its way through the northwestern suburbs of Prague. Scholl stared out of the window, wondering why Abendschon had been so unwilling to talk in his office at the Petschek Palace.

"It was blood poisoning that killed him, you know—not the wounds," Abendschon said abruptly. "Interesting, eh? They turned the Bulkova Hospital into an SS barracks. Doctors were flown in from Berlin—all Germans, of course: they kept the *Reichsprotektor* well away from those filthy Czechs. And yet—Heydrich died."

Scholl began to get an inkling of what the inspector was driving at. He knew at once that this was not a point that could be approached directly: you could only define it by skating delicately around it.

He kept his voice studiously neutral: "But—as you say—the

Reich has been able to salvage something from the wreckage."

"Just so. My friends in the SS tell me that Herr Himmler is heartbroken by the death of his colleague, but he cannot allow his private sorrow to interfere with his public duty."

"Men in the service of the state," Scholl observed blandly, "are often called upon to make such sacrifices."

Abendschon grunted in agreement. "Even friendship must be sacrificed on the altar of Germany. Herr Heydrich himself said something of the sort, the first time we met. You remember? In March?"

Scholl nodded. He stared through the glass partition at the thick, shaven necks of the uniformed driver and the guard in the front seats of the car. The inspector's point was beginning to emerge: the only friendships that had been discussed on that Sunday afternoon were Paul Thümmel's—with Admiral Canaris and Himmler. He remembered with sudden clarity how Heydrich had dropped Himmler's name into the conversation and then paused to emphasize it. After Hitler, Himmler was probably the most powerful man in Germany. But his position was not unassailable. It might be said that he had been rash to include among his friends a senior *Abwehr* officer whose primary loyalty was to the Czech and British secret services.

Or worse than rash.

Abendschon had been in charge, under Heydrich, of the Thümmel investigation. If Heydrich had wanted to discredit Himmler and seize his position, here was a perfect opportunity. Heydrich had the Führer's confidence. All he would have needed to do was convince Hitler that Himmler associated with Thümmel not from friendship but to gain a means of communication to the Allies. As A-54, Thümmel offered Himmler a chance to keep a foot in both camps. That at least was how Heydrich might have presented the matter to Hitler.

There was a rumor that the Führer was obsessed with doubts about the loyalty of those who were closest to him. The curious defection of Rudolf Hess must have multiplied his fears. If Heydrich, with the help of Abendschon, was trying to prove Himmler guilty, if only by association—

"You know that the *Reichsprotektor* was flying to Berlin on the day of the attack?"

Scholl nodded.

"A meeting with the Führer," Abendschon continued. "Great

changes were in the air. Heydrich was late leaving home, and he dispensed with his SS escort. Little things—but curious, don't you think? Then there was the briefcase. During the drive, it was on his lap; they say it contained important papers, something he wanted to show Hitler. But no one's very clear what happened to it after the attack. The eyewitness reports are contradictory. I even questioned the staff at the Bulkova—a policeman hates loose ends. I was so relieved when the SS told me not to worry, that the briefcase had been recovered."

There were fewer houses now, and the motorcade was able to pick up speed. Even here, where the city shaded into the countryside, the soldiers were everywhere. Since leaving the Petschek Palace, the motorcade had stopped for three military checkpoints. In the last few weeks, thousands of people had been arrested; and hundreds had already been executed. Suspects and their families were only a small percentage of these. The Gestapo and the SS had widened the scope of their spring-cleaning to include Jews, Communists, and indeed anyone whose loyalty to the Reich was at all questionable. Seven partisans had been cornered in the Karl Borromaeus church in Resslova Street near Charles Square. None of them had survived. The sweep had been so swift and efficient that Scholl doubted if it could have been the work of inspired improvisation. It was almost as if Heydrich's death had been nothing but a formality, like the signature of a constitutional monarch on a bill, which had already, to all intents and purposes, become law.

"Have you found—" Scholl groped for the correct word—"the culprits?"

Abendschon shrugged. "We think so, though we can't be completely certain. Several of the partisans in the Karl Borromaeus church had been trained in England—the RAF parachuted them into the protectorate. We think two of them were responsible for the attack. We know quite a lot about them—and about the network that supported these criminals. One of the parachutists turned traitor and came to us. Oddly enough, the network had links with Thümmel."

The motorcade turned left off the main road and stopped at another checkpoint. This one was manned by the SS. By the roadside a policeman was using an axe to cut down a signpost. The sign said LIDICE. The NCO saluted and the motorcade moved on.

"Nearly there," Abendschon said.

Scholl wondered whether now was the time to introduce his

reason for contacting Abendschon. But instinct told him to wait. He had been prepared to plead if necessary when he came to the Petschek, but now he realized he was somehow in a position of strength.

The motorcade moved slowly through a green plain toward what looked like a cloud of gray dust, straddling the road. As they drew nearer, men in black uniforms could be seen picking their way among piles of rubble. Flecks of ash appeared on the bonnet of the car. Abendschon tapped on the glass, ordering the driver to stop.

Scholl climbed out. He could see a bulldozer among the ruins. A demolition team was attacking one of the few remaining chimney stacks with sledgehammers. Half a dozen trees were left, but they no longer looked like trees. The foliage had been shriveled off them by the heat; their branches were blackened and twisted.

Abendschon walked around the car to join his guest; the cigar dangled from the corner of his mouth.

"Not bad, eh?" He reached inside his jacket and pulled out a notebook. "By the end of the month there will be nothing here but a bed of cinders." He chuckled and then coughed violently. "By next spring you'd need a team of archaeologists to find the place."

"What about—" Scholl stopped and swallowed. "What about the people who lived here?"

"You military men are all the same." Abendschon cuffed him lightly on the arm. "You like your facts and figures, don't you?" He flipped open the notebook. "We shot all the males over sixteen on June the tenth—one hundred and seventy-three of them. Another nineteen worked in the mines at Kladno: we arrested them later and shot them in Prague. We had to shoot a few of the women, too; you know how it is—they panic and do something stupid. But the rest—nearly two hundred—have been exported to Ravensbruck."

By now they were walking toward the desolation—slowly, like two friends out for a stroll on a summer afternoon.

Scholl said, "What about the children?"

"There were about a hundred of them. One got himself shot—the silly little bugger tried to run away. I ask you—where did he think he could go to? Believe me, most of these Slavs are solid bone between the ears."

"And the rest of the children?"

"Oh, we've spared them. You know the line the propaganda people will take: the Reich does not make war on children and so on.

They'll go to the camps. We may be able to Germanize some of the younger ones, once the racial experts have given them a certificate of health."

Each footstep drove a puff of ash into the air. Abendschon turned to a fresh page in his notebook and scribbled on it with a pencil.

"Do excuse me, Colonel. You know what our superiors are like." The inspector chuckled. "One day they'll want us to give daily reports on the color of our urine."

The heel of the boot attached to Scholl's prosthesis crunched on something. Scholl glanced down. He had trodden on a calcined bone—a thigh bone, by the look of it. It was not a large one.

"You all right, Colonel? You look a bit pale. It's all this ash, you know. It's murder on the lungs. My men here have to work on half shifts."

It was then—as he scraped his heel along the ground to remove the traces of powdered bone—that Scholl lost his faith. It was a faith he had hardly known he had, until it was gone. Physically he felt slightly sick; his mind was merely confused. His memory produced an unexpected and vivid image of a necklace of imitation pearls which had once belonged to Eva. One day—on the concourse of the Friedrichstrasse station in Berlin—the string had broken and the pearls had scattered beneath the hurrying feet of commuters. He could see them now—little beads that danced gaily into oblivion.

"I'm fine," Scholl said. "I was gassed at Arras in 'seventeen—my lungs are still a little sensitive."

"Good, good," said Abendschon absently. He had stopped and was looking around. No one was within twenty yards of them. No birds sang here, and even the soldiers had little to say to one another.

Scholl coughed and wiped his mouth with a handkerchief. "What had they done?"

"The villagers? Someone might have sheltered one of the parachutists, I believe. But the orders for this came from Berlin. It's all for the sake of example. You can't *reason* with these Czechs. You have to show them who's boss." Abendschon slapped Scholl on the back. "Strictly speaking, we're in the middle of nowhere. Lidice no longer exists. Even its name is to be wiped off the maps and the records. That's thoroughness for you."

"We Germans have always been good at that." Scholl glanced

around: they were out of the office, out of the car—*in the middle of nowhere*. He looked up at Abendschon: "Now what do you want to discuss?"

The directness caught the inspector unawares: for an instant his fat, friendly face tightened, as if it was squeezed in a vise. Then the features relaxed.

"My dear colonel—how forthright you soldiers are. It's just a little detail—a loose end, you could say."

Rudi? Scholl thought. *But surely—?*

"Heydrich was a wonderful man—we know that. But even the best of men can make mistakes. Now he's dead, why should we who are alive suffer for his mistakes?"

"A little—how can I put it?—error of judgment concerning Herr Himmler?"

"Just so." Abendschon bowed in the consciously superior fashion of a waiter in a second-rate restaurant. "I know what was in that briefcase. I'm sure that you—as a friend of the *Reichsprotektor*—have some idea of the contents as well. My name wasn't mentioned, of course—nor was yours. But naturally one takes precautions."

Scholl allowed his hypotheses to harden into probabilities. Heydrich hoped to use the Thümmel affair to crush Himmler; Abendschon had been doing the necessary legwork. Himmler, having got wind of the attempt, had quietly scotched it—and had taken the opportunity to remove his rival at the same time. Abendschon, misinterpreting the relationship between Heydrich and Scholl, and exaggerating the latter's powers of inference, feared that Scholl was in a position to betray him to Himmler. There were larger questions—was Himmler really a traitor? had he somehow manipulated the parachutists' attack on Heydrich?—but they could wait. In a sense, they were no longer important to a man who had lost his faith.

"I'm tired." Scholl turned and stumped off toward the car.

Abendschon scuttled after him. His temples were streaked with sweat. "But have you considered the implications?"

"*I'm* not going to mention it," Scholl said over his shoulder. "Are you?"

"It would be a pity," Abendschon panted, "to sully the memory of so great a man. After all, a temporary aberration—"

"Exactly." Scholl put his newfound ruthlessness to good use. "By the way, there's something you can do for me. Your people picked up one of my servants a fortnight ago. He was in Liben at the time of the attack—on an errand for my wife. I wish you'd let him go."

"But naturally. What's his name?"

"Rudi Messner. I don't believe he saw anything worth mentioning. But my garden's suffering from his absence."

"Messner . . . fair-haired? sturdy? about sixteen? I know the one. You can collect him on the way back, if you like. He's of no importance to us."

Magda sat on the edge of the bed, brushing her hair. She was wearing her dressing gown and trying to read as she brushed. Her mother insisted on the nightly hair ritual. Magda complied but without enthusiasm. Frau Scholl was a firm believer in the virtue of at least a hundred brush strokes for each side; Magda thought that twenty was quite enough.

The sound of her father's car in the drive was a welcome distraction. He had not been able to get back to Zbraslav for dinner, but he would probably find the time to come up and say good night to herself and Heinz. And perhaps there would be some news.

The car had woken the dog. Conrad was a new acquisition— half Alsatian, half Labrador, and almost entirely untrained. Her father had bought him at the beginning of June when the security scare had been at its height. As a guard dog, he was not a success. It was true that he barked: but only as a method of demanding attention. His disposition was affectionate and his love for humanity seemingly unbounded. There were no strangers in his canine vocabulary—only new friends.

Car doors slammed and the barking stopped. Conrad would be using his tongue to welcome Papa and Hans Bruckman. That absurd tail of his would be trying to break away from his body.

There was a tap on the door. It opened a fraction, and Heinz slid into the room.

Magda put down the hairbrush. "I've told you to wait till I tell you to come in. How would you like it if I burst into your room?"

"Ssh. Mama will hear." His eyes were bright with excitement. "Papa's brought Messner back with him—I could see from my window. And his arm's in a sling."

"Really?" She picked up the hairbrush and stared coolly at him. "Whose arm? Papa's?"

"No—Messner's." He smiled; and suddenly his face no longer belonged to a child. "I bet they've taught him a lesson. These Czechs deserve all we can give them."

155

Magda brushed the hair across her face: she was sure she must be blushing. "You're going to get a lesson if Papa catches you out of bed. I can hear him on the stairs."

Heinz stuck out his tongue at her and slipped out of the room. Magda got into bed and waited for her father. In a way she was glad she had forewarning of Rudi's return. She could conceal a lot from Heinz, and even from her mother; but her father was more difficult to fool.

She knew her father was tired before he reached her room. She could tell by the way he walked—as if the artificial leg had become attached to a ball and chain.

He clumped across the room, sat on the bed and kissed her. His familiar smell—cigar smoke, soap, and eau de cologne—washed over her.

"Messner's back."

Magda said, "That'll please Miroslav. Is he all right?"

"His arm's badly sprained, and he hasn't had much to eat recently. But he'll survive. He's a tough old character, our Rudi."

"But—had he done anything wrong?"

Scholl's arm tightened fractionally around her. "Of course not. He was more or less on the spot when it happened so the police wanted to talk to him. The assassination's made everyone rather jumpy, so they kept him under lock and key until it was all cleared up. Lots of people were in the same boat."

"And what about the arm?"

"Oh, an accident. He fell out of a bunk, I believe."

Magda judged it politic to change the subject. "You're tired."

"It's been a long day. Some days are longer than others. I must go and say good night to your brother." Scholl kissed her again and stood up. At the door he turned and smiled. "One day this war will be over."

The church clock struck eleven; the stable clock followed suit.

Magda was too excited to sleep. She lay in the darkness, half aware of the noises around her. Her parents came up to bed. They were earlier than usual. Papa wasn't just tired: she knew that; but she was too excited to speculate about the reason. Something about him this evening had reminded her of those dreadful few days after Uncle Franz was killed on the eastern front.

But Papa and his problems seemed much less immediate than

156

the fact that Rudi was back. She hated to admit it, but she had missed him. More than that, she had been worried about him—which was even harder to admit. People were so stupid. Why couldn't these Czech extremists sit down with the *Reichsprotektor* and settle their differences with words rather than bullets and bombs? Anyone who had opened a history book could see that violence bred nothing but violence.

Violence—*His arm's badly sprained and he hasn't had much to eat recently.* It was impossible to imagine herself in Gestapo custody; but what would it be like for someone without her privileges? Surely the uncertainty must be the hardest part to bear—not knowing how long one would be kept there or what was going to happen next. She wondered what it was like to feel afraid, as Rudi must have felt, and whether he would tell her about it. She had always been curious to know what Rudi really felt: there was something elusive about him—a jealously guarded core of independence and privacy, which, when she tried to touch it, slipped out of her grasp; it was like trying to catch water or air.

It was curiosity—of an intellectual variety, of course—that had taken her up to his room a few days earlier. She hardly knew why she had chosen to go on Miroslav's day off, when the old man went to see his daughter in Prague. She had been in the room before but never without Rudi. It was very clean. The narrow bed had been made. There were a few clothes hanging behind a curtain in one corner; socks and underclothes were kept in a battered cardboard suitcase. Between the bed and the window was a pile of old newspapers, both Czech and German. There were a few books on the windowsill, some of which she had lent him and others which he had picked up secondhand in Prague.

It was a room without secrets—a room fit for public display. Yet Magda felt like a trespasser there. The room was like Rudi himself, she thought: it concealed nothing—but nor did it tell you anything.

But there were two items that failed to fit the pattern. One was the knife: it had a stained bone handle and a wickedly sharp three-inch blade. She found it by chance when she sat on the bed—it was tucked beneath the mattress near the pillow, and only the tip of the haft was visible. It had a sheath—the leather looked as if it had been cut from a discarded boot with a pair of shears; and the clumsy stitching made Magda smile. She was almost tempted to take the knife away and make a better sheath for it as a surprise for Rudi's return.

But that would have been foolish.

The other item was the lead soldier—or rather Red Indian—which she remembered from the first time she had met Rudi, nearly two years ago. It was between the pile of newspapers and the wall. She blew the dust from it. Most of the paint had gone. The Indian had also lost its feathers and most of one arm. The base felt rough to her touch: she turned it over and saw that the underside had been scarred and scraped, perhaps with a knife, at some point in its history.

She had run back from the stable block to the villa, feeling slightly soiled; it was almost as if she had violated a confidence. That was nonsense: why should Rudi confide in her, or she in him?

For some reason it was a relief to know that he was back in that room now. It might be fun to slip out and see if he was awake. The idea sent a frisson of excitement through Magda: at night the outside world took on the colors of an unfamiliar dream—an alien place that was all the more attractive because it was forbidden. She wasn't sleepy; she would enjoy a walk outside. It didn't really matter whether or not Rudi was awake.

She pulled on a jersey and an old skirt over her nightdress and tiptoed downstairs, carrying her sandals. There was a side door which she knew from experience could be opened quietly.

Once outside, she jumped from the doorstep over the dangerously noisy gravel path and onto the lawn. The dew was already heavy; and she wished she had thought to bring a pair of socks. A shadow, barking furiously, lolloped across the grass. Magda had been expecting this; she knew no one would come to investigate. During his first week at the villa Conrad had twice disturbed the entire household during the early hours—once when he was making friendly overtures to the kitchen cat, and once when his curiosity had been aroused by a hedgehog.

Conrad slobbered enthusiastically over her hand. He followed her when she set off for the stables. In the distance, the church clock struck midnight. In a few minutes she would hear the other midnight, the second midnight, which belonged to another timescale in another world. Rudi had once made an odd remark about it. *Anything can happen in the space between the midnights.* It occurred to her that Rudi sometimes said things that you could never imagine anyone else saying; whereas with most people it was usually the opposite.

The smell of honeysuckle guided her to Rudi's window. Once she was directly underneath, she could make out a thin line of candlelight where the heavy curtains failed to meet. She found a pebble at the base of the honeysuckle and lobbed it at the window.

The light behind the curtains vanished. The window opened with a scrape of metal from the catch.

"Who is it?"

The first thing that Magda noticed was that Rudi had spoken in Czech; the second was that his voice sounded strained, almost scared.

"It's me, of course." She replied in German; her conversation skills in Czech were limited. "Who did you think it was?" *Someone who spoke Czech?*

"Sorry. I was—nearly asleep."

"Are you very tired?"

"Yes. They kept the light on all the time in our cell. No one slept properly."

Magda felt a little disappointed. She had expected—well, if not enthusiasm from Rudi, at least something a little less dreary. "What happened to your arm? Was it an accident?"

"They wanted me to tell them something I didn't know," Rudi whispered. "I was lucky."

Magda shivered. "What do you mean?"

"One of the men in our cell—he didn't know whatever it was, either. I don't think he'll ever walk again."

Her first reaction was complete disbelief: surely *our* police don't do that sort of thing? But she knew that Rudi wasn't lying. Incredulity gave way to indignation.

"The *swine.*"

Above her she heard a sound that might have been the start of a laugh or a sob.

"That's what they called us," Rudi said.

Magda's anger against the Gestapo converted itself into an equally fierce pity for Rudi. "Is there anything I can get you? Or do for you?"

"No—but thank you. I'll be all right."

The stable clock whirred. The second midnight began to chime.

"I'll show them," she muttered. She was hardly aware of what she was feeling, let alone of what she was saying. "And I'll show you that all Germans aren't like that. It's your birthday next week, isn't it? It must be the twenty-second because I remember you saying it was six days before mine. We're going to drink your health between the midnights. And we're going to do it in champagne."

"It's too tiresome, darling," Betty said. "But Charley's right for once in his life. I'm not likely to get a better chance to see the old man. The doctors give him six months at the outside—more like three."

"Of course you must go." Michael closed his sketchbook with a snap. He flicked a crumb from his trousers to a waiting pigeon. "The war won't be over in six months, that's for sure."

Betty folded the greaseproof paper that had held her sandwiches; these days everything was worth saving. They had met for lunch on adjacent deck chairs in Green Park.

"I can probably get time off from work," she said. "In the circumstances—and things are pretty slack at present. But I'm afraid I shall have to postpone that weekend with Meg."

"Cigarette?" Michael held out his case. "What weekend?"

"Thanks." Betty's hand trembled as she took the cigarette. "We were going down to the Duveens' on Saturday. Meg hasn't talked of anything else for the last week."

Lady Duveen, the widow of a wealthy mill owner, gave regular weekend parties at her house in Oxfordshire. She looked upon them as a species of war work; the majority of her male guests were young, unmarried Allied officers stationed away from home.

"I'll take her, if you like." Michael struck a match. "I haven't seen Laura for ages. She'll be delighted to meet Meg—there's always a shortage of nubile young women at her parties."

"Are you sure it wouldn't be a bore for you?" Betty asked carefully. "I could always take her down later this summer."

"It's no trouble. I'd love to get out of town for a day or two. And I promised Laura I'd try and do her a watercolor of the south front. That was for her birthday—her last birthday."

"Well, that's all right then. I'll have a word with Meg and send Laura a postcard." Betty stood up and stretched. Two Polish airmen were passing: they eyed her with approval. "Will you ring me tomorrow before I go?"

"Of course, darling."

They parted at Queen's Walk: Betty went north to Piccadilly; Michael walked south through St. James's Park on his way to Queen Anne's Gate. She didn't look back and wave. A fear began to grow in her belly like a monstrous and unwanted baby.

Lord Knockroe hitched a ride for himself and his sister on an RAF bomber that was flying to Ulster; he had been at school with the pilot. At Lisburn, he wheeled a car from an unwilling motor transport officer whom he had known at Sandhurst.

Though Ulster was an armed camp crammed with British and American troops, the war seemed remote. There was no conscription here; and rationing was more honored in the breach than in the observance, owing to the difficulty of policing the border with Eire. The Northern Irish, Betty thought, were making war on their own terms.

As they crossed the border and drove down to Dublin, a sense of unreality stole over her. The butchers had meat in their windows; if you had the money, you could buy a dozen fresh eggs in any village shop. Most of all, she was conscious that death would not come from the sky during the night. Eire was too good to be true: it felt as fictional as a country in a prewar novel.

Charley insisted on stopping for dinner in Dublin. They ate at the Shelbourne Hotel, where the head waiter had known their father for thirty years. Charley had not had time to change, and his uniform drew some curious glances in the dining room; subalterns in the Irish Guards had become something of a rarity in Dublin.

Carlow was no more than sixty miles away. They finished the journey in the long midsummer twilight. Castle Leighlinbridge was five miles outside the town of Carlow. The lodge gates were open— no one had bothered to close them since 1917. It was too dark to see much of the park, but Betty could guess the condition it was in. The car bucked and swayed as it jolted over the ruts in the mile-long drive.

The house itself was built of local granite. The bleak symmetry of the design—a central block with two low wings—contrasted oddly with the fussy Gothic trimmings which the first earl had insisted that his architect supply. Only one wing was used now; the other had lost its roof and the central block was given over to rats and spiders. Betty's grandfather had destroyed a pleasant and manageable Georgian house to build this monument to his ambitions.

The next two days convinced Betty that wartime London was preferable to peacetime Carlow. She hadn't seen her father for nearly three years—since the Christmas of 1939. In the interval, he had lost several stone; he was pale and enfeebled; and he had little appetite. Despite the operations, the cancer had recurred. Nowadays he drank very little—it was too uncomfortable with a tumor in his stomach; the resident nurse gave him morphine instead.

Charley had a long talk with their father's lawyer in Carlow; he discussed what the man had said with Betty. There was no question but that the house and the remaining land would have to be sold when their father died. Charley would inherit the title but nothing else. Betty had suspected this for years, but the news seemed to come as a complete surprise to Charley. She in turn was surprised by the bitterness it engendered in him. He took refuge in alcohol, the traditional solace for the males of the Chandos family. Betty was two years older than her brother: sometimes she felt old enough to be his grandmother.

They left Castle Leighlinbridge on Monday morning. Their father was as unmoved by their departure as he had been by their arrival. Cancer and morphine had erected a barrier between him and the rest of the world.

Charley drove fast—partly because they had left later than planned, and partly because it gave some vent to his feelings. Betty offered to share the driving with him, but he refused. They had a packed lunch, which they ate without stopping; Charley brought a flask as well.

There was little conversation on the first leg of the journey. Betty felt that she was traveling from one source of despair to another. Behind them, her father was dying—alone and without dignity. In front was London: if Michael and Meg hadn't started an affair in her absence, she would never believe in womanly intuition again.

"Light me a cigarette, will you?"

Betty lit two and passed one to Charley. They were between Balbriggan and Drogheda, perhaps thirty miles from the border.

"It's so bloody unfair." Charley uncapped the flask with his teeth and drained it. "I'd no idea there was so little money. You know I'll probably have to leave the army after the war. You can't survive in the Guards with just your pay. Not in peacetime."

"What does it matter?" Betty snapped. "You can do something else."

"Of course it matters. I *like* the army. Besides, they need chaps like me. Always have and always will."

"*Balls.*" Betty completely lost her temper. "Officer material from the ruling classes? Don't you know we're fakes? Grandpa bought the title, to all intents and purposes. His father started life as a stonemason, even if he did marry into the gentry. He was even ashamed of his surname—he changed it to Chandos by royal license or something. It was his wife's name. You know what our real surname is? Ruggles."

She began to laugh—partly because she was really Betty Ruggles and partly because it seemed so stupid that she or Charley should be worried by such an absurdity. Once she started laughing, it was hard to stop.

"For Christ's sake, shut up!" Charley screamed.

His foot dug down on the accelerator. The car plunged into a righthand bend at 65 m.p.h. A horn shrieked.

A lorry laden with scrap metal was thundering toward them; it was in the process of overtaking a tractor.

Time slowed and for an instant stopped. *This is eternity,* Betty thought—three vehicles, a blue June sky, and a dusty road somewhere south of Drogheda.

Charley swore, braked, and threw the car over to the left. At the side of the road was a low stone wall topped by a row of iron spikes. There was a gap of perhaps five feet between the off side of the lorry and the wall.

The lorry thudded into the side of the car; the driver's door crumpled inward. The impact of the collision flung the car against the wall. Charley looked so surprised. His hand fell from the steering wheel; his cigarette fell from his fingers. There was a smell of petrol in the air. Engines revved, and people were shouting and screaming. The rim of the steering wheel dug into Charley's chest. The sun sparkled on the broken glass in his hair.

Betty crawled onto the bonnet. She seized Charley's arm and tried to pull him out.

"Please, Chas, help me, please, Chas, please—" She hadn't called him Chas since they were in the nursery. He'd discarded the name when he first went away to school.

The world was suddenly and unbearably bright. Betty heard an explosion. *It must be an air raid. But I didn't hear the sirens.* Her mind shrunk until it had emptied itself of everything except fire and pain.

Then it shrunk still further until there was room for nothing at all.

They were in the space between the midnights.

"I can't open it," Hugh said. "It's impossible."

"Papa says you should hold the cork and twist the bottle." Magda shifted on the bed beside him.

"It's moving—it's coming—it's—"

The cork burst out of the bottle, ricocheted off the ceiling, and knocked over the candle. Tepid champagne frothed over Hugh's hands. He fumbled for the glasses and brushed Magda's leg by accident. She found the matches and relit the candle. Both of them were trying not to laugh too loudly.

"Happy birthday," Magda said. She sipped her wine. "I think this should really be cold. Do you like it?"

"Of course I do." Hugh preferred the thought behind it. Perhaps champagne was an acquired taste. He took another, deeper swallow, bracing himself for the effervescence that had taken him by surprise in his first sip. This time the wine went down more easily. "Will—will the colonel miss it?"

"No. He's got cases and cases of the stuff in the cellar. He hardly ever drinks it. Maybe I'll tell him one day."

Hugh angled the bottle toward him so he could read the label: *Dom Pérignon Tête de Cuvée.*

They were both nervous; and they drank to give themselves something to do. Hugh was refilling their glasses as the second midnight chimed above their heads. This time he didn't spill so much. The second glass went down even more quickly. Magda got the hiccups. They found it almost as amusing as the explosion of the cork.

"Let's go for a walk," she said abruptly. "We can—" a hiccup interrupted her.

"Top up our glasses?" Hugh suggested. "All right—but we'd better not go outside the garden. There're too many patrols around."

Hugh blew out the candle. They tiptoed downstairs; Magda stumbled and would have fallen if Hugh had not caught her. They decided to leave the glasses behind and take the bottle instead.

They walked carefully through the stableyard and onto the lawn. There was no moon. The windows of the villa were dark. The leaves of the chestnuts and ash trees twitched and rustled above their heads.

"Where's Conrad?" Hugh said. "I thought he'd be slobbering all over us by now."

"I don't know. He wasn't around when I came out to the stables. Pass the champagne."

"Perhaps Miroslav took pity on him."

Magda swallowed a mouthful and passed the bottle back to him.

164

He drank without wiping the mouth of the bottle: he felt as though he had snatched a secret, almost sacrilegious intimacy from her. Her next words were uncomfortably close to his thoughts.

"Have you ever kissed anyone? A girl, I mean."

"I—"

Hugh lunged at her—to his own surprise. The bottle jarred against her shoulder. He felt her touch his arm. Panic-stricken, he lowered his head, closed his eyes, and aimed for where he thought her mouth must be. Her breath was warm and smelled faintly of yeast, like the champagne. His lips landed on the corner of her mouth. He kissed her—he could have sworn he felt her lips moving under his—and jerked away.

"I have now," he said shakily. He wanted simultaneously to exult and to despair.

Magda hiccupped and they both laughed.

"I was kissed at a party last Christmas. His name was Otto; he had blackheads."

Hugh drank and held out the bottle. "Then what happened?" he demanded.

"I slapped his face, of course."

Hugh thought that Otto-with-the-blackheads deserved far worse than a slap. But he relished Magda's *of course*. She returned the champagne to him.

"I'm cold," she said. "If you want to kiss me again, you'll have to catch me."

She vanished into the darkness. Hugh, still clutching the nearly empty bottle, set off in pursuit. He hardly knew what he was chasing—the ghosts of running footsteps, the hint of a shadow, or a flesh-and-blood girl. He guessed she was moving parallel with the drive, running over the grass toward the main gates. At this time of night the gates were padlocked.

Ahead and to his left he heard a thud and a gasp. He changed course toward it. The champagne turned sour on him.

"Rudi—I'm here."

Her face was a gray blur in the darkness. She sounded as if she was on the edge of panic.

"What's wrong?"

"I—I tripped over—I think it's Conrad."

Hugh knelt beside her. "It's all right." He felt in front of him until his hands found Conrad. The dog's coat was cold and damp with dew. He ran his hands along the dog's body, but there was no movement. The mouth and the eyes were open. The smell was disgusting, for Conrad had lost control of his bowels and vomited as well.

"I think he's dead," Hugh whispered. He was outraged—less by Conrad's death than by the fact that it had happened now of all times.

Magda grabbed his arm; she was shivering. "But why? How did it happen?"

"I don't know. He's been sick, so maybe it was something he ate."

"You mean he's been poisoned?"

That idea hadn't occurred to Hugh, but, as Magda spoke, he had a vivid mental picture of Conrad—ever trusting and ever hungry—accepting meat from a new friend. Instantaneously he realized the implications.

"Magda, we've got to wake your father and phone the police. If this isn't an accident—"

She squeezed his arm, wordlessly telling him to stop. A few seconds later he understood why. Metal scraped against stone near where the gates must be: someone was coming over the wall, secure in the knowledge that he would no longer have to contend with a ferocious guard dog.

There was a thud and a muffled grunt as the intruder jumped into the garden. It was difficult to estimate distances, but Hugh reckoned that they could be no more than twenty yards away from him.

Two more thuds followed the first. Hugh pulled Magda down to the grass. He wondered whether he should make a dash for the villa, but abandoned the idea for the time being; there was too much risk of noise.

A fourth man jumped down from the wall. One of the party incautiously stepped on the gravel; another swore at him.

The footsteps came nearer to where Hugh and Magda crouched beside the body of Conrad. It sounded as though the four men were having an argument in whispers.

"We should concentrate on the villa." It was the gravelly voice of a heavy smoker; it spoke in Czech. "Jiri is right. You should leave the tactics to soldiers."

"We are all soldiers, my friend. It makes sense to take care of the stables first. There are two Czechs there—an old man and a boy; one is a collaborator, and the other is the worst of traitors."

Hugh stiffened; his skin crawled with fear. He would have recognized that thin voice with the Slovakian vowels anywhere and at any time. Bela had come for him at last.

"We've come here to kill Germans," said a third voice. "I had relatives at Lidice. We know Scholl was implicated: so we kill him first—and his family."

"Jiri," Bela said softly. "If we deal with the small fry first, they won't be able to sound the alarm."

"You take orders from us: we represent the Government-in-Exile."

"Of course you do. But you're not in London now." Bela adopted a more conciliatory approach. "Let's compromise: Ota and I will take care of the stables, while you deal with the villa. Women and children and a couple of old men—you can manage those by yourselves, surely?"

"I don't trust him," Jiri said. "There's something bloody funny here."

Hugh stiffened. The last two sentences had been in English; the accent was a curious mixture of Czech and cockney.

"The poof's playing some private game of his own," the gravelly voice replied, also in English, "and his friend's pissed."

"What are you saying?" Bela spoke in Czech, and he sounded on edge.

Jiri switched back to Czech. "We were just talking it over. All right, we'll split up. You'll come on to the house after you've finished at the stables?"

The four men moved away—Bela and Ota toward the stableyard, Jiri and his colleague toward the house. The second couple passed very near to Hugh and Magda; Hugh could just make out what Jiri was whispering.

"It's a trap," he said, using English once more. "I reckon Bela's betrayed us. You can't trust these Communists."

Gravelly voice said firmly, "We're pulling out."

When their footsteps had died away, Hugh whispered in Magda's ear, "We only have to worry about the ones who've gone to the stables; I think the others are going to double back and escape. Did you leave the side door open?"

"Yes. But—"

"We'll have to loop around by the kitchen garden. Can you run?"

In the event it was too dark to run: it wasn't as if they dared to cross the open space of the lawn. But they walked fast, hand in hand, through the shrubbery, across the kitchen garden, and into the house by the side door. Hugh pushed home the bolts. Magda went on ahead. By the time Hugh reached the hall she was already on the stairs. Now they were in the house the atmosphere between them had subtly changed. Hugh thought bitterly that Magda was the German fräulein once more, while he was the Czech servant.

"I'll ring the police, if you want, while you wake the colonel." He didn't bother to lower his voice.

Magda paused. "All right," she said softly. "Rudi—?"

"Yes?"

"Those men were talking English, weren't they? *And you understood what they were saying.*"

"Is he telling the truth?" Eva asked. "We can't be too careful, Helmuth."

"Why should he lie? He's hardly going to be an *agent provocateur,* is he? Remember that we met him quite by chance."

Frau Scholl shrugged. "I suppose you're right. But isn't there a risk that someone might find out?"

Scholl removed his monocle and began to polish it. They were sitting in the study after dinner, nearly twenty-four hours after the attack on the house. There was now a guard on the gate, linked by field telephone to the house. A patrol checked the grounds every hour with the help of a dog whose attitude to visitors was less friendly than poor Conrad's had been.

"I don't see how anyone could find out," he said at last. "Rudi's documentation is really very good. It's the real thing, you see—not a fake. No one's likely to challenge it now: all the relatives are dead; both here and in Hungary. The boy's got a gift for languages, thank God, so that's not a problem. I wonder if he knows any Magyar—just in case? No one could expect him to be fluent in it still, but it might be worth making sure he knows the rudiments of it."

He replaced his monocle and took a chocolate from the dish beside his coffee cup. He avoided his wife's eye.

"We'll assume he's telling the truth then," she said. "How many people know who he really is?"

Scholl repressed a sigh; he might have known that Eva wouldn't give up so easily. "Well—his father, of course. And whoever his father was working for. But only four other people knew." He held up four stubby fingers and ticked them off, one by one. "Madame

Hase, the aunt of the real Rudi Messner: she was killed resisting arrest in 'thirty-nine. Dr. Spiegel: he was shot by accident during a student riot, also in 'thirty-nine. Jan Masin, whom I killed myself. And this man Bela Juriga—the one who seems to have led the attack last night."

"They might have told others."

"I don't think so. It would have been too dangerous. The man called Ota talked before he died. Abendschon interrogated him. Rudi was just Rudi, as far as he was concerned. Bela Juriga hated him, because he was jealous of his—ah—attraction for Masin; and also because he blamed him—as well as me—for Masin's death. The two parachutists from London know nothing about it. According to Abendschon, they distrusted Juriga partly because he was a Communist and partly because they suspected his motive for the attack was personal, not political."

Eva refilled their coffee cups. "You've thought it all out, haven't you? What's to stop Juriga telling someone?"

Scholl took another chocolate. "No one will believe him," he mumbled. "Rudi made a deposition to the Gestapo this afternoon. I told him what to say. One of the points he had to make was that Juriga was a pathological liar with a perverted lust for revenge. And you've got to admit that the truth makes an absurd story. There's not a shred of evidence. It all rests on the unsupported word of a Czech criminal—a Communist deviant who's known to have a grudge against the boy. Abendschon would laugh in his face."

"Am I to understand, Helmuth, that you plan to keep this—this English adventurer as a sort of family pet for the duration of the war?"

The smile faded from Scholl's face. "What's the alternative? If we tell the truth, they'll chuck him into a camp. I don't know if he'd come out alive."

"Of course he would. You're—"

"Eva," he said quietly, "this isn't like the last war. And the Third Reich isn't the Second. God knows I've tried to pretend it is for long enough. But after Lidice, I can't. We don't *deserve* to win."

"And what are you going to do about it?" his wife said with a sudden spurt of anger. "Run off and join those Russian butchers? Throw a bomb at the new *Reichsprotektor*?"

Scholl shook his head wearily. His memory chose this moment to produce that truism of nursery philosophy: *Two wrongs don't make a right*. Well, what on earth did make a right? Franz had been crucified: and it had taken away no one's sins. The Germans had murdered a village: and Helmuth Scholl lacked the courage even to protest. But he could at least try to look after that boy. It occurred to him that protecting Rudi—or Hugh Kendall—was a moral placebo. It involved the minimum of risk and no effort whatsoever. Nevertheless, it might make him feel a little better.

Aloud he said, "Rudi saved our lives last night. He saved mine when I first met him, and Heinz's as well. We owe him something for that."

"Our lives were only in danger last night because of him." Eva's voice was pettish. Fear often had that effect on her.

"And Heinz? And me?"

Her eyes filled with tears. She dabbed at them with a handkerchief. "I don't deny he's a good boy. He's a good worker, too. But the danger, Helmuth: think of that. What about Magda? And what happens after the war?"

"After the war? We may be thankful for a friend on the winning side."

"But—but we're going to win."

Scholl shook his head. "We didn't last time. I know the news is nearly always good, but I doubt if we hear the whole truth. No, in the end we'll lose. We could have beaten England perhaps. But now America and Russia will slowly crush us between them."

His wife popped a chocolate in her mouth, chewed it, and made a face. "It's a nut. I thought it was one of those orange ones. Is Rudi's father important?"

"He may be. It's hard to tell."

"How could he bear to leave his son here? I'd never do that to a child of mine. And why didn't he come back? The war didn't start for another five or six months."

"Perhaps he's dead." Scholl shrugged. "Perhaps his superiors wouldn't allow it. The needs of the state," he added bitterly, "come before those of the individual."

"Rubbish, Helmuth. This is no time for you to start being gloomy and philosophical. We must be practical. At least *one* of us must be."

Scholl smiled at her. Eva gloried in her pragmatism. Abstractions and generalities—even Nazism and patriotism—were matters of social convenience, discarded like last year's hemline or adopted like this year's collar. They were insignificant beside such enduringly important matters as Heinz's weak chest and tomorrow's lunch.

It was possible that she was far wiser in her simplicity than he could ever be. Last night was a case in point: morality and metaphysics had been obliterated by the need to defend his family and home from intruders. There was joy in action, and in the concentration it demanded. He and Hans Bruckman had once more been a team: they had ambushed Bela Juriga and his confederate in the stableyard, while the police had captured the two parachutists in Zbraslav. Abendschon had been delighted that all four of the criminals had been captured alive; the Czechs tended to kill themselves to avoid arrest.

"Perhaps you're right," Frau Scholl said.

"Eh?"

"About keeping Rudi. It should be perfectly safe. And it wouldn't do us any good if we admitted we'd been harboring an enemy alien for two years. People would think we were either stupid or disloyal. Besides, it's not easy to find trustworthy servants around here."

"But we can't—"

"Helmuth, darling—do be sensible. If we keep Rudi we'll have to treat him in exactly the same way as before. As a servant. You do see that?"

Scholl nodded.

"And that brings me to the other little problem," Eva continued. "Magda. She and Rudi may have saved our lives last night, but we mustn't lose sight of what they were doing beforehand. When all's said and done, they're still children."

Frau Scholl lectured him for some time about the dangers of calf love, especially when allied to unsupervised nocturnal expeditions and illicit drinking. Rudi, moreover, was entirely unsuitable as a friend for Magda. On these matters, Scholl knew, he had no chance of changing her mind whatsoever; argument would only make her more determined. Separation, Eva pointed out, was the only effective cure for an undesirable relationship of this nature. Magda could not be trusted to know her own interests.

Scholl rather feebly reminded her that Magda had been perfectly open to them about Rudi; she had told them at once about his suspicious fluency in a language he claimed to have no knowledge of. Rudi—or rather Hugh—surely deserved some credit for the honesty he had shown in the early hours of this morning when Scholl had questioned him.

Eva ignored all this, as he had known she would. She expanded on the disadvantage of wartime Prague as a place to bring up young daughters. Leipzig, on the other hand, was ideal for this purpose. The educational and social facilities were far superior to anything that Prague could offer; and Eva's Aunt Wilhelmina had offered more than once to have Magda. She reminded her husband that Aunt Wilhelmina was not only unmarried but also their wealthiest relative on either side of the family. As parents they had a duty to give Magda every possible advantage—and that meant Aunt Wilhelmina and Leipzig. Magda, of course, would come back on visits; and no doubt they would often go to Leipzig.

Helmuth Scholl had no defense against this ruthless barrage of maternal logic. He suspected that Eva had been nurturing the idea for some time; the incident with Rudi had merely brought it to fruition.

"Well?" She stared challengingly at him. "What do you say?"

Scholl stood up and stumped across the room to the corner cupboard where the brandy decanter was.

"And that's another thing," Eva said. "Aunt Wilhelmina has been a lifelong teetotaler."

Scholl couldn't help smiling. "At least Magda showed good taste—Dom Pérignon *Tête de Cuvée*. But she really should have chilled it first."

Ten

Muriel Kendall died on March 27, 1945.

"Poor Mother," Meg said to Stephen after the funeral. "It seems so unfair. Why was she always unlucky?"

Stephen shrugged "Someone has to be unlucky."

Mrs. Kendall died in Orpington in Kent. She had never been there before and in all probability she would have never gone there again. She was escorting home a convalescent patient—a cantankerous publican who had lost a leg in one of the December V-1 raids. To make matters worse, she was doing it as a favor on one of her days off.

She was killed by the last V-2 to land in England. She would not have heard the rocket beforehand because it would have been traveling too fast. She must have died instantaneously. Rescue workers found the publican, unharmed in his wheelchair, a few feet away from where most of her body lay. He was crying quietly and monotonously; on his lap was Mrs. Kendall's handbag.

The handbag, which was undamaged, eventually found its way to Meg. She sorted through the contents with an increasing sense of sacrilege. At the bottom of the bag was a battered lead soldier wearing the gaiters and flat cap of a World War I British officer.

Meg was her mother's executor and her sole heir. There was little to inherit: Mrs. Kendall's possessions had contracted over the years to the contents of a second-floor back bedroom in Aunt Vida's house in Richmond. Meg found five other soldiers beneath her mother's handkerchiefs. She reunited them with their officer and put them away in a deed box that she had discovered in the wardrobe. She didn't mention them to anyone.

Nor did she mention the bundle of letters that she had found in the same drawer as the soldiers. They were from her father. Most of them dated back to the last year of the Great War and the first years of the peace. She skimmed through two of them and was disturbed by the love they expressed; it was easier to hate her father than to pity him. A few of the letters, according to their postmarks, had been written since her parents separated; Meg could not bring herself to read any of those.

The letters posed a problem: should she keep them, destroy them, or return them to her father? She hadn't spoken to him for nearly three years, apart from the muttered greetings they had exchanged at the funeral. Aunt Vida had been openly hostile to him, when she remembered who he was. Stephen was still on speaking terms with their father, but treated him with contempt. There was no one to act as go-between.

And there was no one to advise her, either. She dared not ask Wilbur Cunningham; he was at present working a sixteen-hour day at the embassy, and it wouldn't be fair to bother him with personal trivia. Michael—poor, dear Michael whom Mother had liked so much—might have been able to help, but he had been posted to Washington in February. (Meg was privately convinced that he had wangled the posting because of his broken heart. He had actually cried when she told him of her engagement to Wilbur.) Once upon a time she could have asked Betty Chandos; but Betty had become dreadfully serious and unsympathetic since she came back from Ireland.

In the end Meg took the easy way out. She locked the letters in the deed box and deposited it at her bank. In a few weeks she had almost forgotten they were there.

"Will you read the paper to me, dear? My eyes are so tired this morning. Bunnings will clear away."

Meg bit back her impatience. It was typical that Aunt Vida should choose today of all days to be demanding. Usually Meg had the excuse that she had to go to work; she had been a secretary at the Ministry of Information since 1943. But this week she was on leave, and today was VE Day.

She helped Aunt Vida into the drawing room and settled her into her chair. From the dining room came the clatter of crockery. At least she had escaped the washing up.

Her mind drifted back to the question of what she could wear tonight. Wilbur was taking her dancing—at the Mirabelle, the Four Hundred, or Manetta's: the choice was hers. They were celebrating more than victory in the West; Wilbur had promised her that, once the war was won in Europe, they would get married. Marriage would mean the delight of having a home of her own. The whims of two old women would no longer dominate her life.

"When you've quite finished wool-gathering," Aunt Vida said tartly, "I would like to hear the news."

"Sorry." Meg glanced down at the paper. "*The Times* has a headline on its front page."

"Newfangled nonsense," Aunt Vida grumbled. "Come on, girl: read me the Deaths."

There was nearly a column of them today. Meg read slowly through the announcements. Marriage, she was thinking, had one other big advantage. Wilbur was too straitlaced—no, she corrected herself, too honorable—to believe in sex before marriage. Since that last time with Michael, she had had no one. She was surprised how much she missed it.

Aunt Vida recognized no one among the dead. She urged Meg onward to the home, imperial, and foreign news. Even this did not satisfy her: she stirred fretfully in her chair while Meg told her about the crowds celebrating in Piccadilly and the damage to Milan's art treasures.

"Meg, dear," Aunt Vida interrupted. "Is there anything about Czechoslovakia? Or Prague?"

Meg turned over the page. "The Czechs have seized control of Prague radio, and they're appealing for help from the Russians and General Patton. But the Germans are still hanging on, and they've got three hundred tanks." Meg ran her eye down the column. "Oh, and there's a report of a German broadcast from Prague: they're claiming they've surrendered only to the Western Allies—they're still at war with Russia. There's a quote: '. . . the struggle will be continued until the Germans in the East are saved and until our way back to the homeland is secured.' "

"And why not?" Aunt Vida's voice was suddenly louder; it had an edge of hysteria. "Everyone wants to go home, of course they do." Her hands, distorted with arthritis, were trembling in her lap.

"Darling, don't upset yourself."

Meg was already on her feet. To her relief she saw Mrs. Bunnings in the doorway.

"There, there." The housekeeper put her arms around her employer. "It's all right, dear."

Aunt Vida ignored her. Her voice rose to a wail. "If we let them go home, they'll let Hugh come home, won't they? Harry and George and Hugh."

She began to cry.

Colonel Scholl had never understood why they allowed Bela Juriga to survive.

The official story was that he held Slovakian nationality, which put him beyond the jurisdiction of the Reich. That was nonsense, of course—Slovakia's independence had never been more than a diplomatic fiction which existed solely for Germany's convenience.

A more probable explanation was that someone—in the SS perhaps or the Gestapo—had kept Juriga alive to use as a bargaining counter in the event of Germany losing the war.

By now the question was academic. Juriga had spent most of the last three years in the concentration camp at Mauthausen, in Austria. A few weeks earlier, Juriga and three hundred other prisoners had been evacuated by road; their destination was Theresienstadt, a camp to the north of Prague. American fighters had strafed the convoy; many prisoners had been killed; and Bela was believed to have escaped in the confusion. According to the Gestapo, there was evidence that Bela was now in Prague, and actively involved in the revolt. The Petschek Palace had forwarded a brief report on the subject to Scholl. Juriga's hatred of the colonel was on record; it was feared that he might attempt to get revenge for the death of Jan Masin and his own imprisonment.

Scholl had little time to worry about Juriga; his mind was occupied with more pressing concerns. Owing to an acute shortage of professional officers, he was directly involved in the army's efforts to cope with the rebellion in Prague and the Allied advance into the protectorate. He was no longer able to advise from the sidelines. The ground floor of the Zbraslav villa had become the military command post for the southern sector of outer Prague; Scholl's garden was now a tank park; his stable block was a munitions store.

The family and their remaining servants lived on the upper floors of the house. It was a curiously unreal existence: Scholl felt as though he was camping in the ruins of his past life. Eva hated this constriction of her domestic kingdom, but seemed unable—or unwilling—to grasp the wider implications. Heinz, on the other hand, was drunk with the apocalyptic glory of the death throes of the Reich. He was nearly sixteen now, and had announced his intention to live and die for the Werewolf, the German partisan movement which *Reichminister* Goebbels had created in April 1945.

The Werewolf claimed to be the organization of National Socialist Freedom Fighters. Radio broadcasts hammered home the movement's slogans: *Hate is our prayer. Revenge is our battle cry.*

To his father's dismay, Heinz was enchanted by this final outburst of violent idiocy. Scholl felt his son had become a stranger to him. In a sense he knew Rudi Messner better than either of his own children.

For Magda had suddenly become a woman. Scholl had always been shy of women; and he was distressed to find that his daughter was no exception to the rule. She had returned to Zbraslav early in April, since the Americans were threatening Leipzig and Aunt Wilhelmina could no longer take responsibility for the safety of her great-niece.

The future looked bleak. Scholl hoped that the Americans, the lesser of the two evils, would reach Prague before the Russians. But by Sunday, May 6, he knew that the Third US Army was unlikely to advance beyond Pilsen, fifty miles to the west. Intelligence reports suggested that the Allies had agreed to leave the liberation of Prague to the Soviet Army. It was even possible, Scholl considered, that the rising in Prague had been arranged by Czech Communists chiefly to ensure that the Russians would have an excuse to arrive as conquering heroes. Given half a chance, the Germans would have handed over the city to the Czech civil authorities without a shot being fired.

Colonel Scholl's concerns had contracted. He didn't care who ruled Prague—or, for that matter, Berlin and Leipzig. His priority had become the safety of his family. He abused the authority of his position to get them all a place in a military convoy, which was due to drive north on May 8. There was no longer much of Germany left, but at least it was their own country.

A German family could expect little mercy from a Soviet-backed Czech regime; and if Bela Juriga was alive in Prague, the Scholls would be even more at risk. Bruckman would travel with them of course. The Czech servants would have to fend for themselves. It was unlikely that anything very dreadful would happen to them; they had harmed no one; and they had collaborated with the Germans no more than most of their fellow countrymen.

But Rudi—or rather Hugh—was in a different position.

As the Czech-Hungarian Messner, he would not be welcome in Germany. Leaving him in Prague would mean, at best, abandoning him to an uncertain existence as a refugee; at worst it would mean handing him over to Bela Juriga.

But there was a third option; and it was the only one which could ensure Hugh's safety. After all, the Americans were only two hours away by road.

The second midnight was striking as Hugh tapped on Magda's bedroom door. He knocked twice, between the strokes.

There was no answer. Hugh glanced quickly behind him, down the dimly lit landing, and opened the door. He slid into the room and closed the door as quietly as possible. He fumbled around the handle until he found the key. The lock clicked home softly; he had oiled it during the day.

The room was completely dark, for the blackout was still in force. He waited for a few seconds until he could hear her breathing. He moved cautiously toward the sound. His legs were shaking with a mixture of panic and excitement: *Well, what can it matter now?* Despite his care, he stumbled against the end of the bed. The collision made little noise, but to his overwrought mind it seemed loud enough to waken the household.

Progress was easier now he could use the edge of the bed as a guide. He touched a blanket-covered mound and realized it was Magda's leg; he snatched away the hand as if the leg was burning hot. It seemed impossible that he could ever summon up the courage to wake her. There was an almost overwhelming temptation to leave.

Suddenly she stirred. "Who is it?" she muttered.

Her breath was slightly stale with sleep; it swept over him like perfume. He realized that he must be closer to her head than he had thought. There was no going back now.

"It's me. Hugh."

"What on earth are you doing here?"

He swallowed; his mouth was dry. At least she sounded more curious than outraged. "I have to talk to you. I've got to say goodbye."

Magda sucked in her breath sharply. Hugh felt the bed move as she sat up. A match scraped and flared. She lit her candle—the frequent power cuts meant that no one was prepared to rely entirely on the electric light these days. The flame caught on the wick; it streamed higher. As it grew, Magda took form and color from the surrounding darkness.

Three years dropped away from her. Hugh realized that she was—and would always be—the fifteen-year-old girl he had kissed in the garden. They had seen so little of each other recently that he had begun to wonder if she had somehow become another person in Leipzig. Since she had come back to Zbraslav, there had been few opportunities for conversation. One Sunday he had seen her with a young army lieutenant: they had been laughing together; and Hugh had wanted to kill the man.

"What are you staring at?" she asked.

"You." Hugh sat down on the edge of the bed and took her hand. There was a slight tug, as if she wanted to take her hand away; but Hugh held on, and her hand relaxed. There was so little time left that he could only be direct.

"What—" Magda swallowed in her turn and started again. "What time is it?"

"Just after midnight."

"What if someone comes in?"

"I locked the door." Hugh smiled: they had become conspirators. "Look, your father had a talk with me this evening. I can't come back to Germany with you. I've got the wrong papers."

Her fingers were warm. They tightened on his hand.

"But what will you do?" she whispered. "Will you stay here?"

Hugh shook his head. "The Russians will probably take over. And the colonel says that Bela Juriga is probably in Prague now. You remember?"

Magda nodded.

"He knows who I really am, you see. And he hates me almost as much as he hates your father. But there's a chance I can get through to the Americans tomorrow—today, I mean. They'll get me back to England."

He tried to sound as confident as possible. England seemed impossibly far away; and he didn't even want to go there.

Silver glinted in the corners of Magda's gray eyes. Two tears slid down her cheeks. Otherwise her expression didn't change. Hugh was awed by the shattering thought that she was crying for him.

He leaned forward. He could feel the warmth of her body before he touched her. Fine blond hair tickled his cheek, tangling with his stubble.

Afterward it was impossible to tell which of them had started it.

Three o'clock had struck some time ago.

"I must go," Hugh said. "We're leaving at half past four."

"Oh, don't." Magda's arms tightened around him; she pulled him toward her. "Hugh, what are we going to do?"

"I'll come back for you, I promise—after the war." He groped for possible consolations. "And we'll write. We—we can send letters poste restante." He ran his hand down her body, as far as he could reach.

She snuggled closer. "After the war—I can't remember there not being a war. Not really."

Hugh's hand returned to the nape of her neck. He stared stupidly at his fingers: there was blood on them.

"Will they let us?" she said suddenly. "Perhaps this war won't end—the Russians and the Americans might fight one another. Why can't they leave us alone?"

"One of us is *bleeding*!" In his excitement, Hugh raised his voice.

"Sshh." She grinned proudly at him. "Of course I am."

The image of the young lieutenant flashed into Hugh's mind. Relief swept over him. Before he could stop himself, he said, "I thought—perhaps you'd already—?"

"With Otto von Posen? Don't be silly. That was just to encourage you to do something."

It took Hugh another twenty minutes to get out of bed. He got dressed quickly and clumsily; his eyes and his attention were on Magda. It was impossible to believe that he might not see her again for years.

She got out of bed and padded across the room to the chest of drawers by the window. Her naked body glowed in the candlelight. Hugh needed all his resolution to continue dressing.

Magda turned and came toward him with her hand outstretched. "This is for you."

He looked down. In the palm of her hand was a gold signet ring. She took his hand and pushed it on his little finger. The ring was worn; the initials incised on it had become blurred.

"It was my grandfather's. Mama's father, Heinz Kleist. The—the initials fit. You'd better put it in your pocket for now."

Hugh cleared his throat. "I wish I had something for you."

"It doesn't matter."

"Yes, it does." Hugh dug into his trouser pocket and came out with the gray, misshapen figure of Hiawatha. It was better than nothing, despite the inevitable risk of bathos. "It's a Red Indian. I brought him from England. I've had him ever since I can remember."

"I saw him once—no twice, actually. I poked around your room once—it was when the Gestapo arrested you."

Magda took the Indian and began to cry and laugh at the same time. Hugh smothered the noise with his mouth. Somewhere a clock was striking.

In front of the Mercedes was a truckful of soldiers and one armored car; behind it were the rest of the trucks and the other armored car. It was a fresh, fine spring morning. The convoy drove as fast as possible. There was little traffic and, apart from the occasional bomb crater, the road was good.

Bruckman was driving, with an armed soldier beside him. Scholl and Hugh Kendall were in the back. In theory, the troops were going to relieve their comrades on the western front. In practice, of course, it was the other way around: the real fighting was behind them—in Prague and on the eastern front. Apart from fanatical Nazis, few soldiers wanted to fight the British or the Americans. Even Grand Admiral Dönitz, Hitler's successor, was rumored to be negotiating for a separate peace with the western allies.

Scholl's presence with the convoy was perfectly legitimate: his job was to discuss with the commander in the field the eventual withdrawal of all the troops in Western Bohemia to Prague. It was natural enough that he should take Hugh as an interpreter. It might be necessary to requisition transport from civilians who spoke only Czech.

"You have everything?" The colonel spoke quietly, even though the partition isolated them from the rest of the car.

"The money's in the belt." Hugh yawned. "I've got so much food in my pockets I can hardly move."

The boy looked tired, Scholl thought, as if he hadn't had much sleep last night. It wasn't surprising: he must be unbearably excited by the thought of going home after so long.

"You're not worried about what you do when you reach the Americans?"

Hugh shook his head. There was a listlessness about him that surprised Scholl. "I keep asking for the intelligence officer of whatever unit picks me up. Sooner or later they'll check my story with the British and send me home."

"It may take time—"

"I've a lot of that."

Scholl frowned. "Don't you want to go home?"

"I'm sorry. It hardly seems like home. I can hardly remember how to speak English."

"Perhaps it will seem like home when you get there." Scholl rubbed his monocle on his handkerchief. "*I* want to go home, you know. Leipzig may be a ruined city in a ruined country, but I'll still be glad when we get there. Everyone needs a home."

Hugh said nothing for a moment. It occurred to Scholl that the boy had suddenly grown up: he was no longer the gardener's boy or even the Scholl's young protégé.

The colonel said, "What will you do when you get back to England? Or will you leave that for your parents to decide?"

"My parents stopped making decisions for me when they left me in Prague." Hugh hesitated. "I'm sorry, sir. I'm not ungrateful for what you've done. It's just I'm tired of other people telling me what to do and where to go." He jerked his thumb over his shoulder, toward the truckloads of soldiers behind them. "Look at them: they're like animals going to the slaughterhouse. I don't want to be like that."

Scholl successfully resisted the temptation to smile. He could remember when he, too, had indulged in youthful melodrama. Like Hugh, he had been sincere.

"There's one thing I should tell you, sir," Hugh said.

The boy sounded so serious that Scholl was unable to keep his lips from twitching.

"Please go on," he said gravely.

"One day I shall come back for Magda."

Scholl's monocle dropped from his eye. "I see." He looked steadily at Hugh. To his surprise, he found himself hoping that the boy would continue to mean what he said. He could think of far worse potential son-in-laws. "Does Magda know this?"

Hugh blushed. "Yes, sir."

"And how does she feel about it?"

"The same as I do," Hugh said with unconscious arrogance.

Colonel Scholl nodded slowly. "Then I look forward to our next meeting. After the war."

Hugh never learned the name of the village. It was somewhere near Pilsen; and its one street was crowded with troops. Looking at them, Hugh wondered how on earth Germany could be on the verge of surrender. They were well armed and well disciplined; and clearly their morale was high.

He waited in the car while Colonel Scholl interviewed the officer in command.

After ten minutes, Scholl returned. He dismissed the soldier and ordered Bruckman to drive on.

"Along the same road, sir? But that's no-man's-land. The Americans have got patrols out there."

"So have we." Scholl struck a cigar in the corner of his mouth and patted his pockets in search of matches. "Drive on."

Bruckman shrugged and started the engine. He said nothing, but he had the old soldier's ability to express in silence his opinion of his superior's stupidity.

Hugh said quietly, "I could go on by myself."

Scholl lit his cigar before replying. When it was burning evenly, he said, "They'd never let you through the checkpoints. We'll drop you a kilometer outside the village. Then you're on your own."

The second of the two checkpoints was just outside the village. Once they were through, there was a perceptible change in the atmosphere in the car. They were driving along the bed of a shallow valley. On either side of the road were fields; beyond them, as the ground began to rise, pine trees spread up to the crests of the hills. Hugh could see a few scattered farms and cottages.

The landscape was so still that it was menacing. No one was in sight; there was no livestock in the fields; none of the chimneys was smoking; the cloudless sky was empty of planes.

"Half a kilometer more," Scholl said. "Then you'll be beyond the reach of our patrols. Just carry on down this road and the Americans will pick you up. They won't harm you—you're obviously unarmed, and they're not barbarians."

The Mercedes drove into a long, shallow, right-hand bend.

Suddenly Bruckman braked hard. Hugh and Scholl were thrown forward against the back of the front seats. The tires squealed against the road surface. The car jerked to a halt, rocking on its suspension.

Three yards in front of the car was the body of a man.

He lay on his front, spread-eagled across the road. He wore an unfamiliar uniform; his helmet had rolled a few feet away from his head. There was no sign of a wound.

"It's a GI." Scholl frowned. "But there's been no fighting in this sector since yesterday. He should have been picked up by now."

He opened the door and clambered out of the car. For half a minute he stared down at the body; as he did so, he automatically unbuckled his holster. Bruckman swore under his breath. Hugh got out of the car.

The wound was on the far side of the body—a jagged slit in the rib cage. A trail of blood stretched from it to the verge, a couple of yards away.

"I think it's a knife wound," Scholl said; he sounded tired. "We'd better move him off the road. Will you take the head?"

"Stop!"

Two youths scrambled out of the drainage ditch which ran parallel to the road. They carried machine guns, but neither of them was in uniform. The younger one, who couldn't have been more than fifteen, covered Bruckman and the car; the other—perhaps a couple of years older—trained his gun on Hugh and Scholl.

"Keep away from the body," he said; his voice was shaking with excitement. "We've put a Teller mine beneath it."

"You damned fools," Scholl snapped. "What's that going to achieve?"

"*Hate is our prayer. Revenge is our battle cry,*" the younger one said in a singsong voice. "Isn't it, Fritz?"

"We shall *never* bow to the enemy, do you hear?" Fritz shouted. "We guard the honor of the German nation."

"I order you to put down those guns." Scholl took a step forward; his right hand dropped to his holster.

Fritz replied with a burst of gunfire. The bullets ricocheted off the road, perilously close to the corpse of the American soldier.

"No one trifles with the Werewolf. Anything is justified if it helps to damage the enemy." Fritz jerked his gun toward Scholl. "Order your driver to get out of the car."

"Hans," Scholl said calmly, "You'd better do as he says."

Hugh knew instantly what Bruckman would do; much later he

realized that the colonel must have known as well. The little chauffeur had a quick temper; and his loyalty to Scholl was almost fanatic in its intensity.

Bruckman shoved open his door and threw himself out of the car; in one hand he held the machine pistol which was kept by the driver's seat. He rolled onto the road. The pistol spewed bullets, seemingly at random. The younger boy fell backward into the ditch.

Hugh dived into the same ditch—partly for cover and partly because he wanted the machine gun. He was dimly aware of another burst of fire, this time from a different gun.

Fritz was screaming, *"Hate is our prayer! Revenge is our battle cry!"*

The younger boy had crumpled in a heap on the muddy bottom of the ditch. The pool of stagnant water beside him was already stained with blood. The gun had fallen a yard away from his outstretched hand. Hugh picked it up. It was smeared with mud. He looked stupidly at it for a second, wondering if you just had to pull the trigger to make it kill people.

Hugh stood up, still holding the machine gun; the movement brought him head and shoulders above the level of the road; he could feel water seeping into his shoes.

It's all so confused, he thought; *it was never like this for Major Kendall VC.*

Colonel Scholl shouted, "Get down!"

Fritz swung around, the muzzle of his gun pointing at Hugh.

Hugh pulled the trigger, knowing—as if he was in a nightmare—that nothing would happen. He threw the gun toward Fritz: it clattered harmlessly on to the road. Bruckman was trying to reload the machine pistol.

Fritz moved ninety degrees and pumped a single round at Bruckman. The bullet took the chauffeur high in the chest: it flung him back against the car.

Why didn't the colonel fire? Could his gun have jammed?

Even as Hugh watched, Scholl lurched forward, his Luger held by the barrel. His prosthesis caught on the left leg of the dead GI. He was unable to check the momentum of his charge, but the trapped prosthesis deflected it.

The colonel tripped: his tubby body fell heavily on to the corpse.

Another thing that Major Kendall never knew was that courage can be ridiculous.

The ditch saved Hugh. When the mine exploded, he was already falling backward into its shelter, in obedience to Scholl's order. The impact battered his eardrums. Something—perhaps a chip of stone— cut his cheek, inches below his left eye.

At some point he realized he was lying on top of the dead German boy. A column of black smoke contrasted vividly with the blue of the sky. He could hear someone groaning.

Hugh peered cautiously over the rim of the ditch. He tried to analyze what he saw rationally, chiefly as an attempt to stop himself from screaming or vomiting. The force of the blast must have been away from the car. There was no sign of the GI. Scholl's prosthesis lay several feet away from what was left of his body. By some freak of fate his monocle was undamaged. It twinkled in the sun.

Fritz was lying on his back, with his mouth open and the gun still cradled in his arms. He was very fair and his face was covered with freckles. His eyes were the same blue as the sky's.

Hugh hauled himself out of the ditch and stumbled toward Bruckman. The chauffeur was slumped against the running board of the Mercedes, clutching his chest just below the collarbone.

"I'll get the first-aid kit," Hugh said.

"Get away from me, you swine." With his free hand, Bruckman groped for his gun, but it was too far away for him to reach. *"You killed him!"*

Hugh stopped, his hand on the car door. The accusation was so nonsensical that he had no means of answering it.

"He only came here for your sake," the chauffeur snarled. "He would have got that kid if you hadn't stood up. You English bastard: you distracted him on purpose."

Hugh shook his head, but said nothing. He got the first-aid box from the car and insisted on using it, despite Bruckman's protests; the chauffeur was too weak to prevent him. The bullet's entry hole was small, round, and neat; but its exit was much larger and shaped like a ragged star. He cleaned the wounds as best he could with disinfectant and wrapped a bandage around the shoulder. While he worked, his patient murmured a litany of hate.

The accusation made sense emotionally, Hugh thought, if not rationally. Bruckman had been jealous of Hugh for years, seeing him as an upstart rival for the colonel's affections. Now Scholl was dead, the chauffeur could vent his hatred and some relief for his sorrow by blaming Hugh.

As far as Hugh could tell, Bruckman wasn't in immediate danger. There was no need to stay with him, or to go back to the village for help; a patrol from one side or the other would pick him up in a matter of hours. Another reason to leave him suddenly occurred to Hugh: Bruckman knew he was English; he must have overheard something, perhaps years ago. No doubt he had kept his mouth shut out of loyalty to the colonel. But he no longer had any reason to keep quiet.

"You bastard," Bruckman muttered for the twentieth time, "you godforsaken worthless swine, you bloody Jewboy, you—"

Hugh stood up. "I'm going, Hans. I'm sorry, but I didn't kill him. Someone will come for you."

"Where are you going, Judas? Hell?"

Hugh shrugged. "I don't know. I think I'm going home."

III

Postwar
1945–46

Eleven

After lunch, Stephen strolled back through the park. He was not in a hurry to return: the Wednesday batch of reports from Palestine would be waiting on his desk. It was a depressing prospect, and worth postponing for as long as possible.

His office was on the third floor of the house in Old Burlington Street. He shared both the room and a secretary with three other men. As it was a chilly November day, the windows were clamped shut. The air was heavy with tobacco smoke. Edith looked up as he came in.

"His Nibs wants a word with you," she said. "You're late, so you'd better look sharp."

Stephen nodded distantly. Edith was old enough to be his mother, but her vulgar familiarity was a constant source of irritation to him. He hung up his hat and coat with elaborate care; Edith might be in awe of Derek Ingham, but he was not. On his way to Ingham's office, he paused to examine the contents of his in-tray.

He tapped on the door, and Ingham shouted, "Come!"

"You want to see me, sir?"

Stephen noted with approval that his voice was level, pleasant, and casual. His mind, however, was working furiously, trying to find an explanation for this unexpected summons. He was four months through his six-month probationary period with the Middle Eastern section and he couldn't afford to be careless. More than his present job was at stake; if he passed through the next two months without mishap, he would no longer be a temporary wartime employee of SIS; he would be on the permanent peacetime strength.

"Where were you?" Ingham demanded. As usual, there was an unlit briar pipe in his mouth; it had the effect of reducing anything he said to an aggressive mumble. "You should have been back at two."

"I'm sorry, sir. I was late leaving, and then I got caught in a queue."

The excuse was good enough for Ingham, Stephen thought: the behavior of queues was completely unpredictable, rather like the weather. He was aware of a chilly anger inside him. He disliked being treated as a schoolboy by this overweight fool.

"Don't let it happen again," Ingham snapped. Before the war he had been a don; he knew more about the Middle East in the tenth century than in the twentieth, but he had a genius for appropriating as his own the good work of his subordinates.

Perhaps, Stephen thought, it was the analysis he had done on Friday. He had wondered at the time if the pro-Arab bias was a little too pronounced.

"Well—at least you're here now." Ingham ground the stem of the pipe between long yellow teeth. "If you hurry, you'll just have time to get there."

"Where, sir?"

"Twenty-six Albany Court, St. John's Wood Terrace. Three o'clock sharp. Off you go."

Ingham picked up a file, opened it, and frowned at its contents. There was a sudden flurry of rain against the window. Ingham's office smelled faintly of peppermints and wet dogs.

"What happens then? Will someone meet me there?"

Ingham laid down the file with a theatrical sigh. This was a mistake because it enabled Stephen to catch a glimpse of the contents—the quarterly petty cash accounts.

"Just do as you're told, Kendall, there's a good fellow. I'm not authorized to tell you anymore."

"Right, sir. I'll be off then."

Stephen had one more glimpse of the pink bald patch on the top of Ingham's head. He closed the door softly, crossed the outer office, and picked up his hat and coat.

"I have to go out." He gave Edith a rueful smile, inviting her to join him in a conspiracy against Ingham's irrationality. "Not sure when I'll be back."

She smiled back at him—a twist of painted skin on a powdered face. As Stephen clattered down the stairs, Edith's smile and Ingham's bald patch lingered in his mind. His anger focused on them. They symbolized mediocrity, incompetence, and vulgarity.

One day, he promised himself, he would be in a position to sack people like that—or even to destroy them.

Albany Court was an Edwardian block of purpose-built flats. Stephen gave his name to a porter, who telephoned upstairs. Apparently he was expected, for the porter then waved him to the lift.

An elderly maid, primly attired in cap and apron, ushered him into the long, narrow hall of the flat and took his hat and coat. Six oil portraits in gilt frames dominated the hall. A succession of nineteenth-century gentlemen—three civilians, two soldiers, and one bishop—looked down on Stephen, as if surprised to see him there.

"This way, sir." The maid opened a door on the left. "Mr. Kendall."

Stephen found himself in a large drawing room with a big, south-facing bay window. It was cluttered with furniture and smelled of leather and tobacco. The atmosphere was as Edwardian as the flats themselves. A small fire burned in the grate.

"Ah! Your guest, I fancy."

A small man got slowly to his feet. His complexion was purple; a walrus mustache drooped from his mouth; he wore a stained silk dressing gown. He hobbled toward Stephen, walking with the aid of a stick.

Stephen held out his hand, but the man appeared not to see it. He paused in the doorway.

"Ring if you want anything. I'll be in the study."

The maid took him firmly by the arm. "It's time for your afternoon rest, my lord."

The door closed behind them. Stephen's eyes darted around the room. He could see no one. He moved hesitantly toward the fireplace.

"Come and sit down, man. I can't see you over there."

The voice was waspish. Stephen, ever sensitive to possible slights, was prepared to bet that its owner intended to throw him off balance.

Once he had negotiated his way past a sofa, a firescreen, and a tallboy, he could see the man who sat in the deep wing armchair by the fire. He wore a blue pin-striped suit that seemed too big for him; Stephen had often noticed how old people seemed to shrink. Thick glasses sat on a prominent nose; as the chin was large, the overall effect was not unlike an elderly Mr. Punch.

"Sit on the sofa. Did they tell you who I am?"

Stephen shook his head. He lowered himself cautiously onto the sofa and discovered that it was stuffed with lumpy horsehair.

"My name's Dansey." The man gave a wheezing laugh that ended in a hacking cough. He took out a cigarette and tapped it on his case. "I suppose it's true to say I once knew your father."

Stephen had been tense already; the name of Dansey seemed to tighten still further every muscle in his body. Lieutenant Colonel Sir Claude Dansey, KCMG, had recently retired from the position of Vice-Chief of SIS. Stephen had never met him, but he knew him well by reputation. His exploits as a spy stretched back over nearly half a century. According to office gossip, his ruthlessness was as often applied to colleagues as to the enemy; he was reputed to be directly responsible for the demotion of Colonel Vivian, the man who had once been Stephen's chief in Section V. Michael Stanhope-Smith had given Stephen some idea of what it had been like to work for Dansey.

"I can't recall my father mentioning your name." Stephen produced a lighter and leaned across the arm of the sofa. "Did you know him well, sir?"

Dansey sucked hungrily at the flame. "I met him only once; and that was briefly. He didn't know me as Dansey. Stanhope-Smith was there. I believe you know him?"

Stephen nodded. "Very well." He's in Washington at present. But—"

"If he were in this country," Dansey said, "you wouldn't be here."

He fell silent. For a few minutes he sat there smoking and occasionally tapping ash into the fireplace. His silence implied that Stephen was so unimportant that there was no need to make conversation with him unless he, Dansey, chose to do so.

A few years ago the tactic would have embarrassed Stephen. But by now he was too familiar with it to allow it to worry him. SIS was a hierarchical organization. Falling silent was a method of impressing your importance upon those who were—or should feel themselves to be—your subordinates; Stephen had used the same technique on junior officers and the clerical staff.

"Z Organization." Dansey flicked the rest of his cigarette into the fire. "Does that mean something to you?"

"I have heard it mentioned," Stephen said cautiously. "Sometime ago—in the first year or two of the war."

"I've retired now—moved down to the country. Soon after we moved, someone daubed the letter Z on the front door. I hadn't thought about Z for years. It's curious: one starts something and it goes on having effects on other people's lives long after one's forgotten it. And sometimes other people remember that one started it all."

Stephen stared down at his shoes. *Is the old bugger going senile? When's he going to come to the point?*

"The point," Dansey said abruptly, "is this. Just before the war, Stanhope-Smith was working for me. He recruited your father to make one trip to Prague as a courier. For some reason, your father decided to take his son Hugh—your brother, I assume. The job went wrong, and your brother was left in Prague."

This time Dansey's silence was expectant. Stephen's mouth was dry: he would have given a lot to have a glass of water in his hand. The interview had suddenly become unpredictable: he had no idea of what the consequences of his actions might be; Stephen hated to be in that position.

"It was a long time ago, Sir Claude—over six years." Once he had started talking, Stephen found it difficult to stop; somehow it was safer than listening. "Of course I was very badly hit at the time— we all were. I was very fond of Hugh. But these things happen in war."

"How much do you know about what happened to him?"

"Stanhope-Smith and my father told me everything. I gather we had some hope of getting him out until the Venlo Incident destroyed the Z Organization. All the usual checks were made— through the Red Cross and so on. My mother never really gave up hope. I'm afraid we have to accept—"

Dansey held up his hand. "A report's come through from our people in Hanover. It came to me because of the Z ramifications. But I've no intention of wasting my time on something like this. I've retired. In the normal course of things, I'd pass it on to Stanhope-Smith. I've had a word with C: he'll delegate the job to someone else. But in any case, you'll be needed to make the identification. In the circumstances, it seemed better to let you know personally rather than go through the usual channels."

"You've found Hugh?" Stephen said hoarsely. "Is he dead or alive?"

Dansey chuckled. "Dear me. How remiss of me. He's alive—if it *is* Hugh, of course."

He chuckled again. Stephen was not an imaginative man, but for an instant it seemed to him that malice was flooding into the room like poison gas. Outside, the short November afternoon was coming to an end: twilight crept stealthily into the room. The dull red glow of the fire illuminated nothing but itself.

"Where did he spend the war?" Stephen had regained control of his voice. He lit a cigarette to prove that he could do so with a steady hand. "And why is SIS involved?"

"I'm not sure that I should answer that." Dansey had another fit of coughing. When it was over, he blew his nose vigorously. "By the way, don't tell your father until you're sure it is Hugh. One wouldn't want to raise his hopes prematurely. I'm sure it will be a most touching scene when he welcomes home the prodigal son."

The case officer was called Giles Burham. He was so tall that when he squeezed into the back of the Austin his knees nearly touched his chin. He treated Stephen Kendall as if he was one of the walking wounded. Had it been possible, Stephen thought, Burnham would have spent the entire journey trying to make him drink cups of strong, sweet tea.

They drove through the night on nearly empty roads. The weather was foul: it alternated between fog patches and rain squalls. Their driver kept up a constant stream of muttered invective.

Burnham talked a lot. He talked quickly and nervously, treating each word as a bomb that was liable to explode; it was therefore best to get on to the next one as soon as possible. After the first three minutes Stephen realized that there was a very simple reason for this: Burnham felt guilty.

"You know how it is, old chap," he murmured as they drove through Romford on the Chelmsford Road, "there're regulations for every blessed contingency. Priorities and so forth."

"I understand," Stephen said as sadly as he could. "No doubt it's all for the best."

"It's a difficult case, you see. It's not just the fact that every Tom, Dick, and Harry is trying to get into England at present. The question of identity is the least of our problems."

"So I gather from Sir Claude."

"Ah." Burnham sounded relieved. "He explained that side of things to you, did he? Personally, I think it's all ancient history, but Registry likes to bring their files up to date, so to speak. If your brother's story's true—I mean, if it is your brother, of course it'll be true, at least as far as he knows it; it's so often a matter of the correct interpretation, don't you think; and that's where we come in, of course. Where was I?"

"The fact that Hugh might have useful intelligence for us. Which aspects do you think will be the most important?"

"Well—the business about Heydrich was what excited our people in Germany. But I've got a hunch that the Communist angle may be more important in the long run. The Soviets must be working with the local people, and it would be useful to have some detail on them. I don't have to tell *you* that, of course. And there's a very curious link with A-54—did Dansey mention that?"

"Only in passing." Stephen took a chance: "A-54 was before my time."

"I only learned about it recently myself. I'm told that Dansey and Menzies were very discreet about it at the time. Had to be, I suppose. I say, I've brought a flask: care for a drink?"

The whisky was a welcome and warming diversion. But nothing could keep Burnham silent for long.

"I imagine the worst thing about all this—from your point of view, I mean—is the matter of loyalty. Of course one could hardly blame a kid like that, left alone in a strange city."

"No, of course not," Stephen said. The glow of the whisky vanished: he was suddenly very cold and very alert. "Still," he added noncommittally, "it's very difficult for all of us—you, as well."

Burnham sighed. "Evaluation," he confided, "—that's the one thing I hate about my job. It's so subjective, particularly where people are concerned. You have to state your opinion in black and white: it's down there forever on the file. And there's always someone to say you're wrong, or that perhaps your interpretation of the evidence is open to debate—bloody civil servants, all of them. It would have been all right if that colonel was just the normal Vehrmacht career soldier. But this chap seems to have been a Party member and a pal of Heydrich's to boot. I gather that he personally shot several partisans; I know they were Communists, but it still looks bad."

For the last twelve hours Stephen had been angry—with Dansey, with fate, and with Giles Burnham in turn. Now his anger found another, more enduring target—the brother who had come back to haunt him.

The airfield was a few miles south of Ipswich. At first glance it still seemed to be on a wartime footing. The planes still went to

Germany. The only difference was that they carried men and supplies instead of bombs.

The guardroom had been told to expect them: the sentries hardly glanced at Burnham's pass before waving them through. The lamps that lined their route made globes of light in the darkness; needles of rain fell endlessly through the globes. Burnham drained the flask and stopped talking for the first time in two and a half hours. They drove to a block of offices in the lee of the control tower.

The station commander—a dour Scottish group captain whose red handlebar mustache added an improbable touch of frivolity to his appearance—was waiting under an umbrella as the car drew up; he showed them into his own office. He made it quite clear, without using any words, that he considered this visit to be an imposition, and that any courtesy he showed them was due entirely to orders from above.

By this time it was half past three. The transport was due at four. Burnham spent the interval apologizing to the group captain and to Stephen; he also repeated the arrangements for the arrival so often that Stephen wanted to scream at him.

The transport was on schedule. Burnham met Hugh and took him and the two military policemen who were accompanying him to a briefing room next door to the group captain's office. Access to the briefing room was by a door from the corridor but there was also a door from the group captain's office; at one time the room had housed the station commander's secretary.

The second door was left ajar: Stephen was posted in the office, and the light was switched off. Burnham wanted Stephen to see and hear Hugh without being observed himself; there was no question of allowing the brothers to meet at this stage. *Sorry about that, old man. Regulations, you know.*

As the light went on in the briefing room, Stephen took an involuntary step backward. A bar of light shot across the carpet of the group captain's office and crawled up the side of his desk. Stephen was suddenly terrified of what he might see in the next room.

He heard chairs scraping on bare boards.

"Sit down," Burnham said. "The first thing to do is get the paperwork out of the way. Perhaps the sergeant over there can find us some tea while we're doing it. Your name?"

"Kendall. Hugh Henry Kendall."

Stephen shivered. The voice was firm, pleasant, and completely strange to him. Yet he would have known it anywhere. It had the nagging and indefinable familiarity of something heard or seen in a dream. He edged closer to the door.

"Date of birth?"

"June the twenty-second, nineteen twenty-six."

He could see part of the briefing room now—the armed redcap standing by the door and staring at the ceiling, and Burnham's long, stooping back. Only the desk light was on. Stephen craned his head six inches to the left.

"I don't suppose you know your passport number?"

"No. I never had one. I—I traveled to Czechoslovakia on my *vater's*—father's passport."

The young man in the chair had very blue eyes: that was the first thing you noticed about him. The hair was the sort of light brown that had once been fair; the chin was firm; the nose was slim and straight; and there were hollows beneath the cheekbones. He wore British Army battledress without any insignia.

There was a knock on the door and the redcap sergeant came in with a tray. He put it on the desk and handed around the cups of tea. It was an oddly domestic scene; and Stephen felt excluded from it. The man in the chair glanced up at the sergeant and thanked him with a nod and the hint of a smile.

Stephen's last doubts vanished. He had a sudden and desolate vision of the future—of what this man could do to his career with SIS. The man in the chair had their mother's face.

Alfred Kendall was pleased and relieved to find that there was a car waiting for him at the station. He had spent much of the journey from Liverpool Street worrying about the cost of getting a taxi from Ipswich. It wasn't as if he was made of money.

The drive to Albenham Park took no more than twenty minutes. The driver discouraged Kendall's attempts at conversation by the simple expedient of refusing to reply to anything he said.

The park was a couple of miles outside the market town of the same name. There was a checkpoint at the huge iron gates; the lodge cottage had been turned into a guardhouse. The park wall, already seven feet high, had been further fortified with barbed wire. A hundred yards inside it was another line of defense—a ten-foot fence of chain mesh and more barbed wire with its own checkpoint where it crossed the drive.

The house was still invisible, concealed in the folds of its demesne. The park was dotted with Nissen huts and scarred with mud tracks and concrete roads. There was still some snow on the ground. This first winter of the peace, Kendall thought, seemed grimmer than any they had known in the war.

The drive passed through a belt of leafless oaks and suddenly emerged in front of the big house. The graveled forecourt was crowded with cars and lorries. Kendall's chauffeur braked with unnecessary sharpness and pulled up beside a ten-ton truck.

At first sight the building was imposing—a Palladian mansion with a portico in front of the main block, flanked by symmetrical wings. Then you noticed the mud on the flight of steps leading up to the front door, the cracks in the stucco, the missing slates, and the peeling paint.

The driver nodded toward a small door to the left of the flight of steps; the effort of speech was still too much for him. Kendall rang the bell, but there was no answer; he pushed open the door and found himself in a stone-flagged hall. Immediately in front of him was a side table on which stood a hand-painted sign and a decaying spider plant. The sign said RECEPTION.

Further down the hall was a larger table with a corporal sitting behind it. He was a young man with fair, curly hair; he was also grotesquely fat. He was reading a thriller by James Hadley Chase. He put down the book as Kendall came in and stared incuriously at him.

"And who are you when you're at home?"

"My name's Kendall. *Captain* Kendall. I have an appointment with Mr. Burnham."

"Bully for you, old cock." The corporal picked up a telephone, dialed a number, and waited. A few seconds later he said, "Geezer for Burnham. Name of Kendall." There was a pause. "And sod you, too, mate." He put down the phone and picked up his book.

"Well, Corporal?" said Kendall in his most military manner.

The soldier didn't look up from his book. "Someone's coming. Don't fret."

Kendall spent the next five minutes pacing up and down the hall, inwardly rehearsing the reprimand which the corporal so richly deserved. The whole situation was making him uneasy—the house, which should have been in private hands, was deteriorating in the service of the state; the corporal, who should have been respectful to an officer, was treating him as if their ranks were reversed. Everything was topsy-turvy. This war had ruined everything.

The return of Hugh was likely to ruin the peace. Where was the boy to live? What was he going to do? Aunt Vida would probably peg out at any moment; and now there was another potential heir for the estate. It was so unfair.

He looked up as a tall, thin civilian clattered down the stairs at the end of the hall. As the man wore an overcoat, gloves, and a hat, Kendall assumed that he was going out and therefore could not be coming to fetch him. But the new arrival shambled over to him with his hand outstretched; at the last moment he remembered to remove his right-hand glove.

"Captain Kendall? Sorry to keep you waiting. My name's Burnham. I hope Blaines has been looking after you, eh, Corporal?

Corporal Blaines didn't bother to reply; he turned over another page and licked his lips.

Burnham was not disconcerted. Replacing his glove, he took Kendall's arm and led him toward the stairs.

"Bit of a rough diamond, our Blaines," he confided in a whisper that must have been audible at the end of the hall, "but the salt of the earth, believe you me."

He escorted Kendall to an office on the second floor. It had once been part of a much larger room. A paraffin heater stood in one corner, adding little but the smell of oil to the atmosphere.

"If I were you, old chap," Burnham said, "I'd keep your coat on. It's bloody freezing in this place. Only the kitchens are warm. Take a pew. Cup of tea?"

Without waiting for an answer, he opened the door and bellowed! "Tea!" into the corridor.

"I hate January." He sat down behind a large government-issue desk which was covered with files and dirty crockery. "One's had all the fun of Christmas, and there's nothing to look forward to except February. It's so depressing."

"I suppose," Kendall said abruptly, "that there's no doubt about this. It *is* Hugh?"

"Cigarette?" Burnham leaned over the desk with an open packet; for the first time Kendall realized how long his arms were. "No doubt at all, old man. You mustn't worry about that. Your son— Stephen, I mean—made the identification without any hesitation. And we were able to confirm it—we pulled in a chap who was in the same form at that prep school of his. Plain sailing."

Kendall gnawed his lower lip. "But where on earth has he been all this time?"

Burnham lit their cigarettes. "He spent over a year with three of your Prague contacts." He attacked the files in front of him like a dog scratching a pile of loose earth. "Ah. Here we are: Dr. Spiegel, Madame Hase, and Jan Masin." As he said this last name, Burnham blushed. "But from the summer of nineteen-forty until the end of the war, he worked as a gardener's boy on the staff of a German colonel. All quite simple really. Ah—the tea."

A dark girl in VRAC uniform brought in two chipped cups without saucers. Burnham waited until the door had closed behind her.

"I'm afraid everything's a bit primitive. Hope you don't mind sugar in your tea: two spoonfuls are standard issue, as it were. I normally add my own flavoring. Care for a spot?"

Burnham produced a bottle of Scotch from a drawer; he uncorked it and poured a dollop into both cups.

Kendall grinned at his host. He had resigned himself to the fact that there seemed very little chance of a drink.

"Keeps out the cold, eh?" he said. "I always say it's the best form of central heating on the market. You were saying about the boy?"

Burnham laughed. "He's hardly a boy any more. How old was he when you last saw him? Twelve?"

"Good God." For the first time, Kendall thought about the person he was going to meet. It was a shock to realize that it wouldn't be a small fair boy with a sulky mouth and scarred knees. "I suppose he's eighteen or nineteen by now. The same age as Stephen in nineteen thirty-nine."

"Didn't Stephen tell you?" Burnham said gently.

Kendall shook his head. "We don't see much of each other these days. He dropped me a line saying Hugh had turned up and that you people would be getting in touch in due course. I heard nothing more until your letter arrived last week. Stephen's a busy chap, of course—very busy."

Burnham seemed entirely absorbed in stirring his tea. "Of course. I suppose I'd better fill you in on the rest of it. At the end of the war, Hugh managed to get through to the Americans in Western Bohemia. He had no papers and that caused a few problems—they put him in a camp for displaced persons in Austria. Takes a lot of time to deal with these wretched DPs—quite apart from the sheer numbers, half of them are liars. So it wasn't until September that he was transferred to our jurisdiction." Burnham shifted awkwardly on his seat. "Then his story had to be checked and double-checked, both here and in Germany. A drop more?"

"Thanks." Kendall held out his empty cup. His mind was mainly on the golden liquid that flowed so invitingly into his cup; there wasn't much room for Hugh's life history.

"Anyway, we got him back here in November: now's he's been debriefed and he can get back home. But there is one thing—"

"Cheers!" Kendall said.

"Cheers. What was I saying?"

"About going home."

"Ah, yes. Look here, old man, this is a bit awkward. But you've worked with us and signed the Act, so you know what official secrets are all about, eh?"

"Of course." Kendall straightened his spine and closed his mouth. Memories of Prague rushed back into his mind: the diamonds, Madame Hase, who was so nearly a countess, the Michalov Palace, and himself so skillfully persuading those damned Bolsheviks that he was the head of the Central European Section of SIS. It must all be on his file, he thought: young Burnham must know the sort of man he was dealing with.

Burnham ran his fingers through his thinning hair. "The point is, Hugh's told us quite a lot which is still sub rosa, as it were: we're still investigating. So he's signed the Act as well. We don't want Hugh talking about all this—even to someone like yourself."

"Of course." Kendall drained his cup. By God it felt good to be back in this world again: it was as if he had come home. "I quite understand, my dear fellow. You can rely on my discretion."

"Good, good." Burnham glanced at his watch. "I expect you're longing to go home."

"Well—" Kendall could not prevent his eyes from straying toward the whisky bottle.

"I'll take you down to your car. Hugh should be waiting for us."

Kendall staggered a little as he stood up; he hoped he had concealed it from his host. Burnham took him along the corridor and down the stairs, chatting as they went about the iniquities of the meat ration.

"You'd think it was us who'd lost the war," Kendall said.

"Exactly. That's what my wife tells our butcher. Oh, by the way—" Burnham stopped, with one hand on the balustrade and the other on Kendall's arm. "There's one thing I should mention."

Kendall looked up at him expectantly. He had felt too overawed to introduce the subject of compensation—though God knew he deserved it—but had been unable to suppress the hope that Burnham would do so.

"Hugh's English is a bit rusty—don't let it upset you, will you? After all, he's been speaking German and Czech for nearly seven years, so it was bound to happen. He'll soon be back to normal."

Captain Kendall snorted. "You make it sound like he's getting over measles." Disappointment made him bold. "Look here, is there any possibility of some form of compensation from HMG? I mean—"

"I'm sorry," Burnham said over his shoulder; he was already three steps ahead of Kendall. "There's no question of that. I'm afraid we're fully stretched. And of course it's not our responsibility: it came under the jurisdiction of Z Organization. But Z doesn't exist. I wish I could help, but we're hamstrung by the regulations."

They finished the stairs in silence. There was a group of men by the reception desk: they were listening respectfully to Corporal Blaines, who was telling them a joke. As Kendall reached the hall, a burst of laughter rolled toward him. For an instant he was convinced that it was aimed at him.

A broad-shouldered young man in a brown demob suit broke away from the group. Captain Kendall changed course to avoid bumping into him, but the young man changed course as well. Burnham had stopped: he was frowning and hopping from one foot to the other like a huge, ungainly bird.

The young man kept his hands in his pocket. "Hello, Father," he said.

The man's back arched; he clenched her as if he wanted to squeeze her to death; he gave a moan that would have turned into a cry if she hadn't held her hand over his mouth; and then he crumpled on top of her.

Meg wriggled from under him. His head rolled sideways onto the pillow. For a moment he lay still: the eyes were closed; the freckled face beneath the startling red hair was peaceful; he might have been a child.

The eyelids flicked open: the face became alive, knowing, and adult.

"How did I do, ma'am?"

She made herself smile. "I've known worse." *Not many, but a few*. "Come on, Gary, we've got to get up."

He stretched luxuriously. "I wish we could stay here forever."

For an eternity of twenty-second quickies? No thanks.

Aloud, she said, "I bet you do." She glanced at the clock on the bedside table. "It's time you were off to Grosvenor Square. You know what Mr. Cunningham's like if you're late."

He leapt out of bed and began to dress. As she watched him, disappointment gave way to desire. The packaging was good, she thought—the green eyes which were always laughing; the Irish-American voice which was adept at suggesting more than it said; the figure with that trim waist and tight little behind. But the contents were awful.

Sometimes she wondered if her expectations were too high because of Michael: no one since had quite matched his standard. It was stupid to start on the servants: she knew that.

She looked at the clock again: in an hour's time she could legitimately have a drink. Even Wilbur could hardly object, though it was true that Wilbur could usually find an objection to anything if he wanted. That was what Harvard Law School could do to a man.

Meg swung her feet out of bed and felt for her slippers. She pulled on the shantung silk dressing gown that Michael had given her and wondered what she was going to wear tonight. It was just another boring diplomatic cocktail party; the only unusual feature was that she and Wilbur were giving it. Wilbur gave one carefully budgeted party per quarter.

Gary knotted his tie and admired himself in the mirror. "How do I look?"

"All right." She bit back her annoyance: Gary was always asking for her approval. The affair—if you could call it that—would have to stop: it was all risk and no pleasure.

"What about tomorrow?" he said. "I could probably get away in the afternoon."

"Not tomorrow—I've got some shopping to do. I'll let you know."

Usually he tried to kiss her good-bye, but she avoided this by going into the bathroom. Gary was afraid of following her into the bathroom: what she did there must seem unnatural to him. She heard the click of the door as he left. She sat on the lavatory and bit her lip to stop herself crying. The Macy's dress would do for tonight, she decided—the blue one which Wilbur's sister had sent her from New York; Wilbur thought it showed too much of her figure.

The telephone was ringing when she came downstairs. She answered it herself—the maid was busy helping cook in the kitchen. Through the half-open door of the drawing room she could see that the drinks had already been laid out.

"Meg—is that you?"

"Daddy?" She was unable to keep the surprise from her voice. Wilbur didn't encourage her father to make unsolicited telephone calls or visits.

"Hello. Meg?"

"Yes, Daddy," she said wearily. "It's me."

In recent years her father had become increasingly ill at ease with the telephone. When he rang up he never said his name: he knew who he was, and he assumed that the person he was telephoning would know as well. His voice was faint, as if he was holding the handset some distance away from him. He repeated himself on the phone even more than he did in face-to-face conversations.

"I've got some news," her father said. "Some news."

"What is it?" She knew he was drunk without being entirely sure how she knew.

"He's come back. He's here. Hugh."

"Daddy, what on earth are you talking about?"

"Hugh's back," he snapped. "Aren't you listening? Just turned up out of the blue. Out of nowhere. Stephen told me just after Christmas. Didn't he tell you?"

Damn Stephen.

"No—we haven't seen him for months. But where is he—Hugh, I mean?"

"Here, of course. I had to go and fetch him today. They paid my train fare, but that's all. No consideration. Had to take time off work. Just my train fare—can you believe it?"

"Where are you?"

"Here. At the flat." Kendall raised his voice. "Where the hell did you think I was?"

Meg took a deep breath and counted to ten. It never did any good to lose one's temper with her father. Was Hugh really back? Her father had never gone completely off his head, but there had to be a first time. But if Hugh was back he could hardly stay at the flat—which was in fact a bed-sitting-room in Swiss Cottage.

Oh, God—please let it be true—

"Meg? Are you there?"

"Daddy—bring him here. Get a taxi; I'll pay. He can stay with us."

"All right." Her father gave no sign that this was what he had been wanting all along; he made it sound as if he was granting her a favor. "If you insist."

He rang off without warning. Meg replaced the handset and wandered into the drawing room. She poured herself a stiff pink gin and swallowed it with two gulps. She shuddered with relief as the alcohol burned its way down. Her conscience reminded her that she should be making sure everything was ready. But Jane took care of that, just as the cook took care of the food and the men from Harrods had taken care of the decoration. There was nothing left for her to do; the pretense of supervision was merely a substitute for activity.

The maid came in with dishes of lemons and olives. Meg half-turned, so her glass was concealed by her body.

"Everything all right, ma'am?" The maid looked at her sharply, challenging her to take issue with any of her preparations.

Meg nodded. "Jane, is the bed in the spare room made up?"

"Yes, ma'am." Jane put the dishes down with a clatter.

"You'd better air it—we may have a guest tonight."

"And for dinner?"

Meg shrugged helplessly. "Perhaps."

Jane sniffed and left the room. Meg sidled closer to the gin. Another small one wouldn't hurt. Then she heard Wilbur's key in the front door. She hid her glass behind the Cointreau bottle.

"Hello, dear," she called. "Had a good day?"

She knew that was what wives were supposed to say when their husbands came back from work, but it always sounded false when she said it.

Wilbur left his hat, overcoat, and briefcase in the hall; he examined himself in the mirror and straightened his tie; then he came into the drawing room and pecked her cheek. Irritation flickered over his face: he had smelled the gin. He said nothing: he would wait until later. Wilbur always waited for the right time and the right place.

He glanced at his watch. "Are you sure that's quite the right dress? The Margessons are coming. You've just got time to change."

It still surprised her to hear that precise Bostonian voice coming from those well-shaped, sensual lips. It was another case of misleading packaging.

"Wilbur—there's something I have to tell you."

At least he was a good listener. She told him about her father's call; he asked a few pertinent questions. He had known about Hugh for years.

"It's most inconvenient," he said when she had finished. "Assuming, of course, that it's not your father's idea of a joke." He rang the bell and paced up and down in silence while he waited for it to be answered.

"You rang, ma'am?"

"No, Jane—I did." Cunningham ran his fingers through his hair; it was a characteristic and misleadingly boyish gesture of his. "Captain Kendall and—ah—a young man may call this evening. If they do, don't show them in here. Put them in the small sitting room and let me know they're here."

"Very good, sir."

Jane gave a respectful bob and left. Both she and the cook adored Wilbur: most women did. He was very good-looking in that clean-cut American way; despite his prim manner, he could be charming, especially if you liked old-fashioned gallantry; and of course his father was very, very rich.

Meg took a cigarette from the silver box on the mantelpiece. *If they only knew.*

Wilbur struck a match for her. "He'll have to live with your aunt."

"But—I thought perhaps—"

"He can't stay here. Oh, perhaps for tonight—but no longer. In my position I have to be very careful. I'm sure you appreciate that."

The doorbell rang.

Hugh retained only fragmentary memories of that first evening in London. Everything was strange: and the strangest things were the people he had once known well.

The first surprise was London itself. Prague had sustained very little damage during the war. Hugh was completely unprepared for the reality of this blitzed city. Whole streets had vanished; buildings had become holes in the ground. Everywhere he saw rubble, dust, and dirty snow. It seemed a city of the conquered. He wondered if Leipzig was like this.

He had plenty of time for thinking, for his father made few

conversational demands on him. Alfred Kendall spent most of the train journey from Suffolk behind *The Times*. When they reached the Swiss Cottage bedsitter with its haunting smell of cats and drains, he gave the paper to Hugh. It was true that he did ask a few questions during the taxi drive to the Cunninghams' house in Knightsbridge, but he rapidly lost interest when Hugh stumbled over the answers.

Hugh was no longer afraid of his father. He had half expected that. What really astonished him was the discovery that he no longer hated him, either; in fact, he felt nothing for him except a faint distaste. To his surprise, that created a curious sense of loss.

Burnham had told Hugh about his mother's death; his father made no mention of it. The news had upset him greatly, despite the fact that she was by now only a shadowy figure in his memory. One day, he promised himself, he would ask his sister about her.

He recognized Meg at once. She ran across the hall, pushed aside the tight-lipped maid, and flung her arms around him. Her body was warm, scented, and disturbing; even the fabric of her dress felt sinfully soft. But at least she was glad to see him. He was glad that someone was.

They were still in the hall when the guests began to arrive. Hugh had seen Wilbur Cunningham's face. There was an expression on it that reminded Hugh of someone, but he couldn't place it. He sensed that the tall American was not best pleased to have his relatives by marriage in the house.

All the strangers confused him. There were so many of them, and it was sometimes difficult to understand what they were saying. At Albenham he had seen very few people: suddenly the world had become very crowded.

After a few minutes, Meg had to leave them; apparently the two Kendalls were excused from the ordeal of the party. His father fell asleep. Hugh sat in the little sitting room for two hours, sipping the glass of whisky that Meg had given him and luxuriating in the comfort of the armchair and the glow of the fire. The demob suit was ill-fitting and uncomfortable; he was an embarrassment to his father and his host, but at least he was no longer a Displaced Person.

He went to bed early, after what Meg called—with a curious little laugh—"a quiet family dinner." He was in the outside world again, after eight months in institutions of one sort or another; life outside was tiring.

Sleep came quickly. When he woke up, it was still dark. His mouth was parched, probably because of the unaccustomed alcohol before and with dinner. He had a burning desire to urinate.

There was a lamp on the bedside table. He switched it on, reveling in the luxury despite his bursting bladder. Deciding to do without slippers and dressing gown—they belonged to his brother-in-law and were far too large for him—he opened the door as quietly as possible and padded onto the landing.

It was lit by a low-wattage bulb, which was left on all night. The bathroom was at the end of a side landing. He had just rounded the corner when he heard a noise. He glanced over his shoulder. The knob on Wilbur's door was slowly rotating.

There was no reason why he should have pressed himself against the wall: going to the lavatory wasn't forbidden, as it had been during certain hours of the night in the Austrian DP camp. The bulb was on the main part of the landing, so he was in shadow.

The door opened, and Hugh realized that he was being stupid. Cunningham would come to the bathroom and find him lurking in the passage. It would be ridiculously embarrassing for both of them. He was about to cough, in order to signal his presence, when he realized that the man in the doorway was not Wilbur Cunningham after all.

This man was much smaller. He had flaming red hair. As Hugh watched, he turned, raised a cupped hand, and blew a silent kiss back into the room.

At that moment, Hugh remembered where he had previously seen that look on Cunningham's face. It was strange to think that a communist pork butcher of Prague and a wealthy American diplomat in London had something in common.

But where did Meg fit in?

Meg and Hugh went down to Richmond together. They didn't talk much on the journey. Meg had insisted on giving him a five-pound note. "Call it a loan if you must, but just take it, will you?" He carried a battered cardboard suitcase which they had given him at Albenham. It was heavier than it was when he arrived in London: Meg had gone through his few clothes and added some of Wilbur's shirts and underwear.

Hugh decided not to mention what he had seen last night. The redheaded man had slipped upstairs toward the servants' quarters in the attics. Hugh felt it would be wiser to keep his mouth shut until he knew his sister rather better. Years ago, Meg had told him what she wanted from a man—riches, a title, and romantic visits to night-clubs. Cunningham was certainly wealthy: perhaps Meg had decided to compromise. Who was he to judge?

As they walked through Richmond from the station, Hugh was surprised to find that his excitement was growing. He swung the suitcase vigorously; he smiled at passersby, most of whom ignored him. The sun decided to come out, for the first time in days. Even the heavens were on his side.

Meg sensed the change of mood. "Why have you cheered up?"

He shrugged. "I don't know. I suppose I'm beginning to feel I'm coming home."

They turned into Maid of Honor Row.

"You always liked that house, didn't you?" Meg said. "I hated it, especially after Mother died. Alone with two old women. Aunt Vida's very changed, you know. Don't expect too much."

The house was just as he remembered it; perhaps it had shrunk a little, but that was all. The brass mermaid still twinkled on the olive-green front door.

Mrs. Bunnings answered the door. She, too, was unchanged apart from a little natural shrinkage.

"Humph," she said. "Miss Meg and Mr. Hugh. You'd better come in."

Her face crumpled; the stately façade shattered. She flung her arms around Hugh and burst into tears.

Above their heads, a handbell began to ring.

"Oh, God," Meg said. "Aunt Vida's feeling left out."

As far as he could remember, Hugh had never been in Aunt Vida's bedroom before. She was sitting up in bed. His first thought was that she had changed much more than Mrs. Bunnings or the house. She had lost her plumpness; and the gray eyes were vague.

"Come here," she said as Hugh came in. "This side of the bed—the light's better."

He went closer: she waved him nearer still until their faces were no more than a foot apart.

"Harry, darling," she said. "I *knew* you'd come home. Bunnings, you're a silly old woman. I told you Mr. Harry would come back."

"It's Mr. Hugh, ma'am. From Prague."

He bent down and kissed her. She smelled the same—of lavender water and age. Her wrinkles were caked with talcum powder. She raised her hand and touched his cheek.

"It doesn't matter, does it?" she said slowly. "The main thing is that you've come home. Did you ever spend that half-crown?"

Twelve

In the summer, Wilbur Cunningham went back to America for a month.

In Washington he telephoned the British Embassy and asked for Michael Stanhope-Smith. Later that week, the two men met in a motel in Virginia. Dinner that evening was something of a celebration.

"We've cracked it, Mike," Cunningham said. "Truman's seen sense at last."

"It's official?"

"I spent the last two days with General Vandenberg; and I saw the President yesterday afternoon. The Central Intelligence Group is to get the Strategic Services Unit from the War Department. It's not like it was in the old days, but at least we'll have a skeleton organization for espionage and secret intelligence."

"Are they increasing the establishment, too?"

Cunningham shrugged. "A little. That's not important right now: it's the principle of the thing. Truman was terrified of creating another Gestapo—okay, you can accept that; at least the guy's sincere. Now he's finally coming to understand that an intelligence organization doesn't have to go around in jackboots."

"What else?"

"CIG will also get control of the Office of Operations; and it's got the Foreign Broadcast Information Service, as you know."

"There are weaknesses," Michael said. "You're long on military expertise, with all the ex-OSS people, but you're very short on analysts. And what about covert operations?"

"As of now, we've no authority for that." Cunningham smiled.

"But it'll come. Hey—guess who's going to be the new Deputy Head of Station in London?"

"Congratulations." Michael raised his glass. "Is it official yet? When do you start?"

"It'll be official next week, but it takes effect in September. I asked for it to be deferred. While I'm back home, there's some family business to attend to. It's kind of piled up since the old man had his stroke."

"So you're off to Boston?"

Cunningham nodded. "Via New York. Then down to Texas, across to L.A. and back to Boston again."

Michael lit a cigarette, waving his hand to keep the smoke away from Cunningham. "I'm going back to England on Friday week. A month's leave. And long overdue."

"Is that so?" Cunningham smiled. "You must look in on Meg. I know she'll be glad to see you. Maybe you could take her to a show or something. She must be getting pretty bored."

"I'd love to," Michael murmured. He noticed that his fingers had tightened involuntarily; there was a dent in his cigarette. Across the table, Cunningham was staring at him. Michael quickly stubbed out the cigarette.

"Filthy habit," Cunningham said lazily. "Tell me—what's in this for you?"

Meg? What does he know?

Michael had introduced Meg to Wilbur Cunningham in 1943; at the time Meg and Michael were invited everywhere as a couple, though Meg was getting restless with the arrangement. Michael had proposed to her more than once, but she had always turned him down. The trouble was, as she told Michael with that astonishing frankness she was sometimes capable of, if she married him she could never be sure that he hadn't spent next month's housekeeping on last month's burgundy. He was both poor and extravagant. Her parents had been poor: she needed the security of money. In August 1944, Meg became engaged to Cunningham.

Wilbur knew that she had had an affair with Michael, but it didn't seem to disturb him unduly. Indeed, he asked Michael to be best man at the wedding. Michael accepted. But the wedding was postponed until after VE Day: by that time Michael was in Washington so he was unable to fulfill his promise, much to his relief.

Meg, darling—do you ever think of me?

"I'm sorry." Michael lit another cigarette. "I don't quite follow you."

For an instant he could have sworn that there was wry amusement in the American's hazel eyes. He felt a stab of envy, irrelevant but painful, for the man's good looks.

"I mean—you've been very helpful. Oh, I could understand it during the war, when we were trying to get OSS off the ground and SIS was a sort of father figure. But why now? You've been lobbying in Washington and in London. Doing my job for me. Friendship's a beautiful emotion, I know, but that can't be the only reason."

Michael grinned—with relief. "I'm under orders. Menzies and Dansey decided in 'forty-four that we'd need a permanent American intelligence agency after the war. And they were right."

"But the bigger we get—in Europe and the rest of the world—the smaller you'll get."

"We'll shrink anyway. It's better that we ask you to fill the vacuum than let the Ivans take it for themselves. None of our politicians would admit it openly, but we can't afford to take care of ourselves anymore. It's an economic decision really—you know that."

The same figures were in the minds of both men. In order to finance the war, Britain had sold over £1,100 million of her overseas investments and run up over £3,000 million in sterling debts. In American terms that was over 16 billion dollars. Even now, the British economy could only stagger along with the help of another U.S. loan of £1,000 million.

Michael realized—wearily, but without animosity—that Wilbur had known the answer to his question all along; he had wanted to discover merely whether or not Michael was prepared to admit the truth. Someone in the State Department wanted to know if the British lion understood how blunt its claws had become.

The oblique approach suddenly disgusted Michael. It was so typical of the world he lived and worked in. One day, he promised himself, he would escape. The way things were shaping, it was quite possible that they would get rid of him. SIS was changing, for all that C was an old Etonian and the service's reputation was at present second to none. The future lay with people like—

"Have you heard the news about Meg's brother?" Cunningham said.

"Stephen? What's he been up up to?"

Michael was prepared to bet that Stephen would be head of the Middle Eastern section in a few year's time. His single-minded ambition was considered slightly vulgar by colleagues of a prewar vintage. But it would be foolish to underrate him.

"Not Stephen." Cunningham picked up a toothpick and jabbed it into the tablecloth. "The other brother—Hugh. Hey—you've upset your wine."

"Sorry." Michael covered the stain with his napkin. "It came as rather a surprise. It's—it's like meeting a ghost."

"I didn't realize you'd known him."

Cunningham was looking keenly at him, and Michael automatically tried to conceal his shock as efficiently as he had concealed the wine stain.

"Oh, I never knew him," he said casually. "But he's had quite an effect on my life—on yours as well, if you come to that."

The American frowned. "What do you mean?"

"I quarreled with Dansey because Hugh Kendall was left in Prague. Because of that, I transferred to SIS before the war, and eventually got my present job."

Michael threw back his head and laughed as more and more ramifications occurred to him. Hugh Kendall, a boy he had never seen, had changed his life.

"Without Hugh, I doubt if we'd be sitting here now—in all probability you'd've had another SIS liaison. You might have struck someone who was less enthusiastic about a permanent American intelligence service. Stephen wouldn't be working for us. I wouldn't have met Meg. *You* wouldn't have met Meg."

There was a silence. It grew so long that Michael felt uncomfortable. Then Cunningham smiled.

"I guess some people are like that. It's like my old grandpa used to say—the one from Alabama that we weren't allowed to visit when we were kids. Some people and some things are like Benjamin Franklin's nail." His voice lost its usual urbanity and acquired a Southern drawl. " 'You all know 'bout that nail? *For want of a nail, the shoe was lost: for want of a shoe, the horse was lost: and for want of a horse the rider was lost.*' "

Aunt Vida died slowly. The habits that had gripped her mind for a lifetime gradually relaxed their grip. She knew that life was slipping away from her, and the knowledge was painful.

Sometimes she lay there swearing; after a while they got used to that. It puzzled them how and when she learned the words. Her voice changed, too: often it was girlish; the vowels and vocabulary belonged to the rural Gloucestershire where she had grown up, midway through the last century. As she lay there dying, she relived fragments of her life. Death left her no privacy.

The swearing worried Mrs. Bunnings far more than Hugh and Meg. Meg hated the physical tastelessness of dying—the sickroom smells and utensils, the decaying body, and Aunt Vida's inability to control her natural functions. But the gin helped her to bear it. Even Mrs. Bunnings joined Meg occasionally for a glass. The two women were closer than they had ever been. There was nothing like a death-bed, Mrs. Bunnings observed more than once, for showing you who your real friends were.

Alfred and Stephen Kendall had both been told. Alfred sent a letter which Aunt Vida was too ill to read; Stephen sent flowers; neither of them came. Mrs. Bunnings was grateful for this mercy: Mrs. Lane would not have wanted them to see her in this state.

Aunt Vida had bad dreams. During the last few days they invaded her shadowy waking world. It was this invasion that seemed to Hugh the most humiliating feature of dying. On the day before she died she thought she was in the middle of a sea of mud which was inexorably encroaching on the island of firm ground where she lay.

For hours she lay there, clinging to Hugh's hand.

"It's no man's land, Harry," she repeated, time and time again. "I'm scared, I'm scared."

"Hush now," he would say. "It's all right. You're dreaming."

But it wasn't all right, and it never would be. She believed she was about to drown in mud; and the dream was more real to her than the cries of the children playing on Richmond Green or the people who came and went in her bedroom.

Just before she died, she said: "Hugh—go away." Her voice had something of its old vigor. "You mustn't drown as well."

No, he thought, both then and later, it wasn't all right.

Stephen and Alfred came to the funeral.

Afterward, the family returned to the house. Mr. Turnbull, of Turnbull, Truscott and Turnbull, accepted a small sherry and discussed the terms of the will.

The will confirmed Alfred Kendall's worst suspicions about

human nature in general and Aunt Vida's in particular. It had been drawn up on May 10, 1945—after Muriel Kendall's death but long before anyone knew that Hugh was still alive. Mrs. Bunnings received a thousand pounds. Hugh and Meg were left five hundred pounds each. Stephen was given two hundred and fifty pounds—on condition that he did not invest it but spent it within six months, either on a holiday or on luxuries; receipts for his expenditure were to be shown to Mr. Turnbull.

Aunt Vida also bequeathed to Hugh "that freehold property known as Wilmot House," together with all its contents except her clothes and jewelry; these went to Meg.

The value of the estate was smaller than Alfred Kendall had expected: after the legacies and death duties had been paid, Mr. Turnbull thought there would be about fifteen thousand pounds. The residuary legatee of Aunt Vida's estate was the Star and Garter Home for disabled servicemen.

"Preposterous!" Alfred Kendall commented to Stephen. "The woman must have been off her rocker."

Mr. Turnbull beamed at the Kendalls and Mrs. Bunnings. He turned to Hugh. "I must confess that at the time I advised Mrs. Lane against leaving the house to you. It could have caused a great many problems. Still, all's well that ends well."

On the evening of the day of the funeral Mrs. Bunnings went to stay with her married sister in Bournemouth.

"I'm worn to a frazzle, Mr. Hugh, and that's the truth. I'll be back on Friday week."

Meg invited Hugh back to Knightsbridge, and he accepted gratefully. Aunt Vida's death had hit him far worse than he had expected. The boatyard where he was working as a laborer had given him indefinite leave of absence; the manager had been particularly understanding over the last few weeks because Mr. Turnbull was a major shareholder in the yard.

There was another reason for him to be depressed. Magda Scholl was rarely out of his thoughts. He had sent at least a dozen letters to Leipzig, but he had received nothing in reply. The staff at Twickenham post office had grown used to his weekly visits and made a joke of the fact that there was never anything for him in the poste restante section. No one seemed to know much about what was going on in the Russian-occupied zone of Germany.

Hugh's worst fear was that she might be dead.

It was well over a year since he had seen her. At times he found it hard to recall her face. He wished he had a photograph of her. The ring she had given him was all he had left; he wore it around his neck, because people would ask questions if he wore it on his hand. But he would have preferred a photograph.

Magda was often in his dreams. There was always something wrong. If they were about to make love, they would be prevented at the last minute. In one, frequently recurring dream, he would catch a glimpse of her, hurrying away from him on the opposite pavement of a crowded city street; terrified of losing her, he would chase her through the crowds, but when he reached her she had someone else's face.

Another twist to Hugh's unhappiness was the fact that he felt increasingly guilty of disloyalty. Nowadays he found himself staring at some of the girls he saw in the streets; and he couldn't help fantasizing about them. He loved Magda; but he needed a girl. It was a humiliating thought that almost any girl would do, so long as she was reasonably attractive.

Jane waited on them at dinner, making her disapproval so obvious that even Hugh noticed.

"What's wrong with her?" he asked when she was out of the room.

Meg poured herself another glass of wine. "She heard Wilbur saying that I wasn't to have any of my family here while he was away. Oh, and she doesn't like my drinking, either. The silly cow thinks it's unwomanly. Do you want some more?"

Hugh pushed his glass across the tablecloth, knocking over the salt as he did so. He had had two martinis before dinner. The world no longer seemed quite so dreary as it had a few hours earlier.

"Is it all right me staying here? I could easily go back to Richmond."

"Of course it's all right. Jane will tell Wilbur all about it when he gets back. I think he likes being able to disapprove of me. What the hell does it matter?"

They had coffee in the drawing room. Meg dismissed Jane for the night. "Now we can get down to some serious drinking. Do you like my new dress? A friend of mine bought it for me in Paris."

A little later, Meg suggested dancing. Hugh tried to explain that he didn't know how to dance, apart from a rather inefficient waltz. His sister brushed aside his protests.

"I'll just put slow records on. Come on—it'll be jolly good practice for you."

After the third record and two more brandies, they did little dancing: Meg just wanted to stand with Hugh's arms around her, swaying more or less in time with the beat of the music.

How long since I held a warm body in my arms? Not since Magda's.

"I miss this," Meg mumbled into his shirt front. "Wilbur doesn't like dancing, not with me. He used to do it before we married, but that was only because he thought he ought to. But now there's no need."

Her arms tightened around Hugh's neck; she rubbed her body against his and gave a little sigh of pleasure. A shiver ran through him: he tried to back away, but she wouldn't let him.

"I was awfully innocent," she said softly. "I thought he just wanted to wait until we were married. You know what Wilbur is, don't you?"

So she must know about the redheaded chauffeur. Despite himself, Hugh's arms tightened around her. Pity was a dangerous emotion.

Aloud, he said, "There were people like that in Prague." It was the first time he had mentioned that to anyone apart from Burnham. The SIS man had made him feel defiled by association.

"I'd heard about them. Mary—d'you remember Mary? My friend at school? We used to laugh about it and wonder how on earth they could do it. I never thought I'd ever know one of them. Let alone marry one."

She was crying now: the tears seeped through Hugh's shirt to his skin. The record had come to an end: the needle scratched to and fro. Meg was still swaying in time with the nonexistent music. Hugh felt acutely embarrassed.

"People envy me, you know—he's handsome and his family have got pots of money. At first I thought there was something wrong with me. D'you know why he married me? So people would think he was normal. So he'd have someone to sit at the other end of the table at dinner parties. And most of all because of a trust fund his grandfather set up: he could only inherit if he got married."

Suddenly she slipped away from Hugh, changed the record, and poured them both another drink. He sat down on the sofa. She lit a cigarette and sat down beside him.

All alone, a woman sang, *I'm so all alone—*

"Put your arm around me, Hugh."

He did as she asked; it would have seemed churlish to refuse. She snuggled against him.

"People are so stupid about sex," she said suddenly. "It's just a need, like eating or going to the lavatory. But it's so important. There was a man once, before Wilbur. Michael."

She began to cry again. The cigarette smoldered unheeded in the ashtray. Hugh leaned across her and stubbed it out. Meg caught his hand and pressed it against her breast.

"Do you remember? When we were children? We kept each other warm. *Please, Hugh.*"

He pulled himself away, spilling his drink on her dress, and stood up. He was gasping for breath; the room seemed as hot as a furnace. The image of Magda's naked body filled his mind. His own body was screaming for release. He stumbled toward the door.

"I'm going back home," he said thickly, "to Richmond. You must understand."

Meg stared at him: her face was white; her mouth gaped like a red wound.

Hugh opened the door and rushed into the hall. As he reached the front door he glanced back. Meg was on her knees; half supported by the arm of the sofa. The tears were running down her cheeks.

"Michael," she said softly. "Michael?"

All alone, the woman sang, *I'm so all alone—*

Michael came back to a country which seemed grimmer than it had ever been in the war. The people he met were characterized by a dull despair; Britain was dying as a world power; and the Labour government was intent on hammering the middle classes into extinction.

After Washington, London was unbearably drab. Michael reported to Broadway and was granted the honor of a quarter of an hour alone with C. He rang up Betty, to warn her of his arrival. It never ceased to amaze him that her voice was unchanged.

"Too tiresome," she said when Michael told her that he wouldn't be able to get home until the middle of the afternoon. Derek Ingham was taking him to lunch at the Athenaeum; Ingham had supervised Michael in medieval history at Cambridge, and believed this gave him special privileges. Like everyone else in SIS he wanted to hear the latest gossip from Washington.

It wasn't until half past three that the taxi dropped him in Connaught Street, just north of the park. As he inserted his key in the front door, Michael noticed the peeling paintwork; the dustbins in the area were full to overflowing; a weatherstained piece of cardboard had replaced one of the panes of the window to the right of the door.

The hall smelled of old fried fish. As Michael hung up his coat, something moved in the shadows at the far end.

"Betty?"

"Michael." She came toward him. He strained to see her: the light was poor. She touched his arm in a ghostly caress and backed away before he could kiss her. "Would you like some tea?"

He accepted the offer with a heartiness that sprang from embarrassment. Betty went to make it, brusquely declining his help.

Michael climbed the wide staircase to the sitting room on the first floor. It was a big, well-lit room; he kept the best of his pictures here. Like the hall, it smelled of fried fish. The curtains were half drawn. Dust stirred as he moved slowly across the carpet. The top of his Mother's Queen Anne bureau was dotted with bleached rings from carelessly deposited glasses. The empty fireplace was thick with cigarette ends and spent matches.

He pulled back the curtains and opened the window. He had been lucky with this house. He had got it for a song in 1944, from a cousin who was scared of the flying bombs; it was leasehold, and the lease still had twenty years to run. One day, he promised himself, he would spend some money on renovating it.

"I meant to clean up."

Betty was standing in the doorway. She must have had a kettle already on the boil. As she wore slippers, her footsteps had made no sound on the stairs.

"It doesn't matter," Michael said.

For the first time he saw her in a good light. Her hair was longer than it had been last year—she had grown it so it fell in two black wings on either side of her face. It covered up what was left of the ears and also concealed much of the raw, red skin which had been clumsily grafted on to the cheeks. She was dressed in dark gray—a thick jacket, despite the summer weather, and a skirt. Apart from her face and neck, none of her skin was visible. Even her hands were concealed by black cotton gloves. You could hardly tell that two of the fingers were missing from the right hand. Michael wondered what she used to fill the empty spaces in the gloves—cotton wool, perhaps.

"You look well," he said awkwardly. "Much better than you did."

He crossed the room and took the tray from her.

"You don't have to lie." Betty lit a cigarette and went to stand with her back to the window. "I'll leave the pouring to you."

Michael poured the tea. It was Lapsang; and he wondered how she had managed to get tea from China. Like so much about Betty, it was a mystery to him. After her accident in June 1942 he hadn't seen her for two and a half years. She had spent months in the hospital in Dublin, undergoing plastic surgery which was amateurish by British standards. They had sent her home to Castle Leighlinbridge to convalesce: instead she watched her father die and withdrew still further into herself.

After the Earl's death, she was kept in Ireland by lethargy, the fear of exposing herself to ridicule and the need to dispose of the house and estate. Everything took twice as long in wartime: it wasn't until February 1945 that she returned to London, driven there by the fact that she had nowhere else to go.

Michael had written regularly to her while she was in Ireland; and she had infrequently replied. They had met again almost as strangers. His posting to Washington followed almost immediately, so they had parted without becoming much better acquainted.

But Betty had to live somewhere and Michael had offered her the use of his house in his absence, on the understanding that he might come back whenever he chose. Neither of them had mentioned rent. Michael suspected that she couldn't afford anything; and anyway what did it matter? During his absence, the larger, regular bills were sent to his bank, which paid them on his behalf.

Betty took the tea with her left hand; she used the saucer as an ashtray.

"How long will you be here?" she asked.

"About a month. Technically I'm on leave, but I may have to go into the office once or twice."

Betty still knew nothing about Michael's job; she believed he was attached in some unspecified way to the Foreign Office; she never asked questions about it.

"I bought some food when I heard you were coming," she said listlessly. "Do you want me to go away?"

"Why on earth should I? Michael had been wishing that there was some way to get the house to himself: guilt made him vehement. "This is your home just as much as mine."

"That's nonsense, Michael. I'm living off your charity."

Michael felt himself flushing. "I won't have you saying that."

"It's true." She put down her tea cup and lit another cigarette from the stub of the old. "Are you going to see Meg Cunningham while you're here? You'll want me out of the house if she comes here, won't you?"

How much does she know about Meg and me? Who told her?

"I saw Wilbur in Washington," he said as casually as possible. "He asked me to look in on Meg—perhaps take her to a show. Why don't we all go?" He decided it was better to ignore Betty's last question.

"Don't be stupid. Stephen told me all about you and Meg. He's not interested in *me* now, of course; but he wanted to see what my reaction would be. You have some strange friends. Stephen's like children who pull legs off spiders, just to see what happens."

"I'm sorry." Michael sat down and fumbled for his cigarette case. "At the time you were in Ireland; and I didn't want to hurt you. When you got back to London, the—the affair was over, and you were quite depressed enough as it was. So I said nothing. I suppose that was foolish. I should have known that someone would tell you."

"I knew anyway." Betty turned her head: Michael could see her profile in silhouette; it was still beautiful. "I'd seen it coming for years: I knew what would happen when the two of you went to Laura Duveen's for the weekend."

"It's over, Betty: it was over two years ago, perhaps longer. She's married to Wilbur now. She's just a friend. And he's a friend of mine as well."

"That bloody little bitch isn't capable of friendship." Betty laughed—a bitter, rasping sound that contrasted sharply with the gurgles of laughter he remembered before the war. "Anyway, I imagine Wilbur would be grateful if you started—"

"Stop it, will you?" Michael snapped.

"You do know about Wilbur, don't you?"

Michael got up. "I'm going to unpack. I might have a nap after that."

"Then you should know." Something in Betty's voice held Michael at the door. "My dear man, he's as queer as a coot."

"How do you know?" Michael grabbed her by the shoulders and shook her. He released her abruptly and took a step backward.

224

Betty followed him: for an instant he had the uncomfortable idea that she was a predator and he was her prey.

"Charley told me. Oddly enough it was at Leighlinbridge, just before he died."

It was beginning to make sense. Charles Knockroe had been homosexual, though he had never flaunted the fact. Betty used to say that was the reason why he drank so much.

"Did Charley and Wilbur—?"

"No, they didn't." She was very close to him now; he could feel her breath. She had flung back her head to stare up at him. Her hair fell back, exposing her ruined face.

Michael forced himself not to look away. "Then how did Charley know?"

"Wilbur likes the rough trade, like Charley used to. Charley met him one night, when they were both out on the same errand. Piccadilly Circus, I think; somewhere like that. Playing Peep-Bo in the gents. Shits that pass in the night. Oh, Christ."

Suddenly she was in his arms. He held her, rocking gently to and fro, with his head resting on her black hair. She pressed herself against him. Her breasts were as firm as ever. Desire—importunate, inconvenient, and absurd—stirred within him. He caught himself wondering how much of her body had been touched by the fire; and he hated himself for doing so. He felt selfishly glad that Wilbur was homosexual—that it was possible that Meg's marriage was little more than a social fiction. But the news altered nothing. Meg had made it quite clear that she wanted no more to do with him, except perhaps as a friend. He remembered what she had said during that terrible Christmas of 1944.

If you're very, very good. I'll ask you to be Wilbur Junior's godfather.

Moreover, Michael owed something to Wilbur. The man's sexual preferences were irrelevant beside the fact he was a friend; and you didn't make love to your friends' wives. Wilbur Cunningham was also an extremely influential colleague who was making Michael's job considerably easier than it would otherwise have been. If Wilbur became an enemy, Michael's job could become much harder; indeed, it was possible that he might lose his job altogether. Menzies was a realist where SIS was concerned: loyalty to a middle-ranking subordinate like Michael would be less important to him than the need to retain the good will of Wilbur Cunningham; the risk of a disgruntled ex-employee counted for very little beside the advantages which could accrue from an Anglo-American intelligence alliance.

"Betty," he heard himself saying. "Shall we get married?"

Dinner that night was an emotional, drunken affair, despite the fact that Betty had turned down Michael's proposal. Afterward she fell asleep in the sitting room.

Michael watched her for a quarter of an hour, marveling at her generosity and his stupidity. Now she was asleep, he could study the full horror of what had happened to her. The artist in him—constantly at war with the gentleman—pointed out what a marvelous picture she would make. He would do her in profile and with her eyes open, probably in oils. The result would tear your heart out.

Then the gentleman returned: Michael promised himself that he would always look after her, whatever happened; he felt so full of guilt and pity that he would have promised anything.

After his second glass of brandy he could bear to be here no longer. They had eaten early: it was only nine o'clock. The promise he had made deserved a reward. Common sense and duty could both have the night off. Wilbur himself had provided a cast-iron excuse.

He slipped out of the room and downstairs to the hall. It would be better not to use the phone in the house; there was always the chance that Betty would wake up.

The night was warm; Michael decided not to take an overcoat. He walked down to the Bayswater Road and found a phone box.

A maid answered. Michael gave his name and asked to speak to Mrs. Cunningham. A few seconds later she came to the phone.

"Michael! Where are you?"

"On the Bayswater Road. I'm home for a month on leave. Wilbur suggested I give you a ring. He thought you might like a bit of company."

She laughed. "That's an understatement. Do you want to come around for a drink? Hugh's here," she added quickly. "I'd like you to meet him."

"Hugh?" Michael swore at himself: he should have foreseen this possibility.

"My brother—didn't Wilbur tell you? Do come."

Michael, always sensitive where Meg was concerned, wondered

if he had imagined a note of urgency in her voice. "of course," he said quickly. "I'd love to meet him."

He took a taxi to Knightsbridge. The house was just off Lowndes Square, convenient for Rotten Row in Hyde Park, where Wilbur went riding three mornings a week. The Cunninghams could easily have afforded one of the grander mansions in the area, like those in nearby Belgrave Square. But Wilbur, with typical economy, had chosen a relatively modest terraced house. Michael was prepared to bet that the decision had not been made lightly; Wilbur's never were. No doubt the house was guaranteed to be a better investment than its more imposing neighbors. Wilbur always considered investment value of anything he undertook—even, Michael suspected, his friendships; though perhaps he made an exception of those that began in public lavatories.

The prim little maid smelled discreetly of money. Few people could afford servants like that anymore. She showed him into a large, square drawing room.

Meg was sitting in an armchair by the empty fireplace. She leapt up and kissed him on the cheek. Michael tried to hold on to her, but she wriggled from his grasp. The maid closed the door behind him. Somewhere in the house a telephone was ringing.

"Michael—you must meet my brother Hugh. Hugh, this is Michael Stanhope-Smith."

A young man got up from the window seat. Michael held out his hand. Meg's brother came as a surprise: he bore little resemblance to Meg, Stephen, or their father. His handshake was firm, like his chin; his expression was a curious mixture of wariness and relief.

"I was sorry to hear about your aunt," Michael said to Meg. "Wilbur showed me the cable you sent."

"She always had a soft spot for you. Still, she died happy— Hugh had come back."

"She wasn't happy," the boy said abruptly, "not when she was dying; she was scared."

"Hugh, get Michael a drink, would you?"

"Of course. What would you like, sir?"

Sir? Do I look that old?

"Whisky, please. Do call me Michael, by the way."

Meg put her arm through his. "Tell me what you've been up to. We haven't met for ages. How's Wilbur?"

For the next ten minutes, Michael did most of the talking. He chatted easily about Washington, Wilbur, and the shock of arriving in peacetime London. When he showed signs of faltering, either Hugh or Meg would ask him something. He began to suspect that he was a welcome diversion for both of them.

As he talked, he was covertly observing Meg. She was a little plumper than she had been eighteen months ago. Her clothes and makeup had that veneer of simplicity that only money could buy; thanks to Wilbur, she no longer had to make do and mend. She seemed less vivacious and, if possible, more attractive.

Meg suddenly interrupted him. "How's Betty? I haven't seen her for months. She's still at Connaught Street, isn't she?"

Michael nodded. "Her physical health's improved but she's still one of the walking wounded." He turned to Hugh. "I don't know if you've met Betty. She's a friend of ours who was rather badly smashed up in a motor accident. She's looking after my house while I'm stationed abroad."

"You always were tactful, Michael," Meg said.

He saw Hugh look quickly at both of them and then down at his drink. Michael was willing to bet that Meg was well on the way to getting drunk. Neither her speech nor her movements betrayed it yet; but he knew her too well to be fooled. He gave her a warning look, which he regretted immediately.

Meg's color rose. She abruptly changed the subject. "Everyone's furious with Aunt Vida," she said in a high, brittle voice. "She left most of her money to charity. Disabled servicemen—not quite as bad as a cats' home, but almost. Most of us got a few quid; Hugh got the house; and poor old Daddy got nothing. He was *livid*."

Hugh flushed as well. "The house is as much yours as mine as far as I'm concerned. If you ever want to live there—"

"I never want to live there again," Meg snapped. "If you had any sense, you'd sell it. It's a white elephant. You know what Turnbull said: there's dry rot, rising damp, subsidence, a leaking roof, and death-watch beetle. You'd need to spend a fortune on it."

Hugh's fingers tightened around his glass. "I'm not selling it."

The quiet determination in his voice was unmistakable. It suddenly occurred to Michael that the boy might turn out to be the most formidable member of the family.

"What are you doing at present, Hugh?" he asked, hoping to create a diversion.

"I'm working in a boatyard near Richmond—as a laborer." Hugh smiled and his face, serious in repose, became unexpectedly charming. "But not for long. My call-up papers came today. The RAF needs me. That's why I came to see Meg this evening."

Why does he have to explain a visit to his own sister? Michael wondered if the long separation was the only reason for the awkwardness between the two Kendalls.

"But that's absurd," he said. "In the circumstances you should be exempt."

Hugh shrugged. "It's not important."

"If you like, I could see what I could do. I'm sure that—"

"No, thank you," Hugh paused. "You see, I've got nothing better to do."

"What will you do about Wilmot Lodge?" Meg asked.

"Mrs. Bunnings is going to stay on." Hugh grinned. "We're going to find some lodgers. Or possibly start a bed-and-breakfast."

"You can't do that!" Meg began to laugh. "Think what Stephen and Father will say. And Wilbur, too, if it comes to that."

"That had occurred to me," said Hugh dryly.

"But couldn't Father stop you? You're underage."

Hugh shook his head. "The house is Turnbull's responsibility. Aunt Vida asked him to be my trustee, as well as her executor. Until I'm twenty-one, I can't do anything to it without his consent. He thinks the lodging-house idea is perfectly sensible." The grin re-emerged for an instant. "Though he was a little shocked when I first mentioned it to him."

"How on earth did you get Bunnings to agree? Her baronet would turn in his grave."

Hugh turned his answer into an anecdote; it included some wicked mimicry of Mrs. Bunnings and of the titled employer with whom she had begun her career in service. Whether by accident or design, the tension seeped out of the room.

After that, the conversation flowed more easily. They talked about Prague: Michael admitted that what had happened to Hugh was partly his responsibility.

"It wasn't all bad, you know," Hugh said.

But when Michael tried to find out what had been good about Hugh's war, he received no clear answer. Michael began to feel rather sorry for the SIS man who had debriefed the boy. He made a note to look up Giles Burnham while he was in England. Meanwhile, he kept the conversation on more general topics.

Hugh was full of surprises. His English was good and accentless; occasionally he paused to find the right word, but these hesitations were rare. His intelligence was obvious; and he displayed a degree of cultivation that was remarkable in someone who had spent most of the last six years doing menial jobs in a foreign country. Michael was relieved to find that the boy bore no grudge against him.

The evening passed very quickly. It was well after eleven when Meg glanced up at the clock and decided that she wanted a sandwich. She rang the bell for Jane.

Michael stood up. "I really must be going. I had no idea it was so late."

Meg looked at him, and he looked away. Between them stood a ghost; *Betty*.

"I'd better be off as well," Hugh said quickly. "I'm on the early shift tomorrow."

"You rang, ma'am?" Jane stood in the doorway. "You know I go off duty at eleven."

"I'm so sorry, Jane. I was going to have a sandwich, but it doesn't matter."

Jane glanced at the two men. "I'm sure it's no trouble, ma'am."

"It really doesn't matter," Meg said wearily. "Mr. Stanhope-Smith and Mr. Kendall are going now."

"I'll get their hats, then."

"Did I hear the telephone earlier? Who was it?"

"I think it was Lady Elizabeth Chandos, ma'am." Jane shifted from one foot to the other. "She didn't say, but I recognized the voice. She just asked if Mr. Stanhope-Smith had arrived. I said yes and would she like to speak to him or leave a message; but she said, no, it didn't matter, and I wasn't to trouble you."

For an instant, Michael stood perfectly still. The room was suddenly very hot. The clock ticked on the mantelpiece. In the distance he could hear the faint hum of traffic along Knightsbridge; most of it, he thought with irrelevant clarity, would be traveling west at this time of night. Hugh was looking curiously at him; he was frowning slightly, as if Michael were a crossword puzzle.

Meg laid her hand on his arm. It broke the spell.

"See if you can find me a taxi," he barked at Jane; she took a step backward in her astonishment. "Meg, you'd better get on the phone. If she doesn't answer, ring the police."

He strode out of the room. Jane was already running down the steps from the front door. As he reached the pavement, he realized he was not alone.

"What are you doing?" he said curtly over his shoulder.

"Here's your hat," Hugh said. "I'm coming, too."

They could hear the sirens in Park Lane. An ambulance passed them on Cumberland Gate, its lights flashing.

"Just like the war, eh?" the cabbie said. "Them sirens give me the willies."

Outside the house in Connaught Street were two police cars, a fire engine, the ambulance, and a small crowd of spectators. Two firemen were rolling up a hose on the pavement; a third was talking earnestly to a police officer. Another policeman was trying to persuade the spectators to keep away from the front door.

"I'll pay him," Hugh said.

"Not much of a fire." The cabbie sniffed disapprovingly as he pulled over the curb. "Did either of you gents see that one in 'forty-two, when Jerry got a gas main outside Selfridges? Now *that's* what I call a fire."

"Will you shut up?" Michael wrenched open the door and sprinted over the road.

A policeman blocked his way. "I'm sorry, sir. You can't go in there."

Suddenly Michael remembered that night in September 1940 when his landlady Mrs. Granger had died. Betty had been there, holding on to his arm.

The ambulance men came down the stairs and along the hall. The stretcher bumped against the umbrella stand. As the little party emerged onto the pavement, the crowd gave a gasp of satisfaction.

The stretcher held a body; and the blanket had been pulled up over the body's head.

It was a long night, but there was plenty to do.

There were forms to be filled in, cups of tea to be drunk, and questions to answer. The police were very kind, particularly after Michael had phoned the duty officer at Broadway. The duty officer made a few phone calls himself, as a result of which an elderly superintendent who looked like a pipe-smoking teddy bear was routed out of bed.

No one wanted to make a fuss: what was the point? Michael wondered if the police thought SIS had an official interest.

"In cases like this, there's no need to upset the friends and relatives unduly." The superintendent was a Yorkshireman who liked the sound of his own voice. "The lady left a note: it's all quite straightforward. Just you leave it to us, sir."

It was lucky that Hugh was there. Michael found it difficult to get his thoughts in order: he couldn't ask the right questions or make the right replies.

The story wasn't complicated. At ten-thirty, a widow who lived over the road had noticed an unusual red glow behind the curtains on the top floor of Michael's house. She had tried telephoning and banging on the front door. Then she called the police.

They arrived just before eleven, but it was too late. Betty was lying in the bath, she was fully dressed—right down to gloves and shoes. She had slashed both wrists down to the bone. Beside the bath was an empty bottle which had held barbiturates. Betty had been taking no chances.

"We don't know whether she drowned herself, doped herself, or bled to death." The superintendent lit a pipe with great deliberation. "The post mortem will tell us, though. Nothing for you gentlemen to worry about. The point is, the lass is dead."

The bathroom was full of smoke as well; but this was an accident. The police theory was that she had been smoking in the bedroom next door. She had left the ashtray on the bed, with a smoldering cigarette on the edge. The cigarette had probably rolled off and set fire to the eiderdown. The fire had done some damage to the top story, but not as much as it seemed; the structure was still sound.

"More smoke than fire, sir," the superintendent said, rubbing his hands. "It could have been much worse."

The note had been lying on the bathmat. The ambulance men had unwittingly splashed it as they pulled the body out of the bath. The ink had run, but enough of it was still legible. Betty had apologized for dying; and she had sent her love to Michael; but she stressed that she had done it because she couldn't bear to live with her injuries.

At last the superintendent had asked enough questions for the time being. Michael and Hugh stumbled out of the police station to find that London had been transformed by a summer dawn. They walked for miles, while the city came to life around them. They ended up having breakfast at a coffee stall near Waterloo.

"What are we going to do?" Michael said. He swallowed the

rest of his bitter gray coffee. "Shouldn't you be at work?"

"It doesn't matter." Hugh yawned. "What do you want to do? You're welcome to come back to Richmond. Or we could go to Meg's."

Michael shrugged. "I don't know." His voice hardened. "Do you know what the worst thing was? Identifying her. She didn't look like Betty."

Then he began to cry.

Meg saw Michael only once more that summer, and that was to say good-bye. She felt jealous of Hugh: he and Michael had had a five-day walking holiday in the Wye Valley. It was odd how swiftly that friendship had grown.

She recognized that even one meeting with Michael was a dangerous luxury. Their shared past was volatile: it could explode at any moment. Meg had hoped that Aunt Vida's death might have solved at least part of the problem; she could have left Wilbur if she had been a rich woman in her own right. Sometimes she wondered if the price of being rich wasn't too high.

It was more than a matter of money. Betty, even in death, had a claim on Michael, and so did Wilbur. They were claims that excluded her and that she could barely understand. She had some idea of the work that Michael and Wilbur shared. So now she felt jealous of international politics as well.

Michael came to tea on a Sunday afternoon in early September. It was pouring with rain and, despite his efforts with the doormat, he left a trail of damp footsteps across the parquet floor of the hall. Jane forgave him because he was a man.

"I'm leaving tomorrow afternoon," he said. "Courtesy of the U.S. Air Force."

"Do you know when you'll be back?"

He avoided her eyes. "It's difficult to say. Any messages for Wilbur?"

Damn you. Meg shook her head. "I wrote to him yesterday."

There was a moment of silence.

"I managed to sell the house," Michael said, with obvious effort. "Not for very much. I put the furniture in storage. By the way, Laura Duveen sends her love. I spent last weekend at Charne."

This time the silence was longer. Their affair had started at Charne House, that weekend in 1942 when Betty had to go to Ireland. Lady Duveen, a benevolently unconventional hostess, had acted as its godmother—despite the fact that before the war she had her eye on Michael for her last unmarried daughter.

"Really?" Meg gave her tea an unnecessary stir. "Did you ever do that watercolor for her? The south front, wasn't it? I thought that parcel in the hall looked like a painting."

Michael shook his head. "It is, but it's not of Charne."

He looked directly at her. She felt suddenly helpless. He could have asked her any question, and she would have given him whatever answer he wanted.

How could I have been so stupid?

"Do you want to see it?" His voice was rougher than usual. "I'll get it."

He went into the hall. He came back, tearing off strips of brown paper and strewing them over the carpet in his impatience. *Like Christmas morning,* Meg thought. *I want your child.*

It was a small oil painting, perhaps eighteen inches by twelve. The canvas was stretched but unframed. He removed the rest of the wrappings, keeping the back of the canvas toward her. Without warning, he turned it to face her.

A woman lay in a bath. The painter's eye hovered about five feet above the taps. The bathwater was green at the edges but streaked with pink and brown around the woman. She was dressed in gray, from neck to foot, with the exception of black gloves. Her hair floated in the water like two black wings. The features were hardly discernible on the red, shiny face; the skin was pockmarked with craters; its surface bubbled, like molten lava.

"Oh, for Christ's sake," Meg said. "Put it away."

IV

Cold War
1953–56

Thirteen

"We have twelve months," the little man from Moscow said. "The Chief Intelligence Directorate desires that the affair should affect the U.S. elections. The feeling is that President Eisenhower should not be allowed to have a second term." He coughed modestly. "But that of course is a side issue."

Bela lit an American cigarette; like Colonel Nasser, another heavy smoker, he favored Kent when he could get them. With a graceful flick of the wrist he sent the matchstick skimming toward the aluminum ashtray in the center of the wrought-iron table.

"Herr Scholl and I are in a position of some delicacy," he said. "Can I take it that—my ministry has been notified? And Herr Scholl can hardly undertake a mission of such magnitude without the Ministerium für Staats-Sicherheit realizing it. And if MfS knows—officially, I mean—then so will the KGB. And surely, my dear Colonel, the Glavnoye Razvedyvatelnoye Upravleniye does not usually like the KGB to know what it is doing?"

For a moment no one said anything. Apart from themselves the café was empty; the proprietor was paid a substantial retainer to respect their desire for privacy. Its long, white-painted terrace overlooked the Mediterranean, a few miles west of Alexandria. Flights of gulls sheered inland from the sea and swooped away, screaming angrily. In the distance, trucks were changing gear on the main El Alamein road. Mahmoud—the owner and manager—was in the little kitchen at the far end of the terrace, listening to the radio. The three men at the table could hear the Voice of the Arabs inveighing against the evils of Western imperialism on Cairo Radio.

Bela Juriga's use of the full name of Soviet military intelligence was unusual. Most people—if they used a name at all—would use the acronym, GRU. The polysyllabic formality of the full name carried its own encoded message; it was tantamount to saying that official confirmation was needed. Bela wanted to make quite sure of his ground.

Colonel Pakhlanov nodded his broad, heavy head. His suit might have been made in Paris from material bought in London; but the man himself was eternally a Slav; more than that, he was a Slav from east of the Ukraine. A *barbarian,* Heinz thought, *but a powerful one nevertheless.*

"The authorization for this comes from the top. Right from the top." The colonel had a voice like shingle being sucked from a beach by retreating waves. "The Politbureau itself is interested. Departmental—how shall I put it?—rivalries must be suspended."

Heinz Scholl glanced quickly at Bela. If Pakhlanov was telling the truth, then the KGB must know that GRU had penetrated both the Czechoslovak Ministry of Trade and MfS; the KGB regarded MfS—East Germany's organization for state security—as its own private fief.

Pakhlanov patted Scholl's shoulder with a hairy hand. "You must not worry, my friend. We look after our own. It was necessary to disclose our connection with you, but we did not do so without first obtaining guarantees of your safety. We do not wish to lose you."

"How touching," Bela murmured. "I think we need another bottle."

He limped along the terrace toward the kitchen, shouting for Mahmoud. The little Egyptian appeared in the doorway with another unlabeled bottle of pastis. It tasted like absinthe but was at least one and a half times as strong; a friend of a friend was reputed to make it in Cairo; Mahmoud reserved it for favored customers, which generally meant those he was afraid of.

Pakhlanov looked up, a touch of irritation on his face, as Bela returned. "Perhaps we can get down to business, Comrade."

"But of course, Comrade Colonel." Bela uncorked the bottle and poured an inch of the clear liquid into each of the glasses.

"You and your delegation have done well," the colonel said; even when distributing praise, he sounded gloomy. "You've persuaded Nasser to take a great deal of heavy equipment—"

"But we did have to lower our prices," Bela interrupted. "You do realize that Nasser succeeded in playing us off against the West?

Take the MIGs, for example. He beat us down to four hundred thousand dollars each."

"That's absurd," Pakhlanov said coldly. "It's not even cost price. We shouldn't have allowed that, we really shouldn't. Nasser's only real alternative was the Mirage, and that costs well over a million."

"The problem was, Comrade Colonel, that—as Nasser pointed out—the Mirage is a rather better plane than the MIG."

Pakhlanov snorted. "I suppose we have no alternative." He shrugged away a few million dollars of foreign exchange. "But I am not here to discuss arms sales, as you know. I am here because of *you*." With ponderous theatricality, he stabbed a thick forefinger at Scholl. "Your situation paper on Egypt was first class, and it's time we began to act on it."

Heinz Scholl added an inch of water to the pastis. He was suddenly a little scared of what he had done. The situation paper had seemed a good idea at the time—a useful tactic to advance his career; but putting it into practice was quite another matter. Having written it, he had been in two minds about sending it to Pakhlanov. But July had been a lean month as far as GRU was concerned; Scholl had included the report to bulk out the package for the colonel.

"Comrade Juriga's specialty is arms, not the Middle East. Outline the importance of the Suez Canal to him."

Scholl glanced across the table. Bela was lighting another cigarette; one of his eyelids drooped in a wink.

"The Suez Canal," Heinz began, "is important to different people for different reasons. Obviously it carries a great deal of shipping; the Canal Company reckons that fourteen thousand ships will pass through by the end of nineteen fifty-five; and that's a conservative estimate by the way. Perhaps seventy-five percent of the shipping will belong to NATO countries, and about half of that percentage will be British—despite the fact they've thrown India away."

As usual, the sound of his own voice exerted a calming influence on Heinz; and the facts and the figures created their own kind of order. Anarchy of any sort was anathema to him. Bela nodded encouragingly across the table.

"Every year, about seventy million tons of oil comes through the canal from the Gulf oil fields. Almost all of that goes to Western Europe, and it accounts for two-thirds of their oil imports. The alternative route for the oil would be around the Cape, which would make it prohibitively expensive. For a start, they'd need about twice the tanker tonnage they have at present."

"Come on, come on," Pakhlanov said; he glanced at his watch.

"The British also place a high value on the canal's military importance. Churchill saw it as a vital strategic link with the Commonwealth in the event of another world war. I rather doubt that, myself: but the point is, that's what the British believe. Both the British and the French are under the illusion that they somehow own the canal—that's rubbish, of course. The Suez Canal Company, which is registered in Egypt, and in which Britain and France are major stockholders, has a lease on it until 1969; control will then revert to Egypt. The military base in the canal zone provides a degree of protection for the status quo—but the British are gradually withdrawing from it; the last of their troops should be gone by June of next year. The Egyptians, on the other hand—"

"Stop," Bela said suddenly.

Pakhlanov's gray eyes, watchful beneath their heavy lids, narrowed. "The traffic?"

Bela nodded. "Something stopped. A car, I think."

All three of them stared in the direction of the road, a hundred yards away. The wall at the back of the terrace blocked their view.

"Probably parked in the scrub and continuing on foot." The colonel frowned at Heinz. "I thought you said this place was safe. You should have brought some watchers."

Unfair, Heinz thought. *You said no one else was to be involved, you Russian bastard.*

"Perhaps the colonel and I should join Mahmoud in the kitchen," Bela suggested. "That is, unless you need any help?"

Scholl picked up his briefcase, opened it, and took out a pair of gloves. He stood up, slipping his hand inside his jacket.

"I think I can manage on my own."

Stephen Kendall's first warning came on October 12. At the time he didn't recognize it for what it was. It was just an item in the section's weekly roundup of news. The roundup came to Stephen every Thursday, after circulating around everyone else. He read it and decided what should be funneled upward to his director.

Captain Blaines—the Middle Eastern section's latest recruit— had made a note of the brief paragraph in one of the Alexandria papers. Stephen disliked Blaines—the man was obese, incurably vulgar, and impudent—and would have liked to find fault with him.

But Blaines had done his job. The paragraph simply said that Jean-Paul Thierry, an Algerian *pied noir* who sold life insurance, had been found with his throat slit in one of the war cemeteries near El Alamein. Blaines remembered that a man of the same name had once been on the SIS payroll in Oran. He checked with Registry and found that Thierry was now believed to be doing low-level free-lance work in Egypt. His last known employer was the CIA; but that was two and a half years ago.

Despite the worsening situation in Egypt, the section still had a few useful contacts in Alex, both in the police department and elsewhere. Blaines checked these. The police believed that Thierry had been killed by a gang of Arab nationalists who combined political gestures with robbery. No one was trying very hard to find his killers.

But one contact came up with a new, if small piece of information. A year ago, Thierry had done a little legwork for the Russians—though whether he ever knew who his employers were was quite another matter.

Stephen pressed his buzzer and told his secretary to summon Blaines.

The man came bounding through the door as if he hadn't a care in the world.

"And what can I do for you?"

The smell of stale beer washed over Stephen; he waved ineffectually at it. "Sir," he prompted.

"*Sah!*" Blaines replied with parade-ground smartness. For two pins, Stephen felt, he would have saluted, despite the fact he was wearing civvies.

Stephen held on to his temper. Cool superiority was the only way to handle people like that. Someone really should have a word with Blaines about his clothes. That yellow pullover was quite ridiculous.

"Thierry." He tapped the weekly report on his desk. "You've spent a great deal of time on this—and not just your own. And it's been to very little purpose. You've also been in touch with Alex, but you don't appear to have got a senior officer's authorization. I don't want it to happen again, Blaines. Do you understand? Good afternoon."

Stephen bent his head and pretended to be absorbed in the papers in front of him. After a few seconds he heard a small, sharp sound, almost as if that wretched man had clicked his heels.

"Sah?"

Stephen raised his head wearily. "What is it, Blaines?"

"Will there be anything else, sah?"

"No, there will not."

Blaines grinned, almost with affection, and left the office. When Stephen had recovered his temper, he looked again at the Thierry material. It was better to be safe than sorry. He doubted if anyone else had noticed that there was a possible, if remote, intelligence angle on the death of Thierry. The fact that Thierry had worked for both sides made him rather more interesting. People on the fence always were.

Stephen made a note on the margin of the report. It told his secretary to do three things with the report; to include it in the précis which went upstairs; to ensure the information was stored, both in the section's files and in Registry's; and to send a copy over to Grosvenor Square. The last instruction was because there was just a chance that the Cousins might be interested in Thierry; Wilbur had said only the other day that keeping track of free lances was one of his biggest headaches.

The death of the man Thierry seemed just routine at this stage. Stephen devoted far more thought to the disadvantages of seconding army officers who had been commissioned from the ranks. But the chief importance of Thierry's murder was that it enabled him to do his brother-in-law a small favor.

There wasn't much time.

The orders from Moscow had arrived on the daily MfS flight, at least a week sooner than Heinz had expected. Tomorrow morning he would have to leave for Prague, to take up his new post as the East German representative on the Czech trade mission.

He stared out of the window. When he craned his head to the left, he could see the endless stream of traffic on the Unter den Linden at the end of the street. The familiar sight failed to register in his mind. He rubbed the gray, flimsy paper of the Movement Order between his finger and thumb. The decision could no longer be postponed: if he was going to do it at all, it would have to be now. He had done it often enough on behalf of Colonel Pakhlanov and GRU— why should it be more difficult today?

Heinz knew the answer to that. In the past he had always had the reassuring thought in the back of his mind that, if he was caught,

Pakhlanov could be invoked as a last resort; GRU looked after its own—according to the colonel—and the worst that could happen to him was a sideways move to Soviet military intelligence. But that safety net was no longer in place. GRU, MfS, and the KGB were yoked together for the time being in an uneasy alliance. None of them encouraged private enterprise in its operatives.

He left his office and walked down the broad corridor to the lift by the stairs. This branch of the Ministerium was housed in one of the few government buildings in East Berlin to have escaped serious bomb damage. Even the lift was a luxurious antique, with its velvet-covered seats and burnished brass ashtrays.

As the lift took him downward, Heinz felt a twinge of regret that he was leaving the office tomorrow. The huge block with its 1890's décor and its 1950's furniture sometimes seemed the nearest he was likely to get to a home of his own. He had had a Government Worker flat overlooking Alexanderplatz for nearly three years, but most of that time had been spent in the Middle East or Russia; and even when he was in East Berlin he rarely used the flat for anything other than sleeping.

His waking life was bound up with the Ministerium. He had no family ties to distract him since his mother died of pneumonia in 1948. He had quarreled irrevocably with his sister Magda since May 1945. The slut had fled across the border to West Germany a month after their mother's death: the DDR was well rid of her.

Heinz considered friends to be an unnecessary distraction. There were a few exceptions, like Bela Juriga; but Bela was less of a friend than a mentor. It was Bela who had opened his eyes to the evils of fascism and the historical inevitability of communism. It was Bela who had taken the place of his father, if anyone could ever do that. And it was Bela who could help him gain revenge for his father's death.

The lift descended with a decorous absence of speed to the basement. The entire floor was given over to Archives. Above ground the building belonged to the second Reich; below ground it belonged to the third. The Nazis had replaced the original cellars with a bomb-proof warren of reinforced concrete and steel girders.

Heinz joined the queue in front of the counter. To his right was the supervised reading room; behind the counter, rows of steel cabinets and shelves stretched away into the distance. Some of the shelves were mounted on rollers to make best use of the available space. Every now and then, metallic groans and clangs boomed from the bowels of Archives: it was a point of honor among the clerks to handle the sliding shelves as carelessly as possible.

It took Heinz a good twenty minutes to reach the counter. As he waited, he filled in the requisition slip. New arrivals constantly swelled the queue behind him. He had banked on this. Between twelve and two, no more than half the Archives staff was on duty at any one time; the rest was having lunch. But the flow of customers did not decrease correspondingly, so the clerks were always hurried.

"Hello, Klaus," Heinz laid the slip on the counter. "How's the baby?"

He had made it a policy to cultivate the clerks. It was amazing what the occasional cigarette or glass of beer could achieve. Most of their customers treated the clerks like retrieval machines—and it rankled.

The clerk's face lost its harassed look for a moment. "Much better, thank God. It wasn't measles after all—just a rash." He glanced down at the slip. "Trade figures with Great Britain? That's outside your normal line, isn't it?"

Heinz grinned. "You know what they're like upstairs. I'm a Middle East man, so they're sending me to London with a Czech trade mission. Do you want me to get the file? You look rushed off your feet."

Klaus nodded gratefully. "You know where they are? Second section on the left in Area IXB."

"I'll find it."

Heinz passed through the turnstile and strolled into the maze of shelves. He knew his way around almost as well as the clerks. As soon as he was out of sight of the counter, he quickened his pace, keeping a watch for other people in the labyrinth; it wouldn't do to seem in too much of a hurry.

His first port of call was IXB. He picked up two files—one for East Germany and one for Czechoslovakia—and walked between the stacks to Area XIV, where the files for Great Britain were housed.

It was a heterogeneous collection. Many of the older files had been inherited from the Nazis; others were versions of KGB originals, translated and edited by the MfS liaison bureau at Dzerzhinsky Square; only a minority had been compiled by MfS, since the younger organization lacked the resources to do much work outside Germany.

KENDALL. *Hugh Henry: also known as Messner, Rudi: born June 22, 1925—*

It was a thin file. Heinz glanced quickly at the cover: it had a red tag, which meant it emanated from Moscow; it had been opened in August 1945; the last item had been added two years ago, in January 1954. He thrust the file between the two collections of trade figures and sauntered back to the counter.

In the reading room he leafed quickly through Kendall's file. There were two uniformed guards at each end of the room; their eyes swept constantly up and down the rows of chairs and tables; they might have been invigilating an examination—except that invigilators rarely carried automatic pistols.

Some of the material in the file was already familiar to him—which was scarcely surprising, since much of it derived from depositions made by himself and Bela. But this was the first time he had seen the full story. It was all there, in black and white. Heinz flicked over the pages until he came to May 1945. As the familiar names leapt up at him, his sorrow was suddenly as unbearably fresh as it had been a decade ago; and so were the hatred and the anger which had always accompanied it.

A German patrol, probing the extent of the American advance to the east of Pilsen, had picked up the wounded Bruckman. They also discovered the corpses of Colonel Helmuth Scholl and two members of Werewolf, together with the remains of what had once been a GI. Bruckman, who had been devoted to the colonel, was in a state of shock. When the patrol returned to base, the chauffeur was briefly interrogated and dispatched to Prague in a hospital convoy. The convoy was destroyed by partisans before it reached its destination; there were no survivors.

But the Russians had subsequently overrun the command post and captured the regimental records. According to the laconic interrogation report, the Werewolf youths had concealed a mine beneath the GI's corpse. Colonel Scholl had ordered them to defuse the booby trap and, when they refused, had shot them.

Kendall–Messner had taken advantage of the confusion to push Scholl onto the mine. He had then abandoned the wounded chauffeur, whom he believed to be dying, robbed the corpses, and fled toward the American lines.

The Russian compiler of the report had speculated about Kendall's motive. Rather hesitantly, he advanced the hypothesis that the Englishman—young though he was—had been working in some capacity for SIS, but had changed sides during the war. His father and his brother were known to be employees of SIS. The compiler pointed out that Kendall had betrayed several key Communists in the Czech resistance movement, which was of course supported by Britain. The youth had some unexplained connection with the assassination of Reinhard Heydrich, and with the arrest of the Anglo-Czech *Abwehr* source, Paul Thümmel. The attached testimony of Bela Juriga suggested that Kendall's loyalties lay firmly with the Nazis perhaps as early as 1940.

It was therefore possible, the anonymous analyst concluded, that Colonel Scholl had been killed because he knew too much about his guest's wartime activities; Kendall, in other words, was afraid of being exposed as a traitor. Another explanation—equally feasible as far as it went—was that the young Englishman was a psychopath. The attached testimony from the colonel's son, Heinz Scholl—now a member of the Communist Party, lent weight to both hypotheses.

The rest of the file needed careful study, since it dealt with Kendall's postwar career; the material was new to Heinz. Two facts gave him pause for thought: Kendall's brother Stephen was now running SIS's Middle Eastern desk in London; and his brother-in-law Wilbur Cunningham was the CIA's Deputy Head of Station there. Perhaps private vengeance need not be entirely divorced from the official object of the mission.

But Hugh Kendall seemed to have nothing to do with intelligence work these days. He had done his national service in the RAF; he had spent the better part of a year stationed in Hamburg, where—according to unnamed British sources—he had been involved in the black market. MfS agents in the field had been able to confirm that this was at least a strong possibility. Kendall was thought to have been part of a group which traded cigarettes, spirits, and medical supplies for German gold and portable antiques.

It all fit, Heinz thought: Kendall had the mentality of a parasite.

It was believed that Kendall's black market activities had continued for at least a year after he was demobilized. But he had turned his energies to legitimate business as well. Using his flair for languages, he had represented on a free-lance basis a number of British firms which were anxious to break into the Continental market. His profits had been considerable; and he had ploughed back most of them into the purchase and renovation of bomb-damaged property in the West End of London.

In 1950, Kendall went to the United States where he became heavily involved with the commodities market, possibly with the help of his extremely wealthy brother-in-law. He also visited South America, where he bought a controlling interest in a small chain of canning factories in Argentina, and acquired a substantial minority holding in a Peruvian copper mine. In Australia, he invested in the expanding petroleum industry; he was also believed to have lost money in a hydroelectric scheme.

He had returned to Britain in 1951. He lived in what was apparently a family house on the outskirts of London. His business philosophy could be summed up in one word: diversification.

Little information was available on his social life. He was believed to be heterosexual, but he had never married. There had been a number of affairs, however; a London gossip columnist retained by the KGB had supplied a few names and approximate dates, though the list could not be regarded as comprehensive. It was rumored that he was estranged from his father and his brother. He was a frequent guest of the Cunninghams. Among his closest friends was Michael Stanhope-Smith, who had been on file as a British intelligence employee since before the war.

The full extent of his wealth was not known. He was a dollar millionaire, and possibly a pound millionaire as well. As far as was known, he was politically uncommitted; like other minor capitalists he was almost certainly somewhere to the right of the present Conservative government at Westminster.

Heinz closed his eyes and tried to visualize Hugh Kendall as he had last seen him, more than ten years before. The fact that Kendall had dragged him from the Vltava somehow made matters worse: it was intolerable that the murderer of your father had also saved your own life.

That obligation must be ignored: as a person and as a political animal, Kendall had condemned himself by his own actions. He deserved only death.

There was a tap on Heinz's shoulder. He whirled around, automatically sliding the Kendall file beneath the others.

"Are you all right?" Klaus said. "I could see you from the counter: you've gone very pale.'

Heinz forced a smile. Out of the corner of his eye, he could see that one of the guards was looking in their direction. "I'm fine. I just felt a bit tired. Rough night, last night."

He winked, and Klaus grinned back. The guard had looked away. Heinz glanced at his watch.

"Time for lunch, I think. Have you had yours yet?"

It was nearly midday, but the bitter February frost showed no sign of leaving the Fens. The dikes and the flooded fields had iced over; here and there you could see skaters. The snow still lay on the ground; more was forecast in the evening. Land and sky merged together in a gray blur at the horizon. Clouds the color of dirty pewter floated overhead.

Hugh Kendall kept the Jaguar's speed at a sober 40 m.p.h. Occasionally he caught sight of Ely Cathedral in the rearview mirror: from this angle its two towers looked like an earthbound V-sign, directed at the weather.

He reached Cambridge at a quarter past twelve. There was little traffic in the narrow streets around Market Hill, apart from churchgoers returning home on foot. Their faces were chapped with cold, and their breath emerged as plumes of steam; Hugh was unashamedly glad of the heated comfort of the Jaguar. Two tramps sat by the fountain in the marketplace, passing a bottle between them; they stared uncomprehendingly and without envy at the passing car. The sight of them triggered memories. The promise Hugh had made himself, years ago, repeated itself like a litany in his mind.

I must never be poor again. Poor people were pushed around by rich people: it was the way of the world.

He recognized the eighteenth-century façade of Jerusalem College from the Ackermann print in Michael's sitting room. The passage of a century and a half seemed to have had little effect on the place. The clothes of the young men who clustered around the gate had changed in the meantime, and someone had invented the bicycle; but that was all.

A porter directed him to Dr. Ingham's rooms in Front Court. The sitting room was large, airy, and south-facing; it smelled of peppermints, Michael's cigarettes, and old dog. The animal in question—a spaniel—lumbered over from the hearth rug and cautiously inspected Hugh.

"His name's Alcibiades," Michael said. "People have been expecting him to die at any moment for at least five years. How are you?"

"I'm well. Where's Dr. Ingham?"

Michael jerked a thumb at a door set in the painted paneling. "In his bedroom, telephoning my boss. He wants to lodge a complaint against me."

"What's the problem?"

"Have some sherry," Michael said; judging by his breath, he

had lined his stomach beforehand with whisky. "It's a very decent Amontillado. I shouldn't be telling you this, but I've been asking him who he knew at Trinity in the thirties. Everyone at the office is getting hysterical about the third, fourth, fifth man—I don't know; I've lost count. It's a bloody witch-hunt. I'm drunk, you know."

"I had noticed." Hugh poured himself a small glass of sherry. "It's that bad, is it?"

Michael lit another cigarette. "I could more or less stand it until it became *de rigueur* to suspect one's colleagues. Thank God I was an undergraduate here, rather than at Trinity. Derek Ingham doesn't even work for us anymore. Though I suppose he does a bit of recruiting now and then. How was your weekend?"

"Cold. I was glad to have an excuse to leave early. King's Lynn was even worse than here, and the Marchants don't approve of central heating. Do you think our invitation to lunch still holds good?"

"I rather doubt it. We'll have to find—"

The bedroom door opened with a bang. Alcibiades growled. Dr. Ingham flounced into the room with an unlit pipe in his mouth. No one, Michael had once told Hugh, had ever seen that pipe alight. According to Jerusalem mythology, Ingham slept with it in his mouth. The bald patch on his head had turned an unhealthy shade of purple.

"I won't have it, Stanhope-Smith! I refuse to be made a fool of at my age, and I've told Sir James *precisely* what I think."

"I'm sorry," Michael said. He stood up, giving a creditable imitation of being sober. "Perhaps we'd better go."

Ingham turned on Hugh. "You must be Stanhope-Smith's friend. I'm sorry to say that doesn't make you a friend of mine." Rage raised the pitch of his voice; by now it was almost a falsetto. "I'd be grateful if you'd both leave. Pah! The door is behind you."

Michael staggered as they reached the court; he slipped on the cobbles and would have fallen if Hugh had not taken his arm. At the porter's lodge, Hugh glanced back. Ingham was watching their departure from his window.

When they reached the car, neither of them said anything for a moment. Then Michael stirred.

"Sorry about that, old chap. This seems to be my day for apologizing. But I shouldn't have embroiled you. Disgraceful." He shook his head solemnly from side to side and repeated. "Disgraceful. Have you noticed how anger makes people talk as if they were in a Victorian melodrama?"

"It's time you left that job. If you don't you'll either drink yourself to death or get sacked."

"That's plain speaking, old son. It deserves plain speaking in return. Point is, I can't *afford* to. I'm a desk man, you see. Once a desk man, always a desk man—unless you drink yourself to death, of course. Do you know what James said when I told him I didn't want to vet Ingham? He said, *Just be grateful I'm not asking him to vet you.*"

"Wilbur and Meg were at the Marchants," Hugh said abruptly. It was time to try shock tactics.

"No doubt Wilbur was doing his natty imitation of an English gent having a weekend in the country." Michael pursed his lips and added judiciously, "Actually, it's not a bad imitation as these things go."

"Meg said she hadn't seen you for nearly six months."

Michael shrugged. "I'm just trying to be sensible. Better late than never, eh? I can't spend the rest of my life hanging around your sister, much as I'd like to. For one thing, it would get on her nerves. For another, she's married to someone else."

"Not for long. She and Wilbur are talking about getting a divorce."

There was a moment's silence. Michael stared down St. Andrew's Street, his hand plucking at one of the buttons of his overcoat. The color had drained away from his face. He looked as if he was about to be sick.

"She asked me to tell you," Hugh continued. "It's all quite amicable. Wilbur's going to give her some sort of income."

Michael snorted. "She'll certainly need that. If she'd had money of her own, she would have left him years ago."

He sounded so bitter that Hugh wondered if this conversation was a mistake. Most people, however close you got to them, had private areas in their lives—reserved subjects that were fenced off from the rest of the world. For Michael, the usual ones were Meg, money, and his job. Hugh knew he was trespassing; he had a shrewd suspicion that he wouldn't have got so far into forbidden territory if Michael had been sober. But it was too late to pretend that he wasn't there.

Hugh ignored his doubts and came directly to the point. "Meg wants to marry you."

"I can't afford a wife."

"She can afford you. And you can chuck in that job. In any case, you needn't be penniless. That exhibition of yours must have earned you a few bob. If you're painting full time, you'll make enough to live on. Perhaps not as much as you're getting now, but you'll manage."

"I'll make my own decisions, thank you. And I don't propose to become an economic parasite. Painting's a hobby for me: I'm not good enough to earn a living by it."

"That's not what the critics said."

"Ah, *critics*—you can't take them seriously."

Hugh sighed, "Everyone else does, including Meg. Michael, you've got a future as an artist: you just have to grab it. You may not get rich, but you'll be a lot happier than you are now. Especially if you swallow your pride and marry Meg."

The button finally parted company with the overcoat. Michael rolled it over and over in the palm of his hand. For the first time, Hugh noticed the streaks of gray in Michael's hair. His rugger-forward's body was beginning to run to fat. It was a shock to realize that Michael must be in his early forties by now; despite the twelve-year age gap between them, Hugh had always thought of them as being roughly the same age.

"Oh, Christ." Michael turned and looked Hugh full in the face. Suddenly he smiled. "I'd forgotten what it's like to have a future worth grabbing."

Fourteen

One reason for Stephen Kendall's undoubted success in his chosen career was the knack he had of making people beholden to him. He planted favors in other people's lives like other men planted bulbs in their gardens. He made sure the soil was well nourished; he kept the infant plants watered and sheltered from the wind; and eventually he got his reward.

Giles Burnham was a case in point. Burnham transferred from MI6 to MI5 in 1948, and got himself promoted on the way. In theory it was a sensible move. In practice his former colleagues in Six tended to look down their noses at him. Remnants of the prewar antagonism between the two organizations still existed. For some reason, spying was considered a more gentlemanly occupation than catching spies.

Stephen shared this prejudice to some extent, but he was careful to conceal it as much as possible. He and Burnham had been mildly friendly since they had met each other over the business of Hugh Kendall's return in 1945. When Giles announced his move, Stephen congratulated him heartily and made a point of keeping in touch.

The policy had paid off handsomely over the years. Stephen had derived a great deal of professional advantage from having a friend at Five. Giles had even asked Stephen to act as godfather for one of his gangling children. Stephen had been delighted to accept; the other godparents were a member of Parliament and the widow of a baronet.

Since the end of the war, Five's reputation had improved at the expense of Six's. SIS had sheltered too many traitors for its own good; its critics said that gentlemanly dash was just another way of describing bumbling amateurism. A friend at Five was no longer something to be despised.

And Giles Burnham had done well. In the 1953 reorganization of MI5 he had been put in charge of D2. D Branch handled counter-espionage. D1 was the plum post, because it covered the USSR. But D2, which dealt with the Soviet satellites and China, was almost as important, particularly because the Russians used the intelligence services of their satellites for their own purposes.

On the last Sunday in February, Stephen went to the Burnhams for lunch. They lived in a big, late-Victorian semidetached villa in Greenwich. The household was teetotal: to the astonishment of all who knew him, Giles had given up alcohol to please his wife. The meal itself was something of an ordeal: Mildred Burnham had been brought up in India and had not adapted well to a life where the only servant she could afford was an unreliable char who came in for three mornings a week. The lamb was tough and all the vegetables had somehow acquired the taste and much of the consistency of over-cooked cabbage. The two elder children pestered the adults with unanswerable questions, while Stephen's two-year-old godson was sick into his rice pudding.

"It always has that effect on him," Mildred said with a puzzled frown as she scrubbed ineffectually at the tablecloth.

Having tasted the pudding question, Stephen was not surprised.

After the washing-up, Giles suggested a walk down to the river.

Stephen was conscious that they made an odd pair as they strolled through the park toward the National Maritime Museum. He himself was wearing a new navy-blue overcoat and one of his better suits; Giles, on the other hand, shambled down the path in a torn tweed coat that had lost most of its buttons, with a faded ex-army beret on his head. But Giles could do that sort of thing. Stephen had found the Burnhams in Burke's *Landed Gentry:* they owned a substantial slice of Cambridgeshire.

Giles paused to light his pipe.

"This is the life, eh?" He sucked vigorously; the match went out; he tried again. "Nothing like a breath of fresh air."

Stephen nodded without enthusiasm. Fresh air was fine, but he preferred it rather warmer than this. He wondered how many more matches the pipe would need. Five? He introduced another, safer topic.

"Children are looking well."

"Eh? Oh, yes. The children. Expensive little brutes."

Seven matches later they walked on.

"Actually, I wanted a word." He glanced around with theatrical caution. "Something came across my desk on Friday. Thought it might interest you."

"Oh?" Stephen forgot he was cold for a moment. He looked up at Giles, who with infuriating deliberation was trying the effect of another match on his pipe.

"A Czech trade mission turned up on Monday. Semipermanent. Diplomatic status. You know the sort of thing. We ran the usual checks, and a couple of interesting points emerged. One of the senior men is Bela Juriga."

Stephen's balled fist broke through the lining of his coat pocket. After a moment he said, "It's the same man, I suppose?"

Giles chuckled. His face lost its habitually vacuous expression and became briefly and alarmingly intelligent. "I thought you would have read your brother's file. Strictly against the rules." He tried another match. "There's no doubt about it. His job's quite genuine, by the way. He went into the Ministry of Trade after the war, and became a sort of high-powered salesman for their arms industry. He was responsible for that business in Egypt."

Stephen frowned. "The Nasser deal? But what's he doing here?"

"I wish we knew." Giles sucked again: the pipe was apparently blocked; he put it in his pocket. "I thought it was worth mentioning, since there's both a personal and a Middle Eastern connection. You will let me know if you come up with anything?"

"Of course. Are they based at the embassy?"

Giles nodded. "Grosvenor Place."

"What about the rest of the mission? Any leads on them?"

"Nothing so far. But I'll send you the details." Giles paused and looked down at Stephen. "On the understanding, of course, that the information is for your eyes only, and that you don't act on it. Not in this country, I mean. We can't afford a wild SIS operation on our patch."

Stephen smiled. "I promise. Scout's honor."

Meg thought she had never been so happy.

Now the decision was made, she couldn't understand why it hadn't been made earlier. Wilbur had agreed to let her divorce him.

255

Doing it the other way around was inconceivable. Doing it by mutual consent would take too long. She suspected that Wilbur rather enjoyed the prospect of going to a hotel with a young woman; it was such a thoroughly English thing to do that it had the appeal of the picturesque for him. He had read of people doing it in the novels of P. G. Wodehouse.

Michael had telephoned her as soon as he got back from Cambridge with Hugh. That had been last Sunday, a week ago. Since then she had been living in a state of euphoria. She had recovered her faith in the possibility of happy endings.

She spent all of this Sunday at Michael's flat near Putney Bridge. It had been a strange day—bounded by four walls, warmed by a gas fire, and isolated from the rest of the world. In the end they hadn't made love. Now there was no need to hurry, waiting was a kind of foreplay. They wouldn't be rich—not in the sense that she had grown used to with Wilbur—but who cared? They would have each other. It had taken her far too long to realize the limitations of financial security.

Wilbur knew: that was the strange thing. In the last week she had felt closer to him than she had ever done since they were married. The other night he had said to her, "Money's a prison. I've always known that. And that's why—"

At that moment, Jane had come in to announce dinner and he had never finished his sentence. But there was really no need for him to do so. He was trying to explain why he had to take his pleasures anonymously—why he preferred the company of people who didn't know how absurdly wealthy his family was. Once or twice he had forgotten his own rules—Gary Brennan, the chauffeur who had tried to blackmail both of them in 1946, was a case in point. Gary had simply vanished: one day he was there, and the next he had gone; so had all his belongings. It was as if he had never existed. The next chauffeur was a middle-aged man with a squint, a wife, and grown-up children.

Understanding though Wilbur was, he was still careful with his money. His lawyer was drawing up an agreement: she was to divorce him and to receive an annual income of £3000 for life; but in return she surrendered any claim she might have, now or in the future, on his estate. Wilbur was so rich that he couldn't even afford to be generous.

The shocked reactions of her friends—most of whom were connected with the U.S. Embassy or the Foreign Office—had been predictable. Stephen's cold fury had surprised her, however; it was as if he had a vested interest in their marriage. On the other hand, their father had taken the news much better than she had expected, largely because Wilbur did not intend to discontinue the small monthly payments he made his father-in-law; it had always been a tactful arrangement—in theory the money came from Meg's bank account.

This morning, as the taxi carried her through the quiet Sunday streets from Knightsbridge to Putney, she had thought to herself: *I can never be happier than this.* But now, as she lay in bed twelve hours later, waiting for sleep to creep up on her, she knew she had been wrong.

Today Michael had told her he wanted to resign from his job. That made her happy for two reasons—partly because she would have the pleasure of giving him money, but mainly because she knew he needed to paint almost as much as he needed her.

But there was another, more pressing reason for happiness.

"Darling," Michael had said. "You're thirty-two, aren't you? Do you think—I mean, would we be too old to have children?"

On Tuesday, February 28, there was a coincidence. Perhaps coincidence was the wrong word for the curious serendipity that so often occurred in the small, enclosed world of secret intelligence.

In the morning, a messenger brought the little package from Curzon Street. Stephen ripped it open. There were three group photographs, obviously taken without the subject's knowledge. Special Branch had snapped the trade mission once in the arrival lounge at the airport and twice on the pavement outside the Czechoslovak Embassy. Giles had also included biographical notes. Before Stephen had time to read them, he was interrupted by a knock at the door.

It was Johann Eicke. The young West German looked like a fresh-faced peasant, but he was considered to be one of the high-fliers of the Bundesant für Verfassungsschutz. Liaison between SIS and BfV was becoming increasingly extensive: they shared a common enemy, and Germany had developed into the most frequently used battleground of the Cold War.

Stephen pushed the photographs across the desk, more to flatter a potential ally than for any other reason.

"You get a lot of Czechs, don't you? Are any of these chaps familiar?"

Eicke took the photographs and studied them with a lack of haste that Stephen found infuriating. The West German was rather clever at giving the impression that he had the mental age of a sluggish ten-year-old. That was one reason why he had been selected for the London job.

"Bela Juriga," Eicke said at last. "He's the middle-aged one with the face like a skull. I'm sure you know him—their arms man. I don't know the other Czechs, though. Two of them look like bodyguards, don't they?"

"Oh, well," Michael reached out for the photographs. "It was worth a try."

Eicke tapped one of the faces with a thick forefinger. "But I know the East German. Or rather, I've seen a photograph of him before."

"Really?" Stephen's interest quickened. Since the German Democratic Republic was not recognized by the West, its citizens often traveled on the passports of other countries in the Soviet bloc. It was always useful to be able to pinpoint them. Giles would be pleased.

"This one." Eicke passed over one of the prints. "He's saying something to Juriga."

The photograph had been taken outside the embassy. On the right Stephen could see the garden wall of Buckingham Palace; in the background Grosvenor Place stretched up to Hyde Park Corner. The man in question was looking up at Juriga; the camera had caught him full-face. The mouth was open, and the front teeth were noticeably prominent. He was small—probably not more than five feet four—and looked boyishly slim in comparison with the two thugs.

"He looks harmless enough," Stephen said. "What's his name?"

"We call him *Das Kaninchen*." Eicke threw back his head and laughed. "In German that means the Rabbit. Because of the teeth. But his real name is Scholl. Heinz Scholl."

Heinz Scholl was surprised to find that he liked London.

He was a man who preferred cities—landscapes without buildings disturbed him—but he had come to England prepared to dislike everything about it; and London, the capital of the crumbling empire and the product of many centuries of unchecked and ruthless capitalism, could only be loathsome. His impression of the city was chiefly derived from the novels of Dickens, many of which he had read in translation as a boy.

But the real London refused to fit into the stereotype he had constructed for it. He liked the shabbiness, the bomb craters, and the drab crowds that swirled along the pavements; the ceaseless activity soothed him. Certain sights haunted him—a legless war veteran with a tray of matches, sitting on the pavement at Oxford Circus; a ragged boy staring open-mouthed at the red-coated sentry outside St. James's Palace; even the pale office workers, traveling home by tube, sheltering their individual privacies behind newspapers and blank eyes. Compared with Cairo and Beirut, London seemed a paradise.

Heinz was grateful that the work was going well. At this stage it involved a lot of talking, chiefly to diplomats from unaligned nations. Bela concentrated on the military attachés, while Heinz saw the men who masqueraded under a variety of different titles at the embassies, high commissions, and consulates.

There were many arguments to use, from the absurdity of a declining European nation being the world's major Islamic power to the advantages which would accrue if Britain's influence in the Middle East decreased, preferably suddenly. Some discussions were more specific: the arms and economic aid that the USSR could make available to certain countries in certain contingencies was one popular topic; another—and this was Heinz's particular specialty—was the long-term Anglo-American strategy in the Middle East.

As instructed, Heinz avoided the question of ideology in these discussions. Pakhlanov had been very firm about that. Instead, he stressed the geographical importance of the Suez Canal, the imperialist lifeline that bisected the Arab world; he exaggerated what the British and the Americans had done in Iran—restoring the Shah to power in order to safeguard Western oil interests—interests that, properly speaking, belonged to the Iranian people.

To some extent, events played into his hands. The British were trying to establish the Bagdhad Pact, an alliance of pro-Western Arab states against the USSR. The fact that Iraq—and Anglophile kingdom—was the leading member of the pact did nothing to increase its chances of success. The British hoped that Jordan would join, but that hope was destroyed early in March 1956, when young King Hussein was persuaded to dismiss General Glubb, the British officer who commanded his Arab legion. The dismissal was a slap in the face to the British and effectively damned the chances of the pact. The British nursed their hurt pride while the rest of the world considered it a triumph for Arab nationalism. Heinz Scholl's unobtrusive visits to the Jordanian Embassy in Kensington had paid rich dividends.

Colonel Pakhlanov cabled his congratulations.

In the first few months of 1956 there were many signs that Heinz and Bela were not working alone. Heinz was inspired and comforted by the thought that he was part of a secret army—one man among many, all of whom were fighting for the same cause.

Pakhlanov seemed to be the controlling intelligence, but Heinz could never be entirely sure of this. The colonel was certainly responsible for the planning of the Crabb affair. This came to fruition in April, when Krushchev and Bulganin paid a brief visit to Britain. The Russian cruiser *Ordzhonikidze,* which had brought the Soviet leaders, lay at anchor in Portsmouth Harbor. Commander Crabb, formerly one of the Royal Navy's experts in underwater sabotage, vanished in an embarrassing blaze of publicity while apparently examining—or perhaps attempting to sabotage—the cruiser's hull.

There were questions in Parliament. Both the government and the opposition were outraged by the thought that SIS, possibly with CIA assistance, was trying to wreck—in some ill-defined manner—a Russian goodwill visit to Britain. The prime minister, anxious for a thaw in the Cold War, had specifically forbidden any such operation which might offend the visiting Russians. It reflected badly on everyone. Only Colonel Pahklanov and the unfortunate but foolish Crabb ever knew the full story. Heinz suspected that Crabb was blackmailed, possibly with the help of a mole inside SIS or the Naval Intelligence Department. In any case, the truth didn't matter.

What did matter was that SIS was appointed scapegoat for an operation that never really happened. A number of people eventually lost their jobs—including the Foreign Office Adviser to the Secret Service and C himself. The affair caused incalculable damage to morale. The British intelligence establishment was already reeling after the Russians had displayed Burgess and Maclean at a Moscow press conference in February. No one knew what was going on; no one was entirely sure his colleagues were trustworthy; no one felt his job was safe. As Bela Juriga put it, it was all very satisfactory.

Bela and Heinz shared a flat in one of the embassy houses. It was the first time they had been together for so long since those terrible days in May 1945. Heinz found himself thinking—and dreaming—of that time. Bela and the partisans had attacked the villa in Zbraslav just before the last German forces pulled out of Prague. His aim had been to capture Hugh Kendall; instead he got Frau Scholl, Heinz, and Magda, all of them shattered by the news of Colonel Scholl's death. At the time, Bela's conduct had puzzled Heinz. He had set free Magda and Frau Scholl, but kept Heinz with him. At first Heinz believed he was going to be killed—as a surrogate for Hugh Kendall. Instead, Bela patiently reeducated him, exposing fascism as threadbare rhetoric cloaking viciousness, and providing in its place the glorious equalities of communism.

"I don't want to repeat my mistakes," Bela said once. "I tried to rule Rudi—Hugh—by fear; I should have tried to win his heart and mind. A willing colleague is always better than a slave."

Bela had become almost like a father to Heinz. There was nothing sexual in their relationship, though the older man had never attempted to conceal his homosexuality. Bela, Heinz knew, no longer had much interest in sex in itself. Heinz wondered if he was still mourning the death of the Prague butcher who had been his lover; or perhaps he had been castrated at Mauthausen; such things had happened in the camps.

Heinz himself considered that sex was an overrated activity. He had biological needs, of course: but these were easily satisfied once a week and on a commercial basis. The amenities of Soho were another reason for liking London: the women here were cleaner than their Egyptian counterparts; they were less curious about their customers; and you could be reasonably sure that they were not in the pay of the security services.

Yes, London was a good city to be in. All in all, Heinz Scholl was enjoying his visit far more than he had expected.

"I was awfully sorry to hear about you and Meg," Stephen said, with what he hoped was just the right blend of sympathy and diffidence. "I suppose there's no chance that the separation will just be temporary?"

Wilbur Cunningham shook his head. "Not a hope, I'm afraid. In the long run, divorce will be best for both of us. But there're no hard feelings."

"That's something." Stephen strolled over to the window and stared down at the trees of Grosvenor Square garden. Wilbur's office always made him feel uncomfortable: it was four times as large as his, and it was furnished as a luxurious study in a private home. "It's rather awkward that Michael's concerned."

"Not for me." Cunningham joined Stephen at the window. "After all, he's her old faithful, isn't he? She'll be in good hands."

Stephen was irritated by the American's good humor. He had come here with the intention of playing the truly fraternal brother-in-law; he had hoped that Wilbur would feel decently bitter to Meg and Michael. Wilbur had no right to be so cheerful. He could at least have the good manners to define how the divorce would affect their relationship.

"By the way," Cunningham said. "You know that guy Scholl? I checked him out with our people, both in Berlin and Cairo. He's MfS, okay; Eicke was right."

"But is he the same one?"

"As Hugh knew in Prague? Looks like it. He didn't waste time in changing horses—joined the Leipzig CP in November 'forty-five. Maybe Hugh was wrong, and Heinz wasn't such a dedicated junior Nazi after all."

"Maybe." Stephen shrugged. "Hugh was only a kid then: he probably exaggerated it."

Cunningham walked back to his desk and took a slim folder from the center drawer. He scanned the contents quickly, as if refreshing his memory, but didn't offer the file to Stephen. *Special relationship,* Stephen thought: *that means all take and no give.* His brother-in-law looked up and smiled.

"Scholl has some sort of personal connection with Juriga. We haven't been able to figure that out. Details about him are kind of thin on the ground altogether. We know he worked with Juriga on the Nasser arms deal. The East Germans can't afford a full station anywhere in the Middle East, but Scholl seems to represent their interests. A roving commission, you might say."

"Then why's he roving over here?"

"A good question." Cunningham ran his finger along his forehead, just below the hairline; it was a trick that Stephen had noticed before; perhaps the American was afraid of going bald.

"Any answers?" Stephen said.

"A few hints. Nothing certain. Oh—you know that *pied noir* you mentioned a few months back? The one who got his throat cut near Alex? One of the gardeners saw someone walking away from the part of the war cemetery just before they found the body. What *was* that guy's name?"

"Thierry," Stephen said coldly.

"Right. Thierry. Anyway—the gardener said that the man who might have killed him was small and European. There's no reason to trust the gardener, by the way. He might have invented it in the hope of a reward. He says he only caught a glimpse of the face. Apparently the man in question had big teeth. They stuck out at the front."

Das Kaninchen?

"You could show the gardener the photograph," Stephen said. "It could be useful to have a positive identification."

Cunningham shook his head. "We're too late. The gardener fell under a truck last October."

Hugh Kendall maintained a small office in Conduit Street. There were only two rooms—one for himself and one for his secretary, a large woman whose husband had died in a Japanese prisoner of war camp. Mrs. Easton was motherly by nature but childless by misfortune. She had been with Hugh for two years and was well worth the large salary he paid her.

One morning in May, Hugh arrived to find her making coffee at least an hour earlier than usual. As he entered, she looked up.

"You have a visitor," she said quietly. "I showed him into your office. Would you like some coffee?"

Hugh nodded. The unexpected visitor must be unusually important or charming or both. Mrs. Easton did not alter her routines lightly; and few people were allowed into Hugh's office when he wasn't there.

"Such a surprise," Mrs. Easton said with a girlish smile. "It's your brother. Mr. Stephen Kendall."

"I see." Hugh agreed: it was a surprise—more so than Mrs. Easton knew. He hadn't seen Stephen since 1950. His brother had made it quite clear that Hugh was a potential embarrassment to him; he had no time to waste on black sheep. Hugh also suspected that Stephen had never forgiven him for inheriting Wilmot House, after all, he was only the younger son. Occasionally Hugh had news of Stephen through the Cunninghams, but Meg and Wilbur never invited the brothers at the same time.

Stephen, perching on the edge of Hugh's desk, was staring at the pen-and-ink drawing which hung above the gray filing cabinet. The drawing showed an Adam fireplace, its ornamentation picked out in meticulous detail; in front of it knelt two figures, a man and a woman, each holding a toasting fork. It should have been a peaceful and domestic scene, but there were odd overtones of menace. The shadows were very deep; the two humans seemed ghostly and ill-defined. Hugh thought of it as tea time in hell.

As Hugh entered, Stephen slid from the desk and stepped toward him with his hand outstretched and a smile on his face.

"Hugh. You look well."

263

They shook hands as if their separation had been purely a matter of geography.

Stephen nodded toward the sketch. "Michael's good, isn't he? I remember him doing that, starting it at least. It was during the first winter of the war. That's me on the left. The woman was poor old Betty Chandos. The fireplace was in the drawing room of her house in Hill Street. They've pulled it down now and put up a ghastly block of concrete."

Hugh waved his brother to a chair and sat down himself. While they waited for the coffee, Stephen did most of the talking. He regretted not having seen anything of Hugh for so long; he blamed himself for it, while simultaneously hinting that the delicate nature of his job had left him no choice in the matter. He commented admiringly on Hugh's successful career as a businessman—he had obviously kept himself informed, probably through Meg—and even praised Mrs. Easton and the appointments of the office.

"Father would be jealous," he said cheerfully. "Do you remember that dreary place he used to have in Sweetmeat Court? And that awful secretary—Miss Leaming, was it?"

If Stephen had not been his brother, Hugh might well have been fooled. But when you had grown up with someone, you knew them with their defenses down. Stephen had always been selfish, devious, and ruthless; but he was intelligent and curiously sensitive as well, which meant he could be extraordinarily charming if he wanted.

Mrs. Easton brought the coffee. Hugh noticed with amusement that she had used the best china. Stephen didn't know how honored he was.

When they were alone again, Hugh chinked his spoon against the side of his cup. The sudden interruption surprised Stephen into silence.

Hugh smiled. "What do you want?"

Stephen's mouth tightened into a hard line. He took out a cigarette case and offered it to Hugh. Hugh shook his head, but pushed the ashtray over to Stephen's side of the desk.

"I need your help." Stephen shrugged. "Not me personally. You know who I work for?"

"More or less."

Stephen leaned forward. "Before I say anything, I must stress that this is strictly confidential. It's a matter of national security."

"Then perhaps you'd better not tell me."

For an instant, the brothers' eyes met and locked. Nothing had changed, Hugh thought: the old hostility still lay between them. *I've never liked my brother and I still don't.*

Stephen dismissed Hugh's remark with a snicker of laughter. "The point is, we think you may be able to help us on a very delicate matter. Two people have recently arrived in London. Both of them work for Communist secret services. Both of them are doing irreparable harm. And you knew them during the war."

Hugh looked away. He could see a square of gray sky through the window. A police car was using its siren on Regent Street. He felt as though his past was chasing him. For an instant he could visualize Magda as she really had been; usually he could not manage that.

Oh, God, what if one of them is Magda?

"We feel," Stephen said smoothly, "that you may be able to extend our knowledge of them—give us a more rounded picture. Any little details you can remember may be useful. Possibly at some stage we might even ask you to confront them—in properly controlled circumstances, naturally."

"Who are they?" Hugh turned back from the window, relieved that his voice still sounded under control. His hands, concealed from his brother by the desk, were shaking.

"Bela Juriga—the Slovakian friend of your butcher. And Heinz Scholl, who must have been about sixteen when you last saw him."

The tension left Hugh. It seemed perfectly natural that Heinz should have become a Communist spy. Even as a boy he had needed an ideology and an institution. Hitler and the Nazis had offered both, but once they were gone the Communists provided the obvious alternative. In another time and place, Heinz could have been a Jesuit. Perhaps it would have been different if his father had lived.

"Well?" Stephen said. "What about it?"

Hugh shook his head. "I'm afraid I can't help you."

"Why not? Look, Hugh—I don't want to stress this, but it is your duty. Also, it'll do you no harm, you know. You'll earn the gratitude of some very important people. For example, I notice you don't belong to any clubs. We could help you there. It could be very useful for someone in your line of business. It's the way things get done in this country—a word in the ear of someone like Sir Basil Cohen and—"

"I said no." Hugh stood up. "I think you'd better leave now."

"For God's sake, Hugh." Stephen's thin face was flushed with anger. "Common sense and ordinary decency—"

"Don't talk to me about decency. And I don't like your brand of common sense."

Hugh stared down at his brother. Stephen worked for the organization that had abandoned him in Prague. Hugh wanted nothing to do with anyone's secret service. He had no animosity toward Bela Juriga now; in a sense they had both been victims of circumstance. Nor had he any intention of harming Heinz Scholl: Hugh had disliked the boy, but he was Magda's brother and Colonel Scholl's son.

Stephen stubbed out his cigarette and slowly stood up. "I don't pretend to understand you. But I do know you'll regret this. I'll make it my business to see that you do."

Hugh opened the door. Mrs. Easton looked up. Her smile vanished when she saw the expression on Hugh's face.

"My brother is leaving now," Hugh said.

Mrs. Easton quickly found Stephen's hat and umbrella.

Stephen paused at the outer door. "Thank you for the coffee, Mrs. Easton." He lowered his voice and said to Hugh, "You always were a fool. The trouble with fools is that their folly makes them dangerous to sensible people."

Michael Stanhope-Smith discovered that it was harder to leave the service than it had been to join it.

He wrote his letter of resignation in March, but it wasn't accepted until the end of May, and even then there were conditions. The chief of these was that he should agree to stay on until the end of the year.

Sir James, a former diplomat, made this condition seem both a favor to himself and something that Michael should have offered without waiting to be asked. Experienced and trustworthy station controllers were at a premium at present. An extra six months would allow Michael to train his successor. SIS was in a state of flux. As Sir James remarked—with that weary smile that was one of his greatest assets—the service seemed to be afflicted with a positive epidemic of nervous breakdowns at present.

Naturally, Michael deserved something in return: there would be immediate de facto promotion, backdated to the middle of 1955; this would considerably improve his pension rights. He would not be expected to work on a full-time basis, unless staff shortages made this essential. Sir James concluded with a little flattery—so oblique that

Michael only understood it for what it was after he had left the room—about Michael's exhibition and the promising future as an artist that lay before him.

It was delicately done. Another six months hardly seemed to matter after nearly twenty years. The extra money would come in useful. The divorce was unlikely to come through until the autumn at the earliest. Despite everything, Michael still felt a certain loyalty to SIS: it would not be right to leave the service in the lurch.

Early in June he was surprised to hear from Stephen Kendall. In the last few years they had seen little of each other. There had never been a quarrel, or anything like that; somehow they had simply drifted apart. He was rather pleased when Stephen phoned him out of the blue and asked him to lunch at the Travellers'.

The Travellers' Club was in Pall Mall, next door to the Reform. Michael was not a member, though many of his more career-minded colleagues were. It was entirely typical that Stephen should have managed to get in.

They ate dull, nursery food in a large dull dining room. Stephen enlivened the food by ordering an excellent Médoc. When the wine waiter had gone, Stephen raised his glass.

"To you and Meg. I'm delighted that you've got back together. I always felt you two were made for each other."

"So did I." Michael smiled. "I can't say I'll be sorry to leave the service, either."

"We shall miss you," Stephen said. "But I gather you're staying on for a few months."

"Sir James was very insistent. At least it means I'll be financially less dependent on Meg."

"So you'll be making the usual trip to Germany next month?"

Stephen's voice was casual, but Michael was immediately aware that the conversation had shifted on to another plane; the social preliminaries were over. Michael made trips to Germany every three months to liaise with military intelligence attached to the British Army of the Rhine. It was a routine chore which rarely produced anything useful. But the director felt that close links should be maintained. Regular visits by an experienced station controller was the easiest way to do it.

Michael nodded. "It's a bore but I can't get out of it."

"I wonder if you could do me a favor while you're out there." Stephen glanced around the dining room. They were lunching late and there was no one within earshot. "I could go through official channels, but in this case that might cause complications."

"Why?" Michael reached for his glass. It was a good Médoc, but he was beginning to suspect that he would have to pay for it.

"It would mean going through Five. And they'd think I was trespassing on their territory. You know what Giles Burnham can be like. He's so possessive about his little fief."

"Aren't we all?" Michael said dryly. "Why does this affect you?"

"It's really a Middle East matter, you see." Stephen grinned. "Though I doubt if I could persuade Giles of that. But it could be very important to all of us, especially if Nasser jumps the way I think he will."

Michael sighed inwardly. No doubt Stephen had some coup in mind; and no doubt he wanted all the credit for it. Still, there was no harm in hearing what he wanted. Michael felt like a boy on the verge of leaving school: the concerns that had dominated his life for so many years no longer seemed important.

"What exactly do you want me to do?"

"Nothing much." Stephen smiled in his old charming way. "Actually, you'd probably enjoy it. While you're in Hamburg, I'd like you to have a chat with a woman. She's very good-looking, I'm told. Her name's Magda Kleist."

Fifteen

The British summer of 1956 was one of the worst in living memory. When Colonel Pakhlanov summoned Heinz to Egypt in July, he was glad of the excuse to go. It seemed so typically English that their climate and inadequate heating should combine to give one chilblains in midsummer.

A car from the embassy was waiting at the airport. Pakhlanov had taken over the Cairo *referentura* for the time being and was using the local GRU Head of Station as his office boy.

When Heinz was ushered into the big, cool office, the colonel was reading a newspaper; without lifting his eyes, he waved toward a chair. This was politeness indeed.

A few seconds later, Pakhlanov looked up. He was not exactly smiling, but his habitual gloom was not quite so pronounced as usual.

"Things are moving, Scholl. The Americans and the British have finally declined to finance the new Aswan dam."

"So now the USSR can step in?"

The colonel clicked his tongue in reproach. "Of course not, Scholl. Not yet, anyway. We've let it be known that no loan will be forthcoming."

"But Nasser will never survive. It'll destroy his political credibility here."

"You underestimate him." The colonel leaned back and lit a cigarette. "There is one course of action open to him, and he must be persuaded to take it. Quite apart from the obvious benefits to us, we need something to divert the attention of the media for a while. In a month or two we shall have to send the troops into Hungary."

Heinz concealed his surprise. Russian military intervention in the affairs of a Warsaw Pact state was always a delicate matter.

"What do you want me to do?" he asked.

"I've arranged for you to see Nasser. You're going to brief him on the military capacities of Britain and France in the Middle East, and on the likely American reactions. You impressed him last year: he'll listen to you."

"Conventional warfare?"

Pakhlanov nodded. "Even the British would hardly be so stupid as to use the atomic bomb in a case like this. It's a pity, but there it is. You must stress the likely response time, of course—that's crucial. You understand what you have to do?"

Heinz nearly laughed out loud: the more he understood, the better he liked it. The strategy was elegant and economical; the risks, the expense, and the effort would be incurred by other people.

"Permit me to congratulate you, Comrade Colonel. I would not like to play chess with you."

Pakhlanov actually smiled.

Nasser's speech took Heinz by surprise—not in its content, but in the manner of its delivery.

Even the venue was interesting. Nasser spoke from a balcony overlooking Liberation Square, Alexandria. Two years before, while standing on the same balcony, he had narrowly escaped an assassination attempt. In theory, the speech marked the fourth anniversary of the exile of King Farouk; in practice, Nasser was expected to explain—and try to excuse—the fiasco of the Aswan loan. Loudspeakers relayed the speech to a crowd, which some estimates put as high as fifty thousand strong. Simultaneously it was broadcast live all over the country.

Heinz Scholl had previously developed an unwilling respect for the Egyptian soldier. He had many qualities that Heinz admired—tenacity, ambition, and an enviable talent for conspiracy. But Nasser had always seemed gauche in company—almost shy.

The three-hour speech, however, forced Heinz to reevaluate entirely his opinion of Nasser. As he had agreed with Heinz, Nasser began by describing his version of the Aswan negotiations. But, instead of casting it in the form of a sober narrative, he turned it into a distinctly comic dramatic monologue. Moreover, he spoke in *baladi,* the language of the streets and bazaars; it was as if Sir Anthony Eden had broadcast to the nation in music-hall cockney.

The crowd was shocked to find itself laughing instead of booing; and with laughter came sympathy. Nasser began to describe the part played by Eugene Black, the president of the World Bank, which had been heavily involved in the Anglo-American proposals. Without warning, Nasser spoke a single sentence in a flat, completely serious voice. "Mr. Black suddenly reminded me of Ferdinand de Lesseps."

Heinz, sitting unobtrusively in a group of Eastern European diplomats, heaved a sigh of relief. The unexpected comic routine had made him wonder if Nasser had any other surprises up his sleeve. But that sentence, which linked the present problem with the builder of the Suez Canal, was a signal to special units of the army and the police.

As Nasser's speech continued, the units were occupying the offices of the Compagnie Universelle du Canal Maritime de Suez in Cairo, and the company's premises in Suez, Port Said, Port Tewfik, and Ismailia. The last British troops had left the canal zone in June. There was no opposition.

Nasser—drunk with his own audacity, but very much in control—took the crowd into his confidence. At this very moment, he told them, the presses were printing a new law which would nationalize this imperialistic company. Their country no longer needed foreign loans. The canal's revenues would henceforward be used for the good of Egypt and her people—specifically for the building of the new dam and in the battle against imperialism and against Israel.

Nasser laughed in exultation. The crowd clapped and shouted its joy. Heinz Scholl thought: *One day, this man could be dangerous.*

"Today," Nasser said, flinging wide his arms to embrace a nation, "in the name of the people, I am taking over the company. Tonight our Egyptian canal will be run by Egyptians. *Egyptians!*"

Nasser left the rostrum. Heinz went back to the consulate to make a few telephone calls before catching the train to Cairo. Everything was going according to plan: the company offices had been taken over; the crowd was streaming through the streets of Alexandria, shouting its hatred of the British. In the harbor, a visiting British cruiser, HMS *Jamaica,* was at action stations. Military law had been declared in the Canal Zone. The company's employees—foreign as well as Egyptian—had been ordered to stay at their posts.

It was all very satisfactory. Heinz should have been delighted. Instead he felt he had seen—or rather heard—a ghost. His old allegiances haunted him. For once he found himself in agreement with Sir Anthony Eden.

Gamal Abdel Nasser bore more than a passing resemblance to Adolf Hitler.

The BfV office in Hamburg occupied six floors of a seven-story building on the Hermanstrasse. The ground floor housed part of the Ministry of the Interior's statistical section.

Michael's request was treated as a routine favor. The British Council was sponsoring a conference on the origins of twentieth-century Europe; the presence of a prominent Hamburg journalist was desired, but, since the person in question was believed to be a *flüchtling,* a refugee from East Germany, an unofficial security check seemed a sensible idea for all concerned. Perhaps the BfV would permit him to inspect the relevant file.

The senior station officer was delighted to oblige. Not only was Herr Stanhope-Smith vouched for by Johann Eicke, he was also a personal friend of the area director who was the SSO's immediate superior. The SSO settled Michael in his own office, rang down for the file, and sent his secretary in search of light refreshment for their distinguished visitor.

They looked through the file together, since the SSO obviously felt that his verbal commentary might be helpful. Michael could have done without this assistance.

The file was a thick one, partly because Frau Kleist's writings had had a small but noticeable influence on the postwar generation of intellectuals, and partly because her brother, Heinz Scholl, was still on the other side of the Iron Curtain, and known to work for the Ministerium für Staats-Sicherheit. Frau Kleist—or, more properly, Fräulein Scholl—was nevertheless believed to be politically reliable.

The facts spoke for themselves. Frau Kleist had been raped by a group of Russian soldiers while returning to Leipzig in May 1945. Her son, Paul, was born in February the following year. Her mother, who had also been assaulted, never really recovered from the experience. She died in Leipzig in 1948. Frau Kleist, who had graduated from the gymnasium at Leipzig during the war, studied history at the university there. She became estranged from her brother in 1945, on both personal and political grounds. After her mother's death, Frau Kleist escaped to the West. She came to live with her maternal great-aunt, Fräulein Wilhelmina Kleist, in Mainz. The aunt, previously a resident in Leipzig, had moved there in the last year of the war. Wilhelmina Kleist died in 1950, leaving property in Hamburg to her great-niece. There was one condition—that Magda should adopt the surname Kleist and use the title of a married woman.

Meanwhile Magda had studied at the universities of Mainz and Cologne. Her particular interest was the development of political ideologies in the last hundred years. She became disillusioned with the prevalent academic system by which professors took the credit for the work of their research assistants. Her aunt's legacy enabled her to turn to writing. Her work on the origins of fascism had been published in *Der Spiegel;* her articles had also appeared in *Der Stern, Die Zeit,* and the *Frankfurter Allgemeine.* A recurring theme in her writing was that regimes of the far left and the far right shared a common totalitarian denominator.

"As far as we're concerned, she's clean," the SSO remarked as Michael turned back to the photographs inside the front cover of the file. "A pretty woman, eh?" He smirked at his guest.

Michael ignored him. There were two photographs, one full-face, the other in profile. He looked at them with the eyes of an artist and thought that the SSO was a fool. The harshly lit black-and-white prints made it quite clear that Magda wasn't pretty: she was beautiful. The bone structure was good. Her face had less to fear from age than most people's. He made a mental note of the address.

He telephoned her from a public call box—old habits died hard, and there was no point in making a call that could be logged; he knew from the file that she wasn't under surveillance. He pretended to be an employee of the British Council and asked if he could see her to discuss a possible lecture. She sounded interested but not particularly excited by the prospect. Michael offered to come to her flat to discuss the matter, but instead she proposed meeting in a restaurant for lunch the following day. It seemed that she valued her privacy.

She named a restaurant near the university. Michael was five minutes early, but she was there before him. He recognized her at once from the photographs. She was reading a magazine, with a glass of white wine at her elbow. Her clothes were good—a simple navy-blue suit which set off her figure; the fair hair was swept back on either side of a broad forehead. He remembered just in time that he was not supposed to know what she looked like. A waiter ushered him across the room to her table.

"Frau Kleist?"

She looked up. "Herr Stanhope-Smith?"

They shook hands. He noticed that she had pronounced his name in the English way. The first few minutes were taken up with exchanging civilities and ordering lunch. When the waiter had left, Magda suggested that he get down to business. Michael was amused: she seemed to be taking control of this meeting.

"The Council is helping to sponsor a conference in London—at the end of August. You may have heard of it: it's on the origins of modern Europe. University College London is acting as host. We were wondering whether you might care to take part."

"It's very much a conference for academics, isn't it? I'm not sure I'm quite the right caliber for that."

"You underrate your reputation in England, Frau Kleist," Michael said smoothly. "Besides, the British Council would like to—ah—broaden the base of the affair. After all, the subject is not simply the concern of academics."

"Had you in mind a particular topic for me?"

"We thought perhaps you might like to discuss how national influences affected the fascist movements in Italy, Germany, and Spain. It's a theme that would fit in rather well with a number of others."

Gray-blue eyes stared thoughtfully at him over the top of her wineglass. She was silent for so long that Michael began to feel uncomfortable. It occurred to him that Stephen would have relished a situation like this: it offered scope for his talent for manipulation.

"How long does the conference last?"

"A week. We would naturally take care of your expenses, including travel. Most of the delegates will be staying at the Russell Hotel."

He wondered, not for the first time, where the money for her expenses would really come from? Out of Stephen's own pocket?

"There is one problem," she said slowly. "I would not wish to be parted from my son. But I do not think I can afford—"

"I'm sure we can squeeze him in," Michael said with a false heartiness that appalled him.

The waiter arrived with their soup; Michael was grateful for the interruption. This job should have been easy. He was overwhelmingly glad that he was retiring. He had spent most of his adult life in the wrong profession: it was not a reassuring thought.

"By the way, there's something that is puzzling me," Magda said when they were alone once more; she switched abruptly from German to fluent, unaccented English: "I phoned the British Council here this morning. No one there had ever heard of a Mr. Stanhope-Smith."

Damn Stephen: he should have covered that.

"That's hardly surprising, Frau Kleist—I'm on the London establishment, and I've only been working there for a fortnight. But the British Consulate will vouch for me. Or you can contact the director-general."

The director-general's cooperation had been necessary to secure Frau Kleist's invitation. Moreover, there was a standing arrangement by which the British Council, if required, would confirm they employed certain people whose names appeared on a list in the director-general's safe. The cover would not fool a professional; but it was sometimes useful when dealing with members of the public. Michael suspected that Stephen had underrated Frau Kleist.

"I see." She drank some of her soup. "In that case, Mr. Stanhope-Smith, I would be pleased to come. I have never been to England."

The rest of the meal passed quickly. Frau Kleist made an entertaining companion. Her intelligence was tempered by a sense of humor; and it was agreeable to have lunch with such a poised and beautiful woman. It was difficult to believe that somewhere in her memory she must still carry the scars of the rape. She looked a good five years younger than she was. Michael wondered about the ten-year-old son: it couldn't have been easy for her to bring up a bastard; and it must have made it all the worse that the boy was a living memento of violence and degradation.

As they were leaving the restaurant, the conversation turned to the capitals of Europe. Frau Kleist was looking forward to seeing London, the largest of them all. Michael said he preferred Paris—it was more of a unit; London sprawled. Just as she was climbing into her taxi, Frau Kleist remarked that her favorite capital was Prague.

The possible implication instantly shattered Michael's well-fed contentment. There had been nothing on the file about Frau Kleist traveling behind the Iron Curtain. He wondered if the BfV was wrong: perhaps her political loyalties were the same as her brother's.

"I've never been there," he said casually. "They say it used to be splendidly baroque in the 'thirties. But I expect it's changed a lot in the last ten years."

Frau Kleist shrugged. "I've no idea. I only knew it during the war. My father was stationed there with the army."

Michael said good-bye. He stood on the pavement, absently watching the taxi as it threaded its way through the traffic. The mention of Prague had prodded his memory. Scholl was a common enough name. He strained to recall the details which Giles Burnham had mentioned, back in 1946. Hugh would never talk about the Scholls, which seemed curious now that Michael came to think about it.

If they were the same Scholls, what on earth was Stephen up to?

Giles Burnham asked the same question.

One evening early in August, he arrived unannounced at Stephen's flat in Fulham. He was so angry that his face turned a dull purple. He hopped from one foot to the other, breathing heavily. Stephen wondered if he was on the brink of a heart attack. It might make life simpler if he was.

"I saw Eicke today. Why didn't you tell me he'd identified Scholl? It's the one your brother knew, isn't it? For Christ's sake, why didn't you tell me?"

"Oh, do sit down, Giles. Do you want some coffee? A cigarette?"

"I want an *answer!*"

"All right, all right. I was going to tell you. But I wanted to get some more information on him first. And that meant contacting Cairo."

Burnham bent down so his face was level with Stephen's and only six inches away from it. His breath stank of whisky: his teetotal resolution must have cracked at last.

"Balls, Kendall. You're trespassing on my territory. You've had a team watching the embassy. God knows how you got the authorization. You probably didn't bother. I've checked with your director of production: he knows sod all about this. You are not meant to operate in this country: you know that as well as I do. I want an explanation."

Stephen sat down and lit a cigarette. As he had hoped, his calm movements made Burnham feel slightly foolish: they emphasized the unnecessary melodrama. Burnham's color became healthier, and he sat down on the edge of an armchair. It was time to try the frank approach.

"Giles," Stephen said quietly, "I've nothing personal against Scholl, I promise you. The point is, he's vital to a Soviet operation that's probably the biggest thing they've mounted since the war."

"You're paranoid," Burnham said contemptuously. "Reds under the bed."

Stephen flushed but kept his temper. "Let me try to explain."

"I'll give you five minutes."

"My information is that Scholl's working with a Colonel Pakhlanov. Probably GRU. The two of them manipulated Nasser into nationalizing the canal. They were clever: the Soviets pulled the strings but Egypt took the risks. No amount of talking is going to get it back. As a consequence, most of the Middle East will be destabilized: it'll swing toward the Eastern bloc."

"That's rubbish. Nasser can't afford to antagonize us, the French, *and* the Americans."

"Wilbur Cunningham's my brother-in-law. According to him, whatever the Americans say, they're unlikely to intervene substantially on our side. It's election year: Eisenhower and Foster Dulles don't want to offend people. They see this as a colonialist issue. If it comes to a fight, we'll be left on our own."

Burnham took out his pipe and blew furiously into it. An oily shred of dottle flew out. "*If* it comes to a fight, and *if* the Yanks won't back us, I don't see that it's going to matter. A tinpot Arab dictatorship can't take on two world powers. You're being absurd."

"Nasser wouldn't be alone. Most of the Middle East would back him. He'd have world opinion on his side. The Soviets would give him anything he wanted. Eden wouldn't dare to use the bomb against him. The PM hates Nasser, and he doesn't want another Munich; but he's even less enthusiastic about a third world war."

"Stephen, you're overreacting—"

"Without American backing, we can't fight a major conventional war in the Middle East. I don't mean military backing. I mean money. Another dollar loan. Do you know how much oil we've got at present? About six weeks' worth, if that. Then think of the logistics involved: Malta's eleven hundred miles away; Cyprus is—"

"What's Scholl got to do with all this?" Burnham snorted. "*Das Kaninchen!* Bloody Krauts."

"You could think of him as the tip of the knife that the Soviets are trying to put between us and the Americans. And he's damned sharp. All things to all men. He's done the rounds of the embassies in London. Promising this, suggesting that. He's working hand-in-glove with that Czech queer: Juriga does the arms side. *You want a hundred SU-100 self-propelled guns? Then vote with the USSR at the Canal Users conference.* The Rabbit is bloody good at his job. And his job is to destroy this country as a world power.

277

Can't you understand? It's as simple as that."

Burnham stood up, his pipe fixed securely in the corner of his mouth. He staggered over to the drinks tray, barking his shins against the sofa on the way.

"You don't mind? A spot of something to concentrate the mind?"

Stephen nodded.

Burnham poured himself half a tumblerful of Scotch, added a token squirt of soda, and drank.

"Promised Mildred I wouldn't do this," he said. "But you made me so damned angry. Cheers."

"There's another thing," Stephen said. "If we get a bloody nose over Suez, the African colonies won't last another ten years. It's a question of prestige."

"And what do you propose to do about it?"

"Getting American support is the vital thing; but there's not much I can do in that direction. We need time, though—and I can think of one delaying tactic. Nobble the Rabbit. It'd take time for the Soviets to get someone else in position. Third World diplomats are pretty touchy—Scholl seems to have won their confidence."

"Now look here, Stephen." Burnham stabbed the stem of his pipe toward his host. "You're talking about murder, aren't you? Or perhaps a smear job. You're off your head. You can't do that sort of thing without ministerial authorization. Especially not since Crabb."

"You and I could do it between us, Giles. We could use one or two of Five's free-lancers. I could find the money. We could even make it seem like an American operation—now *there's* a thought."

Burnham put down his empty glass on the edge of a table: the glass fell to the carpet and rolled under an armchair. Both men ignored it.

"I may be drunk," Burnham said slowly, "but I'm not stupid. If you ask me, Suez has put your head on the block. I don't know how—perhaps you missed something, perhaps you backed the wrong opinion. There'll be an inquiry when all this is over. I think you're scared of losing your job."

Stephen turned away. There was something in what Burnham had said. He might not lose his job, but he was unlikely to get the promotion to director of production, Middle East, which he had been maneuvering toward. A watchdog which had failed to bark would make an obvious scapegoat when Whitehall apportioned blame for the Suez crisis.

But there was more to it than that. This had become personal, as well as professional. Heinz Scholl was fighting on Stephen's own ground, the Middle East; he had no right to be there at all. And Scholl had this awkward and potentially embarrassing connection with Hugh. Stephen could almost blame Hugh for the threat to his career: *if Hugh had left young Heinz to drown in the Vltava, all this need never have happened.*

"You'll regret this, Giles. Sometimes conventional methods won't work."

Burnham walked carefully across the room to the door. He gripped the doorknob to steady himself and looked back at Stephen. He was struggling to resist the effects of the alcohol. His voice, unlike his legs, was still under control.

"This is an interservice matter. What Scholl does in London is my responsibility. If you don't stop interfering, I'm going straight to the minister. Your ideas aren't just unconventional: they're bloody lunatic. You keep out of my territory."

"Trespassers will be prosecuted?" Stephen said lightly.

"Trespassers will be shot."

Michael Stanhope-Smith found it unexpectedly difficult to get hold of Hugh. Mrs. Easton told him that Mr. Kendall had left for Switzerland on business, and that she had subsequently had a telegram from her employer to say that he was planning to take a fortnight's holiday in Greece. Any urgent messages should be sent post restante to Athens. Mrs. Bunnings had had a similar telegram.

In due course, Michael received a postcard from Heraklion. *For some reason,* it said, *when I ask for yogurt they give me olive oil. Greek more difficult than I had anticipated. Was pink: am now peeling. H.*

Michael was annoyed but not surprised. Hugh had a habit of taking unexpected holidays, usually in out-of-the-way places; he had once told Michael that he liked to remind himself every now and then what it was like to be poor and homeless. Michael decided not to write to Athens: letters were unsafe, and in any case it was difficult to put shapeless suspicions down on paper. Besides, there was no hurry: Hugh might well be back before Frau Kleist arrived in London.

He was aware that his suspicions were not only vague: they were also unprofessional. Stephen was a colleague and should be trusted to know what he was doing. Scholl, as Michael reminded himself frequently, was a very common name.

Meanwhile, there were other things to think about. The backdated promotion made its presence felt in his salary checks. He and Meg spent the Bank Holiday weekend in a Glastonbury hotel. There, for the first time since the war, they made love. The weather was disappointing—there were snowstorms in the south of England—but since they spent most of their time in bed, it had little effect on them.

On the Sunday morning they lay in bed watching the hail flinging itself against the window. The maid had brought the papers with their tea: SUEZ DEADLOCK a headline said. USE OF FORCE NOT RULED OUT.

Meg said, "It's so dreary. Haven't we all done enough fighting?"

She reached out for him, and in the ensuing struggle they upset the teapot over the bedspread and made their neighbor bang indignantly on the partition wall. By the time they had finished, the newspapers had been reduced to tea-soaked pulp.

Stephen Kendall, his professional reputation in the balance, worked an eighteen-hour day, seven days a week, for most of August. The workload of his section had swollen dramatically. British and French military planners had taken over a warren of rooms beneath the War Office in Whitehall. They inundated SIS with requests for information. Stephen's section was supposed to have most of the answers.

By monitoring the requests, it was possible to gain an idea of the plans under discussion. Stephen was dismayed on several accounts. The Task Force seemed to lack clear political guidance on its objectives, and on the means it could use to attain them. It was even uncertain about its destination: would it attack Port Said or Alexandria? The manpower and resources of the Egyptian Army could be estimated with a fair degree of accuracy, but no one was sure whether or not it would prove an opponent worth taking seriously. The requests showed with depressing clarity that the planners were muddled and uncoordinated.

Stephen heard unofficially that the government had accepted the view of the Chiefs of Staff: for logistical reasons, the invasion couldn't take place until the middle of next month at the earliest. In the meantime, the government decided that it had nothing to lose by negotiation, a course of action which was strongly supported by the Americans. On August 16, representatives of the twenty-two powers most dependent on the canal met in London at Lancaster House. In Stephen's opinion, Britain had made yet another tactical error:

having submitted the matter to international arbitration, she could hardly use force without being accused of inconsistency.

Nasser was sent an invitation, but politely refused. The conference lasted a week. Eighteen of the members backed an American-sponsored plan to put the canal under international control. India, however, proposed an alternative plan which respected Egypt's sovereignty over the canal; this was backed by the USSR, Ceylon, and Indonesia, and received much support from Third World countries. Heinz Scholl had achieved another significant success.

The young German was rarely far from Stephen's mind. Sometimes he wondered if the Rabbit could have suborned someone in his own section—Captain Blaines, perhaps. He felt as though he was under constant surveillance. He peered in shop windows in the hope of finding someone on his tail; he sealed the doors in his flat with hairs. He found nothing overtly suspicious, but this did not surprise him; after all, the Rabbit was a professional himself. Sleep brought Stephen little relief, for Scholl was waiting for him—around a corner or behind a closed door: the Rabbit was always invisible but always there.

Matters would come to a head at the end of the month—one way or another. Sometimes Stephen managed briefly to convince himself that solving the problem of Scholl would also solve the problems of Suez and his own future.

Burnham's intervention had made his efforts in this direction much more difficult. Official resources were increasingly closed to him. One couldn't rely on favors forever. He had used Michael Stanhope-Smith once; it would be unwise to use him again. It seemed more and more likely that someone was spying on him—if not for Scholl then for Burnham. He tried to get Blaines transferred to another section, but failed ignominiously. Blaines must have powerful friends.

Stephen knew he needed help—a stringer to do the legwork that Burnham prevented him from doing himself. But the free-lance community in London was small, incestuous, and dominated by MI5 and the CIA, the two major contractors of its labor. If Stephen bought himself a stringer, he could not be sure that loyalty and discretion were included in the purchase price.

On August 18 he realized that there was one stringer available whom no one else would dream of hiring. The man in question didn't even think of himself as a stringer.

If anything, he thought of himself as a patriot.

Alfred Kendall ignored the pains in his chest and forced himself up the stairs, through the barrier, and out into the open air.

The rain had declined to a fine, soft drizzle. From the underground station he could see several hundred yards up the Finchley Road. The glistening pavements were packed with morning shoppers, but few of them had their umbrellas open. You could count them on the fingers of one hand. He therefore decided not to open his own umbrella; it was important to be as inconspicuous as possible. His professionalism pleased him.

A smell of roasting coffee from a nearby shop surprised a memory from him—a café in Na Prikope, where they roasted the coffee beans on the premises; he had waited there for over an hour once; Madame Hase had often been late.

By now the tall man in the tan overcoat was fifty yards away. The coat was open and it flapped as he walked. Alfred Kendall walked briskly after him. He noticed a pub on the other side of the road: it was open, but he had no desire for a drink.

The man ahead was Antonin Tesla. According to Stephen, Tesla was merely a thug. In real life he looked even more stupid than he had in the photographs.

Suddenly Tesla was no longer there. Kendall quickened his pace. The Czech had slipped into a small suburban railway station. Tesla was buying a ticket. There was no one else in the little foyer. Kendall ducked back onto the pavement. The station must be on the North London line, which ran in a northerly loop from the City in the east to Richmond in the west.

Metal-shod shoes clattered down steps: Tesla was on his way.

Kendall ran up to the ticket-seller's grill; he caught sight of Tesla's narrow head and broad shoulders descending to the westbound platform.

"Same as my friend, please."

"Your what?" The clerk didn't look up from his newspaper.

Kendall felt cheated: the trick always worked in thrillers. The rattle of an approaching train forced him to abandon subtlety.

"Richmond, please."

The clerk reached for a ticket. "Single or return?"

"Single. No, better make it a return." The extravagance annoyed him, but professionalism required him to keep open as many options as possible.

"Make up your mind, gov."

282

Kendall paid for the ticket, biting back the desire to make a sharp retort; the railways had gone to the dogs since they were nationalized. He discovered with a sharp sense of anticlimax that he needn't have hurried: the train was going east. That never happened in thrillers, either.

He pretended to read the timetable in the foyer while he waited for the train. It wouldn't do to go down the platform. When the train arrived, he ran down at the last moment and flung himself aboard. He was disgusted to find himself in a non-smoker.

At this time of day, the little train carried fewer passengers than during the rush hour; this made Kendall's job harder, for crowds provided cover. At each station, he peered out of the window, watching for Tesla. Sometimes he wondered if he had made a mistake: perhaps he should have stayed outside the embassy until *Das Kaninchen* emerged.

To himself he always used Scholl's cover name. Stephen had mentioned it, and it was somehow more appropriate for a player in the Great Game. The Rabbit was the most important of the six targets. Bela Juriga was the next most dangerous man, but Stephen thought it better that Alfred should keep out of his way, though the chances of recognition seemed slight after seventeen years.

The Rabbit, however, appeared to be staying in his burrow today. Stephen's instructions had been clear: it was better to follow any of the six, even Juriga, rather than to hang around the embassy. It was safer for a watcher to be on the move.

Tesla's movements were promising. By now the train was in Willesden Junction; and the Czech was still on board. That meant he must be making a detour, because he could have reached here, or any point further west, more directly from central London. Kendall felt instinctively—or so he assured himself—that he was on the right track. What Stephen wanted were contacts and addresses which lay outside the usual diplomatic routine.

The train passed beside a scrapyard, filled with the rusting corpses of cars. At the next stop, Acton Central, Tesla got out. The Czech left it until almost the last moment. Kendall had to jump out while the train was moving: he landed heavily, jarring his body; he stumbled and scraped his knee. By an effort of will he forced himself not to cry out. Tesla did not turn around.

Outside the station Tesla walked quickly with his head down, like a man who knew where he was going. He pursued a zigzag course through short streets of shabby late-Victorian terraces, most of which were named after poets. The sun had come out, and grubby children played on the pavements. One of them asked Kendall for a shilling. Kendall refused with a frown. It was disgusting that children should be allowed to beg in the streets.

Tesla stopped. Kendall darted off the pavement and took cover behind a parked van. There were wing mirrors mounted on the front mudguards. He discovered that if he craned his head he could see Tesla. The Czech had taken a piece of paper from his pocket: he glanced at it and then at a detached house, larger than those in the rest of the road, which stood on the corner. The house was built of dirty yellow brick; to one side of it was a yard which had once, perhaps, been a garden; it was now crammed with cars whose condition was only slightly better than those in the scrapyard which they had passed in the train. At the front, the house was separated from the road by a low brick wall and a strip of garden filled with overgrown laurel bushes. A rusting wrought-iron gate, hanging askew on its hinges, gave on to a short path which led up to the front door.

As Kendall watched, Tesla pushed open the gate and walked up to the house. He let himself in with a key. The gate swung slowly back with a screech of unoiled metal. The door closed with a bang, as if Tesla had kicked it. Kendall could make out the house number just above the knocker: 15.

What would a professional do?

"Go on, mister. Just the price of a cup of tea."

Kendall looked down, ready to snarl a refusal and if necessary reinforce it with a blow. It was the same boy who had asked him for a shilling. He was about ten years old—red-haired, bright-eyed, and with the trace of an Irish accent; he stank faintly but persistently of weeks of dirt.

A Baker Street Irregular, Kendall thought: *If Sherlock Holmes could use them. Why shouldn't I?*

"If you'll do an errand for me, I'll give you a shilling."

The boy glanced around, as if looking for eavesdroppers. "Depends what it is."

"I just want you to buy a stamp and post a letter for me."

"Half a crown."

"Don't be ridiculous."

The boy shrugged and half turned.

"Very well then. Half a crown." Kendall struggled to reassert himself. "But you must run all the way."

"Okay, mister. For half a crown."

Kendall realized the agreement was worth nothing. He had no means of enforcing it. But it was better than nothing. He couldn't leave the house unguarded and give Tesla a chance to slip away.

He wrote the message on a page torn from his diary: *Have followed AT to 15 Keats Rd. Acton. 11.45 A.M. AK.* There was an envelope in his pocket—it contained a circular which had arrived that morning; he hadn't even opened it, but he had noticed it was unsealed. He slipped in his message and gummed down the flap. There was no need to change the address. He gave the envelope to the boy and took out his purse.

"There you are—half a crown. Off you go."

"I need another tuppence ha'penny, mister. For the stamp."

Kendall swore under his breath: *The penny-pinching little bastard;* but he handed over the extra coppers. The boy ran off down the street. Kendall peered again at the house, wishing Stephen had given him a gun.

The upstairs windows were curtained. He could see no sign of movement. No doubt, Bulldog Drummond or Richard Hannay would have charged into the house, but Alfred Kendall was made of subtler stuff than these fictional heroes. It was wiser to watch and wait.

He lit a Gold Flake and crossed the road so he could stand at a bus stop. The move enabled him to see the back of the house, while still covering the front door. No one would look twice at someone waiting for a bus.

The cigarette seemed to last only a few seconds. He flicked the butt into the roadway and reached for another. At that moment he felt a hand on his shoulder; simultaneously something hard was rammed into the base of his spine.

"Captain Kendall." The voice was thin and bronchial. "*What* a surprise!"

Kendall had stiffened with shock and fright, but he forced himself to relax. "Bless my soul," he said as calmly as if he had been Bulldog Drummond or Richard Hannay. "After all these years! It's Bela Juriga, isn't it?"

"How did this happen?" Heinz moved closer to Tesla, who tried to back away. "I want an answer, Antonin."

"He must have followed me from the—"

"And where was your backup, Antonin? I presume you remember the standing orders for coming here?"

Tesla spread his hands out. "Of course, Comrade Scholl. But Vaclav was ill this morning, and we thought if I was careful it would be all right if I went alone."

"But you weren't careful, Antonin. More than that, you were stupid, weren't you?"

Tesla nodded. Scholl stared at him with irritation and contempt. These big men were all the same: they thought their size and strength gave them a substitute for intelligence.

"Kendall is an amateur," Scholl said. "He's old and he's ill. Yet you let him follow you. *Why?*"

"I could have sworn no one was on my tail. I checked, I promise you. I didn't come here directly."

There was a tap on the door. Viston, the garage mechanic in whose name the house was rented, put his head around the door.

"I've locked up," he said. "Anything else I can do?"

Heinz shook his head. "Go to bed. We'll wake you if we need you. Pretend we're not here." As the door closed, he turned back to Tesla. "If you make another mistake, you'll be facing a Court of Enquiry when you get home. Now go downstairs. Viston's got some army surplus jerry cans in the scullery. Wash one of them out, drive up to the canal, and fill it with water. The water must come from the canal."

"But comrade—"

"Do it now, Antonin. Don't ask questions and don't get caught. You know what happens if you make another mistake."

When he was alone, Heinz sat down in an armchair and laughed quietly. It had worked out rather well. In the street below he could hear a man singing uncertainly: *John Brown's body lies a-moldering in his grave.* Glass shattered—probably a milk bottle. It was eleven o'clock and, apart from the solitary reveler returning home from the pub, Keats Road was quiet.

Tesla's blunder hadn't compromised the safe house, thanks to Bela's quick thinking. Bela had realized that Tesla had come to Keats Road alone when he found Vaclav groaning over a basin in one of the lavatories at the embassy. He had reached the house not more than a couple of minutes after Tesla. Kendall hadn't been carrying a short-wave radio; and there wasn't a public telephone box or post box within five minutes' walk. The safe house must still be secure.

Bela slipped into the room. The limp was more noticeable than usual. Before sitting down, he checked that the curtains were secure-ly drawn. His face was pale and worried.

"Kendall will say nothing," he said. "We could make him talk, but that would take time or leave marks. He keeps roaring and spluttering and pretending he's an outraged British gentleman."

"But he admits he knows you?"

Bela nodded. "He calls that coincidence. He just happened to be passing."

"It's encouraging," Heinz said. "First they had a professional team watching the embassy. But they must have decided we weren't worth the expense. Using a stringer implies they don't see us as being much of a threat. Especially one like Kendall: he's just a senile lush."

"We're assuming he's the only one."

"We'd know if he wasn't. The British aren't that good. If you ask me, they're overrated."

"Maybe." Bela lit a cigarette and went into the usual fit of coughing. "But what will we do with Kendall?"

"Need you ask?"

"Is it necessary? You don't think he might have some value as a hostage?"

"It's my responsibility, Bela," Heinz said. "You know what Pakhlanov said: you are in control of the technical side, but operational decisions are to be made by me."

"I know." Bela stood up. "It's easier to be ruthless when you're young. I'll say good night."

Heinz sat there, listening to Bela's slow footsteps on the stairs; the front door slammed; a car engine came to life. Viston was upstairs, pretending to be asleep and no doubt appalled that after ten years GRU had finally asked for something in return for its money. Captain Kendall was in the cellar with Vaclav—whose food poisoning had cleared up with remarkable rapidity since this morning—watching over him. Tesla was fetching water. And Bela was running away from what had to be done.

Pakhlanov had been right. *Juriga has become unreliable in situations where there may be a need for wet affairs,* he had told Heinz. *Don't misunderstand me: he's a good man. But the camps have left their mark. Sometimes people see too much death. They either become inured to it; or they become afraid of it—their own or other people's. That's why you'll make the operational decisions.*

A wet affair was a typically Russian euphemism. In this case, Heinz thought, it was really rather apt.

287

Alfred Kendall waited.

He had nothing left but his obstinacy. They had put him in a wooden chair with armrests. They had padded his arms and legs and tied them to the chair. Twelve hours ago? Twenty-four hours? He had no idea: natural light didn't reach the little cellar, and they had refused to tell him the time when he had asked. Not that he had had much opportunity to ask: most of the time they had kept him gagged.

They hadn't tortured him as badly as he had expected. Perhaps Bela had put in a good word with *Das Kaninchen* for old times' sake. But his own body had humiliated him—the cramps, the cravings for alcohol and tobacco and—most shamefully of all—the weakness of his bladder.

Someone was always with him. The four junior members of the mission took it in turns to sit in the other chair by the stairs. They all smoked, which made matters worse. None of them said anything— they left speech to Scholl and Juriga.

But he hadn't cracked: they couldn't know for sure that he was working for the British secret service. Stephen would know something was wrong when he, Alfred, failed to telephone this evening. If he could only endure for long enough, help must come.

If that brat posted the letter—

The door opened and the Rabbit came down the stairs, two at a time; behind him was one of his thugs, carrying a jerry can in one hand and a briefcase in the other. The guard, whom Kendall had heard addressed as Vaclav, stumbled to his feet.

Scholl said something in Czech which Kendall couldn't catch; Vaclav left the cellar. The other thug strode over to Kendall and pulled off the gag.

"Don't be so brutal," the Rabbit said slowly in German. He smiled at Kendall and switched to English. "I am sorry about this. Would you like a cigarette?"

Scholl lit a cigarette and placed it in Kendall's mouth. The smoke was hot and harsh, but he sucked furiously. Scholl stood beside him: every now and then he would remove the cigarette and tap the ash neatly into the old tobacco tin which the guards had been using as an ashtray.

"Antonin," the Rabbit said. "Bring me the briefcase."

He opened it and took out a bottle of Bell's. Kendall's stomach lurched. It had been so long since the last drink.

"A little whisky? We have no glass, I'm afraid, but I'll hold the bottle for you."

Kendall tilted back his head. He felt Scholl's hand on his shoulder, steadying him. His teeth chattered against the glass of the bottle. He swallowed so much that he retched. Raw whisky ran down his chin and dripped between his collar and his neck.

"Careful now," the Rabbit said gently. "It won't go away. Take it slowly."

He lost track of time. The whisky flowed into him, anesthetizing the pain, the fear, and the shame. At one point there was another cigarette. The Rabbit's hand was behind him, supporting his head.

Thoughts circled through his mind: *This is a good German, a kind German . . . When will Stephen come? . . . If I go on drinking, I'll be too drunk to talk, even if they torture me . . . A good German . . .*

His bladder slackened again. His sense of shame pushed aside the growing numbness.

"Sorry, old man. I need a lavatory—a bath."

"A bath? But, of course. Antonin, fetch the zinc bath from the kitchen for Captain Kendall."

Captain Kendall: even now the use of the title brought a flicker of pleasure.

The thug's footsteps echoed on the uncarpeted stairs. The bottle returned. Kendall noticed automatically that it was already half empty. Of course, some of it had been spilled. He wondered if he would soon be sick.

Suddenly the Rabbit wound his fingers into Kendall's hair and pulled back his head. The whisky bottle stayed where it was, inverted over Kendall's mouth. He tried to pull away, but Scholl was too strong. The spirit cascaded from his mouth and poured over his neck and chest.

Kendall was both puzzled and aggrieved: it seemed such a waste.

When the bottle was empty, Scholl set it gently on the concrete floor. He gripped Kendall's ears and forced back his head. Kendall yelped with pain and struggled ineffectually to free himself.

The Rabbit brought his face very close to Kendall's. "Your son," he said quietly, "killed my father after my father had saved his life."

"Stephen—?"

"Hugh."

A door slammed, and Scholl released him abruptly. The thug put down the zinc bath five feet in front of Kendall. He uncapped the jerry can and poured its contents into the bath. Kendall struggled to keep his eyes in focus.

"The water, old chap," he said. "Look at it. It's dirty."

The Rabbit nodded. "First we shall wash your face."

Scholl took one side of the chair; Antonin took the other. They lifted it and Kendall into the air, and rotated their burden through ninety degrees. Kendall found himself staring at the concrete floor. The full weight of his body tugged painfully against his bonds. He screamed—a high, continuous sound which he could hardly hear above the drumming of the blood in his ears.

His knees and the arms of the chair hit the concrete. The brown water rocked to and fro in the bath. Someone leapt astride him, as if he was a horse. Two hands pushed against the back of his skull.

The water came closer. It smelled faintly of petrol.

What would Bulldog Drummond or Richard Hanney do now?

Sixteen

The corpse was found floating in the Grand Union Canal near Harlesden by children playing hide-and-seek along the towpath. It was identified as Alfred Kendall, first by the papers in his wallet and then more formally by his elder son Stephen.

The autopsy showed that he had been very drunk when he drowned, and that he had probably died late the previous night or early that morning. The water in his lungs had come from the canal. There were no signs of violence on his body. The post mortem also showed that the deceased had been a very heavy drinker and smoker.

At the inquest it was established that Alfred Kendall had been unemployed for several years and that he was in financial difficulties. It was tacitly understood that he had become something of an embarrassment to his long-suffering family. The coroner went out of his way to spare the Kendalls pain. A verdict of accidental death was returned.

Michael escorted Meg to the inquest. Stephen was there, of course, but Hugh was still on the Continent. He was believed to be on his way back to England, but efforts to get in touch with him had failed.

Meg wore black out of deference to the conventions, but on the way home she confessed rather shamefacedly to Michael that she felt a fraud.

"I never loved him, you know, even when we were kids." She stared out of the window of the taxi which was taking the three of them down the Harrow Road. "I don't think any of us did. He was always someone to be frightened of. Then when we were older he was someone to despise. I wish I'd made more of an effort with him, I suppose, but that's just for my own peace of mind. I don't really *care* that he's dead."

"Well, it's too late to worry about him now," Stephen said brusquely.

He was sitting opposite them. Michael noticed that he was unusually pale, and that the hand that held the cigarette was trembling.

"I wonder what he was doing in Harlesden," Meg said.

"You know what he was like," Stephen said. "He liked wandering around London. Especially in the last year or so."

"Did he? I never knew."

"Perhaps I knew him better than you did."

The answer was the verbal equivalent of a slap. Michael was embarrassed. He was annoyed with Stephen for Meg's sake, but he was also annoyed with himself for underrating Stephen's affection for his father. It was always easier to assume that people were worse, rather than better, than they were.

Stephen thought that if the pressure on him continued for much longer he would break apart.

He excused himself from joining Michael and Meg for lunch: he simply hadn't the time. He was due at London Airport at 4 P.M. Before then he had to put in an appearance at the office and try to get through a day's work in a couple of hours.

First, however, he went to Swiss Cottage. There was just a chance, albeit a slim one, that he might find something there. He had tried to visit his father's bedsitter as soon as he had heard about the death. But the landlady had proved unexpectedly bloodyminded: she refused to let anyone up there until two months' back rent had been paid. Stephen suspected that she was hoping to get her hands on his father's possessions.

The taxi dropped him in Eton Avenue. The weather had suddenly turned warm and unpleasantly humid. As Stephen crossed the road he could feel the sweat trickling down his spine. He yearned for a cold bath and a change of clothes.

The house was a redbrick Victorian villa with a stained-glass window, gargoyles, and a small spire; no doubt the architect would have preferred to design a cathedral. It was shielded from the road by a line of lank and overgrown firs.

When the landlady eventually opened the door, he discovered

that she was in a bad temper because he had interrupted her lunch. But she was mollified by the sight of two months rent in cash; and she was overawed by a letter from Mr. Turnbull which informed whomever it might concern that Mr. Alfred Kendall was dead and that Mr. Stephen Kendall was his executor.

The little room was on the top floor, directly under the roof. In the house's more prosperous days it would have housed a servant. The walls sloped; there was a dormer window; and the temperature must have been in the high seventies.

When Stephen was left alone, he removed his jacket and unbuttoned his waistcoat. It was the first time he had seen where his father lived, for on the few occasions they had met recently it had been on neutral ground or at Stephen's flat. Like a valuer, he assessed the earthbound remnants of his father's life: the green linoleum; the wardrobe with the pile of cardboard suitcases above it; the single, unmade bed with dirty sheets and a pillowcase stained with hair oil; the gas fire with the shilling-in-the-slot meter beside it; the unemptied ashtrays; the sagging armchair; the pine table with letters and yellowing newspapers stacked on its cracked top; and—above all—the dust, which covered every surface in the room with a gray shroud.

Stephen gagged. *I'm overworked,* he told himself, *and I shouldn't have come here on an empty stomach.* With difficulty he opened the little window and leaned out. Half a mile away was a green smudge that must be Primrose Hill; London was an endless blur around the horizon.

The tide of nausea receded. He turned back to the room that had been his father's home. He searched methodically, as he had been trained, moving around the attic in a clockwise direction. The suitcases were full of empty bottles. The wardrobe held astonishingly few clothes. The newspapers dated back to the end of the year: Stephen wondered why on earth his father had kept them. The letters were bills and circulars; Stephen crammed them unopened into his pocket; he and Turnbull would need to settle the outstanding debts. There were more bottles under the bed—it was difficult to imagine from whom his father had hidden them, since it was clear by the dust that his landlady had rarely visited the room.

He checked the floorboards and—fighting back a second attack of nausea—the bedding and the mattress. Apart from an envelope full of pawn tickets beneath the pillow, he found nothing. He put the envelope in his pocket: sometime he would have to reclaim the winter overcoat, the dinner jacket, the silverplated cigarette case, and the gold half-hunter that had belonged to his grandfather.

The landlady waylaid him in the hall. "I can't afford to keep that room empty," she told him with a belligerent gleam in her eye. "I want your father's things out by this evening."

"That's quite impossible." Stephen opened the front door. "I tell you what: you can have everything that's up there. Good afternoon."

It was Magda's first flight, but she knew as soon as she entered the long, cramped cabin of the BEA Vickers Viscount that she was terrified of flying. If Paul hadn't been there, she would have invented some excuse to leave the plane. It would mean throwing up the chance to speak at the conference—a pity, since it would enhance her intellectual credibility at home, if nothing else—but peace of mind would have been worth the sacrifice.

Or rather—it would have been worth it if her career was the only reason why she wanted to go to London.

But the presence of Paul made it necessary to pretend that she wasn't afraid. Conscience might make cowards of us all, she thought as the plane lifted itself from the runway with a sickening lurch, but our children made us brave.

Paul, his nose pressed against the cabin window, was enthralled. As always, excitement made him talkative. Did Mama know that the distance by air from Hamburg to London was 741 kilometers? Did she know that British European Airways had twenty-seven Vickers Viscounts 701s in service? Mama not only didn't know; she didn't care, either.

But Magda coped, with the help of a judicious quantity of gin. She doubted if her fear was visible to anyone else. She had learned the hard way, both to hide her fear and to cope with it. Nothing could ever be quite as bad as that day in May 1945, which had begun with the news of her father's death and ended with her mother and herself being systematically violated by a seemingly endless procession of angry, evil-smelling animals in khaki uniforms. A day like that taught one a sense of proportion just as effectively as the study of history was supposed to do. There were worse things in life than wanting to scream your head off in a tin box above the clouds.

According to the captain, it was a smooth flight in perfect weather. Magda thought: *He would say that, wouldn't he?* Nevertheless, she tried to believe it. Paul helped to distract her with his unquenchable desire to receive or impart information. She could tell how excited he was: the sickle-shaped scar beneath his left eye was slightly pinker than the surrounding skin; it was an infallible sign.

The worst moments came at the end of the flight. It seemed impossible that the pilot should not lose control of this metal envelope and send it and its contents plunging to the ground.

Paul, who could be surprisingly sensitive for a ten-year-old, tried to help. "British airlines are very safe, honestly. Did you know that there were only two fatal accidents on their flights last year?"

And that was two too many. "How many people were actually killed?"

Paul smiled, happy to show off his knowledge. "Thirteen passengers and three crew members."

"Oh, my God."

"But remember, that's hardly anyone."

Trust Paul to see the bright side, even where the statistics of death are concerned.

"How nice, *liebling*," Magda said carefully.

"Only one passenger was killed out of every two hundred and twenty-nine thousand and five hundred which the airlines carried." Paul looked at her triumphantly. "So I think we're pretty safe."

"I'm so glad."

The plane touched down with two jolts, and Magda gasped.

"It's all right," Paul said. "We're here."

The letter from the British Council had confirmed the invitation and enclosed their tickets and an itinerary. Magda reread it as they waited in the arrival lounge. Yes, it definitely said that they would be met at the airport.

She had half hoped that Mr. Stanhope-Smith would be there—after all, he was attached to the London headquarters of the British Council; he was tall enough to be difficult to miss in a crowd. As she gazed at the letter, all the old doubts came flooding back.

They were foolish, she knew: she had checked her visitor's credentials with the Hamburg consulate; and the letter and its enclosures were further confirmation. But the invitation still puzzled her.

The obvious explanation was that someone more important who worked in roughly the same field had dropped out at the last moment. That would explain why the invitation had come at the last moment, and why the travel and accommodation arrangements had been so lavish; for example, she had been surprised that the council was willing to pay all of Paul's expenses; such generosity was surely uncharacteristic.

But the explanation was not entirely satisfactory. Magda had an accurate idea of her own status among professional historians: she had done some research which was considered promising, but the fact that she was not established at a university went against her; so did her sex and nationality. She was not unduly modest about her achievements—no one in her position could afford to be—but they didn't merit the red-carpet treatment she was getting. Surely the council could have found someone else at the last moment—someone who was closer to the academic mainstream than herself?

On the other hand, she could attribute the invitation to luck—a bureaucratic blunder, perhaps—and make the most of it. Both she and Paul needed a change of scene; the trip would hardly harm her career, and she might even be able to use it to lay old ghosts.

By now the crowd in the arrival hall was thinning. Paul was quieter: the flow of questions had stopped, and he was no longer prowling around but sitting on their suitcase; she could tell that he was tired. She wondered if she should telephone the British Council, assuming she could make sense of the alien public telephone system. At least her English, though slow, was reasonably fluent. Then she noticed the man.

He was slim, dark, and well dressed. His face was good-look-ing, though at present it looked very tired. He had a thin mustache, like a pencil line defining his upper lip. His face seemed very slightly familiar.

The odd thing was that he was staring at Paul. Given a choice, most men stared at her if they stared at either of them. But there was nothing lascivious in his face. As Magda watched, his unheeded cig-arette burned down to his hand. He swore and threw away the stub. The intensity of the moment disappeared abruptly. His eyes met Magda's; both of them looked away.

Suddenly he was standing in front of them.

"Frau Kleist?" The smile was charming. "I'm from the British Council. I'm so sorry to be late—I underestimated the traffic. My name's Lane—Stephen Lane."

They shook hands.

"This is my son, Paul."

"How do you do?" Lane shook hands gravely with him; his German was good, but he had a slight English accent. "I hope you had a good flight?"

"Yes thank you, sir."

Lane turned back to her. "My car's outside. Let me take your bags."

They drove to the hotel through the rush-hour traffic. Magda was frankly disappointed by her first glimpse of London: it seemed crowded, dirty, and ill-planned—and hardly suited to be the capital of what had once been the greatest empire the world had ever known.

Once they were at the hotel, Lane was in a hurry to be gone.

"I'd hoped I could take you out to dinner tonight," he said just before he left. "But we've got a flap on at work. Can you manage on your own?"

Madga nodded. "Of course."

"I'm sure you'll meet lots of people you know here. Someone from the council will collect you tomorrow morning—I'm afraid I can't make it. But perhaps we could have dinner in the evening?"

"What about Paul?"

"The hotel provides baby-sitters. Or we could have an early meal here. Just as you like."

Once again, Lane's tired, charming smile nudged her memory.

"Oh—I nearly forgot." He smacked his forehead lightly with the palm of his hand. "I'll be forgetting my own name next. There's a cocktail party at India House tomorrow evening. Quite informal. You'll be able to come, won't you?"

"I—I'm not sure." Magda searched for a new excuse, and was forced to fall back on the old one. "There's Paul, you see—"

"Bring him as well. It's not an official do. No one will mind."

In the end she agreed, with the silent reservation that, if she had anything better to do, she could always back out. Lane shook hands with them both and left. Paul was flattered that Mr. Lane had shaken hands twice with him.

Magda managed to persuade Paul to go to bed early, soon after they had eaten. Though he would not admit to being tired, he fell asleep within seconds of climbing into bed.

For a few minutes she sat on the edge of the bed watching him by the light of the shaded lamp on the bedside table. The scar beneath his eye was in shadow. The pink sickle had become a black one.

It was as if the sight of the scar triggered a switch in her mind. It sometimes did, usually when she was tired or overwrought; and at present she was both. The memory of that moment of violence that had marked Paul for life became unbearably vivid. The emotions which accompanied the memory were fresh and immediate: after nearly ten years, they retained their power to hurt.

Suddenly she was back in the little kitchen in Leipzig. Onion soup was simmering on the stove; the couple in the apartment upstairs were quarreling again; her mother was sitting as close to the stove as she could get, rocking to and fro. Magda herself had been peeling potatoes. Heinz was standing directly under the single overhead light and trying to read—a fat, heavy book with stout cardboard covers. Paul, nine months old, was lying in a cardboard box on the table and crying his heart out.

Had he been teething? Or was it the bronchitis he used to get in the first few winters of his life? Perhaps he was merely hungry. God alone knew how hungry they all were in those first two years after the war.

"Can't you stop the little bastard crying?"

Heinz's voice had been high with hysteria; his lips were drawn back, so his face seemed all teeth. They used to call him the Rabbit at school (and how he had hated that) but at that moment he looked like a rat.

"You slut!" he had screamed; he shut the book with a bang. *"Why don't you take him on the streets where you both belong?"*

"Oh, calm down, Heinz," she had said. Her mind was partly on Paul and partly on the potatoes. She now realized that some of the blame was hers: she had had neither the time nor the inclination to think what Heinz was going through. Scraping a living for herself and the baby had been the important thing, and she'd allowed it to dominate her life. Heinz was just her younger brother; his rage had seemed nothing more than a child's tantrum.

But children grew up; and so could their tantrums.

Heinz had lifted the book above his head with both hands and hurled it at the makeshift cot. The box rocked and nearly tipped over on its side. The crying stopped, leaving a silence more terrible than any noise could ever be. Heinz ran out of the room. She could hear him swearing—a high, fluent babble of obscenities—as he ran down the stairs.

Then she had forgotten him—and everything else—in her anxiety to tend Paul. The baby was unconscious; there had been a lot of blood, but there was no lasting damage apart from the scar.

Her mother appeared to have noticed nothing. She sat through the entire episode, rocking to and fro.

Magda had never spoken to Heinz again. *No lasting damage apart from the scar?* Perhaps she had been wrong about that.

The hotel bedroom became real to her again. She was back in the security of the present. The past was dangerous: memory built traps for you there. Paul was breathing, peacefully and deeply. Magda realized there were tears in her eyes, though she could not have said for whom she was crying.

No lasting damage?

She looked at Paul's face. The adult features were beginning to emerge from the chubby plasticity of childhood. The unfamiliar lighting made her see him in a different way; she noticed hollows and planes which were new to her.

The old doubts and hopes resurfaced. They belonged to the old life; and she had sworn she would leave them behind forever. But she owed something to Paul, if not to herself.

Magda quietly left the room. If she didn't do it now, she would never do it. She took the lift down to the foyer. The clerk at reception greeted her with a smile.

"I need a telephone directory," she said.

"A London one, madam?"

Magda fought back the feeling of helplessness that swept over her. "Perhaps—probably, I mean. That will do for a start."

Hugh let himself in to Wilmot House with his own latchkey. He stepped from a sunlit afternoon into the subaqueous calm of the hall. The familiar smell of polish and roses greeted him. This was a moment he always relished—when he crossed from one existence to another. He needed periodically to reassure himself that it was possible to lead other lives in other places. But it was always good to come home.

Mrs. Bunnings bustled along the passage from the kitchen. Over the years she had grown stouter, grayer, and slower.

"Mr. Hugh!" Her small, sharp eyes took in every detail: his open-necked shirt, the deplorable flannels, and the rucksack he had thrown on the Jacobean chest by the stairs. "And about time, too."

Hugh rested his hands on her shoulders and kissed her decorously on the cheek. "How are you, Mrs. B?"

"I'm all right. But I'm afraid there's been some bad news. It's a pity you had to choose now to go gadding off to foreign parts." She sniffed. "And not even an address for you."

"What's happened?"

"It's your father, I'm afraid. He's dead. There's tea in the pot. Will you have it in the kitchen?"

He followed her along the passage. He knew her brusqueness masked concern. He suspected that he could have turned up at any time, day or night, and there would have been tea in the pot in the kitchen. An invitation to the kitchen was an indulgence in itself.

Their relationship was something he found difficult to explain, even to himself. The war had blown down many of the old barriers between masters and servants. Since the war those terms had lost their meanings as far as Hugh and Mrs. Bunnings were concerned. For the first two years after he had inherited Wilmot House, Hugh had been unable to pay her a wage. Instead, she had run the place as a lodging house and shared the profits with him. If it hadn't been for her he would have had to sell it. She had even lent him her savings to pay for essential repairs to the house's structure. She refused indignantly to retire, though she had accepted with ill-concealed pleasure the opportunity to tyrannize over two charwomen who came in for five days a week. Except on special occasions, she refused to sit down and eat with him. *It wouldn't be right. Mrs. Lane would turn in her grave if she knew.*

The kitchen smelled of baking bread. It had hardly changed in twenty years. Hugh had persuaded Mrs. Bunnings to get rid of the range and have a gas cooker instead; there was a refrigerator now, and the plumbing had been modernized. But it was still Mrs. Bunnings' domain; Hugh was as much a guest there as he had always been.

She made him sit at the scrubbed table and gave him a cup of strong, sweet tea. Only then—when the conventions had been observed—did she tell him how his father had died; her information had come from Meg.

"Has he been buried yet?"

Mrs. Bunnings shook her head. "Funeral's on Wednesday."

"I'm sorry." As he said the words, Hugh realized that he was sorry for his own absence of sorrow, rather than for his father's death. The old man had died as gracelessly as he lived.

"If you ask me, it's a blessed relief for all concerned." Mrs. Bunnings snorted. "I was never one to speak ill of the dead, but I don't believe in telling lies about them, either."

"Are Meg and Stephen all right?"

"Miss Meg's cheerful enough. She's so wrapped up in that

young man of hers, she wouldn't notice if old Khruschev dropped a bomb on us. Not that Mr. Stanhope-Smith is exactly young any more. Still, better late than never, that's what I say." Mrs. Bunnings had had a soft spot for Michael since she had met him during the war.

"And Stephen?"

Mrs. Bunnings shrugged. "I haven't seen him. But Miss Meg said he took it badly. I'll believe that when I see it."

Hugh pushed back his chair and stood up. "I need a bath. Then I suppose I'd better ring Meg."

"I've got a nice bit of steak for your dinner. Will you have it at the usual time?"

Hugh nodded. "By the way, where have you put the post?"

"On the desk in the study, of course. Where else? That reminds me, a foreign lady telephoned last night. I left a note with your letters." Mrs. Bunnings raised her eyebrows; clearly fascinated, she reserved the right to disapprove. "She said she was an old friend."

Hugh frowned. "What was her name?"

"Frau something. I can't remember. It's on the note. They've got a nerve, these Germans, coming here after what they did in the war. I mean, think of your poor mother. Frau Whatsername wanted to leave a message, but I couldn't make head or tail of it. Something about the second midnight."

Teatime at the Russell Hotel was in full swing—if anything so sedate could be said to swing.

A pianist, partly concealed behind a row of potted palms, played old dance tunes which managed to be both familiar and anonymous. A few tables had been set up in the foyer; and these were more popular than those in the dining room because you could watch the comings and goings.

Hugh had a clear view from where he sat to the doors from the street. He nursed a pot of China tea and ignored the curious glances of the two plump matrons who shared his table. The clerk at reception had been very helpful: yes, a Frau Kleist was staying at the hotel; she was taking part in a conference at University College; she would probably return late this afternoon or early this evening.

Frau Kleist? It must be Magda: the mention of the second midnight and the coincidence of the same surname as her mother's family clinched it. Unconsciously, he massaged the signet ring on the little finger of his left hand: the monogram was so worn it was hardly legible. Perhaps she had married a cousin. He ignored the stab of jealousy: it was enough that she was alive, and that she wanted to get in touch with him.

Another possibility occurred to him—so suddenly and so shockingly that he spilled his tea. Perhaps Frau Kleist *was* Magda's cousin; perhaps she had come to tell him that Magda was dead. He could accept anything but her death.

One of the matrons clicked her tongue against the roof of her mouth and edged away from the puddle of tea on the tablecloth. Hugh apologized and dabbed absently at the stain with his napkin.

He had had time to bathe, shave, and change at Wilmot House. He was grateful for that: he wasn't the gardener's boy anymore, and part of him wanted Magda to know it. She would have to collect her key from reception; and he had bribed the clerk to point him out to her. If it was Magda, he knew he would recognize her, but there was always the chance that it was someone else.

Then she was standing in the doorway.

There was no room for doubt in his mind. Two images—the girl in his memory and this tall, grave woman—slid together and became one.

"Magda!"

The shout attracted the attention of several dozen people. He stood up, spilling his tea once more, and elbowed his way through the crowd toward her.

"Well, really!" the other matron said to her friend; she didn't bother to lower her voice. "Young people today are *so* uncouth."

Magda peered in his direction. *She's still shortsighted.* Hugh thought with a rush of love, *and she's still too vain to wear glasses.*

But in the few seconds it took them to close the gap between them, the old doubts returned. Eleven years of pain and uncertainty made Hugh stop and hold out his hand.

"Frau Kleist? How do you do?"

"Hugh—"

He saw her face become blank; she too was armoring herself against being hurt. They shook hands: the formality of the greeting instantly made them strangers. Hugh studied her surreptitiously: the years had given her elegance but taken away none of her desirability. He was aware that she was attracting the covert attention of half the males in the foyer.

"Your hand," she said suddenly. "Show me."

Hugh looked stupidly at her. Automatically, he lifted his right hand.

"Not that one."

He could sense the quiet desperation in her voice. He showed her his other hand; her eyes widened as she saw the ring. She opened her handbag and produced what looked like a piece of lead. She balanced it on the palm of her hand and looked up at him. Her mouth was trembling. Memory gave the metal both shape and personality.

Major Kendall, sir! Hiawatha would say. *Thank God we've found you.*

"Magda," Hugh said urgently. "We must talk. Can't we go somewhere?"

"I must do something about Paul first."

Paul? So she's married after all—

She must have read the pain in his face. "He's—he's my son. I'll leave a message at the desk."

He watched her talking to the clerk, and felt jealous when he saw the smile she gave the man. When she rejoined him, she chattered away, giving him no opportunity to speak; in a way he was grateful for that. She spoke in German, taking it for granted he was still fluent in it.

"Shall we go for a walk? It's so stuffy in here. Paul's not back yet. It's rather fortunate—Frau von Hessel volunteered to take him with her children to see the Tower. She'll look after him until—until I get back. Her husband's one of the speakers at the same conference . . . did you know about the conference? At University College? It's one of these academic junkets which everyone takes terribly seriously. It's meant to be *relevant,* you see—that's the fashionable term; but no one seems to know what it's relevant to . . ."

They walked quickly, as if they were in a hurry to reach wherever they were going. They were a few inches apart. Hugh could hardly believe that, if he wanted to, he could reach out and touch Magda; it was as if a figure from history or myth had unexpectedly come to life. She chose their route, though Hugh suspected that she had no idea of where they were going. She stared straight ahead: he stole a glance at her profile. A spasm of sheer lust jolted through him. One thing hadn't changed.

The first drops of rain fell as they were turning into Great Russel Street. Pigeons swooped in their scores around the forecourt of the

303

British Museum; some rash tourist must be feeding them. The rain gathered momentum. Umbrellas sprang up like black mushrooms along the street. The pavements were full of people hurrying home.

Hugh took Magda's arm; she stopped talking in mid-sentence. "This is ridiculous." His voice sounded much rougher than he had intended. "You'll get soaked. We'll go in here."

The little café was squeezed between a second-hand bookshop and a shop that sold musical instruments. It consisted of a long, thin room which was thick with cigarette smoke. They found a vacant table near the window. Hugh ordered two cups of espresso coffee from the surly Italian who presided behind the counter. Most of the clientele seemed to be recovering from a visit to the museum.

Hugh leaned across the table. "Who are you working for?" he said harshly. "My brother or yours?"

"What?"

The surprise in her voice was unmistakable. Hugh found it difficult to believe that she would lie to him, but people could change in eleven years. Besides, she might not be a free agent.

"What are you talking about, Hugh? I'm a journalist—a freelance. I don't work for anyone."

"Which side of the Iron Curtain are you from?"

"This side. I came over in 'forty-eight, after my mother died. I live in Hamburg now."

"Then why—?"

The arrival of their coffee forced Hugh to stop. He was glad of the interruption. There were so many questions, and he didn't know in which order he should ask them. Perhaps some of them shouldn't be asked. Answers could be worse than unanswered questions.

Magda flushed. "Why didn't I write to you after the war?" There was a flash of anger in her voice. "Two reasons: they said you killed my father; and I—I found other interests in the meantime."

In that case why did you telephone me?

Aloud he said, "That's nonsense—about your father, I mean. You must have got that from Bruckman. He never liked me—I think he was jealous. In his own way he loved the colonel. But you must know that better than I do."

"Then what happened when my father died?"

Hugh explained. As he talked, he watched the color ebbing from her face. He could hardly grasp the fact that for eleven years she had thought he was responsible for her father's death.

When he had finished, it was her turn: she told him how Bruck-man had died, and how the remaining Scholls and the authorities had reconstructed the ambush on the basis of a brief interrogation report.

"So no one had any opportunity to question Bruckman. It all fits." She looked at Hugh. "I'm sorry. I should have trusted you."

He put his hand over hers, noticing belatedly that she wore no wedding ring. "It's over now."

"Is it?" She pulled her hand away like someone pulling plaster from a wound. "It's too late to change anything."

"Why? Are you married?"

Magda shook her head. "But I doubt if you'd want me now. I'm—I'm shopsoiled."

Hugh gripped her hand again; this time he refused to allow her to pull away. "We both are. It was inevitable. But it doesn't matter. Not really."

"You don't understand, Hugh." She took a deep breath. "In May 'forty-five, my mother and I were raped by Russian soldiers. Not just once or twice. I lost count of them. They kept us with them for two days. After the first few hours, they reserved me for the officers. But my mother wasn't so lucky. They mutilated her body and took away her mind. I was glad when she died. For her sake as well as my own."

"My poor darling." He tightened his grip. "And Paul?"

"I don't know. I used to pray he was yours, despite—despite . . ."

"Is it possible?"

"It could be." She shrugged. "It's possible but statistically impossible. My periods were too irregular then to be sure, one way or the other. I sometimes think he looks like you—especially now he's starting to grow up. But I'm afraid that could be just wishful thinking. I couldn't even remember what you looked like."

A son? Hugh threw back his head and laughed. "If he's your son I want him to be mine. That's much more important than who his father was in the biological sense."

"You don't care?"

"Of course I care. I care that he's a part of you." A thought occurred to him. "Why did you call him Paul?"

Her eyes met his; he could see a glimmer of amusement in them. "It's one of the few names that's exactly the same in German and English." The amusement faded. "Hugh, we're going too fast, much

305

too fast. What did you mean about my brother and yours?"

"You're not working for either of them, are you?"

She shook her head. "The British Council invited me to a conference here. I think someone must have dropped out at the last moment. I'm rather a lightweight, compared with the rest of the speakers."

He accepted her word without question. He told her quickly about his brother's attempt to enlist him against Heinz.

"Why did you refuse?" Magda asked.

"He's your brother, and your father's son." Hugh grinned. "And I've never got on with my brother, and I don't like the job he does."

She shivered. "Heinz is in *London?*"

"That's what Stephen said. I suppose he might have left by now. And he's some sort of spy. Did you know that?"

"No. We quarreled nearly ten years ago. Heinz threw something at Paul." She added with seemingly inconsequence, "I'm not surprised."

Hugh took her meaning at once. "That Heinz exchanged one Big Brother for another? Nor am I." He smiled across the table. "But I don't want to talk about Big Brothers. I want to meet Paul."

Magda glanced at her watch. "He should be back." Suddenly she frowned. "I've just remembered. I'm meant to be going to a cocktail party at India House this evening. The man from the British Council invited me."

"Cancel it," Hugh said. "There's a telephone box outside. You can ring him from there. We're having dinner together."

She smiled; the tension was gone from her face. "Are we indeed?"

Hugh nodded. "All three of us."

Heinz knocked and pushed open the door without waiting for a reply.

Bela was standing by the open window, crumbling a loaf of bread. The little office was on the top floor of the embassy. Immediately outside the window was a leaded gutter bounded by a low wall. The top of the wall was flat; Bela used it as a bird table.

"Tesla's phoned in." Heinz closed the door behind him. "We're in luck."

Bela brushed the last of the crumbs over the windowsill. "He's back?"

Heinz nodded. "Turned up this afternoon—looking like a tramp, apparently."

Bela limped over to his desk. He ran a bony finger down the day's movement rota. "Tesla should be in Acton."

"I diverted him. It's my decision."

"One day you'll have to explain all this to Pakhlanov. He won't like it."

"You don't, either, do you?"

"Private enterprise." Bela shrugged. "It's always dangerous. I know you can claim you're putting pressure on the other brother, but Pakhlanov won't believe that."

"Pakhlanov needn't know. Even if he does find out, he may not mind. We've done a good job here. Why should he grudge me a little reward?"

The telephone rang. Bela picked it up.

"In five minutes." He replaced the handset. "Vaclav says the car is ready. You haven't forgotten?"

"The India House party? I wish we could get out of it."

"Well, we can't. India's our most useful ally among the canal users. The High Commissioner is expecting us."

"All right." Heinz looked up at Bela. "This other matter: you won't intervene, will you?"

Bela picked up his cigarettes. His mouth tightened, as if he had felt a sudden stab of pain.

"It's an operational decision, Heinz. That makes it your affair."

Seventeen

The delay came as a bitter blow to Stephen. When the woman rang off, he sat at his desk, staring blankly at the window; his thin fingers squeezed the telephone's handset until the knuckles whitened.

He had visualized the scene so often in anticipation that it was hard to believe that it couldn't happen in reality. The party at India House would have been the perfect setting. Heinz Scholl would have been thrown off balance not only by his sister but by his bastard nephew. With a little luck, the meeting might have happened in front of the High Commissioner herself.

Stephen dwelt lovingly on the possible consequences. The news that Scholl had ideologically unsound relatives would be common knowledge in diplomatic circles in a matter of hours. The fact that the Czech Embassy was sheltering an East German could no longer be kept secret. If fortune smiled, there might even be a public quarrel. All the evidence suggested that brother and sister were bitterly opposed. The little bastard added an unexpected layer of icing to the cake.

Scholl would be labeled unstable: he was guilty if only by association; worse, the whole business would make both him and his employers seem ridiculous. GRU would have to withdraw him. Discrediting him would have an incalculable effect on the prestige that Russia and her allies were at present enjoying. And they would need time to find a replacement. In that time, Stephen could begin to repair the damage that Scholl had caused.

If only that wretched woman hadn't backed out at the last moment—

Still, Stephen told himself, it was only a delay—not a cancellation. The conference had another three days to run. He would find another way to bring the brother and sister together.

Before he left the office that evening, he scribbled a note for his secretary: she was to compile a list of forthcoming diplomatic receptions and parties; there were plenty of them at present, thanks to the canal users' conference. It shouldn't be difficult.

He spent the minimum time consonant with politeness at India House, and then took a taxi to Fulham. His flat felt stuffy: the cleaner had forgotten again to leave a window open. Stephen picked up the pile of letters from the mat and went into the sitting room. He made himself a gin and tonic. As he sipped it, he leafed through his letters.

One of them was from Mr. Turnbull. It was a polite and circumlocutory letter, but what it boiled down to was that the solicitor was anxious to settle the matter of Alfred Kendall's estate. First, they needed to prepare a schedule of his assets and debts.

Stephen sighed. He might as well spend an hour or so going through his father's papers. Frau Kleist's defection had left him with the rare luxury of an empty evening.

He poured himself another drink. His father's pawn tickets, his few private papers, and his letters, still unopened, were in a large envelope on the open bureau. Stephen emptied them on to the sofa and sifted through them.

Someone would have to reclaim the items in pawn—perhaps he could persuade Meg to do it. There were few surprises among the papers—except a number of letters from, and photographs of, Muriel Kendall: perhaps the old man had been fonder of her than anyone suspected; Stephen was frankly uninterested. He opened the letters. The two bills went on one side for Mr. Turnbull. A regimental newsletter and a football pools coupon went straight into the wastepaper basket. A pamphlet on Pelmanism ("TAKE UP PELMANISM AND DEVELOP POWER": what *had* the old man been up to?) was about to join them when Stephen noticed the ragged edge of a piece of paper protruding from the envelope.

He pulled it out and discovered it was a leaf torn from a pocket diary. A message in his father's shaky writing sprawled diagonally across three days: *Have followed AT to 15 Keats Rd. Acton. 11.45 A.M. AK.*

Stephen's mind began to work at double speed. The envelope had two postmarks; the later one was dated the day that his father had failed to report back. AT was Antonin Tesla, one of the heavy brigade. Acton was within shouting distance of the Grand Union Canal at Harlesden.

★   ★   ★

So it had been murder.

310

The taxi driver demanded an extortionate bribe before he would agree to take them from Bloomsbury to Richmond. He named a sum which made Magda gasp; she noticed that Hugh paid it without hesitation. The incident, small though it was, started her thinking; she linked it with the quality of Hugh's clothes and with the indefinable air of confidence which clung to him like a second skin. He hadn't spent the last eleven years growing poorer.

During the long drive through the rush-hour traffic she and Hugh said little to each other. He devoted most of his attention to Paul. She watched them as they talked. It was a grave, almost formal conversation. Hugh might have been talking to another adult. She was reminded of two dogs, well-intentioned but unwilling to commit themselves with unseemly haste, circling around each other as a preliminary to friendship.

She was enchanted by her first sight of Wilmot House.

"It looks like a dollhouse."

Hugh grinned. "It's an extraordinary mixture. Wait till you get inside. When I was a kid, I used to think that living here would be like living in a fairy tale."

"I know," Magda said. "I remember you telling me once."

Their eyes met; there was an instant's silence.

"Here's yer change, guv," the cabbie said. "I want to get home even if you don't."

"Keep the change," Hugh said.

When they were all on the pavement, Magda touched his arm. "Are you sure your housekeeper won't mind? It's rather an imposition at such short notice."

"You underrate Mrs. Bunnings's curiosity." He unlocked the door and held it open for them. "Mind the steps down. Besides, I want to show you something."

As he closed the door behind them, a green-baize door at the back of the hall swung open. A sturdy, grim-faced old woman looked at them with interest.

"Dinner at eight, Mr. Hugh." She made it sound like a threat. Her eyes flickered up and down Magda, deferred judgment, and moved on to Paul. "I put the drinks in the—"

She stopped abruptly and blinked. Her mouth was still open. One podgy hand gripped the edge of the door for support.

"It's all right, Mrs. B." Hugh took her other arm.

Mrs. Bunnings sniffed. "All right? Is that what you call it?" She pulled her arm free and pointed at Paul. "Then why's he the spitting image of what you were like, twenty years ago?"

"What are you doing?" Meg said.

"Making an abstract of a couple of files." Michael capped his fountain pen and stretched. "Shall we eat out tonight?"

"That would be nice." She uncurled herself from the armchair and took two cigarettes from the box on the mantelpiece. "We could try the French restaurant Hugh mentioned." She lit both cigarettes and passed one to Michael. She bent her head to read the label on the file. "*FARRAR, Albert George*—who's he?"

"No one of importance. A little man, in both senses of the word. He died before the war."

He took Meg's hand and pulled her on to his lap; she came willingly. He buried his face in the crook between her neck and shoulder. The smell of her hair and skin was the greatest aphrodisiac he knew.

"Michael?"

"Mmm?"

"I thought you weren't meant to bring files home."

He lifted his head reluctantly. "We're not. But these ones aren't exactly top secret."

"You mustn't let them overwork you, darling."

"I'm not working: this is personal. Just satisfying my curiosity about something while I can. If it hadn't been for George Farrar, you and I wouldn't be here now."

His hand moved slowly up her leg, sliding smoothly over the silk stocking. She wriggled around to make it easier for him, and drew a fingernail gently down the nape of his neck.

"You must tell me about him," she said breathlessly. "When we've got time."

Mildred Burnham was clearly surprised to hear Stephen's voice on the telephone. Giles must have given her some version of their quarrel. Judging by the freezing politeness with which she treated Stephen, Giles had probably blamed him for his fall off the wagon.

Nevertheless, she realized that this was not a social call, and did her best to be helpful. Giles was still at work: if Stephen wanted him, he should try Leconfield House.

Stephen took a taxi to Curzon Street, on the assumption that it was easier to grovel effectively in person than over the telephone. A lot of people were working late: it was one of the side effects of the Suez crisis. The headquarters of MI5 was almost as busy as it was by day.

Burnham agreed to see him at once, as Stephen had expected. Giles was rather like Michael in some ways: both men hated unpleasant scenes; and neither of them was the type to bear grudges.

The atmosphere of the office on the third floor was heavy with pipe smoke, but Stephen couldn't detect an underlying tang of alcohol. It smelled as if Giles's lapse from teetotalism had been only temporary. Mildred was a determined woman.

Giles waved Stephen to a chair; he was talking into a telephone and simultaneously initialing the pages of a report. The office was as untidy as it always was; Stephen had never been able to understand how Giles could work in such a mess.

At last he put down the phone and tossed his pen onto the blotter. His hand fumbled toward the pipe in the ashtray.

"Stephen," he said without much enthusiasm. "What can I do for you?"

"I've brought an olive branch." Stephen smiled. "I want to apologize, Giles. You were quite right to bawl me out."

Burnham looked away; his cheeks were faintly pink. "Not at all," he muttered. "Daresay I spoke out of turn as well."

"Oh no." Stephen paused, aware that it would be unwise to lay on the emotion too thickly. Not with Giles: emotion was something he reserved for children and dogs.

Giles rattled the pipe against the ashtray. A shower of blackened tobacco fell out; most of it missed the ashtray and landed on the file beneath.

"I heard about your father, by the way," he said gruffly; he avoided Stephen's eyes and concentrated on opening his tobacco pouch. "Stanhope-Smith mentioned it. Awfully sorry."

The emotional temperature was rising with disturbing speed. But there was one big advantage: Stephen understood at once that his father's death would hasten the process of reconciliation. He hoped that his face showed the controlled grief which was appropriate to the circumstances.

"It was a terrible shock," he said quietly. "Perhaps more so than you know. You see, it wasn't an accident."

Burnham's long, rather grubby fingers stopped quarrying out tobacco. "What do you mean?"

His voice was wary. Stephen knew he would have to be careful: the truth would have to be altered in one or two particulars.

"In a way it was my fault." He paused for a moment, hoping to imply that his sorrow was temporarily too deep for words. "A week or so ago, I happened to mention that Bela Juriga was in London. I was just making conversation—I had no idea of the effect it would have on him."

"They knew each other in Prague?"

Stephen nodded. "My father was very upset, I could see that. I suppose it brought back too many memories. I've always wondered if he was involved with that woman—Madame Hase, was it? I suspect he blamed Bela and Jan Masin for her death."

Giles cleared his throat. "Not . . . not for anything they might have done to Hugh?"

Stephen welcomed the signs of embarrassment. "That may have come into it," he agreed. "But we shall never know for certain."

"What exactly happened?"

"It's hard to tell. Until this evening, I had no idea my father's death wasn't an accident. But I was sorting out his papers; there were one or two letters which hadn't been opened. This was among them."

Stephen tossed the Pelman circular on to the desk. Burnham looked first at the envelope, with its one address and two postmarks. He pulled out the leaflet. The diary page fluttered into his ashtray. He picked it out and brushed away the ash.

"*Have followed BJ to 15 Keats Rd. Acton. 11.45 A.M. AK.*"

It had been easy to alter the *AT* of Antonin Tesla to the *BJ* of Bela Juriga. His father's handwriting had been shaky at the best of times; he had probably written the note while standing up, in haste and in excitement. The alteration had been necessary on grounds of tact. Leaving the *AT* would show that Alfred Kendall knew the identity of Tesla; this might suggest that Stephen had briefed him on the entire trade mission. Burnham might infer, with perfect accuracy, that Stephen had disobeyed his order to stop the unauthorized surveillance.

"You're sure it's his writing?"

Stephen nodded. "And the paper came from his pocket diary."

There was a pause while Burnham lit his pipe. "Go on."

"I think he must have followed Juriga from the embassy. I don't

314

know why—perhaps he had some notion of revenge; or perhaps he just wanted to talk. For all I know he thought he was playing the Great Game; he romanticized this business. He tailed Juriga to Keats Road, but he must have given himself away. After all, Juriga's a pro. I don't know why my father wrote the note. It could be that he knew Juriga was on to him. That's not important."

Burnham absently scratched his bald patch with the stem of his pipe. "No," he said at last. "The important thing is why they ran the risk of killing your father. Juriga wouldn't do it just for the hell of it, or for old times' sake."

"But he might do it to protect a Czech safe house."

The pipe stem began to investigate an ear.

"Um," Giles said. "Very likely. I'm very grateful, Stephen. And very sorry."

"Sorry?"

"About your father, of course."

"That's what I wanted to show you," Hugh said. "Mrs. Bunnings's reaction to Paul."

Their son was stretched out on the sofa, fast asleep. Mrs. Bunnings, delighted to have a child to feed, had stuffed him to capacity. They had drunk champagne with the meal ("What else?" Magda had said), and Hugh had given a glass of it to Paul.

"I can't believe it." Magda slipped her arm through Hugh's.

They were standing by the open window. The little walled garden was in darkness. Hugh could smell honeysuckle. He had planted it himself, because the smell reminded him of his room above the old stables in Zbraslav.

He could feel the warmth of her body through the thin fabric of her dress. "Are you happy?"

"Wrong word." She looked back into the room; her eyes rested on Paul. "Confused. Unreal. Hopeful. Even scared."

"I want to marry you," Hugh said hoarsely. "And I want you to stay the night."

"Paul—?"

"There are spare beds."

"What about Mrs. Bunnings? She won't approve of us sleeping together."

"She won't know. She sleeps in a separate part of the house."

"My clothes are at the hotel. I can't wear a dress like this in the daytime."

"I'll telephone the hotel, and they can send over what you need."

Hugh noticed that Magda had avoided the larger question of marriage. He decided not to press her; there would be plenty of time for that later. He left the room to telephone and to tell Mrs. Bunnings.

The old woman was knitting furiously in the kitchen. She, too, had been given a glass of champagne. She was determined to interrogate Hugh. It took him nearly ten minutes to tell her a condensed version of the truth. He expected her to show some sign of displeasure; Mrs. Bunnings had made it quite clear to him on other occasions that she disapproved of sex before marriage; nor was she fond of foreigners, particularly Germans. But for once morality and chauvinism were swamped by her keen appreciation of another aspect of this relationship.

"It's so romantic, Mr. Hugh. Like something on the films."

Romantic? It was not a word that Hugh would have chosen.

When he returned to the drawing room, he found that Magda was flicking through one of Aunt Vida's photographic albums. Two shelves of the big glass-fronted bookcase were devoted to the albums. She looked up as he came in. Her face was serious.

"Paul and I take after my mother's side," Hugh said. "I'll have to draw you a family tree."

"There's something I don't understand. I think someone must be lying to me."

She spoke quietly, to avoid waking Paul, but her voice was hard with suspicion. The suspicion, Hugh realized unhappily, might well be directed at him. He crossed the room and knelt by her chair.

"What is it, darling?"

She pointed to one of the photographs. It was a snapshot of two men in a rowing boat. They were on the Thames near Hampton Court; Hugh could see Hampton Bridge in the background. Both men were looking upward and smiling, presumably at the photographer.

"Who are they?" Magda said in a tight little voice.

"The one on the left is my brother Stephen. The other one is a chap called Michael Stanhope-Smith."

An elegant fingernail jabbed Michael's throat. "Does he work for the British Council?"

Hugh shook his head.

"He claimed he did when I met him in Hamburg." The fingernail moved to Stephen. "Nor does he, I suppose? He was the man who was taking me to India House tonight. Did you know that? He's calling himself Lane."

"Magda—"

"They're trying to play games with me." The suspicion in her tone was hardening into certainty. "Are you involved?"

The telephone was ringing.

Michael stirred. Meg burrowed closer to him. Her legs were entangled with his. One of her hands lay palm-down on his groin.

The bell pushed back the frontiers of sleep. It was fully dark now; there had still been a trace of twilight when they had fallen asleep. In the end they had done without dinner. There had been better things to do. He guessed it was between midnight and one o'clock. The air wasn't cold enough for the darkness before the dawn. He extracted one of his legs from the tangle of limbs and edged gently away from Meg.

"Don't go, Michael. Leave it."

"I must. It's probably the office."

He squeezed her shoulder, wriggled out of bed, and stumbled across the darkened bedroom; he didn't put on the light for fear of disturbing Meg still more.

The ringing continued. He ran naked down the hall; the telephone was on a table by the front door. He snatched the handset from its cradle, grateful that it was still ringing. Usually his callers stopped trying when his hand was a foot away from the phone.

"Michael? It's Hugh. Look here—"

"Have you heard?" Michael blurted out.

"About my father? Yes, I have. What the hell are you and Stephen up to?"

"I don't understand."

"Pretending you work for the British Council. Dragging Magda Scholl into one of your bloody schemes—"

"Hugh—will you calm down and listen?" Michael explained, as clearly and circumstantially as he could, how Stephen had asked him as a favor to contact a Frau Kleist while he was on a routine visit to Hamburg; how the possibility that she was one of the Scholls whom Hugh had known in Prague hadn't occurred to him until afterward; and how his attempts to get in touch with Hugh had been doomed by Hugh's decision to disappear on holiday.

At some point Meg passed down the hall, draped his dressing

317

gown around his shoulders, and went on to the kitchen. Michael could hear the sounds of tea being made. A few minutes later, she brought him a cup and a lighted cigarette.

"Where is Frau Kleist?" Michael asked, prompted in part by a desire to get his own back. "Do you know?"

There was a silence on the other end of the line.

"She's with me, actually," Hugh said at last. He sounded so embarrassed that Michael suspected she must be in the same room. "At Wilmot House. Look, Michael, what's Stephen trying to do? You must have some idea."

"I don't know." Michael added to himself, *And I don't particularly care, either*. At a guess this business must have something to do with the Scholl brother, the one who worked for the Ministerium für Staats-Sicherheit. Aloud he said, "I gather Stephen stands to lose a lot of face over this Suez business, but I can't see how that connects with Frau Kleist."

"I can see how it could," Hugh said. "There might be a connection through Heinz, Magda's brother. He was in London a couple of months back. According to Stephen, he's some sort of a spy. Stephen wanted me to confront him or something—throw him off balance, I suppose."

"Perhaps that's your answer," Michael said. He knew he should be disturbed by what Hugh was saying: it looked as if Stephen was conducting a lunatic private operation in the heart of London. But at present the antics of the intelligence community seemed very remote. Through the open door of the bedroom he could see that Meg was back in bed. She blew him a kiss.

"First thing tomorrow," Hugh said venomously, "I'm going to find Stephen and strangle him. Slowly. But before that he's going to tell me exactly what he's up to."

"Why don't you ring Stephen and ask him?"

"I tried. He's not answering the phone. Damn Stephen."

Michael chuckled, sensing that the tension was easing on the other end of the phone. "Meg sends her love. Do you want to talk to her?"

"No. I'll ring you tomorrow. I'd like you both to meet someone. Two people, actually."

He put the phone down without further notice. Michael shrugged, replaced the handset, and walked back to the bedroom.

"What was all that about?" Meg leaned forward to take his

hand; her kimono fell open. "Darling, you're cold." She put the hand between her breasts.

Michael told her as quickly as possible. "I think Hugh might be in love," he said at the end. "I've never heard him so upset. Usually he's so self-contained."

Meg nodded. "Always in control. What's she like?"

"Magda?" He remembered just in time that most of what he knew about Magda—the Russian rape and the quarrel with Heinz, for example—came from the BfV file in Hamburg; the old discipline still held him. "Unusual. She gives the impression of knowing exactly what she's doing."

"Is she good-looking?"

Michael cupped Meg's breasts in his hands and massaged them gently; the nipples were hard. "She's one of those blond Aryan lasses," he said tactfully. "A Nordic beauty. A little too statuesque for my taste."

She pushed the dressing gown from his shoulders. "I'm glad Hugh woke us up. Shall we try it the other way around?"

His mother and the big man wanted to talk privately after breakfast.

They told him to explore the house and garden. Paul was happy to do that. He trusted Herr Kendall with his mother, automatically and without reservation. She didn't need him to look after her. He didn't ask himself why he felt at home with a stranger whom he'd known for less than a day, and a foreigner as well. At his age you asked other people questions, not yourself.

The house fascinated him, because it was so different from anything he had known before. Their flat in Hamburg was part of a postwar block; each flat was precisely the same as its neighbors—above, below, and on either side. But it was impossible to imagine that there could be a duplicate of Herr Kendall's house; it was as unique as an oak tree which had grown from a particular acorn in a particular place. It was full of strange smells and old furniture; the rooms were arranged without a rational plan; there were unexpected steps, up or down, waiting to trap the unwary. It seemed to Paul that you could never fully know this house because you could never be sure that you had seen everything in it.

He explored from bottom to top. Instinct warned him to keep away from the kitchen; that was Mrs. Bunnings's territory, and he sensed that you went there only by invitation.

It soon became obvious that the house was much bigger than it seemed from the front. It was shaped like a capital T; and the stem of the T, which lay at the back of the house, was larger than the cross-bar. There was always the possibility—remote enough to be pleasur-able—that he might get lost.

At the top of the stairs he found a landing which ran the length of the crossbar. There were six doors. Four led to small, rather gloomy bedrooms; one belonged to a bathroom; and the sixth, at the far end of the landing, refused to open. Naturally enough, this aroused his curiosity.

Paul examined the door carefully. It wasn't locked; it was more likely that the wood had warped. He took the handle in both hands and wedged one foot against the wall to give extra leverage.

The door flew open: it banged against the wall, which was at right angles to it. Paul lost his grip on the handle and sprawled on the floor. For a few seconds he lay on the bare boards, listening for the sound of adults coming to investigate. Below him the house was silent. He could see a steep and narrow flight of stairs leading upward from the open doorway.

He climbed the stairs as quickly and quietly as possible. He didn't know whether or not what he was doing was wrong, but it made it more fun to pretend that it was. The treads were thick with dust.

There was another door at the top. This one opened easily. Paul found himself in an attic, immediately beneath the slates. Heavy beams supported both the roof and generations of cobwebs. The only light came from a little window halfway along one of the longer walls. A pile of trunks, corded, and labeled as if for a long journey, had been stacked against the gable wall at the far end.

Paul moved slowly along the central gangway. At one point he stumbled against a black box: it fell over and disgorged a top hat, green with age. Dustsheets reduced some of the items in store to a ghostly anonymity. One of the dustsheets had slipped, revealing a dressmaker's dummy with an officer's tunic draped casually around its shoulders.

The detritus of other people's lives oppressed him. He was relieved when he reached the window. He rubbed the glass with a moistened finger, hoping for a glimpse of a real world which belong-ed, at least in part, to him, but the grime was too ingrained for him to shift it. As a last resort he tried the handle. For an instant the window resisted his pressure. Then it swung jerkily outward.

Fresh air rushed into the attic. It was a cool, overcast day. In the distance, in a gap between two houses, he could see a flash of silver, that might be the river Thames. He leaned out and found he could see the road beneath. The railings in front of Wilmot House seemed very far away. It suddenly occurred to him that the spikes were a row of spears, waiting to impale him if he fell.

He was about to pull back when a door banged, far below him. The foreshortened figure of Herr Kendall strode down the short path, out of the gate, and along the pavement toward the Green. Paul, an involuntary spy, watched with interest.

A long black car turned into the road. It drew up beside Herr Kendall. A man got out from the front of the car; in one hand he held what looked like a folded map; no doubt he was asking the way.

It all happened so fast that Paul could hardly take it in. Herr Kendall bent over the map, tracing a route with his forefinger. The other man hit him on the head with something like a short black club, which he had been holding in his other hand. Herr Kendall slumped against the car.

Simultaneously, the nearside rear door of the car swung open. A pair of arms grasped him and pulled him inside, with a little help from the man on the pavement. A few seconds later, the pavement was empty and the black car was disappearing around the corner.

The telephone call came as Michael and Meg were having a late breakfast of coffee, toast, and marmalade. Neither of them had slept much, but they both felt superbly rested.

Michael swore, threw down his napkin, and strode into the hall. "You won't want a phone when we're married, will you?" he called back to her. "I only have the wretched thing because of the job."

"Is that Michael Stanhope-Smith?" It was a woman's voice and it sounded faintly familiar.

"Speaking."

"This is Magda Scholl." She switched abruptly to German. "Hugh's been kidnapped—my son Paul saw it. I think my brother Heinz must be behind it. Hugh told me about you last night, and I know whom you really work for. You must help him."

The voice was clear and suspiciously calm; Michael wondered if she was on the verge of hysteria. He questioned her methodically, noting automatically the lucidity and economy of her answers. He accepted her story at once, despite the fact that it depended on hearsay derived from her son. Magda wasn't a fool.

At the end of the conversation, Michael preempted what was properly Burnham's decision, and told her to stay with Paul and Mrs. Bunnings at Wilmot House; a policeman would be with them as soon as possible; in the meantime, the proper authorities would take the appropriate steps.

"No," said Magda. "I'm coming with you."

"My dear Frau Kleist—Fräulein Scholl—you would only be in the way. You mustn't worry about Hugh: I very much doubt if they'd dare to do anything to him until they're absolutely sure that—"

"Herr Stanhope-Smith." Her voice was louder than it had been before. "If my brother Heinz is involved, this isn't a normal kidnapping. When he hates something or someone, he is no longer rational. He believes that Hugh killed our father. If you take me with you I may be able to help you restrain him. When he is irrational he is like a child again. And when we were children I was his elder sister; he had to listen to me."

Damn the woman.

"I'm afraid it's quite impossible," Michael said coldly. "By arguing, you are merely delaying the pursuit—"

"If you don't do as I ask, I shall tell the full story to the press, both here and in Paris. Then I shall go the the Czech Embassy here and demand to see my brother."

"Very well," Michael snapped. He could envisage the scandal which could so easily evolve, especially when the person who began it was a beautiful and articulate woman. It would be the sort of business which led to questions in the House. The last thing the service could afford at present was more adverse publicity. "Stay where you are for the moment. I'll have them send a car around."

If he had anything to do with it, that car would contain two of the largest women police constables that Special Branch could find. His mind was a mixture of conflicting emotions: anxiety about Hugh; irritation with Magda; curiosity about Heinz; and annoyance that something like this should blow up when he was less than three months short of retirement.

He had to tell Meg what had happened, since his conversation with Magda had been in German. The blood drained away from her face when she realized that Hugh was in danger. She sat down on the arm of a chair and bit her lip. When she spoke, her voice was perfectly steady.

"Can I help in any way? Sit by a phone? Or stay with Mag-da?"

"Yes—perhaps. I don't know. I must phone Giles Burnham. It'll be his pigeon if Heinz is behind this. And someone had better get in touch with Stephen."

"You get on the telephone." Meg got up, revealing a breath-taking expanse of leg as the kimono fell away. "I'll go and get dressed."

When he heard the news, Stephen was tempted to pray for the first time in a quarter of a century.

For an instant a benign providence, like a heavenly case officer orchestrating his life, seemed the only plausible explanation for such a fortunate concatenation of events.

"Our best bet is Keats Road," Giles Burnham squawked in his ear; the telephone wasn't kind to his voice, especially when he was excited. "If your brother isn't there, God knows where they've taken him."

Stephen abruptly lost interest in theological speculation. "Does Branch know?"

MI5 had no executive powers; for arrests and indeed prosecu-tions it relied on Special Branch. If MI5 was the brain, then Special Branch could be considered as the limbs that carried out the brain's commands. Unorthodox MI5 officers would occasionally act direct-ly, but someone like Burnham would never condone irregularities like that.

"Of course they do," Giles snapped. "It's lucky you came to see me last night. I'd already asked them to apply for a warrant for Keats Road. And our chaps have done some background digging."

He's getting touchy, Stephen thought; *can't take the responsibility of a major operation.*

"We're meeting at the Yard at midday," Burnham continued. "Two cars. You'd better come, too. My God, the ramifications of this could be endless."

"Who else is coming?"

"Michael Stanhope-Smith. He knows the background. And Scholl's sister. She's in London, too. There's something bloody odd about that. Did you know she's—ah—emotionally involved with your brother?"

"Good Lord!" Stephen said noncommittally. "Is the house under surveillance now?"

"Eh? Keats Road? Of course it is. Two-man team. I'd arranged that before all this blew up. Unfortunately they didn't get there until after your brother would have done. If he's there at all, I mean."

"Well, I hope to God they keep their heads down. We don't want this thing going off at half-cock." Stephen wasn't seriously worried. Burnham, for all his nervous quirks and moral inhibitions, wasn't a fool. "Why are we taking Magda Scholl?"

"Just in case we get a siege or something like that. She could help to break a stalemate. Not that we have much choice: if we don't take her, she's threatening to run to the press."

"All right, Giles. Thanks for letting me know. I'll be with you in about twenty minutes."

Stephen put down the phone. It was unfortunate that there was no way to avoid the meeting with Magda. Still, Burnham would have to discover sooner or later that Stephen had not been entirely frank at their reconciliation scene last night.

Not that it mattered. Nothing mattered beside the fact that Heinz had in all probability signed his own death warrant, literally and metaphorically. If he was in that house with Hugh, his diplomatic status wouldn't save him. Stephen imagined with relish the story that might reach the press: *an East German, using a false name and traveling on a Czech diplomatic passport, has kidnapped a British citizen in the heart of London.*

Kidnapped? Why not murdered?

It depended how benign the heavenly case officer was feeling. Two birds had been killed with one stone before now.

Stephen found his key ring and unlocked the bottom right-hand drawer of his desk. Whistling silently to himself, he opened the box file it contained and took out the Browning. He checked the magazine and slipped the pistol in his jacket pocket.

The heavenly case officer helped those who helped themselves.

The five Special Branch officers were in the second car, but their inspector accompanied Michael, Magda, Stephen, and Giles Burnham. As they drove west along Bayswater Road, Giles went over his arithmetic for yet another time.

"The five men behind us; plus you, Inspector, that's six; two men there already, to act as backup if necessary. That's eight, and all armed. It should be enough, shouldn't it?"

"Yes, sir," Inspector Barton said. There was a hint of scorn in his voice. He was a big, sandy-haired Yorkshireman who didn't conceal his dislike of having civilians with him on an operation. "And further support can be called up within minutes. Several units are standing by. But there won't be a fight, sir: you'll see."

The inspector was driving; Burnham sat beside him in the front, while Michael, Magda, and Stephen were in the back. The shortwave radio prattled ceaselessly. The unmarked police cars had sirens, but Burnham had decided against their use. A slightly faster journey had to be balanced against the possibility of unwanted publicity.

Michael thought of Meg, sitting by the telephone in the hall of the Putney flat. He wished he was there with her. Strictly speaking, this business was not his responsibility. Nevertheless, it seemed to him that he was inextricably involved with it, because Farrar had died over seventeen years before. For the same reason Meg was waiting for him in his flat.

"Stanhope-Smith!"

"Sorry, Burnham." Michael put the thought of Meg reluctantly to one side. "You were saying?"

"I was asking if you'd heard about Wiston."

Michael shook his head. Who the devil was Wiston?

"Special Branch found him in their registry," Burnham said helpfully. "He's not in ours. Inspector, perhaps you'd care to—?"

Burnham's voice tailed away on a note of interrogation. Barton's eyes met Michael's for an instant in the rearview mirror. Burnham was trying to treat the inspector as an equal, but the very effort he was making smacked of condescension.

"Frank Wiston." Barton sniffed, and his face assumed the blank mask which policemen used when they were giving evidence in court. "Joined the Communist Party in 'thirty-six—actually fought in Spain for a couple of months. He's a mechanic—served in REME during the war. No known political affiliations since 'forty-one. He's been renting the Keats Road premises for residential and commercial uses since 'forty-six. Self-employed and keeps his nose clean."

"Is he Czech or GRU?" Michael said.

Burnham answered, "Probably GRU if the safe house was set up as early as 'forty-six. The Czechs weren't operational then. After all, the country wasn't brought into the Soviet bloc until 'forty-eight."

Stephen leaned forward and tapped Burnham's shoulder. "What's the plan, Giles?" His dark face crumpled into that unexpectedly charming smile. "We can have the history lesson later."

"We stay in the car. The police surround the house and the inspector knocks on the door. We have a search warrant. Scholl and his pals have diplomatic status, so we'll play this one by the book."

Beside him, Michael could feel the warmth of Magda's thigh resting against his. She had neither moved nor spoken since they got into the car. *How she must hate us all.*

He looked out of the window. Notting Hill gave way to Holland Park. *By the book?* He doubted that. If he had learned one thing since he had joined Z Organization as Dansey's apprentice, it was that there was no book.

Inspector Barton cleared his throat. "The other car's no longer behind us."

"I killed your father here," Heinz said conversationally. "He soiled himself beforehand. It was rather unpleasant."

Hugh said nothing. His head was still splitting. He tried to focus on those front teeth. They seemed just the same as they had been in May 1945. Surely that was improbable? They must have dentists on the other side of the Iron Curtain. In another lifetime Magda had told him that the children at the gymnasium had a nickname for Heinz. His head cleared and he remembered it: *Das Kaninchen.*

"I didn't kill your father," he repeated yet again. "Bruckman was lying because he hated me."

Heinz gave no sign that he had heard. "We tied your father to the chair. Just like you. I made him drunk and then I drowned him. It was quite an easy death, I should think. Your death will be very different."

Hugh had no idea where they were. When he had regained consciousness on the floor of the car, he found that they had tied an evil-smelling sack over his head and cuffed his hands behind his back. He had no way of knowing how long he had been unconscious; his watch was out of sight on his left wrist.

The cellar had a concrete floor. The walls were of unplastered brick; in places they glistened with damp. The sole lighting was provided by an unshaded, high-wattage bulb.

Heinz slapped him again. "Listen to me. Did you set your father to spy on me?"

Hugh stared blankly ahead, over Heinz's shoulder. There was no point in pretending to faint again. Last time they had thrown cold water over him. Behind Heinz were the two big Czechs. He had heard them talking in the car. The one who had hit him was Antonin; the one who had pulled him into the car was Vaclav. Somewhere in the house above was a fourth man—an Englishman with a whining voice and a Birmingham accent. As the Czechs hustled Hugh down the cellar stairs, the Englishman had protested to Heinz.

Not another one, mister.

Get upstairs. You know what your job is.

The next slap hurt far more than its predecessors. Something hard—a ring?—jarred against his cheekbone. Blood trickled down his face to his neck.

"Was your father working for you?"

Hugh shook his head slowly. He could see no reason not to tell the truth.

"For your brother Stephen?"

"I don't know." He wondered fleetingly where Heinz had got his information. "If I knew I would tell you."

"Antonin," Heinz said curtly. "Bring the pliers. You and Vaclav must watch carefully. This will be a unique demonstration."

There was a double knock on the cellar door at the head of the stairs. Antonin opened it.

"Pardon me, gents," the Englishman said, "but I thought you'd better know. There's a Riley parked on the other side of the street. Been there nearly half an hour. Two men in it. I reckon they're coppers."

Heinz took a step forward. The overhead light glinted on his hair. "How do you know?"

"Tell 'em a mile off, mister. It's a knack, see?"

"Vaclav, Antonin. Upstairs." Heinz gagged Hugh with a piece of rag. He bent down and whispered in his ear. "We'll be back, Rudi. Don't run away."

Heinz was the last to leave the cellar. As he left, he flicked up the switch at the head of the stairs.

Hugh sat there in the darkness. He spent the first few minutes trying to move, but the handcuffs and the rope that bound his legs to the chair were too effective. He managed to scrape the chair an inch to the right: but what use was that?

A sour and pointless anger flooded through him. He loathed them all—Heinz, Stephen, and the rest of their kind. Even Michael was implicated. Hugh had been on his way to see Stephen—to stop him from using Magda in his stupid little schemes—when Heinz and

327

the Czechs had kidnapped him. Why couldn't they play their games by themselves, without involving outsiders?

The blood clotted. His skin itched as the drying blood contracted. His tongue wrestled vainly to expel the gag. More successfully, he fought a groundless but unsettling fear that he was going to be sick, and that he would choke to death on his own vomit.

Just as he had won that battle, he heard a doorbell ringing, somewhere above his head.

They parked in a street which ran at right angles to Keats Road. The atmosphere inside the car was heavy with unspoken recriminations. It made it worse that no one could be blamed for the disaster; fate made an unsatisfactory scapegoat.

The news had just come over the radio: the second car was a write-off. First, it had been delayed by a pedestrian crossing. Then, near Notting Hill underground station, a bus had pulled out without signaling; at the same time, a lorry coming in the opposite direction had swerved to avoid a cyclist. The police car had been caught in the middle. Fortunately none of the officers was killed, but all of them were injured, two of them seriously.

"The reserve car should be here in twenty or thirty minutes," Barton said.

"Do we have to wait?" Michael said quickly. A lot could happen in half an hour. "We should go in now, with the surveillance team."

"Be wiser to wait." Burnham turned to Barton. "Don't you agree, Inspector?"

Barton nodded. "We don't know for sure how many are in there. At least four. There's no sense in taking risks."

"The delay could cost Mr. Kendall his life," Michael said.

"I doubt it, sir." The inspector turned his head. "We don't even know for sure that Mr. Kendall's in there. We've no reason to believe they want to kill him."

"I feel sick," Magda said suddenly. "Will you let me out?"

Michael got out of the car and held open the door for her. She certainly looked pale. From the pavement he could see the corner of number fifteen, forty yards away.

"Please get back in." She avoided his eye. "It embarrasses me, having you there."

Michael flushed and mumbled an incoherent apology. He climbed back into the car.

Barton said, "What's that bloody woman doing?"

Magda was running down the street toward Keats Road.

She rested her thumb against the bell and pushed. She was still panting after the sprint. The bell rang on and on. She glanced over her shoulder: they weren't following her, yet. There was a small car parked on the other side of the road; she could see two men inside. That must be the surveillance team.

The door opened and a skinny man scowled at her. "Here, piss off, will you? I ain't deaf."

Magda put the heel of her hand on his chest and pushed. The action took him completely by surprise. He fell back into the hall. She followed him in. A large man with a narrow skull slammed the door behind her and enveloped her in a bear hug.

"Another hostage," said her brother Heinz. He was standing in the doorway of what looked like a dining room; he was carrying a pistol. "Put her in here."

She felt a sharp sense of anticlimax. She had nerved herself up to expect a display of emotion. Instead, her brother was treating her arrival as if it meant no more to him than a tradesman's delivery.

"Heinz, you're being stupid," she said sharply. "The house is surrounded. For God's sake, surrender."

"Make sure you gag her, Antonin." Heinz brushed past her without looking at her. They might have been strangers. "Bring up the other one, Vaclav. We have a small change of plan."

Barton, now his hand had been forced, didn't waste time.

The Riley was brought up and parked across the gateway of the yard, blocking the escape of the big Humber that the Czechs had used. The two watchers, who were both armed, covered that side of the house. Burnham and Barton marched up to the front door, with Stephen and Michael trailing behind.

Barton hammered on the door. "Come on, Scholl," he shouted. "The party's over."

"I am ready to negotiate," said a thin, precise voice on the other side of the door. "But if you try to rush the house, the woman dies."

Stephen gripped Michael's arm. "That's Scholl," he said.

Burnham pushed the inspector out of the way. "What do you want?"

"A flight to East Berlin."

"Is Mr. Hugh Kendall there?"

"Yes."

"When would you release the hostages?"

"My sister when we board the plane. Kendall in Berlin."

"I'll have to refer this back to my superiors," Burnham said. "You understand that?"

"Michael," Stephen whispered, "come with me. I've got an idea."

They moved back down the path and onto the pavement. They kept close to the garden wall; the laurel bushes screened them from the windows of the house.

"I'm going in," he hissed. "Scholl's improvising, he must be. We've got to get him now, before he gets himself organized. I'm not letting that bastard escape."

"What are you going to do?" Then Michael saw the Browning in Stephen's hand. "Look here, you can't—"

"Can't I?" Stephen grinned. His face was suddenly lighthearted; he looked young, happy, and full of hope. "Come and watch my back."

He climbed over the low wall and slid through the laurels to the nearest window. The curtains were partly drawn, but the room seemed empty. The door to the hall was ajar. Stephen raised the gun and smashed its butt against the glass, just above the window's catch.

Stephen seemed oblivious of the danger to himself and to the hostages. Michael lunged forward in a desperate attempt to stop him. His limbs felt sluggish and not entirely under his control; it was as if he was drunk or in a nightmare.

The sound of breaking glass was shockingly loud. Barton shouted. Stephen slipped his arm through the hole he had made, undid the catch, and raised the lower half of the window. He threw his leg over the sill. There was a blur of movement in the room beyond. Stephen fired. Someone screamed.

Michael swore. Now that Stephen had acted, there was no going back for either of them. All that mattered was improving the chances of survival for Magda and Hugh. He dived through the window and rolled onto the uncarpeted floor.

As the shot rang out, the man whom Heinz had called Antonin was wrapping the rope around Magda's body.

The rope's tension slackened as his concentration faltered. Magda stamped on his foot with all her strength. Unfortunately, her heels were not as tall and sharp as she would have liked.

Nevertheless, Antonin screamed. Magda jerked herself out of his arms and bolted for the door with the rope trailing behind her.

In the doorway she collided with Hugh. His hands were behind his back. Behind him in the hall she could see Heinz and Vaclav; the shot had clearly distracted the latter from the job of escorting Hugh. The little Englishman who had opened the door to her lay on his back over the threshold of a room on the other side of the hall. A red stain was spreading across the front of his pale yellow shirt.

Hugh's cheek was covered with dried blood; like herself, he had been gagged, but his eyes were bright. He blinked with surprise as he saw her. Then he lowered his head and charged at Vaclav.

The Czech was beginning to turn, but he had left it too late. Hugh's head slammed into his stomach and drove him against the wall. Vaclav slid down to the floor.

Magda saw movement in the corner of her eye: Antonin blundered toward her, bellowing in Czech. She ducked out of the room and into the hall, which suddenly seemed even noisier and more crowded than before. It sounded as though someone was methodically battering down the front door.

Heinz was shrieking at her, his words scrambled with hatred; there was foam on his lips. In the middle of her fear, she felt relieved that he was still capable of emotion.

Stephen Kendall appeared in the opposite doorway with Michael Stanhope-Smith immediately behind him. Kendall raised his pistol and fired at Antonin: the big Czech flung up his arms and was thrown backward into the dining room.

Hugh was beside her, and she tried to smile at him. She realized that he wanted to use his body as her shield. He shunted her backward down the hall, away from Heinz.

There were two more shots, so close together that the second seemed the echo of the first. Magda peered over Hugh's shoulder. Heinz and Stephen Kendall were both on the floor. They lay as if each was the mirror image of the other, even down to the positioning of the wounds on their chests.

As she watched, she revised her first impression: Stephen lay perfectly still, like a sleeping child; but Heinz was moving.

A panel of the front door splintered inward. A hand poked through the hole and fumbled for the Yale lock. The door swung open, and the smoke-filled hall was bright with sunshine. Barton,

Burnham, and the two constables from the Riley hesitated for a fatal fraction of a second on the threshold.

Heinz supported himself on one arm and squinted down the barrel at his sister. His face was pale and pinched: it reminded Magda of how he had looked when they had pulled him half-drowned from the Vltava. Hugh wrenched his head around, saw what was happening, and tried to cover Magda. She wondered which of them Heinz really wanted to kill. Perhaps he would get both of them with one shot.

Michael Stanhope-Smith dived across the hall and landed on top of Heinz. There was a thin, high scream, like a rabbit's in a trap. Then the gun went off.

Epilogue

Vienna: July 1963
The Stanhope-Smith exhibition came to Vienna as part of the Cunningham Foundation's efforts to introduce modern Anglo-American art to mainland Europe. Its previous ports of call had been Madrid, Paris, and Bonn.

The exhibition's reputation ensured that the Austrian opening was well attended. So far, it had proved a popular success; the critics, however, were divided in their opinions, though all of them regretted that the artist should have died so suddenly at the peak of his powers. Some of them discerned an unfortunate love of the macabre in Stanhope-Smith's work. The oil painting known as *Bath Time* was often cited as evidence of an unnecessarily sensational streak in the artist's oeuvre. It detracted from the essential realism which underpinned most of his work. The whiff of critical controversy was at least partly responsible for the popular success.

Mrs. Cunningham opened the exhibition—appropriately enough, since she owned a good two-thirds of the exhibits. She was accompanied by her sister-in-law, Mrs. Hugh Kendall. One of the newspapers which covered the opening printed a photograph of their children—six-year-old Mary Cunningham and five-year-old Eve Kendall—studying the catalogue together.

The party spent several days in Vienna after the opening. Mrs. Kendall had some research to do. At the Hotel Franz Josef on the Plosslgasse, she was lucky enough to find the register of guests for 1939. She photographed one of the pages which covered the February of that year. There it was in black and white—George Farrar's signature.

It was the first objective evidence Magda had found that Farrar had been in Vienna just before the war. Meg had given her access to Michael's papers; and of course Farrar was mentioned there. But for years Magda had wondered if Farrar was just a convenient symbol, created by Michael the artist rather than recorded by Stanhope-Smith the intelligence officer.

She worked her way through the newspaper files and found the brief, carefully worded reports of his death. HOTEL FATALITY said one of the headlines; SUICIDE OF ENGLISHMAN said another.

Farrar was real. The pattern had a beginning. The choice of that beginning was to some extent arbitrary, but it satisfied Magda as an historian as it had satisfied Michael as an artist.

It was possible to say *If a traveling salesman in toys had not quarreled with a secret policeman—* or *If George Farrar hadn't died when and where he did—*then (for example) she might not have married an English businessman; Meg might not have a daughter with one man's name and another man's genes; Britain's African empire and her great-power status might have lasted for a few more decades; Michael and several Kendalls and Scholls might still be alive; a world war might have traveled in a slightly different direction; and no one might have noticed that there was more than one midnight.

The past reached out unexpectedly on the fourth day of the exhibition. During the afternoon, Magda visited it for a second time, hoping to find it less crowded.

She was standing in front of *Bath Time* when a man cleared his throat beside her; it was a polite noise, designed to draw attention. She looked up and saw an old man with a face like a skull and large, faded blue eyes. He was leaning on a stick. His skin had a waxy quality. On second thoughts, she decided he wasn't so much old as ill.

"Frau Kendall, isn't it?" He gestured toward the painting with his catalogue. "Not sensational. All too real."

He spoke in heavily accented German. She knew at once that she had met him before. Most of his features were small and delicate; the exception was the large flattened nose which should have belonged to someone else's face. The contrast gave her the clue she needed.

Magda smiled and held out her hand. "Herr Juriga."

They shook hands. It would have been tactless to ask how he was.

Bela Juriga said, "The doctors say six months." There was no bitterness in his face—only a trace of amusement. "The lungs, you know. The Party sent me to Vienna to see a specialist. They would like me to stay alive for longer."

"And do you intend to oblige them?"

He gave her an approving nod. "I stopped obliging other people in nineteen forty-four."

"Mauthausen?"

"Dear me. You have done your research. You're right, of course. Someone should investigate the educational qualities of the German concentration camp system."

Magda smiled. "I gather that similar educational establishments still exist on your side of the Iron Curtain. Perhaps you should investigate those first."

Juriga smiled, exposing long, stained teeth with receding gums. "Let us not quarrel. I wonder, may we sit down? Standing for any length of time makes me breathless."

In the end, they left the exhibition and found a café where men in shabby evening clothes and dirty shirts played Strauss waltzes to entertain the patrons. Magda could sense that he was lonely and perhaps afraid, but curiosity as well as compassion prompted her to accompany him.

Juriga had met both Magda and Hugh several times in the aftermath of the Keats Road incident. He had been in charge of the Communist side of the cover-up. Magda suspected he had derived an ironic pleasure from the fact that fear of scandal had united the British, American, Russian, and Czechoslovakian governments, albeit briefly. If the full story had got out, everyone would have looked ridiculous. No one wanted it bruited abroad that their secret service personnel went in for private enterprise on the side.

Her feelings for him were oddly ambivalent. She despised what he had done in the war, particularly to Hugh. Yet she sensed that he—and no one else—had mourned Heinz's death; guilt made her grateful.

"I often wonder," Juriga said while they waited for the lemon tea and pastries, "whether your brother realized how successful he was. In professional terms, everything worked out precisely as he had planned: the Middle East destabilized, British prestige damaged, public attention deflected from the Russian invasion of Hungary."

"I expect so. He wasn't a fool."

Juriga lit a cigarette. "I was—fond of him. Like a father is fond. You understand?"

"I think so."

The waitress arrived, providing a diversion which Magda welcomed. Bela, she realized, saw the pattern from a different perspective—so different that it might as well have been an entirely different pattern.

When they were alone again, Bela spooned sugar into his tea and asked if Hugh was in Vienna with her.

"Not yet. He and Paul are flying over at the end of the week."

"Paul?"

"Our son. Hugh had to go to New York on business, and Paul decided it would be educational for him to go, too."

"I have to leave tomorrow. A pity. I would have liked to see him. If he would have allowed it."

Magda said nothing. How could she answer for Hugh?

Juriga looked away. Then he said, "Are you happy with him?"

"Of course." She spoke without thinking. Then she added, "I never seriously wanted to be married to anyone else. And I still don't. Hugh's . . . *natural* to me. Like breathing."

"Will you tell him, please, I was happy with Jan. As you are with him. I did not mean to hurt him." A fit of coughing drowned his last words; to Magda they sounded like "I am sorry."

She covered his hand with hers. The little band swung wearily into "The Blue Danube."

"If we have to blame anyone," she said, "let's blame Farrar."

336